My blood turned to ice and I felt m
creature, a flying demon, circled u
for the kill. I looked up, sheathed n
already-primed crossbow from my back, trying to keep my
hands steady. I had seen a winged one in action before.
Knew that I had five seconds in which to aim and fire a bolt
through its brain. Either that or die horribly in its jaws,
which were lined with razor-sharp teeth, each over thirty
centimetres long. Two of those seconds had gone when
Luca tugged at my trousers.

'I need a wee . . .'

'Not now!' I yelled above the din.

Three seconds gone. I held up the crossbow, ready to
aim, but the demon spotted my move and changed position,
banking left to begin its dive.

'Great!' My legs continued to shake and fear crept down
my spine.

Four seconds gone. The demon began to close in, lizard-
yellow eyes now just slits, and huge wings held back above
its head, touching so that they formed a fin. Luca screamed.
The Hunted screamed. The street ran red with blood and
gore. All around me the Hunt continued unabated, as high
up above the chaos the waning moon disappeared behind
clouds the colour of a purple bruise . . .

Five seconds. Almost gone. I closed my eyes and fired . . .

WITHDRAWN

C0000 002 617 345

ALSO BY BALI RAI AND PUBLISHED BY RANDOM HOUSE CHILDREN'S PUBLISHERS UK

(Un)arranged Marriage
'Absorbing and engaging' – *Observer*

The Crew
'A jewel of a book' – *Independent*

Rani and Sukh
'Heart-wrenching love story that will exert its power
over you long after the book is finished'
– *The Bookseller*

The Whisper
'Unflinching and authentic' – *Publishing News*

The Last Taboo
'This is brave, committed writing . . . it deserves a
large audience' – *TES*

The Angel Collector
'Page-turning thriller' – *Birmingham Post*

City of Ghosts
'A heart-rending tale from a talented author'
– *The Times*

Killing Honour
'Rai never shies away from difficult topics . . .
It's utterly compelling' - *The Bookseller*

For younger readers:
Soccer Squad: Starting Eleven
Soccer Squad: Missing!
Soccer Squad: Stars!
Soccer Squad: Glory!

FIRE CITY

BALI RAI

CORGI BOOKS

FIRE CITY

A CORGI BOOK 978 0 552 55602 6

First published in Great Britain by Corgi Books,
an imprint of Random House Children's Publishers UK
A Random House Group Company

This edition published 2012

1 3 5 7 9 10 8 6 4 2

Copyright © Bali Rai, 2012
Cover illustration © Adam Brockbank

The right of Bali Rai to be identified as the author of this work has been asserted in
accordance with the Copyright, Designs and Patents Act 1988.

All rights reserved. No part of this publication may be reproduced,
stored in a retrieval system, or transmitted in any form or by any means,
electronic, mechanical, photocopying, recording or otherwise,
without the prior permission of the publishers.

The Random House Group Limited supports the Forest Stewardship
Council (FSC®), the leading international forest certification organization.
Our books carrying the FSC label are printed on FSC® certified paper.
FSC is the only forest certification scheme endorsed by the leading
environmental organizations, including Greenpeace. Our paper procurement
policy can be found at www.randomhouse.co.uk/environment.

Corgi Books are published by Random House Children's Publishers UK,
61–63 Uxbridge Road, London W5 5SA

www.**randomhousechildrens**.co.uk
www.**totallyrandombooks**.co.uk
www.**randomhouse**.co.uk

Addresses for companies within The Random House Group Limited
can be found at: www.randomhouse.co.uk/offices.htm

THE RANDOM HOUSE GROUP Limited Reg. No. 954009

A CIP catalogue record for this book is available from the British Library.

Printed and bound by CPI Group (UK) Ltd, Croydon, CR0 4YY

As always, a big thank you to everyone at Random House for taking yet another leap of faith with me. And to my amazing agent, Penny, for the right advice, at the right times. Big respect to Adam Brockbank for the killer cover too – beyond my wildest expectations.

Prologue

Twenty-five years ago the world changed. A great war, which had raged for three years, ended and the Reign of the Demons began. Everything we humans knew was gone, and the imperfect world we'd created was replaced by Hell . . .

The War came as the world's resources began to dwindle. As the human population increased, those with everything began to resent those with nothing. A group of rich and powerful men came together and began to plan for a new future: a future in which the wealthy would survive and flourish, and the rest of us would serve.

Serve or die.

For this new order to come about, the group needed a revolution. They needed a worldwide disaster that would enable them to take control and reshape human society to their requirements. We don't know how they managed to call forth the demons; we only know that they did. And once the demons entered our domain, darkness descended and the War began.

For the first two years, humans across the globe – governments, their armies and their weaponry – came together to fight against the demon onslaught. As the human casualties grew, ordinary people took up the fight too, but it was all in vain. The fighting destroyed whole cities and decimated outlying areas in every country. Massive bombs and demon hordes laid waste to entire regions, and no nation remained untouched. The Hell-kin began to take control, and eventually many of the rulers who had been fighting against them switched sides. Those who had sworn to defend humanity began to make deals with the demons and their human allies. Country by country, the war turned against us, and the new world began to take shape. By the time the fighting was over, less than a fifth of the original human population was left standing.

The leaders of the revolution, aided by their demon allies, now began to implement a new design for the world. Societies were reformed worldwide along simpler, more refined lines. Humans were divided into two groups: the *Wanted* and the *Unwanted*. Cities were rebuilt across the globe, several in each country, and turned into demon-protected citadels to provide homes for the Wanted. Alongside these were outlying satellite settlements, partially destroyed areas in which industrial zones were established – satellites like Fire City. For the new rulers and their Wanted would need goods and services to make their lives complete, and the Unwanted could provide the labour to make or provide those things.

The Unwanted were rounded up and divided amongst the satellites, enough of them to keep the factories running. The new governments didn't care where their workforce lived or what their lives were like. As long as they worked, they were useful. Paid in newly established credits, enough to provide the basics of survival, the Unwanted became nothing more than wage slaves.

But the demons wanted more than just a place at the table. They wanted to reassert their dominance at the top of the food chain. The demon lords, in return for their patronage, demanded a constant supply of humans for themselves. Some they ate for sustenance, body and soul. Others had only their souls taken – a fate that was far worse. These unfortunates developed a crazed blood lust from which there was no escape but death. But the demon lords understood that they couldn't just butcher us at will. That they could not afford for the human race to be completely extinguished.

And so the Hunt began.

Held every few days, in every part of the world, the Hunt took care of those humans who couldn't work, or who rebelled against the new rulers. The old, the sick and the disabled – anyone who didn't contribute was rounded up and sent as prey to the hunting grounds.

They still are . . .

But we humans are resourceful. For every fifty of us who accept the new world, cowering before or collaborating with the demons and their human puppets, there is one who fights – one like me. Our resistance is small, and it is weak, but it exists.

As long as there are people who want to fight, there is hope . . .

Martha

PART ONE

PART ONE

1

I pulled my hood over my head and dropped down from the building, landing in their midst, my heart pounding. My foes roared with anger, their mouths scarlet, teeth clogged with human flesh. Turning away from their prey — a small boy with chocolate skin and bewildered dark eyes — I watched them size me up, and as usual I felt a mixture of anger and nausea. What they saw was a teenage girl — tall, skinny and armed to the teeth. I had their attention now, and despite the danger I managed to remain calm. Before they could react, I drew a great sword from the scabbard hanging at my waist. The blade flashed quickly through the air — three swift arcs — and the cannibals dropped, their heads separated from blood-spouting torsos and rolling slowly into the gutter.

'Luca!' I shouted above the chaos of the Hunt. 'Come here!'

The boy, who I had been desperate to find, didn't move, cowering as a high-pitched scream erupted from above. My blood turned to ice and I felt myself shaking. A winged creature, a flying demon, circled us, preparing to dive in for the kill. I looked up, sheathed my sword and pulled the already-primed crossbow from my back, trying to keep my hands steady. I had seen a winged one in action before. Knew that I had five seconds in which to aim and fire a bolt through its brain. Either that or die horribly in its jaws, which were lined with razor-sharp teeth, each over thirty centimetres long. Two of those seconds had gone when Luca tugged at my trousers.

'I need a wee . . .'

'Not now!' I yelled above the din.

Three seconds gone. I held up the crossbow, ready to aim, but the demon spotted my move and changed position, banking left to begin its dive.

'Great!' My legs continued to shake and fear crept down my spine.

Four seconds gone. The demon began to close in, lizard-yellow eyes now just slits, and huge wings held back above its head, touching so that they formed a fin. Luca screamed. The Hunted screamed. The street ran red with blood and gore. All around me the Hunt continued unabated, as high up above the chaos the waning moon disappeared behind clouds the colour of a purple bruise . . .

Five seconds. *Almost* gone. I closed my eyes and fired . . .

. . . and nothing happened. No bone-crushing collision. No tearing, piercing explosions of pain as the demon ripped open my flesh. Nothing except an earth-shaking thud as the winged beast fell from the sky, smashing into the rusted, burned-out skeleton of what had once been a car. I replaced the crossbow, unsheathed my sword and stepped slowly towards the dying demon, surprised and shocked. What the hell was going on?

The winged demon lay on its back, legs in the air, talons twitching. Its giant wings were twisted and torn from the fall. The jaws, long and powerful, fell open, revealing those murderous teeth, slick with human guts and oozing thick yellow saliva. A single bolt about the length of my arm pierced the breastplate. It was jet black and sleek, tapered at the visible end and crackling with a blue light that I didn't understand. Much as I didn't understand why I wasn't dead. I spun round quickly, scanning the street for clues, but saw nothing. Nothing except the Hunt.

'Luca!'

The boy shook with fright as I scooped him into my arms and made for cover. The street was lined on both sides by five-storey blocks – flats that had once housed families and friends many years ago. I ran to the nearest door, kicking through a wooden barrier to get inside. Rodents scattered in the darkness and my feet slid on something fluid. Something I didn't want to see or think about.

'Need a wee!' wailed Luca.

'Not *now*,' I told him sternly. 'We have to get away!'

From experience, I knew that each block was identical, with a lower corridor, two sets of stairs and a landing on each level. External walkways ran alongside each landing, open to the elements. I took the left side and edged slowly upwards with Luca over my shoulder and my sword ready. These abandoned blocks with their myriad rooms, were a favourite haunt for those we call cannibals – human beings who have had their souls snatched by the demons and develop a lust for the flesh of their own race. The cannibals often set traps for the Hunted, and without the right degree of caution, death could fall upon you quickly and tear you to pieces.

The walkways were how I'd managed to save Luca, dropping from a first-floor landing right into the mix. Even though that stinking, darkened building meant danger, my thoughts were now elsewhere. I wondered who or what had killed the flying demon and where the spear had come from. I'd never seen anything take out a demon so quickly.

Suddenly something moved on the first landing. It was the faintest of sounds but I heard it. Carrying Luca made my sword useless – I couldn't wield it effectively. I turned to my machete instead. It was shorter, lighter and easier to use in tight situations, and did just as much damage. Luca whimpered into my shoulder.

'Gotta be brave,' I whispered into his ear, even though my own stomach was flipping around like a dying fish.

Whatever was on the landing shifted its weight. I sensed that it was coming closer. Three steps separated us. I set Luca down behind me and he whimpered some more.

'Don't move,' I told him. 'No matter what happens.'

Luca nodded slowly, crossing his legs. 'Wee,' he whispered.

I shook my head. Strands of hair fell across my face and I brushed them away. My forehead felt slick with perspiration. 'And if they hurt me,' I added, 'run and hide, OK? The others will find you. Promise.'

I didn't wait for his reply because my promise was probably empty. Even saying the words made me feel bad. But there was no time for guilt – there never is in this world. I jumped onto the landing, rolled across to the nearest wall and sprang to my feet. The stench was unbearable, as always. Rotting flesh. A cannibal lurched towards me, growling. His eyes bulged, the hands outstretched until I removed them with two swipes. He roared and lashed out with the bloody stumps but I'd already ducked under his arms, severing one of them at the shoulder. Before the monster could turn, I'd removed his head too. The rest of him slumped to the floor, blood spraying in all directions.

That was when I heard the others – a gang of them shuffling relentlessly closer from all sides.

'*Shit!*'

How could I have been so stupid? They'd lured me into a trap and I'd fallen for it – like some first-Hunt novice. I chopped frantically at the darkness all around me. A thud, quickly followed by another, stopped me dead. Fewer footsteps. Something flashed, moving the air slightly. Another thud, a groan, some screaming. I crouched, rolled to my right and back down the stairwell. Luca was gone.

'*No!*' I cried. 'Luca?'

A severed head rolled down the stairs and caught between my feet. I kicked it away, more in anger than disgust. Whatever else was up there, it wasn't another cannibal and it wasn't on their side. Thing is, I couldn't be sure it was on mine either. The demons often turned on their cannibal slaves, as well as each other, usually without reason. If it *was* a demon, then alone in the darkness I was in serious trouble. As for Luca . . .

Suddenly all was still. The silence caught me by surprise. A few seconds passed, seconds in which I tried to summon the courage to face my latest enemy. Cannibals were easy, as long as you didn't get surrounded. They moved slowly and, without the demons to guide them, acted predictably. They just walked towards you, the scent of your flesh in their nostrils, and anyone skilled enough with a sharp blade could decapitate one. The bigger the blade, the more damage you'd do too. The demons were different, however. Even the lowest-ranking of them was difficult to kill. The further up the chain you went, the harder it got. If the one on the landing had also killed the winged demon outside, then it would be high-ranking. All of which meant that I was in mortal danger. An image of my mum's face flashed through my mind, and for a moment I faltered, scared and weary.

Footsteps broke the silence. Footsteps moving *away* from me – fast! The thing above had two legs and it was leaving the scene. Any demon would have noticed my scent by now and reacted. I'd be fighting or, more likely, dying. I edged back onto the landing, praying that Luca had taken my advice and found a secure place to hide. I had no choice – the boy would have to wait for now. Too many other humans were being hunted in the streets – I had to help them. I unhooked a dagger from my belt and, dual-wielding it with the machete, I walked slowly along the landing. Through the gloom I counted eleven dead cannibals, including my own victim. Some had been decapitated, others simply torn apart. The corridor stank of death. Ahead, I saw doors, the glass remarkably intact. These led to the walkway, from which I could see the street below.

As I opened the doors, another winged demon flew

past the landing, a man grasped between its teeth, his body limp and lifeless. I knew it was too late to help but I dropped my blades and drew my crossbow anyway. 'He might be dead,' I yelled at the demon, 'but I'll be *damned* if I let you eat him too.'

'You're wasting your ammunition,' said a male voice.

I froze, unsure of my next move. A thousand thoughts flashed through my mind. If he'd wanted to kill me, I'd already be dead. He was three metres away, had the drop on me and, judging by the corpses in the hallway, could kill with ease. Yet I was still alive. If he *was* a friend, however, why hide in the shadows?

'Because I don't trust you,' the man said, guessing my thoughts as he stepped into view, Luca clinging to his shoulder.

He couldn't have been more than sixteen, a year older than me. Yet he spoke with the authority of someone born to survive. An array of weapons, some I'd never seen before, hung from his body, which was wrapped tight in black trousers, black boots and a long-sleeved T-shirt. His dark hair was close-cropped, his sharp cheekbones covered in skin the colour of porcelain, and his eyes shone like ebony beads. Something deep inside me tingled and I cursed myself silently. It was no time to stand and admire his strange yet alluring beauty.

'Who are you?' I asked, before pointing at the little boy. 'And how did you get to him?'

The stranger put Luca down gently, selected a rifle from his armoury and took aim at the disappearing winged demon. His ignoring of my question made me mad and I felt my face flush.

'You're too late,' I snapped, holding out a hand for the boy. 'The demon is too far away.'

The stranger ignored me again and fired once, but the bullet made no sound save for the rush of air it displaced. The demon's head exploded and it fell to earth, crashing against one of the blocks before landing on a mob of cannibals, crushing many of them.

'How many more are there?' he asked, nodding towards the street. 'Down there, I mean.'

I tried not to show how impressed I was, and shrugged. An odd yet pleasing scent drifted through the air. I found myself staring into his jet-black eyes, and felt a sense of longing.

'Valefor has ten legions at his command,' I told him, trying to ignore the emotions he'd ignited in me. 'This is just one of them.'

The stranger nodded, and thankfully he appeared not to notice that I was staring at him, eyes wide.

'*Valefor*,' he repeated.

'You know of him?' I asked.

The stranger looked down into the street. 'Heard the

name,' he said softly. 'Are there many more demons down there?'

'Yes,' I replied. 'Too many to kill in one night.'

'Let's see, shall we?' replied the stranger. 'Come on.'

'So you *do* trust me?'

The stranger may have shaken his head. The movement was so slight that it was hard to tell. I looked at him and again felt something in my belly – like a little fizzing sensation.

'I trust myself and my weapons,' he said without emotion.

His reply made me feel a little uneasy, so I turned my back to him and checked Luca over, making sure he hadn't been injured. I wondered if the stranger was watching me – sort of hoped that he was.

'He's fine,' the stranger told me. 'Apart from the urine.'

I looked down and saw that Luca was standing in a puddle.

'Told you!' he wailed, stamping his feet.

'Hurry!' the stranger snapped. 'People are dying down there!'

'Yeah,' I told him. ''Cos *that* I don't know. Welcome to Fire City.'

2

Aron ducked, using a pile of rubble as cover. Several body parts lay scattered around him. With time he might have reflected on the passing of fellow humans. But time was something he didn't have. In the middle of the Hunt, life and death were separated by a few seconds.

It was hard enough if you were prey. When you were hunting the hunters, it was twice as dangerous. The prey was simply trying to get away – and most failed. Aron and his gang were chasing the predators, and the demons didn't like being chased. He looked back down the street, bordered on each side by abandoned apartment blocks. Some lay silent whilst others burned. The screams of the Hunted and their tormentors filled the night.

He tried to catch his breath, looking around for the others. Martha had disappeared into one of the blocks twenty minutes earlier. Oscar and Tyrell were up ahead, *if* they were still breathing, and Samuel – well, he was dead. Aron felt something tearing at his insides – the guilt and shame that he didn't have time for. That he *couldn't* make time for. Samuel – torn to shreds because Aron had attacked a demon patrol without thinking, without heeding Samuel's pleas for caution. Aron tried to push his feelings away, hiding from them like he hid from most things.

He peered round the rubble, realizing how difficult his position had become. He was trapped, with demons front and rear as well as those patrolling the skies. An army of cannibals three or four hundred strong was stomping through the streets. At least thirty of them blocked the path between him and his destination – a narrow alleyway from which he could access a pre-secured basement and safety. Only now he didn't have Samuel to watch his back, because Samuel was dead – and he was the reason why . . .

Sensing an approaching demon, he rolled his short stocky frame to the left, into overgrown weeds tall enough to have hidden him if he'd been standing. He slid forward on his belly, praying that the demon wouldn't catch his scent. He'd rubbed himself in the oil that Martha's aunt, May, had prepared – jasmine, patchouli and nettle. Enough, May had said, to deceive a demon's sense of smell.

It worked. The hunter, half dog, half something else that Aron had never identified, stalked past, stopping only to sniff at the air for a few seconds. It walked on its

its hind legs, but stooped forward so that its powerful arms hung like giant, hair-covered battering rams, only just above the ground. A thick, muscular jaw jutted from its face, the forehead and eyes deep-set. It was a patroller, one of many that Valefor used as foot soldiers, and Aron was used to seeing them. He had killed more than his fair share too. Patrollers were the easiest demons to slay – they carried no weapons and relied on brute force to take down their opponents. Being the easiest to kill didn't make killing them easy, however. Aron carried the scars to prove it. Samuel's death *proved* it . . .

The patroller moved on, no doubt intent on rejoining its unit. For the Hunt, they worked in threes, with thirty units in each platoon and ten platoons for each legion. Nine thousand demons to contend with *after* you'd dispatched their cannibal slaves. Talk about great odds.

Once the demon had gone, Aron raised himself into a crouch and peered through the tall weeds. The nearest cannibals seemed preoccupied, surrounding a doorway, snarling. The entrance had been barricaded recently with some kind of appliance – an old fridge. Aron had never seen a working fridge – only heard about them from elders like May. The cannibals pushed at the barrier, snarling and growing frustrated but leaving the way clear for Aron to sneak past them to the alleyway. Only he knew that it wouldn't happen that way.

People were trapped behind the barricade and he wasn't about to leave them. Not when he'd—

He took his crossbow and primed a bolt. Aiming for the nearest cannibal, he concentrated on his breathing, feeling the world slow down all around him. He heard his heart thumping in his chest, the steady rhythmic flow of blood being pumped round his body. He *had* to get it right. Ammunition was limited and he couldn't afford to miss . . .

DUUFFFF!

The patroller knocked him sideways with a single lunge, winding him. Aron gasped for air as his weapon shot from his hands, falling three metres from where he lay on his back, unable to move. The force of the impact made his teeth grind. A familiar growling sent electric tingles through his body.

'*Kill us, would you?*' the patroller barked, pinning him down with its limbs.

Aron balked at its fetid breath and the globules of rancid saliva that hung from its jaws. His ribcage felt as if it had been shattered, each breath searing like a hot knife through his lungs. Still he found words.

'Someone has to!' he spat out.

'*Mistake!*' growled the demon.

Aron strained against the powerful limbs, but to no avail. Patrollers were immensely strong and once they had you pinned . . .

'I'm going to cut out your eyes, you unnatural—' he began.

The demon lowered its face to within millimetres of Aron's, stopping his words dead. A stream of thick saliva dripped onto Aron's left cheek, sliding towards his mouth. He clamped it shut quickly, feeling nauseous.

'*No, human, today you die!*' the patroller almost whispered to him.

'Blow me . . .' Aron managed to mumble through gritted teeth. The demon reared back and howled a death cry. Its eyelids closed, massive jaws parted and ready to tear Aron's head from his torso.

WHUMPP!

The patroller collapsed on top of Aron, stone-dead. A single shot had entered through its forehead, taking out the back of its skull, blowing its brain to mush. Aron blinked uncontrollably for a few moments, trying to get his head around the situation. What had just . . . ?

'You gonna lie there all night?' he heard Martha say. 'Only we've got people to save . . .'

'Where the *hell* did you come from?' he gasped as he tried to extricate himself, his face slick with dead demon. 'This butt-faced thing weighs a ton – help me.'

'I'll do it,' he heard a man say.

Two black-clad arms took hold of the patroller, lifting and casting it aside as if it weighed nothing.

'Man – what the—?' began Aron.

'We have work to do,' he heard the voice say. Someone he'd never heard before – a stranger.

'But he might be hurt,' replied Martha, the concern in her voice warming Aron's soul. His actions in recent weeks had forced a wedge between them, mostly because Martha didn't understand his need to protect her. Strong words had been spoken; words that he now regretted. He longed to return to the way things had been, to the shared childhood that bound them together.

'Then *you* look to him,' replied the stranger. 'Or let him die . . .'

Aron, suddenly angered, ignored the pain and sat up. 'Listen you twisted little turd,' he snapped. 'I don't *need* your help, OK?'

The stranger turned his back as Martha checked Aron over. Despite himself, Aron let rage colour his reaction.

'*Gerroff!*' he shouted at Martha.

'Leave her alone!' shouted Luca from behind the girl.

'Sorry,' Aron replied sheepishly, the fire in his heart quickly doused, replaced by yet more shame.

'Come on,' replied Martha, seeming to ignore his latest outburst. 'We need to get you and Luca to the hideout. Now . . . !'

Despite his anger at the stranger, Aron knew that Martha was right. The rest of the patrollers would have sensed the killing. They were coming, and fast.

'Can you walk?' Martha yelled at him.

'Think so . . .' he replied, struggling to his feet and smiling at Luca, who was standing behind Martha, trying to hide. He looked across the street and watched the newcomer engage the cannibal horde. The stranger, no more a man than he was, he realized, moved impossibly quickly, his blade flashing through the air. The cannibals fell without resistance.

'Who *is* that?' Aron asked Martha.

Martha shrugged. 'He was in the block. I got into trouble and he helped me – saved my life,' she explained. 'We fought through two patroller units to get to you. He killed them all.'

'Is he one of us?'

Martha raised an eyebrow. 'What does it *look* like, Aron?' she said, seeming annoyed. 'He just saved your life too. Or did you have that situation under control?'

Hurt by Martha's sarcasm, Aron continued watching the stranger. He stood at the entrance, talking through the barricade to whoever was hiding behind it.

'I don't trust him,' replied Aron. 'There's something strange about him – inhuman almost. No one can kill so many demons. Don't you think?'

Martha sighed. 'Just get Luca to the shelter,' she told him, her annoyance evident.

'Man, who died and put you in charge?' Aron spat without thinking. Samuel's face sprang instantly into his

23

mind and he felt a searing, surging dagger of shame pierce through his heart.

'There's no time for this, Aron!' she snapped. 'Just do it.'

'Aren't you coming?' he asked, the plea in his question completely apparent.

Martha shook her head. 'No,' she replied, looking at the newcomer with what seemed like admiration. Aron felt his face burning with emotion. 'I'm going with him to get the others . . .'

Aron nodded slowly and his stomach sank a little. A torn and broken body flashed into his mind. He had to tell her.

'Samuel . . .' he said.

Martha didn't need to hear any more. The look on Aron's face seemed to tell her everything. She shed a single tear; one that Aron felt the urge to kiss away.

'No time for that now,' she said, wiping her left cheek. 'Come on – let's move . . .'

Feltham Library

Borrowed Items 18/01/2020 12:48
XXXXXXXXXXXXXX9049

Item Title	Due Date
* Fire City	08/02/2020

* Indicates items borrowed today
Thankyou for using this unit
www.hounslowlibraries.org

3

Several hours later, as dawn broke weakly over the city, I helped lead the small band of survivors back into the darkness. The few that we had managed to rescue . . .

The Haven had been a theatre once, many years before the demons came. My mother, her eyes sparkling at the memories, had told me stories about the shows she'd seen there. That was before my birth, the War and the coming of the demons. The theatre's grand dome had since fallen in, the upper floors becoming death traps for humans and habitation for wild and savage animals. Most importantly, it was completely unknown to Valefor, the demon lord who ruled over Fire City, or to the Mayor, his human puppet.

It sat on the edge of the city, just beyond the artificial boundary created by the demons, a symbol of everything that we humans had lost. What remained of the theatre was under the rubble, an underground sanctuary accessed by two secret tunnels. Everyone we saved from the Hunt was taken there until they could be secreted away from Fire City. Away from the madness into whatever lay in the wastelands. It wasn't ideal, but there was no other choice. If they stayed in the city they'd only end up back in the Hunt anyway. A chance at life was better than no chance at all.

The Haven was laid out in rectangles, a smaller one inside another, with an outer corridor round each side. Small rooms lay off each passage and then, on the south side, a single entrance brought you to the inner area, with another perimeter of corridors. In the centre lay the hub of the sanctuary. It was a maze, a thousand square metres that had once housed dressing rooms, stage prop stores and a generator room.

After the War had been lost, one of the survivors, an actress, remembered the basement. The Hunt hadn't been established yet, so one night she dug through the rubble, hoping to find a stairwell leading down there. She didn't. Each night over the next week she tried again, braving the demon and army patrols, and broke through on the eighth night, dropping into the darkness and sending rats scattering.

Within weeks she had organized a small army of helpers – people who were prepared to risk everything to help the Resistance – people like my mother. They made the forgotten basement habitable – creating simple sanitary facilities, organizing dormitories and a canteen area. A second tunnel was dug; a back door to be used in times of trouble, and I'd heard rumours that there was another too – an exit known only to the elders and for emergency use.

The Haven became the focal point for our fight back – vital and secure, sheltering hundreds from the demons. The woman had been called Gemma Martin, and two years after founding the Haven, Valefor's lieutenants took her. My mother had always spoken highly of Gemma, calling her a true heroine: a woman prepared to give her life to fight the spawn of Hell.

'The perfect role model,' I said absently, the fatigue set tight in my muscles.

'What was that?' Aron asked from behind me.

'Nothing,' I replied.

A simple wooden hatch sat at the end of the tunnel. I knocked a secret code, waited and then repeated my actions. The hatch opened and a shaft of light lit up the tunnel. A giant elder with spiked blond hair and pale skin peered into the gloom – Mace, an elder whom I loved like a father.

'Welcome back!' he bellowed, his smile – which was almost as broad as his shoulders – filling me with warmth as it always did. He wore his usual grey cargo pants, stretched to bursting across his tree-trunk-sized thighs, a grey sweatshirt and an unzipped, black hooded top. His trusty machetes hung at each hip, the blades honed to the extreme. The same weapons I'd seen him use to deadly effect against our enemies. Mace was my father, my teacher and one of my heroes. One of the few adults left from my childhood.

'Did Tyrell cover our tracks?' I asked Aron as I crawled out into a grey-walled corridor. As I stood up, I realized that I'd have to speak to Mace about Samuel. I had wanted more time to compose myself, to tell him . . .

'Yeah,' replied Aron, getting a little too close for comfort.

I felt his body rub against my back and moved away. I was too tired to put up with his silly games and too worried about what I had to tell Mace. The giant clapped a meaty hand against Aron's back, oblivious to my furrowed brow.

'How many have we got today?' he asked.

My face fell as I thought about Samuel. I hadn't seen him die, but I had witnessed enough death to know that it would have been cruel and painful. The only mercy was that he hadn't ended up like the cannibals – a soul-less husk thirsty for blood. For a moment I thought that I would burst into tears but I managed to hold my nerve.

'Mace . . .' I began as he took me into his massive arms.

'What is it, child?' he asked, his voice now barely a whisper.

'Samuel,' I managed to say. 'We . . . we lost him.'

Mace let me go and stood for a moment, his eyes growing dark. Then he sank slowly to his knees, his face contorted in pain. I saw the rage building slowly in his broad chest and I thought that my heart would burst.

'I'm sorry,' I told him gently. 'Aron, tell him what happened.'

Aron looked surprised and uncomfortable at my words. He lowered his head, and when he eventually explained he seemed strangely defensive.

'We got split up,' he said. 'That's all. Me and Samuel went into one of the blocks. We got ambushed by patrollers, and Samuel took them on but there were too many. I tried to stop him, honest I did . . .'

I could feel Mace's anger rising, and knew that he wouldn't want to show his emotions – that his pride would stop him. Mace was the leader of our little group and a father-figure to all of us, not just to me. He clenched his jaw – ground his teeth together. The sound of it made me wince.

'I tried to save him, but—' Aron added, but the words stuck in his throat and he began to well up.

Mace looked up at me instead, his expression calmer but still piercing enough to make my heart thump.

'Where?' he demanded.

I shook my head, knowing what he was thinking. Knowing that he would risk his life to retrieve his son's remains.

'There's no point,' I told him. 'There'd be nothing left, Mace. Nothing of Samuel.'

Mace considered my reply before weeping silently, knowing that I was right. Out of respect, I turned away and watched Aron help the survivors into the corridor. There were ten of them – six women, three youngsters, including Luca, and an old man: ten out of the hundred who'd been sent to the Hunt, selected as prey because they served no useful function in the eyes of our rulers. Oscar and Tyrell, two more of our band, followed them; both of them were bloody from the battle and covered in dirt.

The last to enter was the stranger. He stood tall and stretched out his arms, blinking in the harsh light. Mace spotted him immediately and jumped up.

'Who's this?' he demanded, showing little further sign of anguish. I guessed that he'd already buried it some-where inside, somewhere deep. Death was common in Fire City – no one remained untouched by its grisly claws. To dwell on it was to make yourself a bigger target, to soften the hard edges, to blunt the required alertness of mind and body. A little like removing your armour in the midst of battle.

People died in Fire City.

It was one of many harsh realities in the reign of the demons.

I explained that the stranger had saved Luca and me,

before rescuing Aron too. I said that he'd joined us in our battle, and taken down many enemies. Mace seemed satisfied by what I told him. He eyed the young man up and down, taking an interest in the stranger's clothing and weapons. I found myself studying him too, but for different reasons. Reasons that made me feel embarrassed.

'You carry a rifle,' Mace pointed out. 'I haven't seen one of those since just after the War . . .'

The stranger looked at Mace, unblinking. I watched his eyes stay focused and a single blue vein throb with blood, just above his left temple.

'There are more rifles,' he said calmly.

'But where did you come from?' demanded Aron, his tone far from friendly. 'No one just turns up at a Hunt. No one.'

The stranger looked at me and then shook his head. 'Nowhere,' he replied, before nodding towards the survivors. 'I'm from nowhere. Forget about me – some of these people need help.'

Mace agreed and ordered Aron to take them to the infirmary, ignoring his protests. Once he'd gone, the giant turned to Oscar. 'Did you see my Samuel die?' he asked, his gruff voice calm.

Oscar shrugged and bowed his head slightly. Short and wiry, he was often thought of as a weak link. The truth was very different, however. Blessed with quick hands and an even quicker brain, Oscar was no slouch. I had known him nearly all of my life, and he was, like the other boys I'd grown up with, as close to me as a brother.

'The demons attacked from above,' he explained. 'Tyrell and I were already fighting. Aron and Samuel got isolated and after that we didn't see them again. Not until Aron turned up with Martha.'

Tyrell nodded too, his expression cheerless. 'We need more fighters,' he told Mace. 'There are too many of them. We're losing . . .'

Mace shrugged and tried to remain calm, but I knew him too well. His sky-blue eyes flitted from one of us to the other, and sweat beaded his brow. His cheeks and forehead were flushed and his massive hands clenched into tight balls.

'We've been killing demons,' he said. 'Valefor is feeling the pinch and he's reacting with more troops. It is what any general would do.'

'He's no general!' the stranger snapped, making me jump.

Mace looked surprised at the outburst too, and I wondered how he'd react. The stranger, despite his obvious ability, was taking a huge risk. Mace was the strongest, most powerful man I had ever known. He was the leader of our Resistance and I had seen him take on two patrollers at once and win. His temper was as quick as his sword hand. I prayed that he would remain placid.

'No – he's a hound of Hell,' I heard him agree. 'And I aim to send him back there with both of my machetes buried deep in his heart.'

This time the rest of us were amazed. Tyrell looked at me, and raised his eyebrows. I shrugged in reply, before looking to the newcomer again.

'How?' asked the stranger, his expression sceptical.

Mace furrowed his brow. The stranger looked to me, his obsidian eyes as unsettling as much as they were appealing. Something else lingered too, the soft, musky scent that I remembered from the Hunt – *his* scent. I found myself holding his gaze, as though hypnotized by him.

'He has thousands under his command,' the newcomer continued, looking away to Mace. 'How many do you have?'

Mace smiled weakly. 'Perhaps you and I should discuss this elsewhere?' he suggested. 'Let these brave souls rest.'

The stranger nodded in my direction. 'She comes with us,' he said, surprising me. Why did he want me to go with them?

'Isn't that up to Martha?' asked Mace.

The stranger shook his head. 'She comes with us or I leave.'

I agreed to go with them, intrigued. I also felt

foolishly happy that the stranger wanted me with him. I mean, I didn't even know who he was. All I did know was that we needed him. Fire City needed him. Someone who killed demons that easily was always welcome. Being cute with it was just an added bonus.

'We *need* his help,' I said to Mace, who looked thoughtful.

His eyes narrowed and he nodded. 'Agreed, then,' he replied, turning to me. 'Show him where to get washed up and then meet me in the generator room.'

'Where are you going?' I asked, a little concerned at what he might do.

'To mourn my son,' he said, pulling a flask of gut rot from a pocket.

'That's not going to help,' I told him sternly.

Mace roared with fake laughter. 'It's either this or I hang myself from the nearest tree,' he replied. 'And I'm not dying unless I can take Valefor and his puppet with me.'

4

The stranger stripped off his clothes and stepped into the cast-iron bath. A bucket of water, recently heated, was by the plughole, a tin cup floating in it. He sat and examined himself for signs of damage. His almost translucent skin bore a few scratches but nothing too serious. A simple amulet hung from a brown leather thong round his neck. It was a lump of rock, very like granite, given to him by his mother. He fiddled with it for a moment, thinking back to happier times, until tears welled in his eyes and he had to shake his mind free of the memories.

He took the tin cup, filled it with water and doused himself, repeating the action several times. Taking some well-worn soap, he stood and scrubbed himself, his mind focused on a single thing – Valefor. He had waited a long time to catch up with the demon lord, and now that he'd found him his impatience rose. He thought about the girl, Martha, feeling momentarily guilty that he hadn't told her the truth. The guilt disappeared as quickly as it had arrived, however. He wasn't there for her or any other Fire City dweller. He was there for himself. There was nothing accidental, either, about his arrival in Fire City. He was on a mission and nothing would get in his way.

A cough came from behind the tattered privacy curtains.

'I've brought some more water,' he heard Martha say.

'Bring it in, then,' he replied, soaping his armpits.

'Are you decent?'

He shook his head. In a world that had gone to Hell, in which ordinary people lived and worked for rulers who exploited them, hunted them, and ate them – here was a young woman worried about nudity. 'Yes,' he lied.

Martha stepped through the curtain with a wooden pail, just as the stranger washed the soap from his pits. '*Oh!*' she squealed, turning away. 'I'm sorry, I thought you said you were—'

'I did,' said the man.

Martha put down the pail, keeping her back to him. 'Why would you do that?' she asked.

'Because it's only flesh,' he replied. 'I'm sure you've seen many a naked man in your time.'

This time Martha did turn round, hands on hips, eyes narrowed. 'Do you think I'm some sort of slut?' she demanded.

The stranger shook his head, showering her with

droplets of water. A single drop hit Martha's top lip and sat there, trembling. She took no notice.

'I don't make a habit of seeking out naked men,' she told him.

'In the north,' he replied, covering his genitals with his hands, 'we lived together. Ate, slept, bathed . . .'

'You lived in the north?' she asked.

'For a while,' he told her. 'I left to come here.'

Martha looked taken aback. 'You *wanted* to come to Fire City?' she asked, the surprise evident in her tone.

The newcomer hesitated before replying. There was no sense in revealing his true purpose to her. It brought no profit. 'Not Fire City,' he lied. 'I'm headed south – to the Great Citadel. I just wanted a rest.'

'I've never been outside Fire City,' she admitted. 'I'd love to travel the country.'

He shook his head again. 'You wouldn't love it,' he told her. 'The roads are dangerous, patrolled by the demons and their allies. I travelled through the waste-lands, keeping the main trunk road in sight.'

Martha's eyes grew wider. 'But I've heard that the wastelands are treacherous!' she exclaimed.

'Yes, they are,' the newcomer admitted, 'but I'd rather face wild animals, even those that have turned, than actual demons.'

Martha snorted. 'I watched you dispatch demons

37

with ease earlier,' she reminded him. 'I don't believe that you're scared of them.'

'I'm not scared,' he agreed. 'But I'm not stupid, either.'

'How do you kill them so easily?' she asked.

He shrugged. 'Proper combat training, the right weapons and huge doses of luck,' he replied.

'Luck? It doesn't seem that way to me. Aron thinks you're not human . . .'

The stranger moved his hands, looking down at himself. Martha did the same. 'Do I *look* inhuman to you?' he asked her with a sly little smile.

'I have to go!' said Martha, scarlet as she hurried from the room.

Martha's face was still flushed later as she sat with the stranger and Mace in the generator room. Mace's own skin tone was redder than hers, fuelled by alcohol and tears. Martha wanted to leave him to his grief. Besides, she needed to get back to her other life before she was missed. The stranger had changed into some spare clothes that Martha had brought for him, which had once belonged to Samuel. If Mace noticed this, he didn't show it. Instead, he questioned their guest about his weapons.

'We ambushed a shipment,' said the newcomer. 'The government move them around by train. We derailed one halfway between the Northern Citadel and the midlands.'

Mace looked impressed. He took a swig from his flask and shuddered. The alcohol was home-made, from fermented apples, and a little took you a long way towards drunken oblivion. Mace was close to that now. Once he'd composed himself, he moved on.

'How many of you?' he asked.

'Fifteen,' replied the stranger. 'It wasn't guarded too securely, but we still lost seven men.'

Mace shook his head. 'Was it worth it?' he questioned.

The stranger shrugged and looked at Martha. 'Is rescuing ten people from a Hunt worth it?' he asked.

Martha's face darkened. '*Every* human life is worth it,' she insisted. 'Every single one saved.'

Their guest remained unconvinced. 'And how many have you *lost*?'

Martha looked away, fighting back tears.

Mace spoke for her. 'I've lost three sons, a wife and a father,' he revealed. 'And during the War itself I lost four brothers, their families and countless friends. There is almost nothing left in my heart save my hatred for these bastards. And a single strand of hope for humankind. *Without* that strand, I would be no better than the demons.'

'You *must* understand,' Martha added, looking

directly into the stranger's dark eyes, 'that there isn't a human being outside the citadels who doesn't know what loss feels like.'

It was the boy's turn to look away. Martha was right about life outside the seven major cities – the citadels, as they were called. She was wrong, however, if she thought he was driven by some moral cause.

'I don't understand,' he said quietly, 'because I don't let myself. There is only black and white in this world. The demons and their allies are evil and they have to be killed. That's all I think about.'

'That's noble enough a cause,' grunted Mace. 'I agree wholeheartedly.'

'I'm not noble,' he replied.

'Where did you learn to fight?' asked Martha.

'I've been trained since I was a small child,' he said. 'My siblings too.'

'You have brothers and sisters?'

He nodded. 'Yes, although I haven't seen them in a while. A brother and two sisters – all older than me.'

Martha pushed on. '*Why* haven't you seen them?' she asked.

'Something happened to split us up,' he told her, looking down at his feet.

'Do you know where they are?' asked Mace.

'I think two of them are in Babylon or the surrounding area. The other one – who knows?'

'Babylon?' asked a confused-looking Martha.

Mace grinned and offered her his flask, which she refused.

'I spend enough time serving that poison to customers,' she told him. 'If I wanted to feel like I'd been savaged by a patroller, I'd go and pick a fight with one. Empty-handed.' She turned back to face the newcomer. 'What's Babylon?' she queried again.

'It's what the northerners call the Southern Citadel,' the stranger explained.

Martha nodded her understanding. 'And what do they call you?' she asked.

The stranger shrugged. 'Most of the people I've met don't care what my name is,' he said.

'Your parents cared enough to give you one,' added Mace. 'A name *means* something, boy.'

'Well, mine is Jonah,' he told them.

Mace grinned. 'A fine name!' he bellowed. 'Had my wife survived her last pregnancy, we would have called our son the same.'

'How many children did you have?' asked Jonah.

Mace shook his head softly, his expression changed in an instant. 'Five sons,' he said sorrowfully. 'The one who died as he was born took my wife with him. The other two, Michael and Samuel, were killed fighting for the Resistance. The two who remain are called Joshua and Nathan. They're out in the wastelands somewhere –

fighting with the Resistance, if they're still alive. I haven't heard from them in over two years.'

Jonah thought of his own family. How it had been torn apart so long ago. 'I'm sorry,' he said quietly.

'Why? It's not your fault, son,' said Mace, taking another gulp of alcohol.

Martha rose; it was time for her to go. 'I can't be caught,' she said.

Jonah gave her a quizzical look. 'Caught by who?'

'My stepfather,' she replied.

Mace grunted, edging closer to that drunken precipice. Something passed between his eyes and Martha's. Something Jonah noticed but kept to himself.

'Go, then!' the older man told her. 'I'll bring the boy along later. We have much to talk about.'

Martha considered Mace for a moment. 'Talk?' she said. 'I'm surprised you're still moving, you big lump.'

Their guest told them he wasn't staying. 'I need to move on,' he lied.

'Nonsense!' bellowed the giant at his side. 'You'll stay here until you're rested or my name isn't Mace G—' The next sound he made was a thud as he hit the floor.

'Leave him there,' said Martha. 'He'll sleep it off.'

'I was going to.'

'So are you staying for a while or leaving?' she added.

Jonah considered his options. He could leave and hide in the wastelands, relying on his survival skills while constantly watching out for wild animals, many of which were possessed by lesser demons. Or he could stay in Fire City itself, with a few more basic essentials to hand. He'd be closer to his target that way, but also more likely to be discovered.

'I'll stay for a few days,' he eventually decided. 'Besides, I want to go out on another Hunt.'

Martha nodded. 'Get some rest, then,' she told him.

'Where are you going?' he asked.

'Work.'

5

Fire City is a hard place to live. The world in which Fire City exists is a hard place to live.

Back before the demons took over, things were easier, or so my mum and the other elders have told me. I was born and raised here, and this world is the only one I've ever known. It's hard for me to get my head around – the idea that there was a time and place without demons. But there was, once, and even though I've never experienced it, I long for its return.

I was thinking about these things when Tyrell and Oscar walked into the bar where I work. I share my shifts with Faith – an older woman who is also in the Resistance. Today, Faith was in the kitchen, cleaning up, whilst I tended the few customers.

The saloon sits on the ground floor of the Grand, a disused old hotel owned by the Mayor, the human puppet who rules Fire City. The Grand is at the very heart of the city, in what we've always called the protected zone – an area surrounded by an invisible ring of demon energy, which is about four kilometres in diameter. Everything outside the ring is wasteland, and it is illegal for any human to venture out there unless they have permission from the government.

The bar sells cheap government-funded booze, much like the stuff that Mace likes to drink. Many of Fire City's residents squander the few credits they earn in the factories on getting drunk, most to forget how shitty their lives are. The first floor houses an office and living quarters for the Mayor's right-hand man, a mercenary called Stone who makes my skin crawl with his wandering eyes and his unblinking stare. At the rear of the second floor are more rooms, which I'm allowed to use, both for me and for some of my friends. Above that are two further levels, left empty save for the rats and mice. The saloon is quiet during the early afternoon, but by the time night falls it becomes a raucous and often violent place that reeks of fear and desperation.

'Working hard for the old man?' joked Tyrell, settling his massive frame onto a barstool and rubbing his shaven coffee-coloured head.

The look I shot him caused him to grin.

'He's *not* my old man,' I replied, feeling my usual sense of shame and anger.

Tyrell was talking about the Mayor: human ruler for the demons – and my stepfather. There is nothing I hate more than collaborators, and I *detest* the Mayor. The fact

45

that he was once married to my mother means nothing to me. Before she died, my mother had all but turned her back on him anyway. She'd been a secret Resistance member for years.

I don't know exactly how she died, but I do know that she got caught. The Mayor, like the spineless piece of trash that he is, has always refused to talk about it, which makes me hate him all the more. I'll tell you this, though – if I ever find out who killed my mother, I'm going to destroy them, no matter what the cost. Every time I kill a patroller or a cannibal, or I rescue someone, it's payback for what happened to my mum. I understand that I'll probably get caught soon, but I don't care. I'd rather die than serve the Hell-kin like my stepfather does.

'Has he been in today?' asked Oscar, joining me behind the bar.

'Not yet,' I told him. 'But I'm sure he'll bring his fat, ugly carcass over later.'

'Wow!' grinned Oscar, his oriental features lighting up, pale-brown eyes sparkling like gemstones. 'You're an insolent little puppy today.'

'Got it from my mother.'

Oscar's smile faded a little and he shook his head slightly. I looked around, making sure that the few customers we had couldn't hear us. Membership of the Resistance was an offence punishable by death and we took care to speak cautiously when other people were about. However, the customers I could see were too busy getting drunk to even care.

'She used to be so nice to me,' he said. 'Remember that time we knocked May's herb pot over? She shouted at everyone except me.'

'I remember,' I replied with a warm smile and a slight lump in my throat. 'You were always her favourite.'

Tyrell rapped his knuckles against the mahogany bar and broke the memories.

'Service is terrible,' he said, his eyebrows arching.

Sometimes, when I think about how much Oscar and Tyrell mean to me, I get emotional. I don't even know why it happens, but today was one of those days, perhaps because of Samuel. As I wiped away tears, they said nothing and made no judgements. They never do.

The three of us are the same age, and I've known Oscar and Tyrell my whole life. Like most of the human population, they are Unwanted. They've always been around, and as far as I know neither knew his own family. My mother, my aunt and Mace brought them up, and I've always seen them as my brothers.

Two years ago my brothers fell in love – with each other. I remember how nervous they'd been, how reluctant to tell anyone but me. They hid their relationship for nearly six months, though I urged them to speak to the elders, to be open about their love. When they finally spoke up, some of the more old-fashioned people outside our circle made an ignorant comment or two, but everyone soon got used to seeing them as a couple, and for me, it just brought the three of us even closer.

'You want something,' I told Tyrell, 'get it yourself – don't care *how* big you are.'

Tyrell grinned at my childish reply, reached across the bar and pulled me to him with one mighty hand as though I weighed nothing. He used the other to caress my face.

'Little sister . . .' he cooed, like a lunatic. 'Maybe we should get you a man – ease all that tension?'

As I told him to go and stick his head up a patroller's arse, Jonah came into my thoughts and it must have shown.

'She's thinking about a man!' said Oscar excitedly. 'Look at her little face.'

'Martha?'

I shook my head, trying to break free of Tyrell's grip.

'Tell us and I'll let you go,' he offered as he held on tightly.

'I'm not thinking about anyone!' I protested, hoping that he'd believe me.

'Oscar,' he asked, 'do you think our sister is telling the truth?'

'No,' Oscar replied, 'but I think she might suffocate if you carry on. Let her go.'

Tyrell agreed and I pulled away from him, straightening out my clothes.

'One day,' I said, 'I'm going to get you!'

'Yeah, yeah,' he joked. 'Heard it since I was little.'

'*Little?*' asked Oscar. 'When were you ever little, Tyrell?'

We chatted some more before Tyrell, double-checking that no one could overhear us, mentioned Samuel. I knew that he'd wanted to talk about our friend's death from the moment he sat down, but I also realized that he wouldn't just bring it up. I knew why too, and I understood completely. Tyrell's jokes and annoying habit of manhandling me were his way of softening the situation, of checking how the ground lay. For me, just the sound of Samuel's name caused my stomach to churn with grief.

'I'm trying not to think about it,' I replied truthfully. 'It hurts too much. It's like there's this piece of us that's gone.'

Oscar jumped up and sat on the bar. 'I know,' he said. 'Feels like it can't be true, you know? Like any minute now he's going to walk in, pretending to be his dad and ordering us about. Trying it on with any woman with more than five teeth in her head.'

At that last line, the three of us began to giggle, partly

because it was funny and mostly because it was true. Samuel had been trying to charm the women since he was ten years old. I doubted there was an adult female in the city that he hadn't tried to chat up at some point in her life.

'I dunno what happened,' Oscar continued when we'd stopped laughing. 'We were fine until the demons ambushed us. But even then, it's not like we haven't been jumped before. Samuel and Aron just broke away and then we lost sight of them.'

'Did Aron tell you any more?' I asked, picking up a rag and wiping the surfaces, just to occupy my hands.

'Not much,' replied Tyrell. 'He had that shifty look on his face. The one that makes me want to slap him senseless.'

I understood what Tyrell meant about Aron. Like the others, he was part of the family, but recently he'd been acting strangely. In the past few weeks he'd fought with Oscar and Samuel, taken a hiding from Mace for remarks he'd made about another elder called Prior, and given me the creeps by telling me that he loved me. Don't get me wrong; I *do* love Aron, but only like I love the others. Like I said – they're brothers, but nothing more. Nothing like *that*. Thing is, Aron reacted badly when I told him that, and since then everyone else has been paying the price. I can't seem to make him understand my feelings. He thinks that I'll change my mind, but I won't.

'Mace wants to see if the demons left anything of Samuel,' added Oscar.

I nodded. 'I told him he couldn't,' I replied. 'Even if they left something, it won't be our Samuel. Just a few body parts . . .'

The thought of his remains made my stomach turn. I've seen countless deaths, grown up knee-deep in blood and guts, but it doesn't make any difference. Thinking about someone I love being torn apart makes me sick. I'm glad it does too − the day I lose that is the day I've forgotten what being a human really means.

'Aren't you working today?' I asked them both. Most of us had jobs, and the boys worked in factories deep in the industrial zone, where they helped to make clothing for the Wanted. As a result they were always tired.

'Start in an hour,' Tyrell replied through a yawn.

'I'll make you some coffee, then,' I said.

'Thanks − I need it,' he told me, stretching his arms behind his head.

I set about making his drink as my thoughts turned back to Samuel and Aron.

6

The Mayor knelt at his master's feet, in Valefor's inner sanctum, head bowed and stomach churning. The air was fetid, the stench of rotting flesh assailing his nostrils. Other smells lingered too: the metallic tang of iron-rich earth, the alkaline aroma of urine, so rich that the Mayor could almost taste it. His knees rested on a pile of dried dung, fat bluebottles buzzing in lazy arcs all around him. A fresh pile of his master's faeces steamed silently to his right.

'Where did they get these weapons?' asked Valefor.

The Mayor mumbled his reply, aware that one wrong move might end his life.

'*SPEAK UP!*'

'I do not know, great lord,' offered the Mayor as his hands began to tremble.

The demon lord lifted a muscular, fur-covered leg and pushed the Mayor back with his hoof. He landed on his behind, his right hand scattering the fresh pile of excrement.

'You offer nothing,' whispered Valefor.

The Mayor lifted his head, vainly wiping his hand on the stone floor. Valefor remained on his throne, flanked by two patrollers. His eyes, cat-like and violet, bored into the Mayor's face. Giant, pond-green wings with dagger-like golden tips curled away from his feline body. His head, resembling some diabolical reptilian donkey, had a long, thick jaw and dangerously sharp teeth. Teeth that had crunched through the bones of many a poor soul.

'I need some time,' begged the Mayor. 'I'll find them.'

Valefor stood, towering above everything and everyone, unfolding powerful arms that ended in razor-sharp claws. A thick layer of wheat-coloured hair covered all but the very tips of his arms. His wings flapped behind him, a sure sign that he remained unconvinced.

'Each time there is a problem you tell me the same thing,' he said, 'and each time you fail me.'

'I promise to—'

'*SILENCE!*' demanded the demon lord.

The Mayor felt his bowels contract. A layer of greasy perspiration covered his face. His heart thumped inside his chest.

Valefor sensed this and smiled. 'I scare you,' he said softly.

'You are mighty, my lord,' cowered the Mayor.

'And yet you continue to fail me,' Valefor added. 'This situation is perplexing.'

The Mayor sensed that he needed to prove himself. That Valefor would favour strength over weakness. Gambling on this hunch, he rose slowly to his feet, watching his master's every move, nerves jangling.

'They kill your fellow demons,' he said bravely. 'Yet your own kind does less than I to combat their actions.'

Valefor considered this reply, nodding after a short while. 'You speak truthfully,' he admitted. 'But know this, human. I am nothing like those legions that serve me. Ancient is the spore from which I was created and long have I existed – since before your species first took breath. My power is not of your understanding.'

'I know, my lord,' said the Mayor. 'Which is *why* you can trust me. I would never act against your wishes. I am not that foolish. And I value this privileged existence you grant me.'

Again the demon lord considered his reply. 'This is also true,' he agreed. 'I give you power over the pitiful humans – and in return all I ask is that you keep them under control, stop their puny efforts to resist. It is such a small thing to ask. Yet these weapons pose a conundrum. The Unwanted have no access to rifles. How, then, did they come to possess one?'

The Mayor shook his head. 'I don't know, my lord,' he replied. 'Perhaps the Resistance has reached us from the north . . . ?'

Once more, the Mayor gambled. Officially, the Resistance was a major threat: a highly organized, ruthless enemy, threatening the very fabric of the brave new society built after the War. In the citadels, where the Wanted went about their daily lives, they made a convenient scapegoat. Resisters were terrorists and they faced the full might of the government. Citizens were urged to remain vigilant at all times, and their own fear of terrorism kept them compliant.

However, the reality was different. Those who ruled considered the Resistance a futile attempt at creating hope amongst the Unwanted. They saw them as a small, badly trained and disorganized rabble, riddled with infighting and often infiltrated by the human government. Despite some minor losses, the Resistance had caused no real problems.

Not until recently anyway. In the past few months something had changed. To the north of the country, the revolt had grown. Reports had reached the Mayor of growing demon losses. If he'd heard the stories, Valefor must have done so too.

'Perhaps,' replied the demon lord. 'It matters little to me. My legions are mighty . . .'

'Yes, my master,' said the Mayor.

'And you are adept at deflecting your duties.'

'My lord, I—' began the Mayor, only for the demon to interrupt.

55

'Fret not, my deceitful deputy. I almost admire this deviousness,' he said.

The Mayor smiled, watching Valefor's wings grow still. A plump, dark-skinned servant approached the demon lord. Her head remained bowed, her feet shuffling. Lunch was being served.

'Stop this resistance,' warned Valefor. 'My patience will not stretch much further.'

'As you wish,' replied the Mayor.

'I do wish,' said Valefor. 'But I want no more failure. Make use of my legions. My trusted aide, Mias, will be available to you.'

'I shall not hesitate to call on them.'

'And dare not fail . . .'

The Mayor shook his head. 'I won't,' he promised. 'Shall I leave you to your repast?'

Valefor shook his head. 'Remain,' he ordered.

The Mayor watched Valefor approach the servant, his eyes ablaze. The demon uttered words in some ancient tongue, his colossal wings surrounding the woman, binding her in a cocoon. Before he bowed his head to eat, he turned to the Mayor.

'*DO NOT FAIL ME!*' he whispered, the words continuing to echo around the Mayor's head after he'd spoken.

Turning back to his prey, Valefor opened his powerful jaws wide. As the servant's cranium splintered, vomit rose in the Mayor's throat. He fought it back, swallow-ing and rushing to the door. Behind him the patrollers howled with blood lust.

Twenty minutes later, the mercenary Stone drove the Mayor through potholed streets back to his gated residence, rain pounding against the windscreen of the only car in Fire City. Its once sumptuous interior showed signs of ageing, the leather cracked and faded to grey. The transmission rattled and the undercarriage squeaked. Stone had seen other cars, proper cars, in the citadels. To find one that worked outside the citadels was rare.

Not that he *wanted* to be out here. For Stone, assigned to work alongside the Mayor by the human government, his time in Fire City was a necessary evil. Once his assignment was done, he had other plans.

The car sped past an open expanse of green that had once been a park. Most of it was overgrown, the weeds so dense that it was impossible to penetrate them without a machete. A stone arch stood above the tangle of grasses, a crumbling reminder of the past. Hungry rats the size of small dogs prowled the periphery, searching for food. The Mayor's residence overlooked the open space, although once behind the five-metre perimeter walls, it could only be seen from the upper floor.

'Are you listening to me?' the Mayor demanded.

'Yeah,' replied Stone, his tone as sullen as his expression.

'He tried to scare me, Stone. *Me*. As though I were some cowardly unfortunate. I had to set him straight.' The Mayor sat back in the seat.

Stone eyed his employer in the rear-view mirror, raising a solitary eyebrow. Judging by the sheen of sweat on his face and the faint faecal whiff inside the car, the Mayor was being less than truthful. He was a small man with a big attitude, wearing a charcoal-grey suit with shiny black shoes, a white shirt and a pale-grey tie. As usual, Stone let him play out his charade, bottling away his contempt. For as long as the Mayor paid his wages, Stone would put up with his delusions.

'Have you heard anything new about the Resistance here in the city?' asked the Mayor, adjusting his tie before using a handkerchief to mop his face.

'Nothing,' replied Stone, his steel-blue eyes staring straight ahead.

The Mayor eyed the back of Stone's shaven head. 'Can you find out if anything has changed?' he added.

'Shouldn't be a problem,' said Stone, braking sharply as the gates to the Mayor's mansion approached.

'Unlike your driving,' snapped the Mayor.

'Sorry, boss, I was miles away.'

'Valefor wants action,' the Mayor continued.

'And what Valefor *wants*, Valefor *gets*,' replied Stone, trying not to grin.

A couple of armed guards, human mercenaries dressed in combat fatigues, opened the gates and took positions on either side of the car, their guns drawn. Stone shook his head at the unnecessary show of force. No one was going to attack the Mayor; if they did, then he, Stone, would kill them. That was his job and he was good at it. The Mayor liked the pantomime; it made him feel more important. Another little quirk that Stone was willing to put up with. For now.

'I'll ask around tomorrow,' he said.

'Make sure you do,' ordered the Mayor. 'Now stop this damn car and let me out.'

Stone clenched his jaw, working the muscles, silent fury building in every fibre of his body.

'Something amiss?' asked the Mayor.

'No, chief,' lied Stone. 'Everything's just hunky-dory.'

7

Mace led Jonah on a tour of Fire City. During the day, the streets were calm and the population went about their business almost without fear. Life for the Unwanted was a never-ending cycle of work, drudgery and more work. There were no days off, no entertainment, and no schools for the young ones. If you were old enough, you worked. And if you didn't work, you lived on the streets, scavenging for extra food and trying to stay hidden from the patrols looking for victims for the next Hunt. Pockets of danger lurked, however, and murder was commonplace.

Desperate humans turned on each other, often killing those they robbed.

The crazed and hungry cannibals, their souls consumed and their humanity taken, hid in abandoned buildings during the day, butchering and eating the unwary. Strangers who didn't know the city could easily find themselves on that evening's menu.

As for the demons, they could turn on anyone, at any

time, but usually kept their distance during daylight. Valefor and the other lords weren't stupid. They realized that given free rein to kill humans, their underlings would have decimated the population.

'You can't hunt an extinct prey,' mused Mace as they made their way around the city. 'And they don't care too much for the souls of rabbits.'

'Extinction is preferable to this life,' replied Jonah.

Mace stopped and eyed him. 'Extinction?' he asked with a smile. 'I'd rather die.'

Jonah understood that he was supposed to laugh at Mace's joke but he kept quiet. Instead, his eyes continued to scan the streets, creating a map in his mind. He wanted to learn the position of every alleyway and lane in Fire City. Blessed with a photographic memory, once he saw something he never forgot it. When the time came to confront Valefor, a mental plan of the city might be very useful.

A purple hue hung in the atmosphere; the clouds were dulled and grey overhead. A constant barrage of odours assaulted his senses, from the stench of open latrines to the occasional waft of sweet-smelling flowers and aromatic herbs growing wild through the cracks in the pavement. The people they passed seemed to reek of body odour and musty, unwashed clothing stiff with dirt. Some greeted Mace, but most shuffled by with their heads down. Occasional cats and dogs with threadbare, mangy coats chased after rodents, their domesticated ancestors long since discarded by humans because pets were a luxury that only the Wanted could afford. A dog outside the citadels was more likely to be a man's next meal than his best friend. Jonah had eaten a few canines himself out in the wastelands, near-starvation forcing him to act against his human instincts.

He turned to Mace. 'What do they make here?' he asked.

'Clothing, mostly,' Mace told him. 'Undergarments, socks . . . anything they need in the citadels. The factories are in an industrial zone to the east of the city. Most of us work in them.'

'Not you?'

'I'm due to begin my next shift tonight.'

'And Martha?'

Jonah watched Mace raise an eyebrow and wondered if he was suspicious. The last thing Jonah needed was someone asking too many questions about him. The less they found out, the better.

'Martha works in a bar owned by the Mayor.'

'The Mayor?'

'Human ruler,' explained Mace. 'Martha's stepfather – her mother was married to him – although don't tell her I said that. She'll rip my lungs out with a blunt spoon if she finds out I've told you.'

'I won't say anything,' Jonah told him. 'It's none of my business.'

Only something inside made Jonah flinch. It felt wrong that a traitor had raised the feisty, battle-tough girl. He shook her face from his mind, wondering why he was thinking about her at all.

'Don't judge us,' he heard Mace say. 'Life in these industrial outpost cities is hard. Work, death and the Hunt are the only things you can count on.'

Jonah shrugged. 'It's the same up north,' he said. 'Same all over.'

Mace agreed. 'Used to be, before the War, that you worked and got paid,' he told him. 'You went home, because you *had* a home, and raised your family and spent the weekends enjoying life, because you *had* a life. Now we just try to survive.'

'You must have only been about my age when the War ended,' Jonah pointed out.

'If you're sixteen, then you'd be right,' replied Mace. 'I was repeating something my father told me. You have a good knowledge of history, then?'

'It was something *my* father taught me – to study the past,' replied Jonah, paraphrasing the giant without intent. Despite himself, Jonah found that he was warming to Mace, getting to admire and respect him. It was obvious that the man cared deeply for his people, for his family.

'I taught my children to survive and fight,' said Mace with a wistful look. 'There *was* nothing else. No reading them books or playing games in the sunshine. I sat them on my knee and taught them how shit everything is. Here's how you light a fire and here's the best way to skin and gut a rat before cooking it. Potatoes grow best if planted during this month, and this is how you know which *month* it is. Apples make great booze, if you put them in barrels and let them rot a while, and follow your granddad's secret recipe. Here's how to sharpen your blade, to break into a guarded warehouse, to hide from the patrols. And *this* is how you take the life of a demon . . .'

His voice trailed off, eyes moistening. Jonah realized that Mace was probably thinking about Samuel. He felt a pang of sadness for his new friend and wondered how he might ease his pain.

'There was no point in teaching them anything else,' he said eventually, unable to find the right words. 'They should be prepared for life as it is.'

Mace shrugged and wiped away his tears. He took Jonah's arm and walked on. 'Never talk in one spot for too long around here,' he explained. 'Fire City is full of people desperate enough to sell their souls for a piece of bread.'

'Then point them out,' insisted Jonah, feeling suddenly angered, his left hand settling on his sword.

'You're already drawing attention, friend,' Mace pointed out. 'There's time enough to attract more.'

They walked on, past rows of disused buildings and the remains of a complex that had once held shops and bars. Mace explained the history of the city as they went, indicating various landmarks. Jonah listened intently whilst watching out for patrols. The road ahead of them was deserted and littered with debris; the old stores overgrown with weeds. They walked the length of it without seeing anyone else, crossing another road into a park. A single track had been worn through undergrowth that stood a head taller than Mace, leading down to a towpath and river. Again, Jonah took in everything he saw, adding to his mental map of the city.

'Be careful,' warned Mace. 'These weeds often hide a nasty surprise.'

Jonah pulled a small knife from his belt, but doubted there was anything for him to concern himself with. He decided to offer a little information about himself — something that couldn't hurt.

'I spent many weeks in the wastelands,' he revealed. 'I faced all sorts out there. I'm not worried.'

Mace shrugged and lifted his left trouser leg. 'Lost half my calf with *that* attitude, son,' he said, showing off his deformity. 'It was a badger, twice the size it should have been and crazy with hunger.'

Jonah looked down. The half-moon-shaped dent in

the giant's leg was ridged with scar tissue. He wondered how much it had hurt. Pain was something else that Jonah didn't fear – not any more.

'You have good medics then,' he said. 'A wound like that can kill if it gets infected, and put you at risk of being selected for the Hunt . . .'

Mace winked and Jonah found himself smiling back. There was something warm and likeable about the giant man – something about his manner that was comforting.

'I've a stronger will than five ordinary men combined,' he boasted. 'And Martha's aunt works wonders with a herb or two.'

'I know a few remedies myself,' revealed Jonah. 'Perhaps she and I should compare notes.'

Mace told him they'd meet later. 'I wanted to talk in private,' he added. 'No one comes down here, not any more. It's too close to the edge of town. So no chance of being overheard.'

Jonah nodded. 'I don't have much to tell,' he said, a little ashamed that he was about to deflect the truth.

Mace shook his head. 'You have *plenty* to tell,' he replied. 'The weapons you carry, the clothes you wear. The skill and ease with which you kill demons – all of these things interest me. It's obvious you're fighting for the Resistance, so we're on the same side.'

Jonah stepped onto a towpath slimy with bottle-green

moss, looking down at the murky river water. He wondered what to say to Mace. They *were* on the same side, that was true, but their reasons for fighting differed greatly. Mace reminded Jonah of people he'd met in the north – noble warriors with fearless hearts who were fighting for their right to survive. Good, decent men who he welcomed as friends. How then could he explain his own motives, spurred on by nothing more than a selfish need for retribution?

'I fight with you,' he eventually replied. 'But perhaps not in the same way.'

Mace scratched his stubbly chin. 'How so?' he asked.

'It doesn't matter,' said Jonah. 'I guess being on the same side is all that counts.'

Mace grunted. 'I'll accept anyone who wants to kill these inhuman dogs as much as I do,' he said.

Jonah stooped to pick up a blue-grey stone. He looked at it for a moment, lost in random thoughts he couldn't quite place – fleeting, fragmented memories.

'The weapons,' continued Mace. 'You said that there were others.'

Jonah nodded, cleared his mind. 'The northern Resistance has plenty,' he explained. 'They are planning a new campaign. A more concerted effort.'

'How many fighters do they have?' asked Mace.

'Not much above three hundred,' replied Jonah. 'But there are more potential recruits living in the wastelands. The problem is getting them together. It's impossible to live in communities out there without alerting the government.'

Mace sighed and looked down the river, towards a disused mill that had once been converted into luxury homes. One of its walls had collapsed, revealing three storeys of broken dreams. The demons didn't care where the Unwanted lived. Burned-out houses, the few remaining tower blocks still serviceable – wherever. As long as there were enough people to work and a few more to hunt. Each outpost city provided quasi-slave labour, mostly people in their teens and upwards. The work was hard, the hours long, and it took its toll quickly.

Those no longer able to work were taken and held in pens, fodder for the hunters, alongside sickly or abandoned children, the infirm and the disabled. The government sifted through the younger adults and teenagers, taking the healthy and strong to breeding centres. Once there, they were forced to have sex to create the next generation, a never-ending production line of workers for the Wanted and food for the demons. Most lasted no more than a decade before they too were sent to the factories or joined the Hunted.

Their offspring were carefully sorted. Category A infants, the smallest group, were limited in number and certified as genetically superior. Their futures lay in the citadels, with all the advantages that brought. Category B infants formed the largest set, the Unwanted, even though many were perfectly fit and healthy. They were distributed amongst the outpost cities and towns. Local families took some in, with the others left to fend for themselves. Most would end up as workers or prey by the time they reached fourteen. Some, depending on demand, were re-inspected, passed worthy and taken back to the centres to breed more children.

Category C held the disabled. These children were kept in pens, fattened up and then thrown into a Hunt. It was rare to see anyone with so much as a limp, and old people were also uncommon. The brave new world demanded that you served a purpose. Any deviation from that meant certain death.

'What a life,' Mace said, without explaining his thoughts. 'Now tell me more about the north and their resistance plans. We should coordinate our efforts.'

Jonah's face grew dark. He wondered how much he should reveal. Talking about his mission in general terms seemed to be the best solution. It was like lying through a filter of truth.

'The key here in Fire City,' he said softly, 'is Valefor and his human puppets.'

Mace nodded. 'Cut off the monster's head and the rest will die,' he replied. 'A classic tactic.'

Jonah shrugged at the giant man's reply. 'We never

do, though, do we?' he said. 'We waste time and lives fighting the minions, the lesser spawn . . .'

'That's because Valefor and the other demon lords are too powerful,' said Mace. 'No one has ever killed one of them. No one knows how.'

Jonah threw the stone out into the water. It made a single plopping sound and sank to the bottom, leaving only ripples on the surface. Those fragmented memories returned: the agony etched across his father's face, the screams of his mother. He looked into Mace's eyes, his own growing darker still.

'I do,' he said.

8

Two days later, Aron stopped by the bar and sat in silence as I served several customers. It was around eight in the evening, and I was tired and angry. My stepfather was with Stone in his office, stewing after our latest argument. It had been over Faith and the others making use of the hotel – *his* hotel. He'd called me a hypocrite, telling me that I was living in a dream world.

The thing is, I've never accepted the position I grew up in. As a child, I didn't have any choice. My mother and I lived in the Mayor's mansion, surrounded by the same luxuries he now uses as weapons against me. And I'm not going to lie and say that I didn't like him back then, because I did; he was the man who looked after us, made sure that we weren't starving. I remember him being happier and younger, combing my hair and telling me stories before bed.

But those are the memories of an innocent, and I stopped being that a long time ago. The minute my mother began to spend more time at the hotel, mixing with Mace, Faith and the others, everything changed. *She* changed, and the things I then saw, the people I met, they all changed my way of thinking too. I realized that the world was evil and that the Mayor, no matter how good he'd been to my mum in the past, was nothing more than a traitor to humans. As the arguments increased between my mum and the Mayor, I saw her growing apart from him, and watched him change into what he is now. What was I going to do? Follow *him* over her? Never. And then she died . . .

'I want to talk to you,' Aron said as I pushed away the groping hand of a drunken customer.

'Talk, then,' I replied sharply, without meaning to. 'I'm busy though, so be quick.'

'Can't stop thinking about Samuel,' he whispered, his eyes downcast.

I felt that surge of despair I got each time our dead friend's name was mentioned and it took several deep breaths for me not to cry. Instead, I poured two measures of apple liquor into metal cups and placed them on the bar for another customer, taking two coins in return.

'None of us can stop thinking of him,' I said with more warmth, once the customer was out of earshot. 'It's not like you can forget. He was our brother.'

Aron scratched at the wooden bar top with a dirty fingernail. The grime extended up his finger and across his hands. As I came towards him, I could smell his stale body odour, and I wondered when he'd last had a wash. The rooms upstairs were free and I thought about telling him to clean himself up. Only I was worried about his reaction. Recently it seemed that I spent my time walking on eggshells around him.

It was such a change to how things had once been, and it made me sad. Aron, as a youngster, had been full of laughter and fun. He'd be the first to crack a joke or play tricks on people, the one who dreamed up most of our silly games. I remembered how all of us kids would lie in one bed, top to toe, and Aron would draw shapes on my back with his finger, challenging me to guess what he'd drawn. I remembered too the way he'd throw a strop if things didn't go his way, and the fearlessness he possessed, which often got us into trouble with the elders. I wanted that Aron back again – my Aron – and I was scared stiff that he was gone for ever.

'Where are the others?' he asked, interrupting my thoughts.

'Tyrell's at work,' I replied. 'Oscar should be back soon and Faith is sorting something out upstairs. Dunno about Mace.'

He looked up at me and half smiled, which was the most he managed nowadays. 'And the other one?'

'Which other?' I asked, even though I knew he meant the newcomer.

'Jonah,' he said, before looking away again.

At the mention of his name, I began to wonder where Jonah was and, oddly, whether he'd thought about me at all. He'd spent the last couple of days with the elders, getting to know the city and meeting the people in the Resistance. I told myself not to be silly. Jonah had far more important things to think about than me.

'He might be with Mace,' I told Aron. 'I don't really know.'

'Oh,' he replied.

Over by the door, a woman with red hair and freckles slapped one of her male companions. I walked round the bar and across to them.

'Calm it down,' I ordered, keeping a watchful eye on the two men. They wouldn't have been the first to attack me over a bar fight. After facing cannibals and demons, standing up to a couple of drunken thugs wasn't much of a problem. The woman went bright red but both men looked angry.

'Get lost!' said one of them, a tall man with long brown hair and a thick beard.

The one who'd been slapped sniggered. I felt my heart begin to race with adrenaline. Mood I was in, it would be fun to kick some ass. But I held myself in check, and let the feeling pass.

'I'll ignore that for today,' I told them. 'But any more and you're barred, understand?'

The bearded one stood up, towering over me. 'Who's doing the barring?' he sneered. 'You?'

I shook my head. 'No,' I replied. 'Although don't think I can't. No, I think I'll get Mace to do it. He was looking for something to put his fist through earlier.'

I watched the man's face flush and his eyes grow dark with uncertainty and fear. Mace's name did that. Only his friends knew he was Resistance, of course. Most other people were scared of him because he was tough. It took some serious courage to challenge my giant father-figure, and any man who threatened a woman obviously didn't have any.

'Now do you understand?' I asked, giving them a smile.

'Whatever, bitch,' he replied, trying to sound nonchalant but failing to disguise the edge of concern in his voice.

'Great!' I said, ignoring his insult. 'Can I get you any more drinks?'

As I walked away I heard the woman call me a whore, but I was too tired to set her straight. Instead, I went and sat on the stool next to Aron's, taking advantage of a lull in custom.

'You look unwell,' I said to him, causing him to shrug.

'I'm fine,' he replied. 'It's just a bit cold in the place I found.'

Aron had stopped sleeping at the hotel a few weeks earlier, straight after a fight with Oscar. Even though I'd begged him not to go, he'd done so anyway. It felt like he was deliberately pulling away from us and it bothered me that I couldn't stop him.

'Come back and stay here,' I said in hope. 'There's plenty of space. You can even have one of the empty rooms – if you need time to yourself.'

He shook his head. 'Nah,' he said, still avoiding my gaze. 'I like it where I am now. It's all mine. Besides, it ain't that bad.'

'But you could have that here too,' I insisted.

'I'm fine where I am,' he replied.

I nodded and wondered what he really wanted. All those hours spent together as kids meant that I knew him well, and I could see he was holding back. Eventually I had to ask him what he really wanted to talk about.

'I was hoping that we could speak in private,' he said to me. 'I wanted to apologize for the other day.'

I wondered which day he meant – there'd been so many recently – until his obvious embarrassment made it clear.

'It's no big deal, Aron,' I said warmly. 'What you said – it doesn't change anything, honestly. I don't hate you or think badly of you. It's done with. We can go back to being friends, like we've always been.'

'No,' he snapped. 'It's not done with. You don't understand what I meant. I *love* you, Martha. Not like some stupid little boy, but more than that. I want to be with you always. You and me have a bond.'

It was my turn to look away and consider my reply. I thought I'd explained the other day how I felt. How could I make my feelings any clearer without hurting him? What was I supposed to say? I didn't want to upset him, but I couldn't admit to a feeling I just didn't have.

'I really like you, Aron,' I began. 'But not like *that*, OK? You're like Tyrell and Oscar – a brother. That's how I think about you. I love you too, but just like I love the others. Nothing more, I'm sorry.'

Aron shook his head and, without thinking, I sighed.

'I don't believe you,' he continued. 'You and me – we've got more of a connection than the others. I've seen the way you look at me, how you talk to me. I see it in your eyes, Martha. It's something special.'

I put my hand on his shoulder and looked into his eyes, praying that he'd listen to me and understand.

'No,' I whispered. 'Please, Aron – this is hard enough without you making it worse. I don't love you – not in that way. You're family . . .'

His expression changed; a pleading look appeared in his eyes. I felt sick inside. My words weren't sinking in, no matter how much I tried to make it clear.

'Why would it be hard, then?' he asked. 'If you

77

didn't love me, why would it be so hard to say what you are saying to me?'

I sighed again. 'Because I don't want to *hurt* you, Aron, that's why.'

'I don't believe you,' he repeated. 'I never will.'

'Aron!' I said in exasperation, just as Oscar and Jonah walked through the door. Talk about timing . . .

'What's he done now?' joked Oscar, clapping Aron on the back.

'Nothing!' Aron hurriedly replied. 'We were talking. In *private*.'

Oscar and Jonah both looked at me and I nodded. A tiny part of me was pleased to see Jonah, excited that he'd come to see where I worked. But mostly I felt embarrassed, for both Aron and myself. The tension was thick enough to taste.

'Yeah,' I said. 'It was just private stuff. Nothing, really.'

Aron began to make his excuses and stood up.

'Don't go,' I said to him. 'I'm finishing soon and I was hoping to show Jonah some more of the city. Come with us.'

Aron looked at me and seemed to wince a little. I realized how stupid my comment had been – idiotic, even. Jonah was the last person Aron wanted to spend time with.

'Can't,' he lied, obviously. 'I've got stuff to do at my place. I want to make it warmer and . . . I'll see you later.'

'At the Hunt?' I asked.

'Er . . . yeah,' he replied.

He scooted out of the door before Jonah and Oscar had a chance to say goodbye.

'Weirdo,' joked Oscar.

I ignored the comment, shrugged and asked them if they wanted a drink.

9

Later the three of us were about to leave for the Haven when my stepfather appeared at the top of the stairs and asked me to join him.

'Busy,' I replied, not looking at him. After my failed conversation with Aron, the last thing I wanted was another spat with my stepfather.

'*Now!*' he yelled, causing a scene. Customers in the bar stopped what they were doing to stare.

Oscar started in anger, but I put my hand on his arm. One day I'd work out why my stepfather put up with me, but I knew that his tolerance wouldn't stretch to my friends too. There was no way I was letting Oscar put himself in danger, especially not when the Mayor had Stone around – that man was like the worst sort of predator, always on the lookout for his next victim.

'I'll be fine,' I told Oscar. 'Let me see what he wants and then we'll leave, OK?'

Oscar nodded and Jonah gave me a funny look.

'What?' I asked him.

'Nothing,' Jonah replied, but I could sense his disapproval and I felt ashamed – traitorous, even. I found myself hoping that he wouldn't be put off me, and then felt silly for thinking that way. I mean, how much did he really know me anyway? And why did I care so much?

I stomped upstairs and followed my stepfather into Stone's office. The mercenary was standing at the window, a broad smirk on his face, his eyes undressing me. I knew that men found me attractive but most of them knew how to disguise it. Stone was like a lizard watching flies swarming – tongue flicking in anticipation. It was disgusting.

'What do you want?' I asked, tying my hair up on my head, and watching out for any sudden moves from Stone. The mercenary set me on edge whenever he was around.

'Has there been any talk?' the Mayor asked me.

'There's been lots of talk,' I told him, wondering what the hell he was on about. 'It's a bar.'

He shook his head and asked again. I looked at his crumpled grey suit and badly knotted red tie. At the way he had tried to cover his balding pate with the few straggly ends of hair he had left. His eyes were red and I could smell the booze on his breath from where I stood.

'Well?' he pushed.

Stone left his position and walked towards me. I felt

momentarily wary, like a tiger was stalking me. My hands grew clammy and I felt my pulse begin to quicken.

'He's asking if anyone has mentioned the Resistance recently,' the mercenary explained, stopping less than a metre away. 'Anyone who's looked shifty or odd.'

I pretended to think about it for a while as my mind started racing. Did they know something? Was this how my mother had been discovered? And then I realized that it might be Jonah they were interested in.

'Well?' asked my stepdad again.

'No,' I told them, trying to remain calm. 'But then why would anyone mention the Resistance in the bar? That would be stupid.'

My stepfather guffawed like a suited pig. The folds of flab under his stubbly chin wobbled and his eyes narrowed into puffy slits.

'The entire Resistance is stupid,' he eventually replied. 'Otherwise they'd just get on with life and stop acting like morons.'

I shrugged, knowing that our Resistance group, small as it was, was far from being insignificant. Otherwise they wouldn't be asking me about it.

'Nothing to do with me,' I told him. 'Have you finished? Only I've got things to do.'

'Like what?' he asked.

'None of your business, old man,' I replied, still wary

of Stone's presence but unwilling to let my stepfather have his own way.

'If it involves letting your unwashed friends sleep in my hotel, then it does concern me,' he countered.

'Like I told you before – I've told them they can stay and that's that. You don't like it, you can lump it. You kick them out and I'll go too.'

'Now there's a thought – I could just turn my back on you,' he threatened. 'See how you like your life when the creature comforts have been removed.'

I glared at him now, fighting the urge to gouge out his eyeballs. '*What* creature comforts?' I snapped. 'Other than the stinking rooms upstairs, what else is there? Why do you think I live here and not in that stupid mansion with you? I haven't needed your help for years! You make me sick!'

'Of course you don't need me,' he said smarmily. 'Just like your mother didn't need me.'

'*Don't talk about her!*' I screamed. 'Don't *ever* talk about her.'

'The truth always hurts, Martha.'

'You wouldn't know the truth if it stabbed you in the heart. Don't you get it by now? You mean *nothing* to me, and if you want me and my friends to leave the hotel – just say the word.'

'I promised your mother that I'd watch out for you,' he replied, looking almost genuinely sad. *Almost.*

'Well, she's dead so you can forget your promise.'

He shook his head and looked into my eyes. 'What happened to you?' he asked. 'Where did that sweet little girl go?'

'She died with her mother,' I spat back. 'And so did any relationship I had with you. Go to Hell!'

Before he could react I walked out, slamming the door shut behind me. It rocked in its casing and a fist-sized piece of plaster fell from the wall above it.

'*Martha!*' I heard the old bastard yell after me.

I ignored him, rejoined my friends, and we left the bar.

The walk to the Haven began with a stroll through the protected zone of Fire City. I explained more about our daily lives to Jonah, who seemed to be paying close attention to everything he saw and heard. I wanted to ask what was so fascinating about the alleyways and derelict buildings, but I didn't. Instead, I pointed to a couple of greasy-haired young men who were tramping past us.

'Factory workers,' I told him. 'They've just finished so it must be a little after eight in the evening.'

'How do you know that?' Jonah asked, staring at me.

'That's easy,' I said teasingly. 'There're three shifts during each day, and they're all the same length. The evening shift always finishes at eight.'

'Basic maths, Jonah,' added Oscar, before grinning at me. 'Isn't it the same in the northern cities?'

Jonah didn't reply as more people passed us – most of them tired and hungry, probably looking forward to a night spent forgetting that they were alive. We were all paid in credits – cheaply minted tin coins which could be exchanged for the bare essentials of life. The basic diet of the Unwanted was potatoes, cabbage, dried coffee grounds and water, with the occasional turnip or beetroot thrown in. Anything else came from scavenging – rodent meat, wild herbs, the occasional cat or dog. It was no wonder that so many squandered the little they earned on the cheap, strong alcohol sold at the bar. I knew that it helped them to forget the drudgery and, according to Mace, it kept them compliant too – stopped them from rebelling.

I pointed at a hole in the wall of another building. 'State-owned shop,' I explained. 'Where we buy some of the foodstuffs – when they have them.'

'They had these up north but they were bigger,' replied Jonah.

'More people up there,' said Oscar. 'Least, that's what I've been told.'

We walked in and Oscar and I said hello to a tall, slim man with bright-green eyes and sepia-tinted skin. His name was Corey Williams and he was the father of the boy that Jonah and I had rescued – Luca.

'I hear you saved my son,' Corey said to us.

I shook my head and looked at Jonah, touched his arm and felt that buzzing, tingling sensation again.

'Jonah did,' I said without looking away. 'If it hadn't been for him . . .'

Corey stepped forward and stuck out his hand. When Jonah failed to react, I nudged him.

'It was nothing,' said Jonah without moving.

'No way!' said Corey with a beaming smile. 'You save my son and it was nothing? Forget that!' He grabbed Jonah and gave him a hug, and I could see that Jonah was a little uncomfortable with the contact. Again, I found myself with questions about the newcomer. There was a layer of mystery around him and I wanted to penetrate it.

'We'd better get on,' said Oscar, looking up and down the street from the doorway.

'Is Luca OK?' I asked.

Corey nodded and smiled again. His eyes sparkled. 'He's with his mum at the Haven,' he replied. 'Your Aunt May said they would both be safest there. Just in case . . .'

'How did he end up in the Hunt though?' asked Oscar. 'He's too young.'

Corey shook his head, looking ashamed. 'We were walking past some soldiers and one of them said something to my wife. I ignored them but Luca got mad and kicked the soldier on the knee. He's like that about his mum – one fiery little boy. They grabbed him and took him away and we couldn't stop them.'

I nodded, remembering that Aunt May had asked me to watch out for the little boy.

'We found him, Corey,' I replied. 'That's all that matters. If you had tried to stop the soldiers, they would have killed you.'

'I know, Martha, and I'm deeply grateful that you found him. If I could, I'd let you have some free supplies, but they'd kill me if they found out.'

As we walked away from the shop I explained what Corey had meant to Jonah. 'They're all conscripts – the shop workers,' I told him. 'They don't have any choice. If they did, Corey would be with us, I'm sure.'

'He's always there, then?' asked Jonah.

'All the time,' I replied. 'His family lives in a room behind the store. At least, they did.'

Jonah nodded and went back to studying our surroundings carefully. Here and there were human army patrols, three men in each. I pointed to one and asked Jonah if it was the same in the north.

'Yes,' he replied. 'But there are more of them. The Northern Citadel has several satellite towns all round it – most of them like this place. Factories, workers, everything.'

'More rebels too, then?' added Oscar.

'Yes,' replied Jonah. 'Which is why I think the Resistance should be better organized.'

'How?' I asked.

'By joining up and establishing bases in the waste-lands.'

'But what about the dangers?'

Jonah gave me a piercing look and told me that I wasn't thinking properly. 'What's more dangerous than living like this?' he asked, and I realized that he might have a point. It didn't stop me from feeling a bit silly though.

'You're right,' I said. 'Sorry.'

'Don't say sorry,' he replied. 'You can't be expected to know these things if you've never left Fire City.'

'*Sssh!*' whispered Oscar. 'More soldiers.'

The army in Fire City is made up of two types of soldier. The first types are regular recruits, picked from the Wanted and trained to keep order. The second lot are mercenaries – people like Stone – and work for whoever can pay. I don't know for sure, but it seems as though Stone is in charge of the army in Fire City, through his position with the old bastard. I've often seen him ordering the soldiers around.

'How many soldiers in total?' Jonah asked.

'No idea,' I told him. 'I try not to pay them any attention – it's too dangerous.'

We crossed a four-road junction, just past what had

once been the centre of the city, and our going got tougher. We were about fifteen hundred metres from the edge of the protected zone and needed to be careful.

'If we get caught approaching the border, we're dead,' I explained.

Jonah nodded and told me that Mace had explained as much. 'Secret routes,' he added.

'Do you know much about the demons?' I asked as we ducked down a dark side street, one that was barricaded at the end.

Jonah shrugged. 'A little,' he replied. 'Enough to know what kills them.'

'Even the powerful ones?'

This time he shook his head and a thought passed across his face. He kept it to himself and I found myself wishing that he'd tell me.

'There are so many types of demon,' he explained. 'The smaller ones that possess animals aren't powerful at all. Then you have the patrollers who rely on brute strength, then the underlords . . .'

'You're patronizing me now,' I told him, feeling slightly annoyed. 'The elders taught us all about the demons.'

'Really?' he asked. 'Did you know that there are other demons, ones which you've never seen here in Fire City?'

'Describe them,' I challenged. I've had a competitive streak since I was little and it was kicking in.

'Have you heard of succubi and incubi?'

I looked away, shook my head. I had no idea what he was talking about but I wasn't about to admit to it. My plan about not seeming stupid in front of him was failing though. *Badly*.

'A different part of the species,' he continued. 'They're like Valefor and the other ancients – able to possess humans or take their souls. They're just as powerful. Only they don't sit on any ruling council – at least, not on any that I know of.'

'How do you know so much?' asked Oscar.

Jonah stopped and considered us for a moment. He looked from Oscar to me, and back again.

'Because I have to,' he said at last. 'The best way to destroy your enemy is to understand them. It's something I learned in the north.'

'Man, they taught you a lot up there,' said Oscar. 'Maybe that's where I should go.'

Jonah nodded. 'You should,' he said to both us. 'Your skills would be sharpened and you'd be even more effective.'

'Sounds great,' I said, pointing to a hole in the wall ahead of us. 'Through there,' I added, looking around us. When I was sure that we weren't being watched, I ducked into an abandoned shop, its shelves long since stripped bare. 'Quick!' I whispered to my friends.

Once inside, Oscar led us to the rear, where a doorway opened into the cellar and a secret tunnel. We headed down into the darkness as I tried to imagine what life outside Fire City might be like.

10

Aron sat alone, on a wall by the old railway station. He looked up into the night sky as an electrical storm flashed and burned, and giant amethyst-tinged clouds threatened to release the torrential rain that they held. Instead of worrying that he was about to get drenched, Aron went over and over his last conversation with Martha, playing it out in his head. He searched his memory for an inkling of hope, something in her words that proved that he was right about how she really felt. Finding nothing, he put his head in his hands and groaned. How could it be that she didn't want him? They understood each other; the pain of losing their mothers, the darkness that those deaths created inside them, the hatred that became the sole purpose for living. Surely she could see that?

And now there was Jonah too. If the newcomer had turned her head completely, then all was lost. Aron felt sick at the thought, his head beginning to pound as he imagined them together. He shook the image away and began to walk back towards the Haven.

As he crossed a road junction that was shrouded in gloom, the clouds finally broke and giant drops of rain began to pelt the streets. Drains that hadn't been cleared in two decades quickly overflowed and Aron, drenched in seconds, began to shiver. Up ahead, he saw two older men duck down an alleyway. He paid no heed and, pulling up his hood, intended to walk on until one of the men called out to him.

'Hey, you!'

Aron turned and looked up, water dripping down the bridge of his nose. 'What?'

'Give me your clothes!' The man stepped into the street, a piece of wood in his left hand. His friend came after, his eyes bloodshot and a long scar cutting across his left cheek.

'Blow me,' Aron replied, turning away.

The first man attacked almost immediately, just as Aron knew he would. Aron stepped to one side, using the man's momentum to turn and throw him. His attacker landed in the road, face first in a puddle of rain-water and mud. Aron turned to the second man, his fists raised, eyes wide with anger.

'Come on!' he yelled.

The second man hesitated for a split second; just enough for Aron to dropkick him in his right temple. The man groaned and then began to collapse forwards, allowing Aron to follow up with a knee under the chin. The man's head snapped back with a sickening crack and he was unconscious before his head smashed against the wall behind him.

Aron turned back to the first attacker, who was getting to his feet slowly.

'More?' he asked the older man, who sneered and put up his fists.

Aron smiled, pulled back his hood and sprang forward. His forehead caught the older man directly above his left eye, leaving him on his back again with Aron on top of him. Before he could react, Aron felt his anger at Martha surface and began to punch his victim on the side of the head, over and over until the man passed out.

Aron stood and wiped his bloody hands on his trousers, then turned away, ready to make an exit; but once again thoughts of Martha made his head scream. His mind filled with her words of rejection and tears began to stream down his face. He turned back to the well-beaten man on the floor, raised his foot and stomped down on the man's head. The world began to blur around him; his ears popped, his veins throbbed with blood and his foot became a piston, driving down again and again until he heard a woman screaming through the haze. He spun round and ran into the night . . .

Jonah sat down opposite Martha's aunt and asked where she'd learned to work with herbs. May, her long dark hair and grey eyes almost exactly the same as those of her niece, smiled.

'I knew a little before the War,' she explained. 'And then afterwards, I had to learn more. My sister had some books and many of the elders knew stuff too. I just learned as much as I could; then a little is, you know, guesswork.'

Jonah nodded as he watched other Resistance members milling around the Haven, some waiting for the Hunt to begin and others preparing to leave for the city. They were in the main chamber, at the very heart of the complex, and over in the corner furthest from them, Oscar was tutoring some children in martial arts. There were four young ones, standing in a line and throwing out kicks and punches, their faces stiff with concentration. Jonah shook his head softly as he considered how futile such efforts were. The nature of life meant that by the time the children with Oscar were old enough to fight, many of Oscar's generation would be dead, or so broken that they'd be useless to the cause. The only way for them to survive was to leave Fire City and join the proper Resistance out in the wastelands. At least then they'd stand a chance. It bothered Jonah that they hadn't already done so.

'You seem preoccupied,' said May, her smile warm and friendly.

'I was watching Oscar,' he admitted.

'They've all had that training,' she explained. 'Mace started with Martha, Tyrell and the others when they first learned to walk. Martial arts, weapons – anything to help them.'

Jonah nodded. 'And does it?' he asked. 'Does it really help?'

'A little,' she admitted. 'Which is more of a chance than most people get.'

'What else do you teach here?'

May stood and told him to follow her. She led him into the inner corridor and down towards one of the side rooms. Through the door, Jonah saw two young adults – one a tall, brown-skinned man, the other a woman half his height, with pale skin and red hair, neither much older than him – teaching a group of eight children. Jonah recognized one of the children as Luca, and thought about meeting his father: the warmth and relief Corey had shown, the deep love for his only child. Jonah thought back to his own childhood, saw his sisters at play and his mother watching over them, her immense pride always tempered by an ounce of fear.

'What are they teaching?' he repeated, in a whisper this time.

'Oh, just what we can,' she replied. 'Life, the way the

world works, all about the demons. We teach them about the old days and the War too, so that they understand what they're fighting for.'

'So will all of these children *have* to become fighters?' asked Jonah.

May shook her head. 'Not if they don't want to,' she said. 'We never coerce them, not ever. This life isn't for everyone. However, they generally do go on to join us.'

'What about the teachers?' he asked as he watched the man read from a book.

'The man is called Raj, and the tiny woman by his side is Emily. She helps me sometimes too – she's got a fast brain and learns quickly. I'm hoping she'll take over from me at some point.'

'Where will you go?'

May looked bemused and Jonah sensed the reason why.

'Where everyone else goes,' she explained. 'Death. I'm under no illusions, Jonah. None of us are. It's a miracle that I've lasted this long. Me, the other elders like Prior, even Mace and Faith – we're exceptions rather than the rule.'

Jonah shook his head. They didn't have to be exceptions.

'There are many older ones up north,' he told her. 'Men and women much older than any of you here. If they can survive, so can you.'

May chuckled. 'Perhaps they look after them better up there,' she joked.

'Their strength comes from their numbers,' replied Jonah, ignoring May's attempt at humour. 'If your people left the city and joined them, you would lose fewer of them.'

'*Leave?*' asked May. 'How can we leave? There are too many people in the city who aren't Resistance members but they *are* humans. We can't just leave them to their fate.'

'Why do they stay?'

May looked towards the children in the room and Jonah saw that she was sad.

'Most people here are too frightened to leave,' she told him. 'They're so oppressed that they can't see how futile it all is. I don't judge them either, Jonah. People have the right to decide their own destiny, no matter what we think.'

Jonah lied and told her that he understood. But he didn't. For him there was only one choice to make – join the Resistance and fight the demons, or sit around and wait to die. If you chose the latter, you deserved what you got. The demons didn't care whether you were active or passive. To them, humans were a subordinate species to be used and abused as they saw fit. To live like that, to *understand* that and do nothing, was worse than death. It was, to Jonah, a betrayal of life itself.

'Come on,' said May, 'let me show you around the rest of the complex. The Hunt will start in a few hours and we need to prepare.'

11

As soon as we reached the hunting grounds we split into smaller groups. Mace took Oscar, Tyrell and Raj with him, whilst Jonah, Prior and Aron came with me. Marko, who worked with Oscar during the day, led another unit made up of several men I didn't know very well. Most were new recruits who Mace had trained and I could tell that they were nervous.

'Martha, you take the south side,' Mace told me. 'And be careful. You and Prior are in charge, OK?' He nodded towards Aron, who was looking the other way, and I repeated his action. Then I looked at Jonah, pleased that he was with us. He gave me a welcome half-smile.

'OK,' I said, wondering if Aron would act up because I'd been given the leading role. 'And don't worry, Mace, we'll be fine. We'll meet you at the safe house in two hours.'

Mace gave Jonah a look and then my group set off into the dark streets. The safe houses were pre-prepared

– mostly bunkers or cellars which we had fortified. It was impossible to fight for the whole length of the Hunt and we used the hideaways to take shelter and hide the people we rescued.

'There're three tall blocks up ahead,' I said to Jonah. 'They're infested with cannibals but we need to take them.'

'Agreed,' said Jonah as Aron approached us, looking a little sheepish.

'You want me to go with Prior?' Aron asked.

I shook my head, hoping that he wouldn't throw a tantrum at taking orders from me. Mace often put me in charge because I tried to assess situations before engaging the enemy – just as he'd taught us all. Aron was the exact opposite, however, and I knew that Mace's belief that he wasn't as disciplined rankled. I also knew that Aron would always take it personally, whereas I'd always gone with what was best for the group. Lead or follow – it was the group that mattered, not me.

'No,' I told Aron gently. 'This time we stick together, OK? We need you on your game tonight.'

Aron shrugged, seeming to accept my words without fuss, which came as a huge relief. We crept through the shadows towards the first block. A deserted area of tall grasses sat between it and us – an open spot that we had to cross to reach our goal. Its being so exposed signalled danger and we needed to be extra-cautious. Above us the skies were still quiet but very quickly they would be patrolled by winged demons, on the lookout for prey.

'Did everyone use the scent-lotion May gave us?' asked Prior. He was the oldest of the elders in our group, with rough skin that was sallow and dry. His eyes were a dull blue colour, his head shaved, his chin covered in grey stubble, and the fingers of his right hand were stained yellow from the cheap and plentiful cigarettes he smoked incessantly. Recently he'd developed a deep cough, one that had the rest of us worried.

Each of us nodded and then Jonah took out his rifle. I wondered what he was doing. There seemed to be no reason to draw his weapon.

'Jonah, what are you—' I began, but he cut me off. I held down my irritation, remembering how skilled he was. If he'd taken up his weapon there had to be good reason.

'Go now!' he ordered. 'I'll cover you.'

I looked up again, saw that there were no winged patrols, yet nodded anyway.

'But there's nothing out there,' said Aron, looking to me.

'Just get going!' yelled Prior. I could see that Prior was sick, but he was still one of the few men I had ever trusted. If he thought Jonah was right, I wasn't about to argue.

The grasses, although long, were easy to run through. The only problem would be hollows in the earth created by foxes and other animals – or the animals themselves. Thankfully we reached the first block without incident, and I turned to beckon Jonah across. As soon as I did so, I heard the piercing shriek of a winged demon. How could he have known? I asked myself. I made a mental note to ask him later and focused on the immediate threat.

'*Inside, now!*' shouted Prior. 'Before it spots us.'

I knew that he was right, but part of me didn't want to leave Jonah. Even though I was sure that he could take care of himself, I was still worried about him. I wanted to believe that gratitude was making me think that way, but that would have been dishonest. There was something else, something I'd never really felt before. Again I cleared my mind and tried to concentrate. One slip meant death out here and I wasn't ready to die just yet.

'What about—' I began to say.

Prior grabbed my arm and dragged me into the doorway. He was one of few people I'd allow to man-handle me. He was right to do so too and I knew it.

'*Now!*' he yelled into my face. 'He can take care of himself. If that winged bastard spots us, we're done for!'

The ground floor of the building was dark and deserted. On one side were lifts, both of them ruined.

To the other side I saw three doors and the bottom of the stairs, which went up to each of the eighteen floors. I could hear the faint growling and snarling of cannibals from above us. I remembered my initial Hunt and how scared I'd been on hearing my first nest of cannibals. Mace had called it my coming-of-age. The thought made me smile. A lot had changed since that night.

'One floor at a time,' said Prior. 'We only need to secure the first two. Anything above that, we leave alone.'

I turned again and looked out into the night but saw no sign of Jonah. The winged demon was still patrolling, banking left and right and swooping in low to check for humans. I felt a sense of dread, just for a moment, before the adrenaline began to surge through me.

'Come on!' said Prior. 'Before the winged one calls for backup.'

With Aron leading the way, we climbed the stairs to the first floor, moving slowly with our weapons drawn. The steps were slimy with moss and the entire shaft stank of decay. Something skittered along the first-floor landing, squeaking as it found cover.

'I can hear them,' whispered Aron. 'Coming from the left.'

I stopped and listened for movement, and sure enough I heard shuffling footsteps. The landing had a door on each side and Prior pointed to the one on the right.

'We go in that way,' he told us. 'My lead. Aron, you cover my back. Martha – cover him.' He pushed past Aron, his machete drawn, and edged into the pitch-black corridor. Before I had the chance to register anything else, a cannibal screamed in blood lust and Prior roared.

'*Shit!*' yelled Aron, running straight into the battle, head down.

'*Aron!*' I screamed, part scared, part angry because I knew that Prior could handle a few cannibals alone. Once Aron charged in though, any others waiting to ambush us would smell his blood and go crazy. Any scent of human flesh and they swarmed like wasps around a broken jar of honey.

I had no choice but to join the fight, and cursing Aron for his stupidity, I ran in too. In the dark, the weirdly translucent pallor of the cannibals' skin stood out, luminous and green. Prior was to my right, surrounded by a gang of four monsters, and I went to him first, chopping and cutting at cannibal flesh, ignoring the screams and the blood.

'There's loads of them,' shouted Prior. 'Come on!'

The corridor was long and narrow, with twenty apartments leading from it. Aron was six or seven metres away, trying to push back a surge of cannibals ten strong.

I rushed towards him and began to help, and slowly we managed to kill all of them. Behind us, Prior was wheezing and trying to catch his breath.

'You OK?' I asked.

'Don't worry about me,' he said, glaring at Aron. 'Just get ready to fight. With all three of us in here, they're going to think it's a human hog roast.'

'What now?' Aron asked, compounding Prior's anger.

'You're the hero!' the old man snapped in sarcasm. 'You tell *us*.'

When Aron failed to answer, I pointed to the far end of the corridor. 'The last apartment on the right,' I said. 'We clear that.'

Prior understood my reasoning immediately. Once we took the apartment, we could use the narrow doorway to our advantage. The cannibals, blinded by their blood lust, would fight each other to get to us, blocking the entrance. As they broke through, we could pick them off with ease.

'*Go!*' he yelled as we heard more snarling coming from the stairwell.

I went first, my feet sliding through blood and flesh, and kicked down the door to the last apartment. Knowing that there'd be something just inside, I rolled forward underneath the attack and stood up. My senses made out four cannibals, two behind me and two to my left. My blade made short work of them as Prior and

106

Aron joined me. We turned to the doorway, took a breather and waited for the onslaught.

The snarling grew louder and my stomach began to turn over. I knew that the corridor was filling with cannibals, many more than we'd imagined. They moved slowly and purposefully towards us, eager for a meal. A simple fight was beginning to look much more deadly.

'Brace yourselves,' Prior told us, drawing his second machete.

Aron looked at me and shrugged. 'I'm sorry,' he said. 'I didn't mean to mess things up. I thought Prior was in trouble.'

'Forget it,' I told him. 'We need to concentrate.'

The first wave of sickly green faces appeared at the entrance, five of them, each trying to beat the other into the room. They snarled and spat and screamed at us, arms outstretched, fingers bony, nails like claws.

'*Now!*' ordered Prior, and between us we began to push them back. Arms, hands and fingers went flying and blood spurted everywhere, but we didn't stop. Any let-up would allow them to break into the room, and if they managed that . . .

CRASH! The glass of the window behind me shattered. I spun round and a winged demon, its talons clutching the window frame, shrieked in at us.

'*Prior!*' I screamed as the demon tried to force its way through.

'I'll do it!' he shouted, turning to fend the monster off.

Its claws occupied, the winged being snapped at Prior with its beak, the teeth murderously sharp. Prior bobbed and weaved, avoiding the attack and trying to chop at the creature's legs. From the screams, I counted that he'd succeeded twice, but then the cannibal onslaught increased in ferocity and I was drawn back to the doorway.

'*Martha!*' hollered Aron.

Despite my arms feeling like lead, I increased the speed of my attack, even though I knew we were in serious trouble. With the demon at our backs we were trapped, and the cannibals were beginning to get a foothold. I could see Aron begin to falter, and then he caught a fist in the face. He stumbled backwards and his attacker managed to break free and enter the room. I swung my sword, slicing through the cannibal's jaw, but in that split second two more broke in and Aron and I were forced backwards.

'*Shit!*' I heard myself say, just before there was an almighty crash and the ceiling caved in above us.

I fell backwards, dazed, as a lump of concrete smacked into my right temple. Aron fell on top of me, putting his arms round me he rolled us to the left. I tried to see what Prior was doing, but with Aron's weight on me I was unable to move. Ignoring my attempts to push him off, Aron stayed put and I screamed at him to move.

Suddenly the screaming of dying cannibals flooded my senses and I felt myself begin to drift. The blow to my head was worse than I'd thought and I was moments away from passing out. I tried to shift Aron again, but I was too weak, and then I caught Jonah's unmistakable scent in the room. I calmed a little, thinking that if Jonah was with us, we might just survive . . .

Aron looked into my eyes, whispered something I didn't understand and then, out of nothing, tried to kiss me. Horrified, I turned my head and his lips caught the left side of my neck. I screamed at him, shocked at what he was doing. He tried to turn my head back towards him and I fought against it. I wanted him off me, and despite myself I began to cry. Then, in an instant, his weight was gone and I saw Jonah looking down at me.

'Come on,' he said gently as he lifted me onto his shoulder.

Before I faded into unconsciousness, I caught sight of Prior, hacking up lumps of phlegm. In another corner sat Aron, glowering at me. I wanted to yell at him, to slap his face, but I didn't have the strength. Instead, I felt myself pass out . . .

12

The Mayor stood looking out of his living-room window. One of his servants, a plump girl called Louisa, was weeding his garden, her rounded rump facing him as she worked on all fours. The view cheered him; the girl had shown previously that she was willing to take some extra credits in return for services rendered.

Behind him, on a walnut table, stood an open bottle of wine and a half-empty glass. The Mayor sighed to himself and looked at his watch. 'Better draw yourself a nice, cleansing bath,' he said out loud.

'You do carry an unsavoury odour,' he heard Valefor hiss.

Startled, the Mayor felt his heart contract as he turned to find the demon lord sitting on a leather couch that had been empty five seconds earlier.

'Sire, I—'

Valefor raised a hand, silencing the Mayor instantly. 'DO NOT SPEAK!' he ordered.

The Mayor nodded, his trembling legs carrying him

towards an armchair. He sat down, his eyes never leaving Valefor's, his bowels barely under control.

'My legion report more Resistance activity from last night,' said the demon lord.

The Mayor was about to open his mouth but stopped short, annoying Valefor, who was as happy to kill him as let him live.

'There is a stranger with them,' continued the demon lord. 'An individual with weapons he should not have. Last night he is said to have wreaked havoc. So I will ask you a question, wretched man, and you will consider your answer carefully. If I am satisfied, you shall live. If, however, your answer displeases me, I will order my patrollers to tie ropes to your arms and legs and to pull your feeble little body apart. Is that clear?'

The Mayor nodded.

'Good,' said Valefor with a sneer. 'Can you find this stranger and bring him to me?'

The Mayor took his time as a single bead of sweat crept down the right side of his face. Eventually, as the bead dripped from his jowl onto his grey shirt collar, he spoke.

'Yes, my lord.'

'Are you sure?'

The Mayor nodded again. 'Yes, my lord.'

Valefor stood, his huge wings curled up and over his head in a sign of aggression. 'I do not believe you,' he whispered menacingly.

The Mayor flinched, even though Valefor had made no move to attack him. The single bead of perspiration was joined by many more until he was dripping. The stench of it amused the demon lord.

'I sense that we have an understanding,' he told the Mayor. 'Do what you must to find out whatever you can. I want to know who this stranger is. I want to know why he is here. Is that clear?'

'Absolutely, my lord.'

Valefor relented and his wings returned to their normal position. His purple eyes mocked the Mayor. 'Now go and take your bath,' he told the pathetic little human. 'Although why you'd want to rut with that creature outside confuses me. Kill her and eat her, Mayor – you'd find the taste of her flesh divine. I could show you, if you'd like—'

'No!' yelped the Mayor.

'Such a shame,' the demon lord teased. He closed his eyes, smiled, and then vanished before the Mayor could blink.

'Bastard,' mumbled the Mayor as he stared at the space in which Valefor had been standing.

13

The following evening Stone looked on as Martha polished the mahogany bar with a dry cloth. A couple of male customers sat on battered wooden stools, nursing their drinks, avoiding conversation or eye contact with each other. Like most of the population of Fire City, both men had sallow, parched skin and sunken cheeks. Their clothes were basic: denim trousers and loose, badly sewn shirts made from thick cloth, one grey, the other black. Each wore cheap work shoes without socks, in keeping with their fellow citizens. The older of the two had maybe one more year of use left in him, if that, thought Stone, before he'd join the prey at a Hunt, the younger not much longer. Until then they'd work for the Wanted, doing whatever menial job they were given. Stone, whenever he considered his lot in life, thanked the stars. Life for society's dregs was tough. They were nothing but poorly paid slaves.

Martha interrupted his thoughts by dropping and breaking her third glass of the afternoon.

'You're not having a good day, are you?' joked Stone.

Martha scowled at him as she took hold of a broom. 'Unless you want me to shove these splinters up your arse,' she snapped, 'keep your thoughts to yourself. No one *asked* you to be here.'

Stone smiled. Despite her bravado, he knew that she was scared of him. The thought of it made him happy.

'Your father asked me,' he said, knowing that she'd react with rage. A fourth glass smashed against the wall behind Stone, barely an inch from his head.

'*He's not my father,*' Martha replied through gritted teeth.

'Of course he is,' teased Stone. 'You live in his building. He puts up with your tantrums. He used to have sex with your mother . . .'

Martha picked up another tumbler with her free hand.

'OK, OK!' said Stone, holding up his hands and grinning. 'You win!'

Martha shook her head.

'You look tired,' said Stone, attempting to placate her. She was a fiery beauty, he thought for the hundredth time. Her eyes, impossibly silvery, sparkled with light. High cheekbones flanked her perfectly symmetrical nose. Her Cupid's-bow lips were full and naturally scarlet. He even admired her athletic build despite usually liking his women with a little more meat on their bones.

'And you're a perverted old man with a scavenger's gaze,' she told him, looking sickened at his too-obvious gawping.

Stone cursed wordlessly, anticipating the day when Martha's stepfather wouldn't be around to shield the girl. He'd tamed plenty of wild animals – she wouldn't be the last.

'Have you heard any rumours?' he asked her in a less friendly tone.

Martha, for her part, swept the broken shards into a corner, just across from where Stone was standing. So close that she could smell his body odour. She answered with her back to him. 'What rumours?'

'About a newcomer,' Stone told her. 'An outsider, talking treason.'

'Er . . . no,' she said, failing to disguise the hesitancy in her reply.

Stone noticed immediately. 'You don't sound too certain,' he said.

Martha thought rapidly as she turned to face him. Her involvement with the Resistance was a secret. If she were discovered, Valefor would have her killed, regardless of her guardian. The same was true of Jonah. No matter how easily he killed Valefor's lieutenants, he stood little chance against the demon lord himself. One week in his presence had convinced Martha of the outsider's worth. The last thing she wanted was for him to get caught.

115

'It's a bar,' she said to Stone, praying that Mace, who was with Jonah, wouldn't pick that exact moment to walk in with him. 'People come and go. Am I supposed to remember everyone?'

Stone shook his head. His ice-blue eyes were piercing. He hadn't blinked once – he hardly ever did. The veins in his neck were fat, his jaw muscles twitching. He scared Martha almost as much as the demons did. She was damned if she was going to show it, however.

'No – not everyone,' he told her. 'Just strangers.'

Martha shrugged. 'Isn't that *your* job?' she asked. 'You're the mercenary.'

'*Security* consultant,' replied Stone. 'Security.'

'Whatever,' Martha said. 'Is there anything else? Only I've got work to do.'

Stone smiled. 'Go ahead,' he said. 'I'm enjoying the view.'

'I've met scab-infested demons with more appeal than you,' she sniped.

'Soon,' he said with a wink. 'We'll see how noisy you are then, shall we?'

Martha shuddered as she walked away. Ten minutes later, as Stone disappeared up to his living quarters, she approached the two customers Stone had been watching. One of them was Raj, the other Prior. The elder began to nod before she'd stopped moving.

'I heard everything,' he said in a whisper.

'Go now, then,' advised Martha. 'If Stone's looking for a newcomer, Mace can't bring Jonah in here.'

Prior gave a smile, revealing missing teeth and rotten, inflamed gums.

Martha smiled back. 'Hurry!' she added.

In his office, Stone removed a framed print of fading sunflowers from the wall above his desk. Behind it lay a combination safe which he unlocked. The heavy, vaulted door fell open and he reached inside for a phone. After the War the mobile networks had been taken over by the new government and all communications were now strictly controlled, with only the upper echelons allowed to converse with handsets outside of the citadels. The Unwanted had nothing – no media, no print, nothing with which they could correspond easily with others in the same situation. Rumours were the only news currency out here, unless you were one of the fortunate, like Stone.

He placed the phone on his desk and opened a small, square locket that hung on the chain round his neck with his dog tags. Inside was a sim card, which he inserted into the device before switching it on. As he waited for the covert network to kick in, he walked over to the door and listened for any sounds. Only the person who had supplied it knew about the phone. No one else – not even the Mayor – knew that it existed, and Stone was under strict orders to keep it that way. A hired gun named Pearson had seen it accidentally, some months back. To preserve its secrecy, Stone had broken Pearson's neck with his bare hands, dismembered him and fed each part to the giant rats that plagued the city.

Satisfied that no one was listening, Stone sent a text message. Within seconds the phone vibrated in his hand. He answered quickly.

'You have news?' the caller asked.

'Yes, master,' replied Stone. 'I think he's here.'

'You *think*? I don't pay you to *think*, Stone. I *pay* you for answers.'

Stone felt his face flush with nervous energy. He was thankful that the phone was an old, pre-war model. A newer, face-to-face device would have shown up his emotions.

'I'm trying to find out,' he told the caller.

'Is Valefor aware of him?'

'Yes – the order to find him came directly *from* Valefor, via the human slug I'm working for. Word is that a stranger is in town, killing demons.'

The caller chuckled. 'The Mayor is a tedious little man, isn't he?'

Stone agreed. 'I want to tear out his eyeballs and feed them to him,' he admitted.

'That would be . . . *inopportune*,' replied the caller. 'The Mayor has his uses. However, the very moment he has served his purpose you may kill him. You have my word.'

'I'm going to hold you to that, master.'

'Please do, Stone,' said the caller.

'What about Valefor and his lieutenants?' asked Stone. 'They want the stranger for themselves.'

'Absolutely out of the question!' snapped the caller. 'They cannot be allowed to take him. Is that completely understood?'

Stone told him that it was.

'Do *whatever* it takes, Stone,' ordered the caller.

'*Carte blanche?*'

The caller chuckled once more. 'A mercenary with an education,' he said. 'One of your many admirable qualities, my friend. Yes – *carte blanche*, and that includes the demons.'

'Understood. I'll call again when I have more news, master.'

'I look forward to it, Stone. Good day.'

14

Two hours after my run-in with Stone, Prior was back in the bar, but he shook his head when I asked if he'd found Mace and Jonah at the Haven.

'They weren't there,' he told me in a low voice. I looked around, searching for anyone taking too much interest in what we were saying. Then I cursed, wondering where they were. The thought of them walking in and being discovered by Stone set my nerves on edge.

'At least they haven't come in here,' I said.

The bar was now half full and noisy. Outside, the sky had darkened, the day shifts were over and the Hunt was barely hours away. I needed to sleep before it began and time was getting on.

'Do you want me to ask around some more?' asked Prior, wheezing and rubbing his chest.

'No point,' I replied. 'They could be anywhere.'

'What about that idiot Aron?' Prior asked.

'What about him?'

Prior smiled and made a kissing sound and I realized he was making fun.

'Stop it,' I told him in annoyance. 'He's just confused, that's all. He's one of us, Prior. One of the family.'

'Pah!' spat Prior. 'Aron might be your friend but he has the heart of a gnat. Look at what happened to Samuel!'

'Aron's as brave as any of us, Prior!' I heard myself snap.

I was more surprised at my reaction than Prior. After everything Aron had done, especially attempting to kiss me in the heat of a fight, I should have been much angrier with him. Only . . . what was the point? Aron had problems that couldn't be dealt with by being mean to him. And, deep inside, I still felt a little of the warmth I'd always had for him. It wasn't about to die completely just because Aron was acting odd. There was always hope that he'd move on from what had happened, and we'd go back to how things were. At least, I hoped so.

'Samuel's death wasn't his fault – we've all watched someone die!' I added, defending Aron some more.

Prior shrugged slowly and apologized. I said nothing, poured the man a drink and watched him down it with a single swallow. Samuel's death still seemed unreal. So many of us had died fighting the demons that dealing with loss should have been second nature. Only it wasn't – not really. I knew that some people had lost that

121

kernel of empathy that made them human, often without even realizing it. People who'd become so worn, so defeated, that they just shrugged and moved on, hoping to stay alive for another day. With them, the demons had won the mental war as much as the physical, and that made me hate the Hell-kin all the more. Well, they'd never defeat me mentally, I told myself. Not ever . . .

A sudden commotion at the door made me look up. A group of men were shouting and watching something happening on the street. Curious, I stepped away from the bar, sliding past a drunken woman sleeping with her head on a table, and approached the men. Tyrell, who'd been chatting to Faith by the staircase, appeared at my side, his ebony-coloured head shining, his shoulders threatening to tear the fabric of his hooded, once-red top.

'Let me deal with it,' he demanded, doing his usual big brother thing.

'You don't work here,' I reminded him.

'Don't care,' he said, making me smile. 'I protect my sister, no matter what.'

I felt safe and warm whenever Tyrell was around, like nothing could harm me. We'd been friends ever since we'd met, and grown even closer over the years since. Tyrell, alongside Oscar, was the most loyal ally I'd ever had. Once I'd have said the same thing about Aron too, but I couldn't any more.

'Clear the doorway, then,' I said to him as we approached the entrance.

The men at the door stepped aside when they saw Tyrell, watching over his shoulder as he looked out into the street. I could hear a commotion so I followed Tyrell outside, with Prior right behind me. Across the road some patrollers had cornered two homeless youths, neither more than thirteen years old. The youths, barefoot, with grime-covered faces, trembled in fear as the demons moved in, growling.

'Don't get involved!' whispered Prior. 'It's too dangerous.'

Tyrell shook his head. 'What – I should stand here and watch instead?' he asked. 'Never!'

I felt my stomach twist and turn with dread. Like Tyrell, I wanted to rescue the boys, but I also understood Prior's warning. There would be another patrol close by, and another after that. Taking them on without weapons and in full view of everyone was suicide. With Stone asking questions about Jonah too, the last thing we needed was to draw attention to ourselves. I knew what Mace would say in our shoes so I backed Prior's warning.

'Wait!' I said to Tyrell. 'Let's just see what happens.'

One of the patrollers, over-sized, with black fur and a wide head, howled. The other, shorter and skinnier, with chocolate-brown markings on white fur, gave one of the youths an almighty slap that knocked him flying to the ground.

'They're going to kill them,' said Tyrell. 'You know it.'

Behind them, and from every other occupied building, people were beginning to pour into the street – some of them looking fearful, the others angry. 'Leave him be!' one brave voice called from the crowd. The patrollers sensed the mood, saw that they were outnumbered and paused. Any second they would call out, asking for assistance, and the street would fill with demons. If that happened, I knew that no one would survive.

'Damn!' I shouted, caught between urging the crowd to flee and helping Tyrell rescue the boys. I searched up and down the street, watching for demon reinforcements. I didn't have to wait long.

'HOLD!' came a deep, resonant call.

I turned to my right, saw the owner of the voice and shuddered. My legs felt like jelly and my heart was racing. Mias, underlord and lieutenant of Valefor, was striding towards the fracas with nine more patrollers in tow. His arms, covered in thick black fur, hung low, a silvery stripe cut through his powerful chest, and the eyes of his simian face blazed scarlet. Many in the crowd scuttled away when they saw him approaching, right to be alarmed. Mias was sadistic, and well known for enjoying his work. The rumours claimed that he preferred to torture his victims before killing them, inflicting terrible pain. Apparently mercy was something he didn't understand.

'Get everyone inside,' I whispered to Prior, knowing that we had to act. 'Quick!'

The patrollers with Mias sprang forward, taking up positions on each side of their fellow demons. Each resembled a wild dog, jaws snapping and globules of thick saliva flying in every direction. Every growl sent humans running.

'YOU DARE TO DEFY US!' screamed Mias, his words echoing. I could feel my heart pulsing, hear the blood thumping through my arteries. One of the dog-demons, a bloated Alsatian with the mouth of a barracuda, faced us, snarling. The fuzz round its jaws was smeared with fresh blood.

I felt myself shiver with fear, even despite all my experience in the Hunt. Thing is, this was different. Neither me, Tyrell nor Prior were armed and we didn't have the others backing us up either.

'Don't move!' the dog-demon ordered, viscous russet spit dripping to the ground and steaming.

Tyrell clenched his thick fingers into fists and I knew that he was seconds from exploding. Before we first met, a patrol had killed his father, tearing him to pieces in front of his young eyes. His hatred was so deep that he began to shudder.

'Tyrell . . .' I cautioned under my breath.

Mias loped towards the cornered youths, looking this way and that, daring someone to interfere. A single person stepped forward, an old man who I knew as Turner. He was clothed in a tattered grey cloak, stained white T-shirt and once-blue trousers. His feet were bare and caked in filth, like they always were. Often, I'd let him use the rooms above the bar to have a wash. He was a strange one – a loner who often talked to himself. Tyrell started to tense up, so I put a hand on his chunky arm, hoping to hold him. Turner might be odd but he wasn't a child – he knew the dangers of confronting an underlord.

The demons, I had been taught, had their own hierarchy. Valefor and the other lords were true breeds, ancient beings with powers no human could counter. The underlords weren't as strong – often the offspring or favoured servants of the lords. Demon underlords such as Mias were, however, more than a match for any of us. At the bottom were the minor demons, such as the patrollers, and they too were still formidable foes. Turner's act was idiotic – akin to jumping off a cliff into a sea of pain. I wanted to drag him away but I was frozen – scared and angry and unsure of my actions. I longed for my weapons but they were hidden away, deep inside the Haven.

'They weren't doing anything, my lord,' said Turner,

keeping his head bowed, his eyes averted. A gasp rippled through the onlookers.

Mias turned slowly, his mouth set wide in a smirk. 'You dare to tell me . . .'

'They've done nothing!' Turner insisted, looking up.

'They were setting a fire!' growled one of the patrollers who'd caught them.

Both youths shook their heads, two pairs of eyes almost bursting from their respective skulls.

'We were hungry . . .' one of them managed to say, his hands trembling as he held out a limp, lifeless rodent.

Mias ignored them, his attention fixed on Turner. 'How long have you lived, creature?' he asked, his voice rasping.

Turner shrugged. From where I was standing, I could see the sly little smile that had broken on his face. I gulped and held onto Tyrell's arm, squeezing hard. I'd had enough conversations with Turner to know that he was about to sign his own death warrant. I prayed that I was wrong.

'Long enough to *know* your mother,' Turner chuckled. 'Your father too.'

Mias looked bemused. 'My mother?' he asked. 'I *ate* my mother a thousand years before your father spilled his seed.'

Turner smiled again and my stomach turned over. I wanted to shout at him, tell him to run, but it was already too late. Turner was going to die and there wasn't a damn thing I could do to help him.

'I bet she tasted like a turd too,' he replied. 'Like the *rest* of your godforsaken kind.'

'Ha!' spat Mias. '*God?* That infant's myth, which your species thought would stop us? Tell me, old man, where is this god now?'

Turner shook his head. 'You'll never understand us,' he replied wearily. 'We are more noble and righteous than you'll ever comprehend. Each of us carries a god inside. You carry nothing but iniquity in your soul . . .'

Mias began to clap his hands together slowly. Sarcastically. 'Which soul?' he asked. 'I have consumed so many . . .'

Turner sighed. 'Leave these children alone,' he ordered. 'If you want to fight, fight . . .'

Mias' arm was just a blur. His fingers tore through Turner's chest, returning with his still-beating heart in their grasp. As Turner collapsed, Mias turned towards the rest of us. He held the deep purple vessel above his head and squeezed, a rivulet of blood dripping from his hand. I felt bile rising into my throat.

'*No!*' cried Tyrell, trying to reach the demon but slamming instead into the closest patroller. The two of them locked arms and hit the ground. The dog-demon snapped at Tyrell's neck with its teeth, trying to sever an artery. Tyrell managed to roll the thing onto its back and pin it with his knees before drawing back his right fist. I felt my knees quiver. My mouth went dry. I scanned the street again, desperate and no longer concerned that my secret life might be discovered. I couldn't lose another brother. I *had* to help Tyrell.

Before I could move, however, Tyrell had pounded the demon's head into the pavement with a mighty punch. Mias roared, dropped the heart and used his ape-like gait to scamper towards Tyrell. The other demons began to bait him, shrieking. Mias pounced on Tyrell, knocking him aside. Tyrell's strength was useless now, his lungs emptied of air, his ribs probably cracked where Mias had caught him. The underlord pinned my friend, took hold of his throat, moved his head in close. A crack of lightning preceded an almost instantaneous explosion of thunder. Torrential rain burst through the clouds.

'You're a strong one,' Mias observed, his fur beginning to drip with water. 'A soul *worth* taking . . .'

'*Tyrell!*' I screamed as the demon drew back his head, baring his teeth . . .

15

Stone heard a commotion down in the street. Intrigued, he walked over to the windows, across creaking oak floorboards, and pulled back half-rotten, permanently drawn blinds. He watched as a patroller unit backed two homeless youths up against a tailor's shop. Disturbances in the heart of the protected zone were rare; such was the fear of the people. No doubt the youths had broken some minor rule and now they would be severely punished. From the look of them, Stone saw that they were useless anyway. Homeless, malnourished and probably riddled with fleas and disease, they were fit for death and not much else.

The lead patroller, a particularly ugly specimen with a head that seemed three times too big for its body, slapped one of the boys, sending him sprawling. From the left he heard someone shouting, then someone else. To the right, a group of male workers stopped to watch. Another shout, this time from directly below, caused Stone to open one of the dirt-smeared windows and listen more closely.

'Leave him be!' he heard a man yell.

The street was now filled with people and Stone smiled. The Hunt was an event he rarely witnessed because he wasn't foolish enough to trust the demons – they were just as likely to turn on the Wanted during their blood lust as anyone else. Here, though, *was* a chance to watch some sport. Very soon other patrols would arrive and take care of the crowd. If he was very lucky, some of the Resistance might show their faces, making his job of hunting them down even easier.

Not that he was ignorant. He had his suspicions about who might be involved. Suspecting someone and catching them was not the same thing, though. Had *he* been in charge, Stone wouldn't have let ridiculous ideas about evidence prevent him from acting. The Mayor, in some myopic quest for personal popularity, insisted on following protocol, such as it was. Time and again Stone had pointed out that laws were for the Wanted. The dispossessed were chattels, and they deserved no favours. He might as well have been talking to himself, for all the good it did.

He walked back to his desk and picked up his coffee mug before returning to the window. More people were gathering now and a familiar voice boomed across the scene – Mias. Things were getting very interesting indeed . . .

★ ★ ★

Mace stopped, held out his arm and told Jonah to wait. They had reached a crossroads and Mace sensed an enemy presence.

'Careful,' he told Jonah.

Jonah raised his head, shoulders tense, fists clenched. They had managed to avoid the patrols during the afternoon but now, back in the protected zone, there were demons close by. He could smell them. The sky had turned from purple to deep, dark blue and the buildings each side of the street cast long shadows. Mace gestured towards a burned-out shell.

'Walk in the lee of the buildings,' he whispered. 'They'll give us cover.'

They moved quickly, silently, every sense on alert. Jonah, following Mace's lead, crouched and waited. Up ahead of them, past a bus abandoned where the two roads crossed, a patrol unit came into view. One of the canine demons stood guard. The other two cautiously approached a disused building. A tattered and faded sign told Jonah that it had once been a shop. The letters that remained spelled out *AX* and *OBS* but gave no clue about what sort of business it had been. The larger of the two demons gestured towards the entrance with his oversized head. The other one, much smaller, with tiger-striped brown on white fur, nodded. They flanked the doorway, waiting. Jonah lifted his nose to the evening air. There, above the stench of sewers, was another smell, smoky and dense – fire. He saw the faintest of orange glows coming from inside the building.

'Homeless kids,' whispered Mace.

Suddenly the patrollers broke cover and sprang through the door, howling. Jonah waited a second and ran across to the bus, fifteen metres from the demon on point.

Mace cursed Jonah's mother, but followed anyway. 'Don't get involved!' he spat when he reached the young man. 'You'll get caught.'

Jonah ignored the giant, his attention fixed on the shop. Seconds later two shapes crashed through the window, splintering the wooden planks that had been nailed across it.

'They're just boys!' said Mace.

Jonah saw that Mace was right. Each kid wore tattered clothes, black with filth. They ran to the left, barefooted. The patrollers followed moments later, pursuing their prey on all fours. Jonah peered round his cover and saw that the third patroller in the unit was watching the action. He took a dagger from his belt and set off towards the unsuspecting demon, keeping low. Mace looked on in disbelief as Jonah made up the ground with almost inhuman speed. Before the demon could react, he jumped onto its back, reached round and slammed the dagger into its left eyeball. The patroller fell to its knees, barely making a sound as Jonah took another, longer knife and cut off its head. The body slumped, head rolling right and Jonah left. Calmly, Jonah got up, bent over the severed head and retrieved his dagger, wiping the blood away on the demon's fur.

Mace joined him quickly.

'You take the street,' Jonah ordered.

'What are you—' began Mace as Jonah took three strides towards the nearest building, managed to find some form of grip and scaled the wall to the roof. He disappeared within seconds.

'What the hell!' Mace exclaimed, unwilling to trust his own eyes. He caught himself quickly. The boys on the street needed his help. There was no time to stand and gawp. Drawing his long sword, he turned and pounded towards them . . .

Up on the rooftops, Jonah made ground more quickly, careful to avoid any crumbling rafters. The buildings adjoined each other until the next road created a break, and he wanted to reach the end before the demons. He stayed as close to the edge as he could, his eyes flitting between watching his own path and scanning the street below.

The patrollers had set off fast but their prey was nowhere to be seen. He saw the demons come to a stop, panting and sniffing the air for a scent. He let them alone and continued towards the end of the row. Once there, he crouched low at the corner and waited. His eyes searched the street, trying to sense the whereabouts of the youths. He took slow, deep breaths and cleared his mind. A heat signature, something he had been trained to look for, emanated from behind a dumpster. The youths were there, and Jonah could hear their hearts beating out a frightened rhythm as clearly as if it were a march being played on a drum. Through sheer luck rather than skill they had managed to avoid the demons, but not for long. The patrollers had sensed them too, and before Jonah could react they charged, the largest colliding with the bin, sending it crashing into the nearest wall. The youths set off again, right underneath Jonah's position.

He wondered whether to drop down and head off the demons but stopped short. It would be quicker to get across to the building opposite. He considered the gap for a moment before backing up by five metres and taking a deep breath. Then he ran forward at a sprint. Using his left leg to pivot from, he pounced from the edge, out into thin air, his arms outstretched. His momentum lifted him high, and seconds later he crashed onto the opposite rooftop. He took a breath and moved on, eyes once again fixed on the street below, which was filling with people . . .

★ ★ ★

Mace felt his lungs burning as he ran after the demon patrol, sword heavy in his hands. He wondered where Jonah had gone, why he hadn't dropped from the rooftops and taken on the patrollers. Looking upwards, he scanned the buildings but there was no sign of the young man. Ahead of him, across another junction, lay the centre of Fire City. If the patrollers managed to chase the youths as far as the hotel, all bets were off. Attacking a patrol there was suicidal and would bring other demons to the fight. It would also reveal who was fighting for the Resistance, and if the battle for the youths didn't kill them, the discovery of their clandestine struggle would see them executed for sure.

Yet what choice did they have? They couldn't ignore the youths' plight and let them die. That was what collaborators did, the scum that Mace hated almost as much as the demons. Despite all the problems it would bring, there was no other way. They had to rescue the boys; otherwise any faith the general populace had left in the Resistance would disappear.

'Goddammit!' he cussed as he crossed the junction and hid in a doorway.

The youths were running blind now, unconcerned that they were heading into bigger trouble. They were only metres from the hotel, and about to be caught.

Mace scampered from doorway to doorway, slowing his approach. When he was within twenty metres of

136

them he ducked down an alley, sprinting to the end where he knew a covered passage ran parallel to the street behind the row of shops. He walked into the darkness slowly now, switching from his long sword to a machete. The shorter weapon would be easier to swing in the narrow passageway, which was prime rodent-nesting territory, and although the vermin wouldn't kill him, they could inflict serious injury, especially when protecting their young. Mace stayed alert as he moved, and made it to the end without incident. Once there, he turned left into another alley so narrow that his shoulders brushed against both walls. Ahead of him lay the main street. He came to a stop just before the end and crouched low, using the darkness as cover once more. Peering out into the street, he heard a voice that made him tremble with fear . . .

Jonah stepped from one roof to another, taking his time to avoid a gaping hole in the tiles. Once he was sure of his footing, he took up a position opposite the hotel. Four large windows ran right to left across the first floor, mirroring the second above it. There were two smaller windows on the third floor, parallel with his eye-line. The panes on the first floor had drawn blinds, but a soft light illuminated the room inside and Jonah could make out a figure observing those below. At street level, a single opening about two metres high and four across had been boarded shut. To the left of it was an entrance, and he raised an eyebrow as Martha and Tyrell stepped out, followed by Prior with his sallow and wrinkled skin. The tatty sign hung suspended by rusty chains from a bracket above the doors. Only three letters remained: T, E and L. He watched as Martha said something to Tyrell, placing a hand on his right forearm. The older man said something too, drawing an angry glance from Tyrell.

A movement in the first-floor room alerted him. Whoever was watching had moved away. Once again, Jonah tried to read the heat signature, but the glass panes prevented it. The skill, taught him by his mother, needed more practice. Instead, it was his regular vision that informed him of the watcher's return. The blinds parted slightly but not enough for Jonah to get a clear view.

Unconcerned, his attention reverted to the street, where the patrollers had now captured the homeless youths and were being surrounded by a mob. He winced as the larger demon slapped one of the boys. A flicker from the first floor opposite told him that one of the sash openings was being drawn upwards. He paid it no mind as he saw someone moving through the crowds, an old man in a grey cloak.

Suddenly a roar went up, a new voice bellowed out a warning and he smelled and heard the arrival of more patrols. As some of the crowd ran for cover, Jonah sensed the presence of another demon too, something older and more powerful than the rest. He turned to his right and saw him.

At nearly two metres in height, the demon was shorter than many of his patrollers, but the power in his limbs was far greater. His mouth gaped open as he sped towards the crowd. Crimson eyes sat underneath a heavily pronounced and ridged brow. Below the eyes sat a wide, compacted nose and the powerful jaw that nearly all demons possessed, which extended outwards, with jagged teeth that were yellowing and dripping with saliva. A single slash of silver diagonally bisected the otherwise jet-black fur that covered his chest.

The old man, his face weathered by time, each wrinkle lined with dirt, confronted this demon. He was barefoot, and wearing clothes that were outsized and in tatters. They exchanged words, the man standing his ground as the demon began to clap slowly. Jonah tried to spot Mace, but to no avail. He wondered where the giant had gone as he watched the scene unfold beneath him. Another movement on the first floor opposite took his attention for perhaps half a second. He scanned the windows but saw nothing new. All around him the wind began to pick up, biting and cold.

Suddenly Tyrell cried out. Jonah looked down and saw the old man slump to the uneven tarmac. The demon had plucked out his heart and was holding it aloft, squashing it between powerful fingers. Tyrell, meanwhile, had wrestled the nearest patroller to the ground and was dodging its mouth, pinning it to the ground. He watched Martha falter, as though her legs had grown suddenly weak, and then the lead demon pounced. Tyrell was sent flying by the impact but his attacker remained in control. Within seconds, he had taken hold of Tyrell's throat. Lightning forked in the sky, directly above Jonah's head. Immediately a sonorous boom of thunder rattled the window frames. Rain poured from the clouds, an instant deluge. More of the crowd scattered as Jonah heard Martha scream. In front of her, the demon said something to Tyrell and then he bared his murderous fangs . . .

16

The black shape stopped me in my tracks just as I had decided that somehow I would have to try and tackle Mias. The shape moved faster than I could comprehend, smashing into the demon. The force of the collision sent out shock waves, like an earthquake. The ground began to undulate, sending people flying and causing buildings to shake. I scrambled forward, desperate to reach Tyrell as loose stone, bricks and roof tiles crashed around me.

The rain was thundering down now, almost obscuring the opposite side of the street, and Mias was nowhere to be seen. The ground around Tyrell was steaming, as though it had been heated, and the temperature was at least ten degrees higher than the surrounding area. I knelt at his side and felt the heat against my skin, unable to understand what was happening around us. The demon underlord was gone, the rain was so heavy that I found it difficult to see or breathe, and a circle of impossible warmth radiated around Tyrell. What the hell was going on?

I heard a roar from behind me. So loud that it rivalled

the thunder. As I checked Tyrell for a pulse, I felt the force of two objects colliding. Again, the impact sent out shock waves and I fell to the right before looking up in astonishment.

Mias was back. He had grown to twice his normal size and his eyes flickered as though they were on fire. Jonah faced him, a short sword in one hand, the other holding a tapered spear. Something in his stance reminded me of a predatory cat, like the tigers that my mother had shown me pictures of. The spear he held crackled and buzzed with a blue light, as though it had been energized. Again, comprehension escaped me. I couldn't work out where Jonah had come from. All I knew was that I was pleased to see him.

Pleased, but worried too . . .

Mias stepped towards Jonah and swung out a fist. I gasped in fear as Jonah waited until the very last moment before stepping inside the blow, cutting into Mias' arm with his sword. The demon seemed to feel nothing and repeated his move with the opposite hand, deadly claws outstretched. Again Jonah timed his escape, and again he swiped out with his sword.

This time Mias bellowed as if hurt and I grew more confident. Somehow Jonah had *hurt* the monster, something I'd never imagined possible.

He struck again, and one of Mias' fingers flew into the air, blood spouting from the wound. I watched in growing awe and admiration as Jonah somersaulted through the air as though his legs were coiled springs.

Mias stopped and studied his wound. He roared in defiance and set off towards Jonah. My confidence ebbed as I saw the rage in Mias' face. I could see that he wanted to kill my new friend and the thought sickened me. Only Jonah managed to evade injury again, with yet another impossibly high somersault taking him over the demon. He landed on his feet behind Mias, and used that advantage to stab the demon with his spear. As the demon shrieked, I sensed a presence behind me. Springing to my feet, I turned to find Mace standing at Tyrell's feet.

'We've gotta go!' the giant shouted through the pounding rain. '*Quickly!*'

I nodded, and despite being torn about leaving Jonah to fight Mias alone, I knew that Mace was right. I just had to hope that Jonah would win – any other outcome was unthinkable.

'Where are the other demons?' I asked.

'Coming!' yelled Mace as he grabbed Tyrell and hefted him across his right shoulder. 'Get back into the bar.'

We ran for the hotel's entrance, where Prior and some others had already set up barricades. They let us through before closing ranks again, just as something large and weighty slammed into the closed doors. I shuddered as the doors wobbled in their frame, and led Mace to a table, sweeping it clear. As Mace laid Tyrell down, I saw that the bar was packed with frightened people. Huddled in one corner, shaking with shock, were the two youths whose lives had just been saved.

'What the hell happened out there?' I asked Mace. 'What was that thing that attacked Mias and where did Jonah come from?'

'I don't know what that thing was, but Jonah was up on the roof,' Mace admitted. 'We saw the youths running from the patrollers and came after them. I was watching from the alley across the street when it kicked off. Next thing I knew I was sitting on my arse, with a patroller at my side. The blast wave sent everyone flying. I killed the patroller before it came to, and then Jonah appeared . . .'

I nodded and thought about the intense temperature around Tyrell when I'd reached him.

'That weapon he used to attack Mias – it created some sort of heat circle round Tyrell,' I said. 'I've never seen anything like it.'

Mace shrugged. 'I'll be having a chat with that boy later,' he told me. 'If he survives. Mias looks pretty upset.'

'He'll kill Jonah if we don't do something,' I urged. 'We have to help him.' That was the moment when I knew for sure that my feelings for Jonah were different to any I'd had before. Even though it felt strange to be so attached to someone I'd only just met, I couldn't pretend otherwise any more. He *had* to survive.

Mace grunted and I'm sure I saw a slight smirk too. Was I that obvious?

'We can't help him if we're dead,' he pointed out. 'Let him handle Mias. We need to stop the patrollers from breaking in.'

I didn't reply because his answer wasn't the one I'd wanted to hear. It was the right answer though, no matter how much I didn't like it. We were trapped in the hotel and the demons had *our* scent, the aroma of *our* blood in their nostrils. Suddenly I had an idea – something Mace had once told me about when I was younger. I ran behind the bar and set out a line of empty bottles.

'Something I was thinking about earlier,' I told Mace and Prior when they gave me confused looks.

On the table, Tyrell had begun to regain consciousness. He raised his head and asked where he was. No one replied so he grunted and rubbed his big head, sitting up.

'What are you doing?' Prior asked me. 'We've got to defend the door.'

'Wait a minute,' I demanded, concentrating on filling each bottle with alcohol. When that was done, I searched around for some cloth. Eventually I gave up and began to remove my long-sleeved top, relieved that I'd bothered to put on an undergarment.

'You're stripping in the middle of a battle?' asked Mace. 'Martha, I don't think—'

'*Sssh!*' I ignored more strange looks and tore my top into strips after wringing out some of the excess rainwater. Then I stuffed each bottle with a single rag, leaving a little to overhang. I worked quickly and without a word, and Mace was obviously the first to understand what I was doing.

'Firebombs!' he said, almost delighted.

'Exactly!' I replied. 'Quick – find some matches and get these to the front!'

Prior and Mace gathered the bottles and ran to the entrance. They set their bombs down and began to look for matches. Prior hacked up phlegm, his face bright red, eyes streaming.

Faith, who after fetching a secret stash of weapons from the kitchen was helping to hold the door, took a box from the pocket of her trousers.

'You looking for these?' she asked Prior, who was wiping his mouth, his breathing laboured.

'Light two of the rags,' he gasped. 'Quickly and there's a drink in it for you.'

Faith shook her head, her blonde hair tied into a knot on her head. 'A drink with you?' I heard her reply. 'No thanks – I'd rather amputate, pickle and eat one of my own toes. Now if Mace was asking . . .'

'I'm asking, then!' yelled Mace. 'Just light the bloody bottles, woman!'

Faith did as she was told, her wide face flushed. 'The rags are too wet,' she told them. 'They won't light.'

'Use *your* shirt, then!' ordered Mace. 'You didn't go outside!'

'But I'm not wearing anything else!' Faith protested.

'So what?'

Faith shrugged and looked at me. I shrugged back.

'Bloody hell!' she cursed, starting to remove her top. 'Turn round, then!'

Prior and Mace looked away as she replaced the wet rags speedily. When she was done, she used her hands to cover up her heavy breasts. I looked over at one of the male customers and ordered him to give me his shirt. When he started to protest, I pointed at Mace, using him as a threat. The man shook his head, swore at me but did as I asked.

'There!' Faith snapped at Mace and Prior.

I watched the men take a bottle each, both of them smirking like little boys.

'Nice view . . .' joked Mace as I handed Faith the shirt I'd been given so reluctantly.

'Thanks, missy,' said Faith, using one hand to take the garment and turning her back to the rest of us.

'Can you stop being childish and deal with the problem!' I said to Mace, who nodded sheepishly.

147

'Crack the door open a little,' he said, raising a blazing firebomb level with his shoulder. Tables that were being used to barricade the doors were pulled away. One of the other men, Raj, took a deep breath and then did as Mace asked. A giant hand groped through the gap, almost tearing his face off. Raj slammed the door shut again, his knees weak.

'*Bollocks!*'

Mace steadied himself and waited a few more seconds. The makeshift bomb threatened to go off in his hands.

'You've got to get it right!' I shouted from behind him. 'If it hits the demon it'll set light to its fur. Quick!'

'I know that!' yelled Mace. 'I taught you about these things, remember?'

Raj asked Mace if he was ready, took a deep breath and opened the door again. This time a canine face loomed. Mace grinned, punching the demon square on the jaw. It stumbled backwards, away from the entrance, and Mace threw his firebomb. The bottle shattered against the patroller's head, coating its face in sticky fluid. The flaming rag licked against its fur – just above its green eyes – and in an instant its entire head was alight. The demon dropped to its knees, screaming in pain.

'*Now!*' hollered Mace.

We burst into the street with a collective snarl, no

longer thinking about whether we'd get caught or not. I think we knew without saying that if we let the patrollers overrun the bar, we were probably all dead anyway. Raj and Faith set about a shorter demon, using machetes to hack chunks of flesh from its body. Prior set another one on fire, before stabbing the next in the eyes repeatedly, his face slick with demon blood, his coughing ever worse. Behind them, I lit more rags and passed the bottles on. Within minutes the entrance was clear.

Mace led the charge into the rain, splitting skulls and cleaving limbs. The firebombs had given us a big advantage, and we were winning. Between us, we dispatched the patrollers quickly and without a single injury.

Finally I turned my attention back to Jonah and Mias, a little fearful about what I might find. I walked across the street to where Jonah had slumped to his knees. I couldn't see Mias anywhere. As I moved closer, I saw that Jonah wasn't moving. I called out to him and felt the same increase in air temperature as earlier.

'Jonah – are you hurt?'

Jonah lifted his head but didn't reply. He seemed to be in a daze, eyes wide and mouth drooling. He was holding one of the black spears and turned to look at me.

'Where's Mias?' I asked gently.

Jonah shook his head slowly. 'He's gone,' he replied. 'Dunno where . . . hurt him.'

I crouched and put a hand on his shoulder. Kinetic energy coursed through my arm, making the nerves tingle. I felt my face flush. A warm sensation spread in my belly and I felt elated that Jonah hadn't been badly injured.

'You need to hide,' I said, shaking my head free of the sensations that touching him had brought. 'Before they send more patrols. This is going to get bad.'

And then I saw Jonah's eyes. The pupils were dilated, the irises unfeasibly black. Something else was there too, something almost as impossible as the ring of warmth surrounding him and the defeat of an underlord at the hands of a human. A circle of orange flame flickered round the edge of each iris. I gasped . . .

'Need . . . to . . . sleep . . .'

I yelled to Mace for help and he ran over, concern etched across his face. Between us we lifted Jonah to his feet. As I looked up, I thought I saw the blinds on the first floor of the hotel twitch. I paid it no mind though. My head and heart were too full of Jonah.

17

As Aron and Oscar made their way back from work, it became apparent that things weren't right. Torrential rain pounded streets that seemed unusually empty. Lightning crackled overhead, followed by explosions of thunder. The pavements steamed, and everywhere a tart, almost cloying aroma hung in the air. The patrols seemed to be extra aggressive, if that were possible.

'Something's wrong,' said Aron.

Oscar nodded; his angular, tapered eyes watching each passing patrol keenly, the rainwater dripping from his chin.

'Trouble,' he said softly.

'More than just trouble,' replied Aron, wiping water from his face.

The industrial zone sat parallel to the protected part of the city, connected by a narrow passage of dark streets. From the sky, the layout would have resembled a figure of eight perhaps, or more accurately, two enclosed rings of similar diameter linked by a short corridor.

Usually that corridor was full of workers coming and going. Today the flow was in a single direction, away from the factories.

'Where is everyone?' Aron added as they passed a gang of human mercenaries standing on a corner, pensively smoking damp cigarettes and soaked to the skin.

'Dunno,' said Oscar. 'Just keep moving.'

The next patrol was demon; two half-canines supervised by a simian with dripping ginger fur and clawed hands. Oscar kept his head down but Aron managed to incur their ire, stopping to stare at them with his bright blue eyes.

'Move forward, wretch!' spat one of the half-dogs.

'But you're so pretty,' replied Aron with a smirk.

'Walk on!' said the ape-like one. It held out a hand, showing fearsomely long daggers for fingers.

'I think you might need your nails clipping,' continued Aron, unaware that another patrol was closing in from behind.

Oscar did see it though, and he tugged Aron by the arm. 'Shut the hell up!' he whispered to his friend. 'You're going to get us killed.' He disliked Aron's arrogant streak. Aron was always pushing things too far, never apologized for his actions, and seemed to enjoy trouble. More than once his big mouth had led Oscar and Tyrell to risk their lives for him. As if life wasn't hard enough.

'I'm just toying with them,' Aron protested. 'Relax.'

'*You* might have a death wish,' Oscar told him, 'but I don't. They're surrounding us, you dick.'

Aron turned and caught sight of the other patrol. A crash of thunder shook the buildings lining the street. Somewhere close by a window imploded.

'So we run, then, do we?' he asked. 'Not me . . .'

Oscar shook his head. 'No weapons,' he whispered. 'And no support or cover. Are you *insane*?'

'No,' replied Aron, 'but I'm not scared either.'

Oscar ignored the barb, aware that he'd annoy Aron.

'I'm not crapping my pants,' Aron added, trying again to get a rise out of his companion.

'You're too obvious,' said Oscar, 'and it never works. You can't wind me up – now, come on!'

He walked on, hoping that Aron would follow and growing livid when he didn't. Then he stopped, sighed and surveyed the scene. Things had suddenly got a lot, lot worse. Three patrollers flanked them to the rear. Further away, the mercenaries numbered four, although they wouldn't intervene if the demons attacked Aron. It was more than their lives were worth. That left two more patrollers and the beige, wolf-like demon that looked to be in charge. Every doorway and window along the street had been barricaded, offering no escape route. Ahead of them were several more patrol units. If it kicked off, they were dead.

'*Make* me move,' Aron said defiantly, eyeing the ape-demon.

The patrollers growled as their supervisor told them to hold still.

'But, Lord Saarl . . .' one of the canine monsters protested.

Saarl smiled at Aron. Oscar, on hearing the demon's name, shuddered. He was one of the most vicious of all Valefor's underlords, second only to a sadistic brute named Mias. Oscar remembered seeing Saarl in action and had no wish to repeat the experience.

'You are a foolish animal,' said the demon, his emerald eyes seeming to grow larger as the already tiny pupils shrank further.

'*I'm* not the animal,' snapped Aron.

Lord Saarl let out a high-pitched cackle. All around him vapour rose through the rainfall, white and hazy.

'We're *all* animals,' he replied. 'Some are born to hunt and others . . .'

The underlord flexed his murderous fingers and changed stance slightly, ready to pounce. Aron, caught up in his own stupidity, failed to notice.

Oscar didn't. 'Aron!' he cautioned, drawing closer to his friend.

'I would heed your friend,' warned Saarl, cocking his head to one side. Like his fellow demons, he had an elongated jaw with rows of saw-like teeth.

'If I was you,' replied Aron, 'I'd possess something less ugly. I bet you've never had a girlfriend.'

Saarl pounced before Aron's words had finished resonating; a glancing backhand that sent him sprawling. Aron landed on his back in the road, winded.

The demon turned to Oscar. 'If he speaks again, he will die.'

Oscar nodded his understanding before seeing to Aron. His friend was dazed, a livid welt across his right cheekbone, his already shaggy blond hair even messier. Oscar knew that Aron was lucky. Another underlord would have torn him to pieces.

'What the—'

'*Ssh!*' ordered Oscar. 'If you say another word I'll kill you myself!'

The sound of a car's brakes screeched through the air. Heavy doors were opened and slammed shut again.

'Lord Saarl!'

Oscar turned to see Stone glaring at him. Beside him was the Mayor. It was his voice Oscar had heard. Oscar looked away, not wanting to give Stone any excuses to react. The mercenary was as dangerous as any demon.

'Lord Mayor,' he heard Saarl reply. 'What brings you out in this delightful weather?'

The Mayor replied, but the sound of an explosion drowned out his words.

155

'What the hell was that?' asked Aron, sitting up and rubbing his wound.

'Not thunder, that's for sure,' said Oscar. 'Sounded more like a bomb.'

They watched as various patrol units came running. Lord Saarl was listening to the Mayor when he cried out suddenly. He grabbed the Mayor by his collar and pulled him close. Another explosion reverberated through the night.

'Where are all the people?' asked Aron.

'I don't know,' Oscar replied with impatience.

He was too busy watching the Mayor turn cherry red and hyperventilate, his double chin wobbling visibly. Saarl seemed to be spitting words at him, each one making the human flinch. Then, just as suddenly, Saarl let him go. He turned to his troops and barked an order before loping off into the night. His minions followed quickly. The Mayor straightened his clothes, trying in vain to regain some dignity.

'*Stone!*' he shouted.

His right-hand man moved to him slowly, hands in pockets. Chunky wraparound sunglasses obscured his cold blue eyes. His shaven head glistened with water.

'Clear the streets. *Now!*'

As the Mayor stomped back to his car, Stone approached Oscar and Aron. 'I'd run and hide if I was you,' he said with a smirk.

Aron got to his feet and told the mercenary to shove his advice up his arse. Oscar fought away the urge to punch his friend on the jaw, and asked Stone why they should take cover.

'Because someone fought and hurt Mias,' replied Stone.

'Huh?' both boys said in unison, their eyes wide with shock. No one attacked an underlord. No one would dare.

'There's a stranger in town,' said Stone. 'Someone I need to find. There's a large reward for information.' The last part was stretching the truth but Stone cared little. 'Dark hair, dark eyes, dressed in black,' continued the mercenary. 'He carries strange weapons too.'

'Sounds like your ideal man,' replied Aron.

Oscar cursed silently at the change in Stone's expression. He had been expecting them to cower and run away. Yet Aron was cracking bad jokes and Stone had grown suspicious.

'We have to go,' Oscar said.

'You *sure* you haven't seen him?'

Oscar shook his head quickly. 'We've just finished our shift,' he explained. 'Haven't seen anyone but other workers.'

'What about you, smart mouth?' Stone asked Aron. 'Have *you* seen him?'

'I don't talk to collaborators,' Aron snapped in reply.

'Even if I had seen this . . . person, I'd cut out my own tongue before I told you.'

Stone removed his sunglasses and put them in the pocket of his fatigued combats. He clenched his fists, the knuckles cracking. His stare was unblinking.

'I'm going to ignore that remark,' he said softly. 'But next time we meet, you *will* talk to me . . .'

'What's happening in the protected zone – the explosions?' Oscar cut in, before Aron talked himself into an early grave.

'What do you think?' asked Stone. 'Valefor is pissed off at what happened to Mias. I think they're like demon best buddies or something. All sounds a bit gay to me.' He looked at Oscar with a smirk.

'We'd better leave, then,' said Oscar, looking down at his feet.

Stone nodded. 'I would,' he advised. 'Tonight this city will earn its name . . .'

18

An hour later, I sat in the Haven and listened to my aunt describe the chaos in Fire City. May had only just arrived, bringing a few terrified residents with her. The hideaway was full already and they had been the last to gain entry. Now Oscar and Raj were up at ground level, guarding the entrances. Our sanctuary was too important to lose, even if that meant turning people away.

'Every street, every alleyway,' she told me, her grey eyes wide. 'Saarl is killing everyone he can find. Half the buildings are on fire and you can't see the sky for the smoke.'

I rarely look at Aunt May without pining for my mother. She talks, walks and acts just like her and sometimes, if I close my eyes, it's like my mother's still with me and the world will be OK. The feeling only ever lasts a few seconds before reality slams me in the face with its fist. As May continued to explain what she'd seen, I felt my stomach turning somersaults.

'What's *he* doing about it?' I asked my aunt.

'You mean the Mayor?' replied May, pulling a face. 'What *can* he do, Martha? He's a puppet and a coward. That animal Stone and his cohorts are warning people but it's too late.'

'I wish Mum was here,' I said without thinking, causing Aunt May to furrow her brow.

'We all do,' she replied. 'What made you think of Maria?'

I shrugged. 'Just stuff,' I said, thinking how my feelings for Jonah were so new, so different. Inwardly, I was longing to be able to talk to my mum about them.

'You know,' said Aunt May, putting her arm on mine, 'you can always talk to me about things.'

'I know that,' I replied with a nod. 'I'm still feeling a bit down after what happened to Samuel last week.'

'And the other thing?' she whispered, allowing for Aron's presence in the same room.

We were in one of the old changing rooms, slumped in moth-eaten armchairs that were musty and damp. A broken mirror ran along one wall with a worktop attached below. Mace and Aron were leaning against it, their expressions sour. I nodded again as my aunt glanced at Aron.

'We'll talk later,' I said in a low voice.

Mace asked us what we were whispering about.

'Girl stuff,' replied Aunt May. 'Nothing to worry your pretty big head about, Mace.'

'You know this is all *his* fault,' said Aron out of the blue. 'Jonah, I mean.'

I glared at him and shook my head in disbelief. 'He's not to blame,' I snapped. 'No more than anyone else is. This is our life, Aron.'

'He attacked an underlord,' Aron countered. 'It was bound to cause trouble. I told you something isn't right about him.'

Mace told us to shut up as I recalled what I'd seen in Jonah's eyes. The flames dancing around his irises, like circles of fire. A little part of me wondered whether Aron was right, but only for a split second. My mother had always taught me to judge people by their actions, not their words, and Jonah had proved he was with us, even if there was something odd about him.

'No!' Aron shouted at Mace. 'Why *should* I shut up? He's only been here for just over a week and the city is being destroyed.'

'And it was perfect before he came, wasn't it?' said Aunt May, shaking her head. 'Things were wonderful?'

Aron snorted and I fought back the urge to slap him. What was *wrong* with him?

'Things were bad,' he admitted, 'but not like this. Valefor and his demons are going to kill everyone.'

'No,' said Mace. 'No, they won't. They can't afford to

kill everyone because the factories won't run. Valefor isn't stupid – he has a chain of command to worry about.'

Aron looked incredulous. 'You mean the government? Like *they* can control the demons.'

Mace sighed and shook his head. 'Not them,' he explained. 'The *other* demons. Valefor might be an ancient, but he's not in charge. Otherwise he'd be in Babylon City – not stuck out here.'

'There's a ruling council of demons,' said Aunt May, adding to Mace's explanation. 'Valefor isn't on it. He can't be if he's in Fire City. Whoever calls the shots is going to stop this . . .'

'But not before Saarl and Valefor gain some satisfaction,' continued Mace. 'Until then, we just have to hope that people find good hiding places.'

'Hope?' asked Aron. 'What happened to *helping* our people? We should be out there, like during the Hunt. Rescuing our own from them!'

I watched Mace and my aunt exchange knowing looks. They were old enough to remember the War and everything that had happened since. They knew that the demons weren't stupid enough to annihilate every human. In the world before the demons, the human race had been at the top of the food chain. Now the demons had taken their place. For a food chain to exist at all, though, there had to be balance. Mace had taught me that.

'Why do you think they have breeding centres?' I asked Aron, even though the thought made me wince inside.

'To create more prey,' he replied in a sullen voice. 'I'm not stupid.'

'Not *just* prey,' I told him. 'Workers too. The Wanted need clothes and food and all those other things, and the Unwanted make them. That's how this world we live in works. The demons rule, the Wanted come next, and then there's everyone else.'

Aron shrugged. 'Dunno what this has to do with Jonah,' he replied. 'We were talking about him.'

'No,' I told him forcefully. '*You* were talking about him.'

Aron refused to back down. I could see that touch of defiance and arrogance in his eyes – something that I'd always found annoying, but more so recently.

'He's trouble,' he insisted. 'I think we should just tell him to go.'

'Tell *who* to go?' came Tyrell's deep voice from the doorway.

I dismissed Aron with a wave of my hand and turned to Tyrell. We had more important things to think about.

'How is Jonah?' I asked.

'OK, I suppose. He's up and about but his wounds are bad. Faith sutured a few of the deepest ones but he says he's fine.'

'I'll go and talk to him,' I said, a sense of relief washing over me, touched too by a little excitement.

'But *we* were talking!' Aron wailed.

I shook my head at him and felt myself getting angry. 'No, Aron,' I told him. 'You were moaning and the rest of us were getting annoyed. It's not the *same* as talking.'

'I'm coming with you,' said Aunt May. 'Make sure there's nothing else Jonah needs.'

Aron's expression made me even angrier. His sulking meant that any sense of sympathy I had for him was beginning to dry up. Mace seemed to feel the same thing and he told Aron to grow up.

'We *need* Jonah,' he said, almost in exasperation. 'I don't know how, but he managed to hurt Mias. That's reason enough to thank him. Can't you see that he's an asset, Aron? Are you that blinded by—'

'*Thank* him?' asked Aron. 'What about all the people who are going to die because of what he's done? And what am I being blinded by anyway? What the hell do you know about me, old man?'

I watched Tyrell put a meaty hand on Aron's shoulder – a little warning about upsetting Mace. He was calmer than me after Aron's last jibe. Mace had brought us all up, wiped our arses and taught us everything we know. For Aron to question his love for us was more than just wrong. It was nasty.

'People are going to die,' Tyrell pointed out as I

whispered 'I love you' at a visibly upset Mace. 'Don't matter if it's tonight, tomorrow or next week. Unless we try to fight back, these bastards will kill us all anyway.'

'But we had our system,' Aron whined. 'Jonah's messed it up!'

'Aron, please!' Mace pleaded. 'Our system is useless. Rescuing a handful of people from the Hunt and watching ten times as many perish. Losing our family and friends, and fearing discovery every day. Maybe the time has come to retaliate more openly?'

'But we're not ready for that – you said so yourself.'

'Aye,' replied Mace. 'I did and we're not – not yet. But with Jonah's help—'

'We don't *need* his help!'

Tyrell's grip on Aron tightened. 'You sound like a child,' he told him. 'We need all the help we can get.'

Aron's sullen, defiant expression told me that we were wasting our time. Suddenly he snapped. He shoved past Tyrell and walked out of the room, slamming the door shut behind him.

'This is all about you,' Tyrell said to me. 'He's worried that you'll take to Jonah. He's jealous.'

I shook my head. 'It's not about me,' I replied. 'None of this is about me. He's losing his mind – I can feel it. We need to watch him, help him if we can.'

'If he'll let us help,' said Aunt May, shaking her head in sorrow. 'I've seen too many end up like Aron.

165

The pressure gets to them – this shitty life that we lead.'

'I know, I know,' said Tyrell. 'No need to say it.'

Mace took out his flask and chugged down some booze. 'I can't believe he said that to me, though,' he whispered. 'He's as much a son to me as Samuel was.'

'Don't get upset,' I replied. 'He didn't mean it, Mace. He was just angry.'

Mace considered me for a moment, shook his head and took another swig.

'Come on,' Aunt May ordered. 'Let's go and see Jonah.'

19

Stone coughed as the fumes from yet another burning building poisoned his lungs. He was guarding the hotel, part of him relishing a confrontation with some patrollers. Not that it would happen. Saarl, crazed as he was at Mias' humiliation, would think twice before attacking the Mayor's property, even if the owner *was* cowering in his mansion, surrounded by armed guards.

'No one comes in!' he told one of his men.

The soldier nodded silently and held more tightly to his machine gun. His acne-scarred face was flushed and sweating, the thick black monobrow above his eyes twitching. 'No problem, boss,' he replied.

'I'll be back in a minute,' Stone added. 'Got something to finish in my office.'

He took the stairs two at a time and, once inside, bolted the office door. He turned on his phone, dialled and waited for a reply.

'Tell!' demanded the person on the other end.

'I've found him.'

'Good, good,' came the reply. 'Is he in your custody?'

'No, sir. I haven't yet—'

'Then why are you calling, Stone? I thought I'd made my position explicitly clear during our previous conversation?'

'You did, sir, but there's a little local difficulty preventing any action.'

Stone heard his controller sigh before speaking again. 'Difficulty, you say?'

'The city's in flames,' explained Stone. 'Valefor and his underlords are wreaking havoc.'

'Why?'

'Because of the boy; he nearly killed an underlord named Mias.'

'You saw this?'

Stone sensed the excitement in his controller's question. 'With my own eyes,' he said, 'and I have to say that—'

'Silence!'

'But, sir, I—'

'You saw nothing, Stone – is that understood? You saw nothing and you tell no one. That is a direct order!'

'Yes, sir.'

'Discretion is a virtue that I admire, Stone. Having said that, it is splendid news. I wish you to proceed immediately in capturing the youth.'

'But, sir, the demons are—'

'I'll take care of that, Stone.'

'Yes, sir.'

'Can you get to the boy?'

Stone thought about what he'd seen and how it would help his plan. He decided to run it by his master. 'I've been thinking about how, sir.'

'Consideration is always useful, Stone. Impatience leads to defeat in every case and patience to victory. There's an old saying about donkeys and patient men but I won't bore you with it. What have you been thinking?'

Stone explained his thoughts quickly, outlining every part of his plan. His master waited a few moments before replying.

'The success of your plot rests on a few variables,' he said. 'I don't *like* variables. They are, by their nature, unstable.'

'I agree, sir, but I'll deal with any sudden deviations. The main points should work, however. Can I progress?'

'Absolutely,' said the controller. 'Let me make a few calls and sort out the little difficulty with Valefor. In the morning you may begin.'

'Thank you, sir.'

'And where is your Mayor?'

'With some whore,' revealed Stone. 'It's his default reaction to bad news.'

'Nero fiddled . . .' said the caller gleefully.

169

'Sir?'

'Never mind, Stone. I look forward to our next chat. Keep the phone with you from now on – I may call at any time. Good evening.'

20

The Mayor studied himself in the mirror, holding his stomach in and his shoulders back. The years hadn't been too unkind, he thought to himself. Yes, lack of exercise had made him flabby and withered his arm muscles, but on the whole he was in good shape. Good enough to entice his fair share of young women. The latest, Bella, was seventeen and waiting in his bed. Ordinarily, she worked as a maid, but the promise of an extra two months' salary had encouraged her to take up new duties. Not that he needed to pay – he *was* the Mayor, after all. It didn't hurt to spread some wealth around, though.

Several stray hairs poked from his nostrils, mostly grey. He rummaged through the bathroom cabinet, found his scissors and clipped them away. Next came his ear lobes and eyebrows. Finally he lathered himself in fine cologne, one he'd had delivered from the Southern Citadel. One day, he would be rewarded for his hard work and retire amongst the other Wanted, away from the hell of Fire City. He fancied a place by the sea, perhaps close to the city that, during his youth, had been known as Brighton. It was a smaller citadel but with clean, fresh air – ideal after years spent amongst the Unwanted, suffering their stench. He'd always been loyal to his masters and had often gone beyond the realms of duty. He would suggest retirement – it was the least he deserved.

His thoughts turned to Martha, his wayward and sullen stepdaughter. He'd spent years looking after the girl, keeping her on out of some pitiful sense of duty when his ex-wife had died. Perhaps Martha had also been his way of keeping hold of the Maria he'd fallen in love with – the simple, beautiful woman he'd first met. It was the only way to explain his continued tolerance of the girl. Yet in return for his kindness, Martha gave him abuse, sarcasm and very little else.

He had rescued her mother from desperate poverty, yet the same woman had betrayed him, cuckolded him. How striking Maria had been, with her sparkling grey eyes and burnished skin and a fire in her heart. He'd fallen for her instantly, unconcerned that she came with a child. Having Maria by his side was all that mattered. Only she hadn't felt the same – for Maria, the Mayor had been nothing more than an insurance policy. He'd been a convenient sap, a fool willing to provide for her, in exchange for sex. Soon that dried up too and she'd taken to drink, spending her time with lowlifes and traitors. In the end, her death had been unavoidable, a simple trade-off for continued power. Maybe he would have given up everything if she'd loved him – it was hard to know – but he *had* loved her, more than any woman he'd ever met. Such a shame then that she'd betrayed him . . .

He put any thoughts of his ex-wife away, splashed a little more cologne round his chops and made his way into the bedroom. The girl, Bella, lay on her side, facing away, towards the French doors. Her skin was pale, her bony hips visible. He wondered whether she'd be grateful, this one. Whether she'd be worth keeping and fattening up. The thought of an heir and a woman to see out his days with grew more appealing each time. Someone young and vibrant, malleable even.

'Would you like some wine?' he asked her, removing his silk robe and getting into bed.

Bella said nothing and kept her back to him. He reached out a hand and touched her bare shoulder. Her skin was burning up.

'Shall I open the doors, my dear?' he asked, running his fingers down her back. 'You're awfully warm.' He heard her sob a little. 'Don't cry, my dear,' he said in a soothing tone. 'I'm not a monster. I'll be kind.'

Bella stirred a little then, whispering to him. 'I've never done this before,' she said, her voice sending ripples of excitement coursing through him. 'Will you close your eyes?'

The Mayor smiled and did as she asked. Her weight shifted as she turned and straddled him, an intense, earthy aroma filling his senses. He made to look at her but she stopped him.

'Not yet,' she purred into his left ear, her breasts brushing against him, her breath as hot as lava.

'Yes . . .' he murmured, feeling utterly at ease. 'You're a very good girl . . .'

He felt her sit back and run her fingers through the hairs on his chest. Her hands felt calloused, her nails a touch too long – minor details that he would fix when he made her his favourite. He'd make her grow her hair too, make her eat a little more to fill out those sunken cheeks and put meat on her bones. Make her more like Maria . . .

'You can look now,' she told him, leaning in once more, her mouth barely an inch from his, her weight increasing as she pressed herself into him.

The Mayor waited a moment, wanting to prolong the feeling. She was surely going to become his most wanted. Such a delicate face, such a pretty smile, such an uncanny resemblance to . . . He reached out to caress her hair and something felt wrong. Something felt awfully, dreadfully wrong. He opened his eyes and saw mauve feline irises staring back.

'Still as pretty?' he heard Valefor ask playfully.

The Mayor's heart felt as though it was being crushed in a vice. He screamed, trying in vain to get away. Valefor chortled in amusement.

'I hope you weren't fond of that one,' he said. 'It's just that once I consume them, most humans are never the same again.'

The Mayor tried to speak but his chest was being compacted and his lungs were aflame with pain. Valefor sensed this and sprang away suddenly, the movement so fast it was almost imperceptible. The Mayor gasped and drew down as much air as he could manage, spluttering. He scrambled away, falling to the floor and crawling back towards the bathroom, away from the demon. Valefor stalked him, his expression sardonic.

'Your wretchedness amuses me, Mayor. Wriggle some more.'

The Mayor turned onto his back, used his hands to cover his genitals and begged for mercy.

'If I wanted you dead,' Valefor told him, 'you would be.'

'I d-d-don't understand,' the human stuttered. 'What have I done to displease you, lord?'

Valefor saw a glass of red wine on a walnut bedside table. He picked it up, sniffing at the contents. 'This wine you drink – what is the attraction?'

'I-I . . .'

'Mind if I try some?' The Mayor watched Valefor down the glass in one, his grey-green wings outstretched, twitching. 'Terrible,' the demon said, his mule-like jaw convulsing. 'Now tell me about the stranger.'

'The stranger?' the Mayor asked him.

'The one I asked you to find. The one who nearly killed Mias,' replied Valefor in a menacing tone. 'Did we not speak of this already?'

'I've heard nothing since then,' the Mayor managed to say. 'My men have been asking around.'

Valefor growled and pounced on the Mayor once more, pinning him to the floor. Thick, warm drool hung from his mouth. 'You *should* know by now,' he spat.

'I – I've been b–busy . . .' whined the Mayor.

'I want him found!'

The Mayor nodded.

'You understand, then?'

'Yes, my lord – please – you're hurting me!'

Valefor relented and stood up, turning his back on the human. He eyed the furniture in the room, the king-sized bed and dark-wood armoire.

'Your position has given you many comforts,' he told the Mayor. 'I hope you haven't forgotten your place.'

The Mayor stood up gingerly and put on his robe. His chest hurt and his legs wobbled. 'Never, my lord,' he replied.

'Something is amiss in the city,' Valefor explained. 'No ordinary human could have hurt Mias – he is of pure breeding, only a little less powerful than I. It bothers me that a creature as venerable as he should suffer. I want this stranger.'

'And you shall have him,' replied the Mayor. 'Just give me a few more days.'

Valefor twisted his neck from side to side. 'Meanwhile, I will have my revenge,' said the demon lord. 'Tonight the factories can remain empty. Any human found on the streets will die. As payment for the injuries inflicted upon Mias.'

'But what of the council, my lord?' asked the Mayor, trembling.

'YOU DARE TO SPEAK TO ME OF THE COUNCIL?' Valefor bellowed.

The Mayor cowered, begging forgiveness. 'I did not mean to—'

'ENOUGH!' demanded the demon lord. 'I want this stranger found and the Resistance crushed. Anything less and I will carve out your heart and feed it to you.'

'As you wish, master,' the Mayor whimpered.

'I have been summoned to the Southern Citadel,' Valefor added. 'I shall return after the Hunt tomorrow. I expect news.'

'I understand.'

'I hope so.'

The Mayor shuddered as he watched Valefor open the French doors and fly off into the night, his giant wings silhouetted against a teal sky. He stumbled into the bathroom, knelt before the toilet bowl and vomited until his stomach burned.

21

Aron sat with Prior, his head still spinning with rage. They were in the central chamber of the Haven – a large rectangular basement with smaller rooms and corridors round each side. The older man took occasional sips from a flask, wincing each time he swallowed. Aron realized that Prior was growing weaker, his breathing more coarse. The veins in his arms and neck had grown black, his feet were swollen and what hair he had left hung limp and greasy. These were tell-tale signs of disease and malnutrition that afflicted many of Fire City's residents, and Aron knew it wouldn't be long before Prior passed on.

'Did you know . . .' said Prior, 'that I've not left this city since the end of the War?'

Aron shrugged. Around them the people lucky enough to have made it into the Haven tried to rest. Some were napping on the cold stone floor; others sat huddled in groups, too worried to sleep. No one knew what the morning would bring.

'I've *never* left it,' Aron replied. 'How sad is that?'

Prior took another swig, swallowed and belched. 'What's stopping you?' he eventually asked.

'Let's see,' said Aron. 'Demons, cannibals, dirty collaborating humans in soldier-boy outfits, wild animals, more demons . . .'

'You know, son, I'm not too ill to give you a slapping,' joked Prior, misjudging Aron's mood completely.

'Go ahead, old man,' Aron sneered. 'You'll have a heart attack before you reach me. I'll be fighting demons long after you've kicked the bucket.'

Prior looked down at his feet. His heart ached to show the boy he was wrong. His head knew that Aron was right. The fight outside the hotel bar had nearly done for him. Every bone in his body ached, his muscles felt knotted and his lungs fought for every breath. Physically he was close to the end but he still had his wits.

'Aye, I'll be gone soon,' he replied softly. 'People I know will miss me, some will even cry. Tell me, lad – who will mourn for you when the time comes?'

Aron looked startled. The sneer faded, the little boy appeared. 'I've got friends,' he said quickly. 'People who love me.'

Prior smiled but with sadness rather than glee.

180

'People who'll *stop* loving you if you carry on,' he told him.

'I don't understand,' said Aron.

'You upset people, lad. You act like you're untouchable, you hurt people with your words.'

Aron shook his head. 'What do you know?' he asked, his scorn returning.

'Aron – just listen to yourself!' Prior insisted. 'You don't think about what you say.'

'What – and you do?'

Prior nodded. 'Yes, I do,' he replied. 'And when I get angry, it's because I've earned the right.'

'*Earned* it?' snapped Aron. 'What sort of bullshit is that?'

Prior saw that he wasn't getting through. He decided to be brutal, hoping that the boy would see sense. 'Do you know what people say about you?' he asked.

Aron shook his head. 'I don't care either,' he added.

'They call you names,' continued Prior. 'They say that you're sullen. People don't like you.'

'Rubbish!'

'And they question your heart, son . . .'

Aron leaped from his chair and sent the old man sprawling. A group of women, two with children, gasped. A baby began to wail. Aron stood over them all, raging.

'I'm not your son, you old bastard!' he screamed. 'You ever question my heart again, I'll kill you!'

Prior didn't reply. Instead, he sat where he'd landed and shook his head. One of the women, dark-skinned with a broad nose and plaited hair, stood and faced Aron.

'You have no shame?' she chided. 'Throwing your weight around. Push *me*!'

Aron glared at the woman but only for a moment. He ended up staring into space.

'Back off!' she shouted. 'Back off or God help me I'll beat that look off your face, boy!'

Prior told her to leave Aron alone. 'He's not worth the trouble, Diane.'

Diane nodded. 'He should be ashamed!' she replied. 'Lord knows how many people have died tonight and he's here throwing old men around? You want to fight, you little rat, go outside and fight!'

She cursed some more, daring Aron to react, as more people started to gather. Faith, who'd been tending to an expectant mother, appeared and helped Prior to his feet. He thanked her and found a crate to sit on. His breathing had grown worse.

'You need to get some rest, Prior,' warned Faith.

'I'll happily lie with you,' he joked, trying to lighten the mood and assuage the guilt he was feeling. He had pushed the boy too far.

'In your dreams,' said Faith, but without her usual sass. She took Aron by the arm and pulled him away.

'Gerroff!' he complained, but she held on as he swung his arm.

'You need to cool off,' she warned. 'Either that or deal with Mace – understand?'

Mention of the giant calmed Aron almost immediately and he stopped struggling. Faith walked him out of the main chamber and down a dimly lit corridor, past several side rooms.

'Oscar and Raj need to be relieved,' she told him. 'And you need time to think.'

Aron shook his head. 'Nothing to think about,' he replied. 'I didn't do anything. Prior called me a coward.'

'So to show you're *not* a coward, you pushed a dying old man around? If the cap fits . . .'

'I'm not what he says!' protested Aron.

'OK, OK . . .' said Faith, trying to calm him again. 'You just need to cool off, Aron. We're all tired and sometimes things get to us. It'll be fine in the morning, trust me.'

As they passed an open door, Aron glanced in and saw Martha leaning across a makeshift bunk on which a man was lying. His heart sank. Was she kissing someone? She pulled back and he saw Jonah. Their eyes met and Jonah smiled. Aron felt his stomach turn and ran for the exit hatch.

'Aron?'

When he failed to reply, Faith sighed and turned back. Round the corner, by a sick bay, she bumped into Mace. His expression was dark with rage.

'Where is he?' Mace demanded.

'Leave it,' said Faith. 'I've sent him to relieve Oscar and Raj.'

'On his own?'

Faith shook her head. 'No – I was going to ask Tyrell to join him.'

'Tyrell's done enough for today,' Mace told her. 'I'll get someone else to go up.'

'I don't know what gets into him,' she admitted. 'These last few months he's been unbearable.'

'He's obsessed with Martha,' revealed the giant.

'Tell me something new,' said Faith, running a hand through her blonde hair. The skin around her blue eyes was dark and creased. Mace felt the urge to pick her up and take her to bed, and not just because she was so lovely.

'He follows her around,' Mace continued. 'She's had to warn him off. He tried to kiss her or something the other night.'

'That explains a lot,' said Faith. 'But it's his reckless-ness that's going to get him killed.'

'I know,' Mace admitted. 'Trouble is, he'll take some of the others with him.'

'They say his father was a killer.'

Mace shook his head. 'He went insane, Faith,' he explained. 'Happened to a lot of people after the War. He flipped and killed some people before the Mayor caught him. And then his mother . . .'

'Waking up in Hell will do that,' Faith suggested. 'Drive you crazy, I mean.'

'It happened to many, remember?' Mace reminded her. 'The War turned us all into animals. In the end.'

'Sometimes I forget what it was like,' said Faith. 'You know – before the demons came.'

'You and me both.'

'I dream about it sometimes – the world I was born into. Feels like it only ever existed in my head, y'know?'

'Yeah,' replied Mace, burping.

Faith asked if he'd been drinking.

'What else is there to do?' he replied. 'You look like you could use some.'

'I've got injured people to tend to and some poor scared girl who couldn't keep her knees shut eight months ago . . .'

'Huh?'

'She's pregnant,' Faith explained.

'Oh – that,' said Mace.

'Yeah, *that*,' she replied.

'You've a tremendous pair of breasts, by the way.'

Faith gave Mace a filthy look before breaking into a

grin. 'You're *such* a little boy,' she teased, turning her back and walking away.

'Not so little,' boasted Mace.

Faith stopped and looked back over her shoulder. 'So I hear,' she replied.

Mace watched her leave, scratching his head as he did so, and wondering exactly whom she'd been talking to . . .

22

Aunt May had given Jonah some more herbal tonic —
made from ginger and rosemary — before leaving us
alone. She insisted that he should rest too, and gave me
a funny look on her way out of the room. I glared at her
but she just smiled and I began to get paranoid. Did she
know? Was I *that* obvious?

'If I catch you disobeying me,' she'd told him, 'I won't
be happy.'

Jonah had grunted his assent but was on his feet the
moment she'd gone.

'You heard what she told you,' I said with a warm
smile. 'Lie down.'

I was standing by a makeshift bed — an old door that
had been placed on two crates and covered with a thin
and mouldering mattress. Dark stains dotted the fabric
and I felt thankful that I didn't know their exact origin.
May, Faith and the others must have treated hundreds of
people in these rooms, many of them seriously

wounded. How many had died right there on that bed? How many bodies had been taken to the boiler room and cremated in the furnace?

'I'm fine,' Jonah replied, stretching his arms. 'Haven't you got anything else to do?'

I sat down on the edge of the bed, his scent filling my senses. I still couldn't put my finger on what it was, but something in his smell was unavoidable and enticing. I felt my heart begin to race.

'I've got loads to do,' I told him. 'But I'm more interested in you and what happened with Mias.'

Jonah pretended to study himself in a mirror which ran the length of one wall, only his eyes were fixed on mine in the reflection. I tried to look away but it was no use. Instead, I found myself studying his almost too-perfect features and his lean, muscled physique. I wondered what it would be like to be held by him, to be kissed by those bow-shaped lips . . .

'What was this room used for?' he asked.

'Same as the others,' I replied, snapping out of my reverie. 'They were mostly changing rooms. Make-up, clothing . . . for the theatre.'

'I don't understand,' he admitted.

'People would act out stories, up above us, when the theatre was still standing. My mother used to go every week. She used to sing me the songs and tell me the tales.'

'Why would people act out stories?' he asked, causing me to smile.

'Entertainment,' I explained. 'Surely you've heard about the world before this one?'

He nodded, but something in his expression told me that he was unsure.

'I've heard many things,' he said. 'Mostly from people in the north. We discovered a room full of books up there, in the wastelands around the citadel.'

'I love books!'

'Don't you have them here?'

I shook my head. 'Only a few. The Mayor has some at his mansion, but he won't let anyone near them. They were my mother's.'

'Why did your mother live with him?' he asked.

'He's my stepfather,' I said, confused by his question. 'But you know all of this. When I was little, my mother married him.'

'But *why*?' he repeated. The look of disgust on his face set off an alarm in my heart. I thought quickly, hoping to make myself clearer. Hoping to defend my mother and to stop him thinking badly of me.

'She wasn't like him,' I insisted. 'She was one of us.'

Jonah looked unconvinced and, despite my feelings for him, I found myself getting annoyed.

'How was she one of us?' he asked me. 'She was

living with one of their puppets. I hate collaborators almost as much as—'

'I do too!' I said, interrupting him. 'And so did my mother. She made a mistake. She was young with a baby and she was scared. She wanted better . . .'

'Marrying a traitor was better?' he said. 'I'd rather die.'

I stood and approached him, my temper rising. 'You don't have kids to feed!' I snapped. 'You know nothing about being a woman in this shitty world!'

Jonah must have seen that he'd upset me. He held up his hands, shook his head. 'I'm sorry,' he told me.

'You'd better be,' I replied as I felt my eyes begin to water and grew annoyed that I was crying in front of him. 'My mother gave her life for the Resistance . . .'

Jonah returned to the bed and sat down. A thoughtful look passed across his face and he began to finger the amulet round his neck. 'What happened to her?' he asked. 'Your mother?'

I wiped away my tears and took a deep breath. I found it hard to talk about my mother without showing the strong emotions that came with it. Yet there was something about Jonah that made me want to confide in him – a softness in his eyes that made me trust him. I wanted him to reciprocate too – I wanted to know everything about him.

'I don't really know,' I admitted. 'Prior told me that

she was caught helping the Resistance. She worked at the bar, same as me, performed the same role. My mum was a healer. She helped to run the Haven with May and the others.'

'Who caught her?'

I shuddered at my vague memories of her death and the aftermath and looked away for a moment.

'Mias,' I revealed, pretending to be interested in the far wall. I wiped away more tears. 'From the little I was told, she was taken to Valefor, who executed her. My stepfather didn't help her, no one did . . .'

'What could the Mayor have done?' asked Jonah. 'He exudes spinelessness from every pore − every turncoat does. That's why they join forces with the demons − because they're cowardly.'

'A *real* man would have done something,' I replied, looking back at him.

'Is there any such thing?' he asked. '*Really?* Seems to me that human beings have become animals. Look at how they live.'

'They,' I said, wondering what he meant. 'You said *they* . . .'

Jonah shrugged. 'You know what I meant,' he replied.

Only I didn't. Suddenly I flashed back to the look in his eyes, the way he'd fought with Mias. The almost superhuman speed and agility he'd shown. Was there something inhuman about Jonah − something to be wary of? And if there was, how would I stop myself from being drawn to him?

'What *are* you?' I blurted, determined to find out.

Jonah looked back towards the mirror and fiddled with his amulet some more. 'I'm tired,' he deflected. 'Maybe your aunt was right.'

'Jonah – I saw your eyes after you fought Mias. They were on fire.'

'You were mistaken,' he told me, as though I was stupid. As though I hadn't seen his eyes. 'How could they burn? I'd have gone blind.'

I told him that he wasn't listening properly. 'They weren't *literally* on fire,' I explained. 'The flame colour circled your irises and your pupils were huge . . .'

This time Jonah smiled and made me feel like a little girl. A silly little girl. I wanted to be angry with him but I couldn't. Even though we were talking about other things, in my heart I just wanted to kiss him. His eyes, his mouth, the pale skin of his face, and the heat from his body – all of it entranced me.

'The entire street was ablaze,' he said. 'All you saw was a reflection, Martha. Do you think I'm a demon? I'm no less human than you – *remember*?'

I blushed at the recollection of his naked form, but I refused to be beaten. He was trying to change the subject and I wasn't going to let him, no matter how attractive he was.

'That's another thing,' I added. 'You hurt Mias, yet when I found you he'd disappeared – where did he go? And what about the fancy somersaults? No ordinary person can do those things.'

'I told you before,' he said, looking annoyed and making my heart sink a little. 'It's just training, that's all.'

'What sort of training, Jonah? I've never heard of such a thing.'

'I was trained by the northern Resistance,' he explained. 'The uprising is stronger there. They have weapons and a structure. They taught me combat skills and martial arts. That's where the somersaults and all those things come from. It's nothing weird.'

He watched me as I digested his words, and I thought I saw a tiny flicker of guilt in his eyes. I guessed that I might be pushing him too far, making him reveal things he'd rather keep hidden. I cursed myself silently for being such a freak. So what if he had secrets – everyone else had them. I nodded to show that I was satisfied with his explanation, and he seemed relieved. Yet there was still the issue of where Mias had gone after the fight.

'What about Mias?' I asked.

'I don't know what happened to him,' he told me. 'We were fighting and I used my spear, and then he vanished. The ground started to burn all around me, like the earth was on fire. I was stunned and I couldn't think properly . . .'

'I'm not convinced,' I told him, 'but I can't believe you'd lie to me either. You don't seem to feel the need.'

Jonah nodded in agreement. 'Most of my skills can be taught to anyone young enough,' he said. 'They just require practice and dedication. The weapons I've got are better too. They are more powerful than yours.'

'Which is why I'm pleased you're here,' I admitted, although I knew it wasn't the only reason. 'You can teach us, maybe share your weapons.'

Jonah looked away again. 'There's a cache of arms out in the wastelands,' he revealed. 'I've spoken to Mace and we can go and get some. We've come up with a strategy to take the demons on – but Mace will tell you when the time is right. Thing is, after that, I won't be staying. I have my own business to take care of.'

'What business?' I asked, although I wasn't really listening; I was feeling sick. My stomach had somer-saulted at the mention of his going away. And the scent that clung to him – that aroma that made me feel dizzy with a lust that I couldn't understand – seemed to grow more intense. Something in that earthy, spicy, almost animal odour touched me at the basest level, no matter how hard I tried to fight it. I wanted to kiss him more than I'd ever wanted to kiss anyone.

'My siblings,' said Jonah, giving me a strange look.

'You want to find them?' I said, snapping out of it. Again I felt my face take on colour and I wished that

I hadn't made my desire so obvious. Only I couldn't help it.

Jonah nodded in reply. 'Yes,' he said. 'They're in the Southern Citadel, like I told you.'

'But if they're living down there, you know where to go,' I pointed out. 'You could help us first and still find them.'

'I can't do that,' he told me as a wave of tiredness seemed to overcome him. He yawned and his eyes began to narrow.

'I think you should nap,' I said. 'You look shattered.'

Jonah lay back and closed his eyes. Despite myself, I leaned in and kissed him gently on the cheek. The musky scent overpowered my senses and I felt something in my belly. I pulled back before I had the chance to make a fool of myself.

'Thank you,' I whispered. 'For saving Tyrell and the others from Mias.'

Jonah turned to his side, opened his eyes and smiled weakly. I waited a moment, wiped his brow with a rag and left him to his slumber.

23

When Mace emerged from the Haven a day later, the streets were deserted. The smell of burning carried on the breeze, and everywhere already decrepit buildings smouldered. Dead bodies, all human, littered the pavements, rodents and wild dogs feasting on their flesh. The demons had obviously run amok and the innocent had paid a heavy price.

Mace shook his head in sorrow as he recognized the corpse of a young woman he'd known as Sara. She was on her back, her mouth frozen in terror and bloody sockets where her blue eyes had once been. Her chest had been slashed open and the insides exposed. Mace kicked out, sending a rat scurrying, but not before it had taken another mouthful of Sara's guts with it.

'I'm gonna puke,' said Faith, covering her mouth and fighting the urge.

Mace, wary that they might be attacked at any time, pulled her towards him. 'There's nothing to be done, Faith.'

Behind them, Prior coughed into his hands before wiping them on his trousers. 'Damn bastards!' he spat, raging at his own impotence.

The three elders had formed an advance party, making sure that the killing was over and the city calm before allowing the others to leave the Haven. Each had had no idea of the death toll or the destruction that awaited them.

'This is insane,' whispered Faith as she saw a man slumped against the remains of a car, his lower jaw torn off, blackened tongue hanging to one side. 'How can they justify this?'

'They won't,' said Mace. 'They'll just say they were teaching us a lesson. Revenge for what Jonah did.'

'So many bodies,' she continued as they rounded a corner towards the centre of the protected zone. About one hundred metres ahead of them, a flatbed truck pulled up and four human mercenaries jumped out. Faith watched in horror as they picked up the discarded bodies and threw them into the back as though they were nothing. She started forward, only for Prior to hold her back.

'Don't,' he said in a soft voice. 'There's no point in causing more trouble.'

'They don't scare me,' she said defiantly.

Mace agreed with Prior. 'Nothing to do with being

scared,' he told her. 'We'll have *our* revenge for this, Faith. Just not here and not now.'

'Revenge?' she questioned. 'How can we take revenge without *this* happening again?'

Prior told them he had to stop. His lungs ached and his chest felt tight. 'I'm dying,' he panted, leaning forward, hands on his knees.

'Stop being so negative,' replied Mace. 'May's herbs will sort you out.'

Prior looked at him and smiled warmly. 'Not this time, my friend,' he said. 'I'm done for, and to be honest I'm happy about it. Gotta go sometime, big man.'

'But—' began Faith.

Prior shook his head. 'No, Faith,' he added. 'It's my time and you all know it too. And before I go, I'm taking some of these godforsaken monsters with me.'

Mace was wondering if he should tell his closest friends the plans in his mind. He'd discussed his ideas with Jonah when he'd shown him around the city. Down by the riverside they'd talked about linking up with the Resistance from the north. But was it too soon to tell the others? The last thing they'd need would be false hope. No hope at all was preferable. At least that way you weren't kidding yourself. You just faced reality and dealt with it. With hope, your judgement was clouded by something over which you had no control.

You made yourself weak, and susceptible to attack even.

Yet Mace also knew he had no choice. He'd known for a long time that they'd been losing their fight against the demons, and this latest outrage just made things clearer. What good was a Resistance that couldn't protect the people from a massacre? A Resistance that didn't, as a *minimum*, make the *human* collaborators pay? From everything Jonah had said, it seemed that the northern uprising was growing in strength. Surely it was better to join forces with other fighters than take on the demons alone?

'There's a plan,' he eventually said, decision made. 'A strategy I've developed.'

Faith was looking into a supply store, its meagre stocks ruined, the walls black with soot. Corey Williams had run this particular place, ordered by the government to do so. Now he lay dead on the counter, his arms hanging limply and his neck twisted at an unnatural angle. His fuzzy, copper-coloured hair had gone, burned off his scalp, and his face was one giant blister, oozing beige pus.

'What did you say?' she asked absentmindedly as she recalled the way Corey's fingers had felt as they'd brushed away the hair from her teenage face, many years earlier.

'I'm going to make contact with the north,' Mace revealed. 'Jonah tells me that the opposition up there is

199

getting stronger. They've plans to move south, and I think we should get involved.'

Faith turned away from the remains of her former lover and crossed herself, mimicking something her own mother had often done. 'You remember Corey?' she asked.

'Yeah,' said Prior, who was now sitting at the kerb. 'He owes me a drink . . .'

'He's in there,' she told him. 'He's dead.'

'Like every other poor sod out here,' Prior replied.

Mace sighed and put an arm round Faith's waist, thinking of all the people he'd lost too. He pulled her to him. She didn't resist, burying her head into the giant's chest and wailing. They stood that way for a good few minutes until Faith ran out of tears.

'I was completely besotted with him,' she said, wiping her nose on Mace's hooded top. 'He was my first. My dad hated him because he wasn't white, so my mum used to let me sneak him into the house. He had these amazing eyes – green and sparkling. I thought we would last for ever.'

Mace ignored the saliva and snot on his clothing and told Faith to take heart. 'We're going to lose many more loved ones before we die,' he reminded her. 'We can't let it stop us, Faith. We can't give up.'

Faith stepped back and ran her fingers across Mace's

face. 'Thank you,' she whispered, before regaining her composure.

'What's this plan, then?' Prior asked after another cough.

'It's about rebalancing the odds,' explained Mace. 'In *our* favour. Jonah knows about a cache of arms, buried about two days northwest of here. He says that there are others living out there, hiding in the wastelands – people who might join us. They can also take a message to the fighters around the Northern Citadel.'

'You want to start a war?' Faith asked, her eyes questioning him.

'Not *start* a war,' Mace parried. 'Just fight it properly.'

'Guess a war is on, whether we contest it or not,' she said sadly. 'It was a stupid thing to say, Mace. I'm sorry.'

'Don't apologize, beautiful,' he told her. 'Just tell me what you think.'

'Can we trust this boy?' she asked.

'Yes,' the giant man replied. 'After the incident with Mias, we can. Whatever Jonah has learned up there, he's better than any of us. We *need* his skills.'

'What about Valefor? You can see evidence of what he'll do all around us.'

Mace looked into Corey's supply store and nodded. 'We won't be here when he reacts,' he declared with a sly grin. 'We're moving out.'

Both Prior and Faith shot him looks that were at once bemused and shocked.

'Moving out?' asked Prior. 'Are you out of your tiny little mind?'

Mace grinned. 'Just trust me, will you?' he said.

Martha ladled soup into tin cups. It was thin and watery, made of wild young nettles and lavender. It wasn't much, but once you dipped a chunk of stale bread in it, it was enough. The stores at the Haven had run dry and May had done her best with what remained. The queue for food was long, full of tired people with haggard expressions. Many were nervous about what awaited them above ground, worried that they would find loved ones dead. Most were bewildered and didn't understand what was happening, beyond the gossip that they'd heard.

Martha was trying her best to be cheerful but Aron was making it difficult. Standing to her left, handing out the bread, he interrogated her about kissing Jonah.

'On the cheek,' she said for the fifth time.

'I *saw* you,' Aron whined. 'Or was that just my imagination?'

'I was thanking him for saving Tyrell's life, Aron.'

Aron dropped a hunk of parched bread into someone's hands and snorted. 'Yeah, right,' he replied.

'The only reason I'm explaining myself is because

we're supposed to be friends,' Martha snapped. 'Although *that* can change.'

Aron shook his head. 'I can't believe how you've all fallen for him,' he accused. 'It's like you've gone blind. All the trouble out there — *he* caused all of that.'

Luca Williams and his mother, Mica, came forward to get some soup. Martha said hello and gave Luca a little extra. His mother's face was drawn, her cheeks hollow. Martha knew that Luca's father was outside and Mica was worried.

'Corey's a clever man,' Martha told her, before smiling at the little boy. 'He will have found somewhere to hide.'

'I hope so, Martha,' replied Mica. 'I can't bear to think about—'

'Hey, Martha!' said Luca as his mother's sentence remained unfinished.

'Hey!' Martha replied cheerily. 'You been a good boy?'

'*Yeah* — I've been playing with Tommy and Hardeep!' he replied excitedly.

'Are they your friends?'

The boy nodded.

'Well, enjoy your soup, Luca.'

When the little boy failed to reply, his mother nudged him.

'Oh. Thanks, Martha,' he mumbled.

Martha watched them move on, hoping in vain that Aron would relent.

'You're not even listening to me,' he moaned. 'Might as well be invisible.'

'We wish,' said Tyrell, who was standing to Martha's right.

'You what?' demanded Aron, his face flushed. 'What did you say?' He shoved past Martha and confronted Tyrell, who smirked.

'You gonna push me too?' he asked Aron. 'Like you did with Prior?' Tyrell's voice was calm but the challenge was clear.

Aron felt rage welling up inside, a fury that he'd carried since he could remember. He struggled to control his temper. He hadn't done anything but regard Jonah with suspicion because it was the correct reaction. The stranger seemed to have cast a spell on everyone, and only Aron could see the truth. Jonah was *trouble*, and if he stayed around things would only get worse for everyone. Too many people had paid the price for what Aron saw as conceit. There was something very wrong about Jonah, and Aron decided that he had to know what that was. He had to protect his friends because they were too ignorant to see things clearly. A sense of purpose flooded through his heart, a feeling that he had found his role.

'Sometimes,' he heard Martha say, 'I wonder why I bother with you.'

He flinched inside but kept his face straight. 'Then I guess you're about to find out,' he replied, without looking at her. His eyes were still locked with Tyrell's.

'What does that mean?' she asked.

'You'll see,' he told her. He broke Tyrell's stare and stomped off towards the sick bays.

24

Faith poked her head round the corner, watching out for demon patrols. She was hiding in an alleyway, between two five-storey blocks, with Prior and Mace behind her. The intersection was clear so she urged the men forward. Mace went first, sprinting across the road and into a doorway on the other side. Prior waited until Mace was out of sight, took several deep breaths and did the same. Once he too was hidden, Faith followed.

They were edging back towards the Haven, using one of several trusted routes. The key to avoiding patrols was to assume that they would turn up everywhere. That way, you remained on guard, always wary of threats. They were skirting round the eastern edge of the protected zone. Another five hundred metres and they'd be safer, having crossed the invisible line that marked the beginning of the wastelands. The Haven sat another few hundred metres from there, surrounded by dense weeds, deserted ruins and narrow streets filled with rubble.

Most of the dead from the night before had been

cleared, and human soldiers were now driving through the wreckage, urging the population through loud-hailers to return to work. Slowly but surely, Fire City reawakened. It was late afternoon and the sky was steel grey, with little flecks of rain falling. Between them, Faith, Mace and Prior had covered most of the protected zone, and they were content that people could now return without fear of further retribution. Bar a couple of patrols, the demons were absent anyway. The only officials they'd managed to spot were Stone and the Mayor, standing outside the hotel, heatedly discussing something.

'Probably wondering what to tell their masters,' Mace had guessed.

This particular route to the Haven took them inside an old office block, a tall structure once painted blue. A network of tunnels started in the basement, leading in many directions. Only those in the Resistance knew which led where, another security measure to protect their shelter. Mace led the way, holding one of his machetes, guarding against danger. A stairwell opened before him, only just visible in the gloom.

'All clear,' he whispered. 'I'm heading down.'

He descended slowly, using his weapon as a guide. The grey light from the surface began to ebb away as he progressed, until it had almost vanished. Faith and Prior followed behind, with Prior's laboured breathing the only sound other than their footsteps.

Mace knew this route well. He moved forward five footsteps before crouching and feeling the wall to his right. Within seconds he'd located a false panel and removed it. He used his machete to check the entrance to the tunnel and, finding it clear, went headfirst through the gap, downhill at an angle of forty-five degrees. Three metres along, the tunnel levelled out and he sat on his haunches, his scalp almost brushing the roof. He edged forward for another ten metres until finally the tunnel widened and he could stand, albeit with his head lowered. Over the years, the tunnels had been made wider and timbers used to reinforce them. Despite the darkness, the damp and the decaying odour, they were as safe as they could be.

Mace felt around for the oil lamp he knew was there, before striking a match. An orb of light flickered to life around him, illuminating Faith and Prior as they caught him up.

They followed the tunnel for nearly a kilometre, underneath the border between the protected and abandoned zones, and as they went Mace told them more about the plan he'd devised with Jonah. Faith was beginning to grasp his meaning, but she was still unsure about the consequences.

'We can't move so many people,' she pointed out. 'That's just ridiculous.'

'Yes, we can,' said Mace. 'We're talking about a long-term thing, Faith. It won't happen overnight.'

'Moving people in small groups?' asked Prior. 'That's liable to get us caught.'

Mace agreed. 'There's going to be a risk,' he admitted. 'We know that. Besides, the people we save from the Hunt end up in the wastelands anyway. This is the same but on a larger scale. Anything is better than what we have now.'

Faith questioned whether that was true. 'What are we prepared to accept?' she asked. 'Fifty deaths? A hundred?'

'I don't see how that differs from the current situation,' replied Mace. 'We lose as many in the Hunt, and then there's sickness and other killings. Look at how many have died since Mias was injured.'

'But that was *because* of Jonah,' Faith pointed out. 'If he hadn't been here, it wouldn't have happened.'

Mace knew that she was right, but he also believed in his scheme. Jonah's presence and actions had made a terrible situation worse, but if he left, what *was* there to go back to?

'I agree that fewer people would have died,' he told her. 'But they were going to die anyway, sooner or later. The key to this idea is that we make a stand. We take our people and set up a new life out in the wastelands. It might not be much but it's a chance to give us a better future.'

They came to a fork in the tunnel and went left, climbing over a pile of rubble. The passages stank of iron-rich earth and were damp, with water dripping from the roof. The soil underfoot clung to their boots.

'How do we know it won't be worse out there?' asked Prior. 'I mean – can we even survive, in such a large group?'

'That's something I'm going to think about,' revealed Mace. 'I'm going out there, with Jonah, to the weapons cache he told me about. It's about two days to the site and two back. I'll see for myself what it's like.'

'And these people you mentioned – the ones already living out there – you think they'll help us?'

'Yes,' Mace told Prior. 'Jonah is absolutely certain of it.'

Prior scratched his scalp as they approached another turn, the Haven drawing nearer. The closer they came, the more warren-like the tunnels became, new routes veering off in every direction. This subterranean labyrinth would play a vital role in Mace's plans.

'Jonah is certain,' he replied. 'Not you.'

Mace sighed. 'Unless we go out there and try,' he told them both, 'we'll never know. We *have* to do *some*thing.'

Faith touched Mace's arm gently. 'I agree with the last part,' she told him. 'We can't go on like this.'

'You said it earlier,' Mace told her. 'The War is on anyway – we either fight or we die. It's simple.'

'Simple, until we have to make difficult choices,' said Prior.

'I guess so,' replied Mace as he pictured Samuel's face in his mind.

'You know most of the population won't come with us, don't you?' Prior added. 'They're too scared, too lost . . .'

Mace nodded. 'We'll take anyone who wants to come,' he replied.

Prior and Faith looked at each other, and Mace saw the doubt in their eyes.

'It's just an idea,' he told them. 'We'll work out the details later.'

Jonah was washing himself with a damp rag when Aron burst into his room.

'You think you're clever, don't you?' Aron yelled.

Jonah dropped the rag and pulled on his clothes, eyes fixed on Aron. 'What are you talking about?' he asked.

'All this stuff!' Aron retorted, his eyes wild, his face the colour of ripened strawberries.

'You're not making sense,' said Jonah. 'Take a breath, Aron, and calm down.'

'*No!*'

Jonah pulled on his boots and sat on the bed, hoping to defuse the situation. 'Calm down,' he repeated. 'Just relax and tell me what's wrong.'

'You!' Aron accused, stabbing a finger in his direction. 'You're what's wrong. Ever since you got here, you've caused problems.'

'I've been helping,' said Jonah, 'because Mace asked me to. I was just passing through.'

Aron shook his head. 'That's crap and you know it,' he countered, his voice calmer. 'Who would just *pass through* Fire City? It would have been easier to avoid.'

Jonah nodded, knowing that Aron was right. 'I *was* trying to avoid it,' he replied. 'I got caught in the Hunt and I rescued Martha and the little boy. You too . . .'

'I didn't *need* your help!' spat Aron. 'None of us did. We know how to fight the demons.'

Jonah understood that Aron was upset over Martha – a blind man could tell he was obsessed with her. Yet he was also talking rubbish. Aron would have died that first night, had Jonah not saved him. The same was true of Martha.

'You were stuck underneath that patroller,' he reminded him. 'Remember?'

He watched the other boy grow angrier still. 'You ain't normal!' Aron yelled. 'I know you're hiding something!'

'We're all hiding things, Aron,' replied Jonah calmly. 'I'm just better at it than you are.'

'*Yeah?*' Aron sneered. 'What secrets do I hide so badly?'

'Martha,' offered Jonah. 'You hide your fixation with her. Very badly.'

'You don't know anything about me and Martha!'

Jonah nodded slowly. 'I know plenty,' he countered. 'I know that you follow her around, that you get jealous of other men, that you think you love her.'

'I *do* love her!' Aron protested. 'I don't just *think* it!'

'And she doesn't feel the same,' said Jonah.

'Shut up!'

'No, Aron, I won't,' insisted Jonah. 'Think about what you're doing here. This is ridiculous. I haven't done anything to you . . .'

'Not me, no,' agreed Aron. 'Pity about all those dead folk outside though.'

Jonah felt a spasm of guilt and looked away.

'See?' jeered Aron. 'You know I'm right. You killed all those people – *you*!'

'I was saving Tyrell,' Jonah replied. 'Would you rather I'd let Mias take him?'

Aron nodded. 'Yeah,' he said. 'Better that it's one person than lots who die.'

'But Tyrell is your friend,' said Jonah.

'So was Samuel and *he* died,' replied Aron. 'And I could list another fifty, starting with my mother, but what's the point? People die.'

Jonah fixed him with a stare. 'Which is exactly why

213

I'm trying to help,' he explained. 'To stop so many people being killed.'

'Crap!' Aron retaliated. 'You ain't here for us!'

Aron was as close to the knuckle as Jonah was prepared to let him go. His next retort would hurt, but Jonah knew that it couldn't be helped. He stood and readied himself for Aron's reaction.

'There isn't anything between you and Martha,' he said. 'That *thing* you have, it's all in your head, Aron.'

'No!'

'Yes,' Jonah replied. 'That's why you're angry with everyone. It's because you understand that. You know it, you just don't like it.'

Aron threw himself at Jonah with a grunt. Jonah sensed the move and stepped aside with astonishing speed, watching Aron crash into the makeshift bed and send it crashing against the far wall.

'Don't,' he warned.

Aron looked up at him and started to weep. Jonah shook his head and left the room, feeling ashamed.

Fifteen minutes later, Mace was overseeing the return to the surface when he heard a woman scream. He spun round and saw Aron across the Haven's main chamber, waving a long sword at Jonah.

'What the—' he began.

Jonah's attention was focused on Aron's advance.

'Move now!' he shouted at May and Tyrell, who'd been helping him to manage the exits.

Aron swung the weapon at Jonah's head. Yet the moment the sword should have cleaved through Jonah's skull, he was gone, ducking down to the left and round behind his attacker. He locked Aron's arms in a powerful hold, forcing him to drop the blade.

'*Let me go, you bastard!*'

'*Aron!*' Jonah heard Mace bellow. '*What the hell are you doing?*'

As the elder approached, Aron looked up at him, his eyes red and watery. He tried to speak, but all that emerged was a guttural, bestial sound. He struggled to break free, kicking out and catching Mace on the knee. Martha and many others had gathered too. Aron searched their faces, his expression pleading.

'This is too much,' he heard Martha say. 'You need to go, Aron!'

Jonah relaxed his grip and Aron sprang forward, running into Mace, who took hold of him.

'What are you doing, son?' Mace demanded, shaking Aron as though he weighed nothing. 'Haven't we seen enough death?'

'His fault!' spat Aron. 'All his fault!'

Mace continued to shake the boy until his bones rattled.

'Gerroff me!' yelled Aron. 'I'm gonna kill him!'

The sound of Mace's slap echoed around the room. The force of it sent Aron sprawling to the floor. He looked up at them all, shaking his head, crying.

'Get out!' Mace demanded. '*Now!*'

Aron scrambled to his feet, glaring at Martha. She shook her head in sadness and turned away.

'You bitch!' screamed Aron, running for the exit. Behind him, every face was filled with surprise, anger and amazement.

'Should I go after him?' asked Tyrell.

Mace shook his head. 'No,' he said gloomily, reaching for his flask. 'Not this time . . .'

PART TWO

PART TWO

25

Valefor's lair was located in the old marketplace, an ornamental two-storey structure with high windows and a domed clock tower. A curious arch, with stairs to each side, stood in front of the main entrance, the grey stone crumbling and covered in dingy green moss. Every window had been barricaded, and to the rear the roof had collapsed.

The building sat in a wide square, surrounded on all sides by narrow lanes and deserted blocks that had once held shops and offices. Nothing remained of the market stalls, save a few pieces of rusting iron. Poisonous hogweed, intertwined with ragwort and nettles, had grown all around the square. In turn, these were dwarfed by knotweed that in places was almost three metres high. Thick brambles added to the density, alongside the occasional tree and overgrown shrub. A single pathway had been cleared round the entrance, and Mias limped down it, having been summoned by the demon lord.

Although his heart still burned with fury, Mias would

follow Valefor's orders. There was a natural order to the world, one that he had to accept regardless of his feelings. The human pests were necessary to that order, and Mias had never disobeyed his masters. Several patrollers stood guard at the entrance, and he ignored them as he entered. These canine demons weren't worthy of the name; they were inferior beings, lacking both the breeding and the powers of true ancients. Many patrollers had flanked him on the night he'd been humiliated yet not one had come to his aid. He would never again trust their competence.

Inside, the air was thick with the stench of decay. Mias welcomed the warm and inviting aroma. His master was waiting in a cavern down a narrow set of steps, its low ceiling strung with entrails and gleaming white bones.

'Welcome, my brother,' rasped Valefor, sitting on a throne-like chair flanked by his guards, his giant wings flapping.

'Master,' replied Mias, kneeling before his lord.

Valefor told him to rise, and stood himself. 'Are you recovered, brother?' asked the demon lord.

Mias nodded. 'Almost.'

'What news is there?' Valefor enquired.

Mias shook his simian head. 'None of the stranger,' he confessed.

'You've searched for him?'

'Yes, master, and he is nowhere to be found,' replied Mias. 'I will resume my search immediately.'

'And you?' continued Valefor. 'Can I trust that you are willing to forget your rage? The factories must run – the council demands it.'

Mias looked away momentarily. When his gaze returned to Valefor's he nodded. 'It is forgotten, master.'

Valefor extended an arm, resting a clawed hand on Mias' shoulder. 'To forget your anger is not to forget your honour,' he said. 'You are a true ancient and this stranger will pay for his actions.'

'Thank you, my lord.'

'When we catch him, I will tear his soul to pieces, brother, and I will leave the last morsel for you.'

Mias howled and began to stamp his feet in excitement.

'Patience, brother,' demanded Valefor. 'Is the city back to normal?'

'Almost,' replied the underlord. 'The workers have returned, the factories are open. By this evening, it shall be as it was.'

Valefor removed his arm and walked towards his throne, thinking about his meeting with the ruling council. 'How many humans died?' he asked.

'Two or three hundred, my lord,' offered Mias, bowing his head.

Valefor saw this act of contrition and told Mias to

stand tall. 'There is no shame in this!' he declared. 'The council is aware of the situation. You and I have its blessing.'

'I am grateful,' replied the underlord. 'I did not mean any disloyalty.'

'A few hundred vermin mean nothing – no more than three nights of hunting. And we shall suspend the next Hunt to make amends.'

'But—'

'Silence, brother,' Valefor admonished. 'It is the ruling I was given and it shall come to pass.'

'Yes, lord.'

'And before long, we shall feast on the bones of this stranger.'

Mias howled once more, causing the patroller guards to follow suit. Valefor waited a while before silencing them all.

'Do you have any further orders?' asked the underlord.

Valefor shook his head. 'Nothing more than I have already asked,' he added.

As he watched Mias leave, Valefor considered the events of the past few days. A stranger, a human, had humiliated his second-in-command, the most powerful of Valefor's entire legion. He wondered how it was possible, and whether Mias would fare much better in any return encounter. It mattered little anyway. If Mias failed, then Valefor would take matters into his own hands. There was not a human alive who could challenge his power.

'Summon the Mayor!' he barked as he retook his throne.

Stone skirted the square's edge, mindful that his actions might look suspicious. He was heading a patrol on the Mayor's orders, rounding up any remaining reluctant workers. After abdicating his role for nearly two days, the wrinkly old bastard had finally reappeared, flabbier and more nervous than before. Stone hated to take orders from such a weak man, his subservience being a mere façade. The citadels, the social structure, the entire world had been rebuilt on the principle of survival of the fittest and best, yet everywhere such pathetic humans remained. The Mayor belonged with the Unwanted, and once Stone had finished with Fire City . . .

A vibrating pocket curtailed his thoughts. Stone told the two men with him to continue as he ducked into a small square once named after dolphins.

'News, Stone?' demanded the caller.

'Nothing to report,' admitted the mercenary. 'Valefor has returned and the Mayor is back on his high horse.'

'And your plan?'

'Moving slowly, sir,' replied Stone. 'The city is getting back to normal so it's only a matter of time.'

'Excellent. I know that his council has admonished Valefor. The needs of the economy must always be paramount.'

'Yes, sir.'

'Tell me, Stone, how much do you understand of the bargain between ourselves and the Hell-kin?'

Stone moved down the alley, towards the point where it opened out into a new street. Ahead of him, across another, bigger square also overgrown with weeds, was a waterless granite fountain. The boy, Aron, sat leaning against it, talking to himself. Stone raised an eyebrow. He recognized him as one of the young men who hung around the hotel bar.

'Only what I see,' he replied, wondering what Aron was doing alone.

'I was part of the original approach, my friend. It was a marriage of convenience, based on a decade-long strategy, worked out by like-minded souls from across the world, all of it done in secret . . . a miraculous *coup d'état.*'

'Er . . .'

'You sound distracted, Stone.'

'I am,' Stone admitted.

'Should I take your lack of interest personally?' the caller chuckled.

'Not at all, sir,' Stone replied. 'I need to learn more of what happened before the War. Only I've spotted one of the people I told you about.'

'The plan?'

'Yes, sir.'

'Well, in that case, I'll stop my rambling and hang up. Perhaps we can resume later?'

'Sir?'

'When you've talked to your quarry, Stone.'

'Oh,' said Stone. 'Yes, I'll keep you informed.'

'Make sure you do, friend. Good day.'

Stone replaced the phone, turned and caught up with his patrol.

'Go on ahead,' he told them. 'There's someone I need to speak to.'

Moments later he approached Aron, who seemed oblivious to his surroundings. 'I told them, Mama,' he heard the boy mumbling. 'I told them and they didn't listen and now I ain't happy.'

'Aron?' said Stone, thinking that the boy had flipped.

He saw it all the time, an endless procession of people who lost their minds. They ended up wandering the streets in a daze, until they were rounded up for the Hunt. Part of him understood why it happened too, and he was surprised that any of the Unwanted remained sane.

Stone proceeded cautiously. Cannibalism worked

rapidly. Losing a finger was the last thing he needed. That would upset him.

'Aron?' he repeated.

The boy looked up at him and smiled. 'Collaborator scum,' he said. 'Welcome . . .'

'Who were you talking to?' asked Stone.

Aron shook his head. 'You think I've lost it,' he said. 'I haven't. I always come here and talk to my mum.'

'You been drinking?'

Aron glanced at the flask in his right hand. 'S'pose . . .'

Stone looked around the square. The old town hall sat on the eastern side, most of it destroyed by bombs. The rest was overgrown and Stone could hear rodents shrieking and scurrying through the weeds. The fountain itself was intact. Four cast-iron, winged lions stood at each corner of a crossed plinth, with a two-tiered column rising in the middle, bisected by two platters, the lower one twice the diameter of the one above. The whole structure stood in a granite bowl perhaps three metres across. Little of the bronze that had gilded the ironwork remained yet it was still impressive. The water pump had long since perished.

'Why this place?' enquired Stone.

Aron snorted. 'This is where they killed my mum,' he revealed. 'Smashed her skull in.'

Stone watched as angry tears streamed down Aron's

face and he felt like smiling. His controller had mentioned the variables in his plan, the little things that might send it awry. Yet here was a variable that would work in its favour, completely unexpected. Anger, Stone had been taught, was an emotion that could be controlled, used to mould people. He sat down beside the boy and asked where his friends were.

'What friends?' Aron replied.

Stone pulled some weeds from the earth and worked the stems in his fingers, thinking hard about how to proceed. Something had caused a rift between Aron and the others, a crack that might be of use.

'I don't need her anyway,' the boy added.

'Who?' Stone asked him.

'Martha . . .' he replied. 'She can . . .'

Stone sat silently as Aron began to wail, his head in his hands. Sometimes, he thought, life made your choices for you.

26

Jonah, Mace and Tyrell left the following evening, heading northwest. They moved cautiously for the first five kilometres, grateful for the cover that darkness provided. Random demon patrols outside the protected zone were not unheard of, and Valefor and the Mayor were searching for Jonah, which made for slow going.

Jonah took his companions back along his original route into Fire City, retracing his steps easily.

'You have a good memory,' Mace had said as Jonah pointed to an abandoned bus.

'What's a bus anyway?' asked Tyrell, eyeing the double-decker vehicle rusting in the middle of a wide cross-junction. To the north lay open land, and bomb-damaged buildings lined the roads on each side.

Mace grinned at the young man. 'You're joking, right?' he asked. 'There are derelict buses all over Fire City.'

'I know that, old man,' Tyrell retaliated. 'I just don't

know what they were for. You never taught me about them.'

'They were passenger vehicles,' Mace explained. 'Back when ordinary people had places to go. When we were *allowed* to travel freely, many people took buses . . .'

'They must have them in the citadels,' replied Tyrell. 'Do you think?'

Jonah shook his head. 'Not in the north,' he revealed. 'There are cars and people use trams, but mostly they walk.'

'Trams?'

Jonah waited for Mace to add another explanation. 'Carriages on tracks,' he said when Mace failed to reply. 'So that people can move from one part of the citadel to another. In the south, some of the carriages travel along tunnels underground.'

'No way,' Tyrell blurted. 'Underground?'

'I've never been there,' Jonah admitted, 'but I've heard it said.'

'I haven't been out this way since just after the War,' Mace reminisced. 'This area was known as Abbey Field. The crossroads used to be packed with vehicles and people.' He pointed to the southern corner, at the remains of a glass structure. 'Used to sell cars there,' he said wistfully. 'Big shiny ones. I collected toy versions of them as a boy.'

'Long time ago, then,' joked Tyrell.

'A better time, son,' Mace replied, his eyes glazing over with memories of a half-forgotten past.

'We should keep moving,' Jonah cautioned.

'I reckon we're safe now,' Tyrell told him. 'From Valefor at least.'

Jonah pointed towards the north. 'That way,' he told them, setting off once more.

'We're far from safe,' Mace said to Tyrell, 'even out here. Keep your wits about you.'

They trekked for another three hours, following the main arterial road but never openly. Jonah had warned them about wild animals, and even wilder humans, not to mention the army. Venturing into the wastelands was officially forbidden and the penalty for breaking the law was death. Regular government patrols searched the main routes for escapees, so the only safe way to travel was off road.

Yet, even then, danger was everywhere. In the time since the War had ended, most of the countryside had returned to the wild. Dense forests covered the land and many fields had disappeared under thick, overgrown vegetation. The only remaining agricultural land was used to grow food for the Wanted, but much of this had been placed under giant glass domes, protected day and night by the army.

Escaped zoo animals had proliferated, meaning that non-native species such as lions, tigers, gorillas and even elephants had taken hold. Wolves, foxes and rodents were also a major problem, as were some of the feral human tribes that were scattered about. The only currency that mattered in the wild was strength, and there were creatures far more powerful than humans out hunting for a meal.

Around midnight, Jonah told them to take a rest, sensing that his companions were tired. Tyrell sat down on a stone wall and blew out his breath.

'Knackered,' he said, reaching down to massage his calves.

'How far have we come?' asked Mace, taking a swig of water from a flask they'd brought with them.

'Dunno,' said Jonah. 'About seventeen or eighteen kilometres maybe.'

They were outside an abandoned village. All around them houses sat in darkness, their windows and doors destroyed, gardens grown wild.

'There's a cellar in the village,' Jonah revealed. 'I used it on my journey to the city.' He led them down the deserted main street, past a stone monument shaped like a needle, and the remains of several cottages.

To the left stood three walls of a larger building, the rest destroyed. Tyrell was reminded of the Haven, even though it was several times the size of this place. However, the Haven held the promise of sanctuary whereas the heap of stone before them seemed dark and forbidding.

'Round the back,' Jonah told them, climbing over a mound of rubble. 'Come on.'

A few moments later, they found themselves staring at a hastily arranged pile of spherical rocks, each about the size of a man's head. Jonah wore a puzzled expression, his brow furrowed as he studied them.

'What's up?' quizzed Mace.

'They weren't there when I left,' Jonah explained, before looking around. Mace's eyesight, like Tyrell's, had adjusted to the darkness quickly but Jonah could see further. He searched for heat signatures, present as green and orange shapes in his eyes, but found nothing save for a few blurred forms which were too small to indicate any real danger.

'I can't see anything,' he said.

'It *is* dark,' Tyrell pointed out.

Jonah ignored him, crouched and moved two of the grey stones. He rapped the ground with his knuckles and the resulting noise, part wooden, part metallic, indicated a hollow beneath the ground. One by one, he shifted the other stones too. Brushing aside the dirt with his hands, he revealed a timber hatch, remarkably well preserved.

'Are we sure about this?' asked Mace. 'Maybe someone has been here since last week?'

Jonah nodded. 'They have,' he replied. 'The stones didn't arrange themselves.'

Mace took no offence, already used to Jonah's matter-of-fact responses. Instead, he stood watch as the hatch was lifted slowly and a set of stone steps exposed. A sour and fusty smell greeted them.

'Have you got a match?' asked Jonah.

Mace pulled a box from his pocket. 'Here,' he said.

'Wait here whilst I check it out,' Jonah ordered. 'I left a lamp down there. Keep an eye out for any movement.'

Both Mace and Tyrell stiffened, wary of any threat. Jonah pocketed the matches and drew a short blade from his belt. He took the steps quickly and without caution. If something or someone *were* below, the sound of the hatch being lifted would have alerted them anyway. At the bottom, he knew that there were two rooms, one on each side. He went right, into the larger chamber, and sensing no presence, human or otherwise, found the lamp he'd hidden behind some old beer kegs and lit it. Slowly, as the flame danced into life, the rest of the basement came into view. Three rows of barrels, some wooden, others steel, led to the old pump system, some of the clear plastic pipes still connected. The remnants of liquid inside had turned black with bacteria, and the same was probably true of the contents of the wooden casks. Jonah had wondered, though, whether the steel casks had preserved their wares. Without a working pump system, it was hard to know.

On the stone floor, a five-centimetre layer of dust

had settled. Insects of all kinds crawled through the gloom and huge cobwebs hung in each corner, over-loaded with cocoons, some fresh, silken and gleaming, others petrified. A squeak told Jonah that rodents were still using the walls for shelter – he'd eaten two of their number a fortnight earlier. Their resilience continually amazed Jonah. No matter what the circumstances, rats, mice and their other cousins survived and flourished.

He turned to the stairs, broken glass crunching underfoot, and explored the left side of the cellar; once again, he saw nothing out of place. An old generator sat in the far corner, the green paint flaking from its sides. He studied it, wondering again whether it could be resuscitated. He could think of many situations in which a liquid pumping system might prove useful. A few more rusting beer kegs stood next to the machine, some banded with green and red stripes and others stamped with unfamiliar logos. A makeshift tent made of weather-beaten faded canvas, and held up on thick wooden poles, sat to the right. Jonah approached and found that the only scent was his own – a faint, linger-ing trail that he'd left during his last visit. Other than that, nothing and no one had been there.

Satisfied, he turned back up the steps.

'All clear,' he told them as he got halfway. He waited a moment for Mace to come pounding down. Nothing happened. 'Mace?' he called, holding up the lamp, its glow revealing moss-covered walls, glistening and wet. 'Tyrell?'

Worried when he heard no reply, Jonah set down the light and emerged onto the street. Mace and Tyrell were nowhere to be seen. One of the stone spheres caught his eye and he crouched to study the dark liquid that stained it. He removed some with his forefinger, sniffed, then tasted it.

It was blood. Human blood . . .

27

Aron stepped through the door and into the bar, wary that he'd immediately become the star attraction. A group of young men, all around his age, stared openly, their expressions angry. Around the crowded room, various other people did the same, whispering to each other or shaking their heads. He ignored them all, concentrating instead on Martha, who was busy behind the bar. She hadn't seen him enter but Oscar had, and Aron saw him lean across the faded mahogany counter, tapping Martha on the arm.

Aron walked over to them, forcing a smile he didn't feel. 'Hey!' he said, hoping that they'd return the greeting.

Oscar turned to him and nodded once, the movement almost imperceptible. Martha just stood and glared, her mood apparent.

'What do you want?' she asked, setting a limp dishrag down on the bar.

Aron looked to his feet, his pale skin blushing.

'Well?' Martha demanded. 'After what you've done, you're brave to venture in here, Aron.'

'I'm sorry,' he said softly, looking up at her, his light-blue eyes filled with regret.

'Sorry doesn't cover it,' she informed him. 'You've gone too far this time.'

Aron turned to Oscar, who shifted on the balls of his feet, ready for a fight. 'I'm not going to attack you,' said Aron.

Oscar shrugged at him. 'Who can trust you?' he asked accusingly.

'But you *know* me,' Aron protested, turning to Martha too. 'Both of you.'

Martha shook her head defiantly. 'No,' she answered. 'We *knew* you, Aron. But that was before you started acting like a madman. In the past three months you've attacked Oscar, Faith, Prior and now Jonah too. You've argued with almost everyone we know, thrown tantrums, made hurtful comments, lied . . . shall I go on?'

Aron felt the resentment growing in his belly. He tried to hold it back, but his expression gave him away, as always.

'See?' continued Martha. 'You've got that look on you again. Like you're the victim and everyone is just picking on you. Thing is, you've done all this yourself and you can't even see it. You're rude and arrogant and I don't want to be near you.'

'Don't say that,' Aron pleaded. 'We've got a con-nection, Martha, one that can't be broken.'

Martha huffed, her grey eyes sparking with irritation. 'I used to think that,' she replied. 'Used to think that no one could stop us being friends. Never dreamed the person to ruin it would be you, though. I dunno what's happening to you, Aron. It's like you've changed into someone else.'

'No,' he retaliated, feeling his ire escalate. 'I'm still me. It's *you* . . . chasing after Jonah like he's some messiah. Completely pathetic!'

Oscar stood forward and poked Aron in the chest. 'You don't talk to her like that,' he said, his calm expression contradicting the menace in his words. 'Understand?'

They stood at similar heights, and Aron found him-self staring directly into Oscar's pale tan eyes. He smiled, pushing Oscar's hand away.

'Don't push your luck, slant,' he warned, making reference to Oscar's oriental heritage.

'How clever,' Oscar countered. 'Must have took all day, thinking up that one. I'm impressed.'

Aron shook his head. 'At least I don't hide behind my boyfriend,' he spat. 'Everyone knows about you and Tyrell. It's unnatural and so are you!'

Oscar's fists, hanging at his side, clenched. 'And we're *friends*?' he asked. 'Don't make me laugh. Besides, I might not be *your* idea of normal, Aron, but that's fine with me. What's *normal* about you?'

'I think you should leave,' Aron heard Martha say. 'Now!'

He looked at her, shook his head. 'This is a bar,' he told her, 'and I want a drink.'

'No,' she replied. 'You're not welcome, not any more. I thought you'd come here to apologize, maybe talk to Prior – make it up. But not you.'

Aron smirked. 'Yeah, *that's* an idea,' he jeered. 'Why don't I find your boyfriend and beg him too? You'd love *that*!'

'You won't find him,' revealed Martha, looking away. 'He's not here.'

'What – has the hero run off and left you all?'

'No,' said Oscar. 'He's with Mace and Tyrell. Risking his life to help us. You know that shit that you claim to do? Well, he's out there, in the wastelands, *doing* it.'

Aron shoved Oscar backwards. 'Claim?' he spat. 'I don't *claim*, you slope-eyed rat, I act!'

Oscar pushed him back and they squared shoulders, neither willing to back down.

'You ain't got Tyrell to hold your hand now,' Aron mocked. 'Who's gonna save you this time . . . ?'

'I am,' he heard Faith say, just before something solid and heavy smacked against his head. He slumped into

Oscar, and just before passing out he heard Prior order his removal.

'Sometimes you just can't rebuild a burned bridge,' the old man added.

Stone decided that he'd seen and heard enough. He was standing underneath the tall stone arch in the park opposite the Mayor's mansion, watching Valefor humiliate his employer again.

Mias stood guard, flanked by several patrollers, whilst two mercenaries made up the human contingent. Torrential rain pounded rhythmically against the ground, dark grey clouds enveloping the sky. A strong wind whipped around them, causing tree branches to creak and moan. The weather reflected the Mayor's own actions as he whined and trembled before the demon lord, rain dripping down his fleshy features.

'I grow tired of your excuses, human,' Valefor declared. 'My patience wears as thin as your hair.'

Stone saw the demon's powerful jaw begin to grind, giant wings quivering in the wind behind him. Much as he detested the Mayor, he would not watch Valefor kill him. There would be far too many questions from the government. He stepped forward, clearing his throat.

'Stay!' ordered Mias, sensing Stone's movement.

'I don't take my orders from you,' Stone replied.

Valefor turned to face him, lilac eyes half lidded. 'You wish to speak?' he asked.

Stone determined that his best course would require deference to the demon's ego. 'Yes, my lord,' he replied, drawing amusement.

'I can sense your feelings,' Valefor reminded him. 'Your reverence is as false as your employer's words are. Tell me why I shouldn't consume you.'

Stone looked directly at the demon lord and smiled. 'You can read my thoughts,' he quipped, 'so you know why.'

Valefor considered Stone's reply carefully, nudging Mias into impatience.

'Shall I take him, lord?' Mias trembled with delight.

'No, brother Mias,' Valefor commanded. 'Let him speak.'

Stone explained that he had a plan. 'They must have a headquarters,' he continued. 'Somewhere secret we don't know about. I'm going to find it for you.'

The Mayor looked shocked, his face filled with surprise. Stone knew that he'd complain afterwards but it wasn't important. Stone, when faced with his employer's questions, would simply point out that his actions had prevented certain death. Enough, surely, to warrant the interruption.

'If they did, we'd know,' replied Valefor.

Stone shook his head. 'Only inside the protected

zone,' he pointed out. 'What if it's outside that limit? Your sense abilities are restricted to the central zone, aren't they?'

'Perhaps,' Valefor confessed, impressed with the human's knowledge of his species. 'You understand our ways?'

'I'm paid to,' Stone explained. 'I like to provide an excellent service.'

'You say that you can find them?'

Stone nodded. 'If I find their hideaway, I'll find the stranger. We can handle two issues at the same time . . .'

'Agreed,' Valefor replied. 'The question is, can you succeed where your employer has failed?'

'Absolutely,' Stone boasted. 'In fact, I was about to brief the Mayor before this meeting. I just forgot to, so he hasn't really failed. Yet.'

Valefor laughed. The Mayor glowered at Stone, anger making him shake.

'I like you, human,' said Valefor. 'What do they call you?'

'Stone, sir.'

'Well, Stone – how long before you have news?'

Stone shrugged. 'One, maybe two days,' he suggested. 'No more than that.'

'Very well,' agreed Valefor. 'And if you fail me . . .'

'I won't fail,' Stone assured him. 'I *never* fail.'

28

Tyrell felt the back of his head. The wound was still wet and painful to touch. An unpleasant odour permeated the air around him – a vile blend of faeces, vomit, body odour and feet. The heat of other bodies, perhaps twenty of them crammed into a tight space, caused sweat to trickle down his face. Still groggy, he looked around, trying to work out where he was, hampered by the lack of a light source. Suddenly he heard a door slam, and raised voices that belonged to humans.

Soon, whatever he was in began to move, and to his left someone stirred. The vehicle rode over some bumps and Tyrell tipped backwards until someone's stomach got in the way. Whoever it belonged to didn't complain.

'Mace?' he whispered, aware that in the darkness he had to be alert.

'Who?'

Tyrell's eyes began to adjust and he made out a shape. He felt around with his hands, catching bare feet, arms and a mouth, the lips cold and clammy.

'He's dead.'

Tyrell tensed as the man continued to talk from about two metres to his right. Was he talking about Mace or some other person? As if he could sense Tyrell's thoughts, the man clarified:

'Poor kid – they snapped his neck.'

'Where are we going?' asked Tyrell, thankful that it wasn't Mace and slightly ashamed of his relief.

'You don't *know*?'

'Wouldn't have asked if I did,' Tyrell replied abruptly.

'Round-up zone, about ten kilometres north of here.'

Tyrell tapped the side of the vehicle and felt cool metal. Someone moaned softly, a woman somewhere to his left.

'Where were you hiding?' the man continued.

'I wasn't,' Tyrell told him as he felt a slight tremor of fear. 'I was with two others, heading north. We came from Fire City.'

'Oh,' the man replied.

'Are my friends in here?' Tyrell asked. 'Big, bear-like man with bright blond hair and fists like boulders, and a tall, skinny younger one, dressed in black?'

'Not that I saw,' the man told him, 'and I was watching them throw people in. I was the first one they picked up.'

'Who are *they*?'

'The army,' said the man. 'Don't you know *anything*?'

Tyrell ignored his reply and tried to sit up properly. His head was throbbing, as though a thousand boots were stamping across his forehead. A wave of nausea overcame him and he shuddered.

'I'm Negus,' the man told him. 'You got a name?'

'Tyrell.'

'Well, I hope you ain't badly hurt,' Negus added.

'Why's that?'

'Because when we get to the round-up zone, they're going to shoot anyone who isn't able-bodied immediately. Everyone else gets sent to herds around the country – ready for the Hunt. At least with the last one, you stand some chance.'

'How many people?' Tyrell asked.

'Depends on how many they catch tonight.'

Tyrell wondered what had happened to Mace. He thought back to the moment when Mace had said he was going for a dump. Seconds later, as the giant had disappeared into the bushes, something hard and heavy had smacked Tyrell in the face. The subsequent blow had knocked him out cold. It was hard to believe that Mace hadn't heard something or suffered himself. But if he had been caught too, why wasn't he in the vehicle? Perhaps he'd put up a fight and been killed, his body left where it had fallen? Alternatively, maybe he and Jonah had escaped and were on the run. No matter what,

245

Tyrell knew that the situation was bad and that his options were severely limited.

'I need to get out of here,' he said. 'Now.'

'Relax, brother,' Negus replied. 'The doors are re-inforced and we're in a convoy. Even if you escape this van, which ain't happening, the bastards behind us will shoot you.'

'How come you know so much about it?'

Negus chuckled. 'Because this is the third time they've caught me,' he boasted. 'And they ain't held me once.'

'So you know how to get away?' said Tyrell, his excitement rising.

'We'll see,' deflected Negus.

'I need to go now!' Tyrell demanded. 'Get me out!'

'That would be suicide,' Negus warned. 'These patrols are supported by other units, and the whole convoy is tracked from the sky. The government follows them on remote monitors too, back in the citadels.'

Most of his reply made no sense to Tyrell and he wondered what could track something from the sky, other than a demon.

'I just want to get out,' he said again, though less forcefully.

Negus told him that he wanted the same thing. 'Just get some rest, brother,' he advised. 'You're gonna need it, trust me . . .'

Mace watched Jonah crouch and examine the ground. He'd returned to the hatch just after Jonah had emerged from the cellar, both of them perplexed about Tyrell's disappearance.

'See anything?' he asked, his mind racing.

Jonah shushed him and tried to concentrate. He wondered how his senses had been fooled by whoever had taken Tyrell. Perhaps the fight with Mias had taken more out of him than he'd imagined. The only culprits he could think of were the army round-up patrols or some tribe of wild humans, probably cannibals. The latter would have been far from silent, and he would have heard them, even from underground. That left the soldiers, and if they had taken Tyrell, then all bets were off. They'd be miles away already, heading for one of the round-up zones that Jonah had seen on his journey to Fire City.

In that case, Tyrell was alone, and Jonah was surprised at how angry he felt at such an outcome. His mission didn't involve getting attached to the humans he met. It was not his way, yet something was beginning to break that resistance down. He shook that thought – and a sudden image of Martha – from his head and turned back to the task at hand.

'I was only gone for five minutes,' Mace confessed. 'How the hell could anything have happened in such a short time?'

'It's not your fault,' Jonah reassured him. 'Out here, the blink of an eye is sometimes too long.'

'I should have stayed put,' the giant man replied guiltily. 'I should have watched his back.'

'Then you'd both have been taken,' Jonah pointed out. 'I think it was soldiers. They would have just killed you if you'd resisted.'

Mace growled. 'I would have taken a few with me,' he declared.

'I know that,' said Jonah, understanding that Mace did not make idle boasts. 'But the others would have shot you. They move fast and they have specialist equipment – night goggles, machine guns and the like.'

Mace shrugged in defeat, knowing that Jonah was right. Yet it did nothing to assuage the shame he was feeling. Tyrell was gone, and for the giant it felt the same as losing another son.

'Sometimes,' he said wearily, 'I wonder if this is worth doing. Seems to me they always win anyway: the demons, the government . . .'

Jonah stood and put a hand on Mace's left shoulder. 'I'm sorry about Tyrell getting caught,' he said, 'but you can't blame yourself.'

Mace smiled. 'I can,' he countered, 'and I will.'

Jonah shook his head. 'They'll take the convoy north,' he revealed. 'There's a round-up zone close to where we're going. That's where they'll take him, I'm sure. We can get there in time . . .'

'Catch up with army vehicles?' Mace asked. 'I fought in the War, Jonah. I know we can't *catch* them.'

'We can try though, can't we?' challenged Jonah.

Mace shrugged again. 'What about taking a rest?' he asked.

'I'm not tired,' Jonah replied. 'You?'

Mace considered his aching calves, the soreness of his feet, and lied. 'I'm fine,' he answered.

'We're going to have to take risks,' Jonah admitted. 'But staying on the road will be quicker.'

'I'm ready for anything,' Mace told him.

Jonah pulled out one of the two spears he carried on his back, and handed it to Mace. 'It's got an energy field,' he fibbed. 'We stole them from a convoy we ambushed in the north. It will fend off attacks quickly.'

Mace looked at the sleek ebony javelin in his hands. It was about a metre long and weighed more than it should have. Perfectly balanced, it tapered at both ends into murderously sharp points.

'Where does the energy come from?' asked Mace.

Jonah shook his head and lied again. 'No idea,' he said. 'Whatever it is, the power has faded but it's still worth carrying. Coupled with your other weapons, it will help.'

'Are we guaranteed to meet enemies on the road?' Mace added.

'Yes,' Jonah replied as he wondered whether he could energize a spear that wasn't connected to him. They would find out soon enough.

'When Aron said that you're not normal, he wasn't lying, was he?' said Mace.

Jonah eyed the giant and nodded. 'There's plenty to tell,' he admitted, 'but not now. We need to get moving.'

'Tell me something,' Mace insisted. 'One thing.'

Jonah looked away, his thoughts blurred into one, his heart racing. He'd known that their trip into the wastelands would lead to this moment, and partly he'd welcomed it. Mace was an elder, and wiser than many of the other humans. He would see much on this trip that would be hard for Jonah to explain. Perhaps the best course of action was telling the truth? Yet to do that Jonah would have to do something he'd never fully done with anyone, not since his family had been torn apart. He'd have to trust Mace completely.

'Things aren't always black and white,' Jonah said cryptically as he searched for the right words.

'I guess not,' Mace told him in reply. 'All I ever see is grey. Your answer doesn't tell me much though.'

'Sometimes things happen, and consequences occur, and there is no helping the outcome.'

Mace asked Jonah to face him. The younger man turned, his eyes still downcast and half closed.

'Jonah . . . ?'

'You must try to understand,' Jonah whispered. 'You *have* to understand. I didn't have any control over what happened.'

'Understand what?' demanded Mace. 'What are you talking about?'

Jonah opened his eyes and looked up. Mace gasped. He stumbled backwards, holding the spear between himself and Jonah.

'My mother wasn't human,' Jonah declared, orange and red flames dancing around his irises. 'She was a demon.'

29

The Mayor demanded to know what Stone was up to.

'You think you can belittle me?' he yelled, his face almost purple with rage and rivulets of sweat running down his jowls.

Stone held up a hand, attempting to pacify his boss before he had a coronary. 'I was helping you out,' he insisted. 'Valefor was after blood.'

'Valefor is no concern of yours!' the Mayor spat. 'You seem to have forgotten your position.'

Stone was glad of the privacy that his apartment afforded. The thought of being chastised in public was too much. Stone doubted that he'd have been able to control his actions in full view.

'I know my position,' he countered. 'It's to protect you. Suppose I'd stood there and let Valefor humiliate you further? In front of my men . . .'

'So *you* humiliated me instead?'

Stone fingered the paperweight on his desk, a smooth glass block, hard and heavy. In another world, he took the weight and smashed the Mayor's head in until all that remained was a mess of pulped brain, blood and fragments of bone. Back in this one, he smiled.

'Don't be so paranoid. All I did was offer to solve Valefor's problem, and by extension yours too.'

The Mayor, who'd been standing by the windows, walked across the room, sitting down in a threadbare armchair. He faced Stone. 'Tell me about your plan,' he said. 'You know – the one you forgot to mention.'

Stone sighed. 'I didn't really forget,' he explained. 'That's just what I told Valefor – not that it matters. When he's that close to any human, he can read everything they think and feel.'

'That's even better,' the Mayor replied with sarcasm. 'He *knows* you lied to him.'

Stone wondered how much more stupid the Mayor could be. 'Of *course* he knows, sir,' he replied, trying to hide his exasperation. 'And he doesn't care. All he wants is this stranger . . .'

'The stranger that I told you to find,' the Mayor reminded him.

Stone nodded.

'And the plan?'

'You won't like it,' Stone warned. 'It involves your stepdaughter.'

'Martha?'

'Yes, sir.'

253

The Mayor shook his head. 'I don't understand, Stone,' he admitted. 'Explain.'

'She's a member of the Resistance and she knows the stranger. And before you begin to doubt my words, listen. This isn't second-hand information, sir. I saw the evidence for myself. I saw *her*.'

The Mayor considered what he'd been told for a while. Stone got up and poured them both a drink. The Mayor took his glass and drank half of the amber-coloured liquid quickly. 'Are you sure?' he asked, his voice quieter, his tone less arrogant.

'Completely sure,' Stone insisted. 'You may think I've done nothing for the last few days but that's not true. I'm one conversation away from finding their HQ.'

The Mayor finished his drink, stood and walked back to the windows, looking down to the street below. At nearly two a.m. a few people still walked the streets, mostly drunken men and the odd homeless scavenger. Across the far side of the city, east of his mansion, he knew that the Hunt would normally be in full swing.

He'd heard about the Resistance and how some of the prey had been rescued, and had long wondered what happened to the liberated. It made sense that they had some secret location, a hideaway to which they could take people. Valefor's powers, as Stone had said during their meeting with the demons, extended to the edges of the protected zone, and no further. That covered only several square kilometres, and beyond lay the outskirts of the city and the wastelands. It was very probable that the Resistance secreted the saved outside the protected zone.

It was also more than likely that his stepdaughter was involved. Physically and emotionally, she was the same as her mother, and the Mayor had tried for years to make her see sense. But Martha was headstrong and arrogant and she hated him, despite everything he'd done for her. The death of her mother was self-induced; no one had forced the woman to become a traitor. The Mayor had tried his best to help. Blinded by a foolish love, he'd gone cap in hand to his superiors, begged Valefor to intercede, all for nothing. And now Martha was following in her mother's footsteps. It would be a shame to lose her; in the correct situation, with the right amount of moulding, she would have made a fine substitute in his affections. However, it was not to be, and there were plenty of other girls desperate to rise above their sorry lives.

He turned to Stone and shrugged, relieved that giving up on her was a choice that had been taken out of his hands. 'Is she downstairs?' he asked.

'Martha?'

The Mayor nodded.

'No. Her shift finished at midnight. Who knows where she is?'

'She's not in her room here?'

'I've no idea,' Stone admitted. 'You want me to check?'

'I'll do it,' the Mayor told him. 'Leave her to me.'

'You're the chief,' replied Stone. 'Do you want me to give her a pass when the time comes?'

The Mayor shook his head. 'No point,' he explained. 'If we protect her, Valefor will kill us. No, when the time comes, you must kill her. But make sure it's quick. Despite everything, Stone, I'm not an animal. I loved that girl and her mother once, and no matter what, I don't want her to suffer.'

Outwardly Stone agreed, but inside he felt another wave of revulsion for the Mayor. Stone had no family, none that he was aware of anyway, and was a mercenary with the blood of hundreds on his conscience, yet even he was appalled at the Mayor's appetite for self-preservation. The stories about the Mayor's former wife, Maria, were rife in Fire City. Stone pondered the worth of a world in which spineless slugs like the Mayor prospered, and valiant women – even misguided ones such as Maria – were killed.

'Who is your mole, Stone?' the Mayor enquired.

'Aron – one of the boys Martha is friends with,' Stone admitted. There was no mileage in hiding the truth. 'I've already spoken to him and I'll find him tomorrow, set things up.'

'I know who the boy is,' said the Mayor. 'But why tomorrow? Why not right now?'

Stone gave the Mayor a hard look, making him flinch. 'Because I'm tired and I'm going to sleep,' he snapped. 'I'll deal with it tomorrow.'

The Mayor asked who'd be driving him home.

'Ask one of my men,' Stone told him. 'They're downstairs.'

Stone waited for the Mayor to leave before taking out his mobile phone. His handler answered on the second ring, despite the hour.

'I've been waiting up for you,' he told Stone.

'I thought you might,' replied Stone. 'I've had another idea.'

Across the city, Valefor stood on the roof of a deserted apartment block and looked over his domain, Mias at his side. With the Hunt cancelled, Mias had set the patrollers a new task, searching door to door for the stranger and rounding up anyone who got in their way.

'Any sign of the Resistance?' asked Valefor.

'No, my lord.'

'And no news of the stranger?'

'No,' admitted Mias. 'My legion searches for him but no word as yet.'

'I cannot sense his presence either,' Valefor revealed. 'Perhaps your rampage taught them a lesson?'

Mias smiled. 'I've always said that these animals need

a firm hand,' he gloated. 'We are too soft on them.'

'Perhaps that is true,' replied Valefor.

'Do you trust the human soldier to find them?' asked Mias.

'*Stone?*' said the demon lord. 'I think he will do his job.'

'And then . . . ?'

Valefor's wings flapped behind him, his jaw muscles flexed. 'Once we have what we need, you may dispose of him. The Mayor too.'

'But what of the council, my lord?'

Valefor shook his giant head, his eyes on fire. 'I care not what they say,' he confessed. 'I am an ancient and my will shall be done. If the council wish to inform Asmodeus of my actions, so be it. I was feasting on souls with the Great Lord before most of the council existed. We are kin, the Great Lord and I.'

Mention of Asmodeus, the most powerful of all demons, caused Mias to drop to one knee and bow his head. Rarely seen or heard from, the Great Lord was ruler of everything on Earth. Through his majesty had the reign of the demons been re-established, returning them to their rightful place at the top of the food chain.

'I shall follow your lead, brother Valefor.'

'And for that, you shall have great reward,' Valefor replied.

'Do you wish to feed?' asked Mias, rising to his feet.

'Yes,' Valefor told him. 'This stranger is powerful. I shall build up my strength for our meeting. I shall tear the meat from his bones and torture his soul until it screams. Until then, have your patrollers bring me some sustenance.'

'At once, sire,' said Mias. 'Should I resume my search?'

'Not tonight,' Valefor replied. 'They are not here. Tomorrow, go into the city and question the people. You have my permission to use whatever force you require. If anyone stands in your way, brother, kill them.'

'So we do not wait for Stone to deliver?'

Valefor looked into Mias' scarlet eyes. 'I grow tired of waiting,' he replied.

30

In the half-hour since Jonah's revelation, Mace had spoken only once. The word he'd uttered, as his mind performed cartwheels and his heart almost entered his throat, was 'shit'. Since then, he'd followed Jonah's lead as they moved quickly through the night, along deserted streets and out into what had once been called the countryside. He wanted to ask questions but couldn't think of the correct ones. What *were* you supposed to ask? The usual stuff just didn't seem to apply. It was only as they entered another village – roads filled with derelict houses – that Mace finally gave up and let his mouth take over.

'It's not possible,' he blurted as Jonah held up a hand, the signal for Mace to stop.

'Movement,' Jonah warned, ignoring Mace's remark. 'Up ahead, to the left.'

Mace failed to see anything. Despite having grown used to the darkness, his eyes weren't that attuned. Heavy cloud obscured the stars, and the moon was absent.

'Is that one of your *demon* powers?' he asked, hoping to sound jovial rather than inquisitive, and failing.

'Yes,' Jonah replied, without elaborating further.

'What can you see?'

Jonah approached a car and crouched, beckoning to Mace to do the same. He peered into the night, looking beyond the thirty metres that Mace's human eyes could just about decipher. Possible shapes in Mace's vision became heat signatures to Jonah's eyes. There were several of them, all human judging by their scent.

'Humans,' Jonah eventually revealed. 'Keep quiet and follow my lead.'

He waited a few seconds before scampering to the cover of a building, keeping low. Mace did the same moments later, with difficulty. Running whilst doubled over wasn't something his giant frame managed easily.

'Something's happening,' Jonah whispered. 'One of the human forms is on the ground.'

He moved again, forward by twenty metres this time, keeping to the shadows. Mace waited before following, his eyes fixed on the road ahead. The possible shapes were real now and he could hear them too – shrieking and snarling.

'Cannibals,' said Jonah.

Suddenly the scene became clear to Mace. A group of flesh-eaters surrounded a vehicle in the middle of the street. They held clubs and used them to beat their victim, who lay motionless on the ground beside it.

'We've got to help him!' Mace insisted.

Jonah didn't wait to agree. He sprinted forward, drawing his blade, and into the mêlée. Mace, despite having seen him in action, was again amazed at his speed. It took only seconds for Jonah to despatch the flesh-eaters, gutting every single one of them. By the time Mace had joined him, the fight was over and Jonah was busy checking the pulse of their victim – a soldier, his face flecked with blood and gore, his eyes impossibly wide and black.

'He's dead.'

Mace looked down at the corpse. The left side of the soldier's face was a bloody mess, the skull split open, eye socket caved in and jaw bone smashed. He lay at an awkward angle, one of his legs hanging by a thread of skin beneath the knee. The other leg and both arms lay a few feet away, the flesh gnawed. The cannibals had obviously been at their attack for a while. The question that arose, once the horror of the incident evaporated, was why the victim had been there at all. Mace said as much.

'I don't know,' Jonah admitted, 'but it doesn't look good.'

'Did he get lost?'

Jonah shook his head and pointed to the army-issue jeep. 'Each vehicle has satellite navigation,' he explained.

'I haven't seen one of those in years,' replied Mace, recalling a small black box that he'd bought as a teenager. It had plugged into his car's cigarette lighter, and never kept its signal. He'd stamped on it in the end as it tried to direct him down a one-way street, *against* the flow of traffic.

'If the soldiers were searching the village, the whole unit have got to be close,' Jonah added. 'They wouldn't have left someone behind though. He was probably bringing up the rear. But that also means they missed the cannibals, and I don't understand how.'

He turned to study the street, noting the redbrick semi-detached houses on both sides, each with a small front garden. A few cars still stood in the driveways, most beyond repair, and each building was silent and dark. He could smell something in the air, but the thick walls of each abode blocked his other senses.

'What do we do?' asked Mace.

'Take the jeep,' Jonah told him. 'Make use of our luck.'

Mace walked round to the driver's side and saw keys dangling from the ignition. He leaned in, ready to start the engine.

'*Help!*' came a cry from the deserted houses.

'That was a kid!' Mace declared, turning round.

'Don't move!' Jonah ordered, scanning the darkness once more.

'Jonah – that was a little girl. We've got to help her!'

From the right, a metal dustbin rattled and glass broke. A bare-footed figure about five feet tall ran into view. It was a female, maybe ten years old, with long dark hair and wearing an adult's shirt. She ran to a hedge and hid behind it, whimpering.

'Wait!' Jonah demanded. 'It smells like a trap!'

Mace shook his head. 'I don't care!' he roared. 'I'm going to get her.'

He ran towards the girl, his heart pumping overtime. There was no way he was watching her become someone else's dinner. He'd seen too many humans end up as food for the flesh-eaters. He got to within less than a metre when the girl sprang at him, her mouth open and teeth sharp.

'*Shit!*'

She clamped her jaws round Mace's left forearm and tore into it. The giant swung her away from his body, trying to ignore the pain, but the girl held on like a rabid dog with a side of beef, yet almost weightless. Her legs swung through the air, her arms flailing for some kind of purchase as though she were drowning.

'*Gerroff!*'

An ear-splitting cry pierced the night and more cannibals streamed from their cover. The bait had worked. Mace thought quickly, deciding to use the girl's slight form as a weapon, despite how sick it made him feel. He threw out his arm, the girl still attached, and her legs deflected the first attacker. The cannibal, a tall, gangling male, fell to the ground, allowing Mace to stamp on his face, knocking him out cold. Two more males, both bigger and heavier, emerged, their eyes blazing.

'Great!' Mace groaned, cursing his luck. He was in trouble now. One attacker was easy, but if they both jumped at the same time . . .

He balled his right fist and began to punch the girl, hammering the side of her face until she let go. Her tiny body slumped to the ground and she scampered away, spitting blood and teeth, just as the two men attacked.

The first came from behind, trying to bring Mace down. He spun round, using his attacker's momentum against him. The second man was too powerful, however, and he dived into Mace's midriff, bringing him crashing down on top of the first one. The giant lifted his head and then slammed it back down, smashing the first attacker's nose beneath him to a pulp, before turning his attention to the second. He had barely done so when Jonah speared the cannibal through the ear with a smaller blade, ripping through his brain.

'*Get up!*' Jonah bellowed as the rest of the cannibals lurched into view.

Mace rolled left, untangling himself from the first attacker before breaking his neck with one twist of his

265

huge hands. Another flesh-eater came forward, a cricket bat in her hands. She must have been about his age, heavy round the middle with pendulous breasts that hung free. Open sores, oozing yellow pus, covered her belly and upper thighs and her toenails resembled claws. A band of teeth laced her neck, her face painted with what looked like blood.

Mace drove a fist into her mouth, aiming for a spot some thirty centimetres behind her head. The woman fell immediately, and Mace used his heavy boots to finish the job. He pounded her to death, ignoring the feeling of cowardice his actions provoked. He told himself over and over that she wasn't a woman, she was a cannibal, but it didn't help. It never did.

As yet more cannibals appeared, joining in from all sides, Mace realized that they couldn't fight them all, not even with Jonah's powers. He sprinted to the jeep, jumping in and turning over the engine in one movement. A metallic grind accompanied his first shift as he slammed a foot down on the accelerator. It had been nearly fifteen years since he'd driven a car and the jeep lurched forward, the momentum causing Mace to smack his head against the roll bar.

'Jonah!' he called above the engine noise and the howling blood lust of the cannibal tribe. '*Get in!*'

The half-demon, surrounded by attackers, somersaulted over them backwards, landing like a cat. Staying on all fours, he ran towards Mace, his pace incredible. He pounced into the passenger seat as Mace found the right gear and urged the jeep down the road. Behind them, the flesh-eaters shrieked in anger before turning on the smallest of their tribe, the girl they had used as bait, and tore her to pieces. Mace continued to hear her screams for what felt like a mile.

'Next time,' Jonah told him angrily, '*listen* to me.'

Mace knew that he'd made an error and said nothing. Jonah wiped the blood and guts from his face and settled into silence too.

31

Ten kilometres north, the van carrying Tyrell and Negus turned into a large compound ringed with barbed-wire fencing. Other than the narrow approach road, the perimeter was surrounded by forest, a hundred acres deep on three sides. As the vehicle scrunched to a halt on the loose gravel, Tyrell tensed, ready for whatever lay ahead.

'Wait until they call you out,' Negus told him. 'Don't make any sudden movements, don't try to run and don't mouth off. Any one of those reactions and you'll be picking a bullet out of your skull.'

Tyrell looked over at his new companion, wondering what he looked like in daylight. He'd already established that they shared a skin tone, but Negus' hair was longer, and in the darkness of the van it resembled dancing serpents. As the doors were thrown open and artificial light flooded it, Tyrell squinted. Three soldiers looked in, two with their guns trained on the captives.

'*Out!*' one of them ordered, his accent unlike any Tyrell had ever heard.

He followed Negus' lead, stepping into the cold night with the other conscious occupants of the van and looking his captors up and down. Each wore standard-issue camouflage fatigues, heavy black boots with rubber soles, and blue berets. One was brown-skinned but paler than Tyrell, with beady eyes and a sneer. The second, who held a torch and gave the orders, had pale, almost translucent skin covered in freckles. His eyes were deep blue and a scar ran from his left ear to his nose, bisecting the cheek. The final soldier was a similar height and build to Tyrell, but white, and he wore dark glasses despite the time of day. A cigarette hung from his lips, the tip glowing, and he squinted as smoke twirled up into his eyes.

'Any more live ones?' asked the freckled one, glaring at Negus.

'Not that I know of,' Negus replied.

Tyrell saw his hair properly now. It had grown thick and knotted, and had been twisted into clumps at the scalp. The resulting locks were of different lengths, some hanging down, others sticking out at odd angles. His skin was slightly darker than Tyrell's and had an almost purple hue in the torchlight. It was shiny and healthy and gave Tyrell no clue as to the man's age, other than his obviously being an elder. Negus was also short, not much more than five feet four, yet his build was wiry, his bare arms corded with muscle. Tyrell thought of Oscar, another slightly built man who people often under-estimated, and he felt suddenly alone. He wondered too about Jonah and Mace, and prayed that they were still alive.

'Go back in and check!' the lead soldier ordered, gesturing into the van.

Negus shrugged and held out his hands. 'Can't climb back in with these on,' he said of the silver handcuffs that bound him.

The pale soldier shook his head and slammed the torch against Negus' temple, sending him sprawling. Tyrell twitched but stayed calm. The soldiers wore nameplates on their uniforms, and Negus' attacker was called Boyd.

'You!' he said to Tyrell. 'You ain't wearing any cuffs. Check out the van!'

Tyrell nodded, understanding that he had no choice but to obey. Reluctantly he stepped back into the gloom, being careful not to tread on anyone. Several bodies lay unconscious, all of them adult and male. Two women, barely older than him, huddled in the far right corner, whimpering. Tyrell approached and crouched, telling them to follow him. One of them looked up into his eyes and shook her head.

'Scared,' she replied softly. 'Don't want to go out there.'

Tyrell put a hand on her arm. She was thin, her face

gaunt and her breath rancid. The skin around her mouth was flaky, and her lips were so dry that they'd cracked and bled in two places. Greasy strands of blonde hair hung from her head.

'If you don't do what they say,' he said in a soothing voice, 'they'll kill you.'

'No!' she whined. 'Don't want to die.'

Her friend was in a similar state but larger and dark-skinned, with short black hair. Her eyes remained closed and Tyrell noticed a deep gash in her side, oozing blood. Neither woman was much older than him and he began to grow angry. He wanted to fight but knew that it would be suicidal. Instead, he decided to protect them as best he could.

'What's your name?' he asked the first girl.

'Jodie . . .'

'Well, I'm not going to let them hurt you, Jodie, I promise. Just come with me . . .'

'But I can't leave Saira,' she replied, stroking the second woman's face. 'She's been stabbed.'

Tyrell remembered what Negus had said and wallowed. 'You have to,' he explained. 'Please, Jodie. If you don't come now they'll kill both of you.'

The woman shook her head, pushing Tyrell's arm away. '*No!*' she insisted, raising her voice.

Tyrell heard one of the soldiers enter the van behind him, and he fought back the urge to react.

'Get out!' the one called Boyd ordered, pulling a gun from the holster attached to his belt.

Tyrell took hold of Jodie and stood, lifting her easily and ignoring her struggles to escape. He turned and edged towards the doors before jumping to the ground. He held Jodie close, covering her ears with his large hands. Two shots rang out from inside the van.

'Get those unconscious rats out of here and burn the dead,' he heard Boyd say. 'I'll take the rest to the holding pens.'

Tyrell felt a tear run down his face as rage built inside his massive frame. He placed his mouth against Jodie's head and whispered, 'Dead man. He's a dead man . . .'

Twenty minutes later, Tyrell, Negus and Jodie stood amongst a handful of other captives, naked and shivering, having been hosed down with cold water. The others numbered ten – seven adult men, two women and a young teenage girl, no more than fourteen. One of the older women shielded the youngster with her body, forgoing her own dignity to protect the teen. They were in a wooden enclosure about six metres by four, with five soldiers leering in, laughing at their discomfort. The cage was fenced with thick barbed wire, like a giant chicken coop.

'Can we keep the little one?' he heard one of the

soldiers ask. The raucous laughter that followed made Tyrell feel sick.

'Prefer the fat ones myself,' said another. 'They squeal more.'

Tyrell told the women to ignore them, and one of the captive men, an older guy with grey chest hair and wrinkled skin, chastised him.

'Shut up!' he spat. 'You want them to kill all of us?'

Tyrell eyed his accuser, ready to knock him down, but Negus stopped him. 'He's right,' he whispered. 'Just let it go.'

Moments later, Boyd appeared with two civilians, both dressed in white lab coats. 'The medics will check you over individually,' the soldier told them. 'If anyone acts up, I'll kill you, understand?' When no one replied, Boyd sneered. 'Thought so,' he said.

Tyrell looked at Negus, wondering what their examinations would yield. Hadn't his new companion explained the set-up already? The weak were killed and the rest went to the Hunt. There was no need for any more assessments.

'I don't know,' Negus whispered, second-guessing Tyrell. 'They've never done this before.'

'When do we escape?' Tyrell asked, already checking his surroundings for a means of breaking free. If Negus didn't come through, he wanted to be ready with a plan of his own.

'Later,' Negus said from the corner of his mouth. 'We'll talk later.'

The gate to the pen was thrown open and a skinny soldier not much older than Tyrell ordered one of the men out at gunpoint. Instinctively Tyrell sought out Jodie's hand, but she refused his show of support, pushing his arm away.

'It'll be over in ten minutes,' said one of the doctors, a balding man wearing large spectacles. 'Try to remain calm and nothing will happen to you.'

Tyrell closed his eyes and waited, wishing that Mace and Jonah were at his side.

Afterwards, when the captives had been assessed, clothed and given a place to sleep, Dr Rogers turned on his computer and tapped into the Net. His colleague, a student called Kira Hamley, had retired for the night, leaving Rogers free to contact their boss. The young woman was unaware of every aspect of their work, and Rogers preferred it that way. Hamley, although a promising student, was naïve and a little too emotional. Her liberal attitudes towards the Unwanted ensured that her clearance level stayed minimal.

The screen in front of him in his makeshift office turned sky blue. He waited for the desktop to appear before signing in. His employer's face appeared almost instantly via the in-built camera.

'Anything of note, Dr Rogers?' asked Senator Wise, his honey-coloured eyes sparkling.

'There's one,' Dr Rogers informed him. 'A black male – big and strong and free of disease. I'm amazed that he's ended up out here. I suggest we re-evaluate our sorting process at the breeding centres.'

'How old is he?' asked the senator.

'Seventeen, maybe a year younger?'

'Then perhaps he was born out there, *before* the War,' Wise suggested. 'I don't pay you to suggest changes to our fine system, Doctor. I pay you to do your own job.'

Dr Rogers looked away, cursing silently. 'Just waiting on the blood test results for final confirmation of health,' he said after a moment.

'Excellent. If all is well, I want this specimen fast-tracked to my institute. Tell Boyd to handle it.'

'Yes, Senator.'

'And what of the delectable Miss Hamley?' Wise added, a smile creeping across his face.

'Her work is excellent,' Rogers admitted. 'However, she is prone to sentimentalism when it comes to the Unwanted. She thinks that they deserve better treatment.'

The senator's weary sigh sounded loud, even through the computer's small onboard speakers. 'It's nothing more than a trend,' he told Rogers. 'The younger generation looking for a cause to fight for. It happened in our time too, Rogers.'

'Yes, but the War was supposed to end all of that nonsense,' Rogers reminded him.

'And it did,' Senator Wise replied. 'What we have now is a few liberals wringing their hands. Five minutes in the wastelands and they'd be backing extermination. Let them have their whims, I say. The illusion of free speech keeps them happy.'

Rogers shrugged and flicked a beetle from the work-top on which his computer sat. 'And if they get too vocal?' he asked.

'Then we throw them out of the citadels,' Wise replied. 'As I intimated – there is no cause for concern.'

Dr Rogers nodded and asked the one question he always asked. 'How long before I can get back to civilization, sir?'

Senator Wise seemed momentarily distracted by something off-camera. Rogers watched him press the mute button and bark some orders. When he returned to the conversation, he seemed highly annoyed.

Rogers repeated his question.

'When I tell you!' the senator snapped.

'You've been promising me a return for months now!' Rogers retaliated in an agitated tone.

'I *could* leave you out there,' Senator Wise warned.

Dr Rogers shuddered at the thought, but failed to be

moved by the senator's threats. He was a highly respected member of society in his own right. Wise would never dare to turn on him – not really.

'We'll talk about this next time,' Rogers said in defiance. 'I'm not some bimbo intern you can boss around, Senator. With all due respect, of course.'

Wise dismissed him with a wave of the hand. 'I'll see what I can do,' he relented. 'Just get me results!'

'That's precisely what I'm doing, sir.'

'And send the bimbo back with your specimen, if he checks out.'

'You want Kira to return?'

'Isn't that what I just said?' asked Wise. 'Let me know the final outcome as soon as it is confirmed,' he added.

'That might be anytime, sir. It *is* very late. What if you're sleeping?'

The senator chuckled. 'I don't sleep, Rogers,' he replied. 'You should know that.'

As the screen went blank, Rogers swore out loud. 'You might not sleep,' he imagined telling Wise, 'but I bloody well do, you shrunken little shyster!'

32

Martha awoke with a start, nightmares fading into her subconscious. She was in one of the many spare rooms at the hotel. Faith and Prior were asleep on the floor, lying on blankets. They'd returned from the Haven three hours earlier, just as dawn broke over Fire City. Normally the women slept in their own room, but Prior had insisted on staying with them, worried about further repercussions. Neither woman had complained.

Martha left her makeshift bed and crept softly into the washroom. Once there, she stripped and used a cloth to wash herself with cold water. A cracked and stained mirror hung on one wall, throwing her reflection back at her. She avoided it and continued cleaning herself, wondering how long it would take Jonah and the others to return. Unwilling to face the bloodbath without Mace and Tyrell, she hoped it would be in time for the next Hunt. Jonah's plan worried her too, particularly when she'd realized that leaving would mean abandoning those who stayed to their fate. It felt wrong, yet she understood why such a move was their only option.

Once she was done in the bathroom, she dressed and made her way down to the bar. A couple of customers slept in a corner, having passed out at closing time. Prior had wanted to throw them out but Faith had told him to leave them alone; they were harmless enough and it wasn't the first time it had happened. The tables were a mess so Martha set about tidying up, clearing away glasses and wiping down. Faith joined her after a while, her face drawn and lined.

'Prior sounds bad,' Martha said to her as she fixed a pot of the brown dust that passed for coffee.

'I know,' Faith replied with a look of sadness. 'He's not going to last much longer.'

'He's better off here then,' Martha told her. 'He can't sleep out there any more.'

Although their lodgings were far from luxurious, the hotel still afforded a lifestyle of plenty compared to the slums on the edges of the city. That was where the majority of the population survived, without even basic amenities, living off scraps. Until a few weeks earlier, Prior had been out there too, unwilling to leave the shack he'd called home for over a decade. It had taken stern words from May to make him see sense.

'You OK?' she heard Faith ask.

'Yeah,' she replied. 'Just thinking about this plan.'

Faith jumped up and sat on the bar, crossing her legs and pushing her blonde hair back. The coffee maker slurped away on the worktop opposite her.

'Sounds crazy to me too,' she admitted. 'I just don't see how it's going to work.'

'I can't see most of the people coming with us anyway,' Martha commented.

'Prior said the same thing,' Faith told her.

'Jonah must have it worked out,' Martha thought aloud.

'Let's hope so, Martha,' Faith replied. 'He's an odd one, isn't he?'

Martha nodded. 'I can't work him out,' she said. 'There's something about him that . . .'

'Smells wrong?' offered Faith.

'Yeah, but not literally . . .'

Faith smiled. 'From what I've sensed, he smells rather enticing,' she said, her expression mischievous.

Martha blushed and agreed. 'Thank God!' she exclaimed. 'I thought it was just me.'

'Whenever I'm near him, I start to think very naughty thoughts,' revealed Faith.

'Faith!'

'A fine specimen but far too young for me,' said the older woman. 'I like my men with a little more . . .'

'Muscle?' teased Martha. 'Big, broad-shouldered men

who smell of sweat and liquor? Hmm . . . who do we know fitting that description?'

'You know you're not beyond a slapping, young lady,' warned Faith.

Martha giggled and started polishing the bar. A loud knocking made Faith start.

'That'll be the door, then,' said Martha. 'Way too early.'

Faith shrugged. 'Might as well let them in,' she replied. 'Not much else to do.'

As Martha walked to the entrance, cloth in hand, Faith heard Prior make his way downstairs, his wheeze growing stronger each day.

'Coffee?' she asked him, jumping down from the bar.

'That piss?' asked Prior, shaking his head. 'That ain't coffee, Faith. In my day . . .'

Across the city, close to where Valefor's legions were stationed, Aron raised his weary head and groaned. His clothes felt stiff with dirt and his stomach grumbled with hunger.

His shelter was a three-storey terrace, one that he'd checked for threats and then made his own. It was basic and it protected him from the elements, but not much more. His bed was a length of board raised on a single layer of bricks. A musty sofa had provided seat cushions for use as a mattress, and once past the smell of mildew

281

and grime, it was almost comfortable. He sat up and scratched his head, blinking in the fingers of light that filtered through the boarded windows. His bladder screamed for release and he made his way down to the ground floor, where he'd raised the floorboards and dug out a latrine. He relieved himself slowly, ignoring the flies that buzzed up around him and the pervasive stench. Finished, he walked back through two empty rooms and into the hallway.

He was about to head back upstairs when he noticed that the doorway, little more than a barricade, had been pushed open slightly. Sure that he'd secured it, his senses kicked into overdrive. Someone – or something – was in there with him, and they had to be upstairs, otherwise he'd have seen them already. He unsheathed his knife and took the steps slowly, wary of every angle of possible attack. When he reached the first landing, he crouched and waited, ready for anything. A minute passed before he moved on, heading towards the room he'd slept in. He entered slowly, wielding his weapon, and was greeted by a lazy, arrogant laugh.

'Nice place,' Stone said in a mocking tone.

Aron sighed and replaced his dagger. The mercenary intrigued and angered Aron in equal measure. He wondered what Stone's life was like. How he lived with what he did every day. 'What do you want?' he eventually asked, rubbing his face.

'You,' Stone told him. 'I want you.'

Aron walked to his bed, found his trousers and put them on. He wasn't about to stand there and talk to this guy with his tackle on show.

'This must have been some house once,' continued Stone. 'You know, back *then*.'

'Probably,' Aron replied. 'Why do you want me?'

Stone was standing by the window, hands in the pockets of his combats. He wore a black sweatshirt with two holsters strapped across each side, both holding guns. His eyes bored into Aron's face, unblinking as always.

'We can help each other,' he offered. 'You give me what I want, and I'll sort you out.'

Aron shook his head. 'Why would I want to work for you?' he asked. 'I hate people like you.'

Stone took his hands from his pockets, found a cigarette and silver lighter in another flap on his combats and lit up. He took a couple of drags, exhaling the smoke fully before responding. It swirled around his head in a blue-grey haze. 'You don't know who I am,' he parried.

'You're a collaborator,' Aron offered in rebuttal. 'A scumbag.'

'The world is more complicated than that,' Stone explained before taking another drag.

'You work for the demons,' Aron replied, watching

283

the smoke curl around Stone's cold features. 'That's all I need to know.'

Stone considered the boy and his surroundings before deciding to change tack. 'You hungry?' he asked.

Aron nodded. He'd been hungry for over a day and his head felt light. 'I've got some bread,' he added.

Stone smiled. 'A bit of mouldy crap, no doubt,' he scoffed. 'I've got steak and eggs, part of my ration. I'll make you some — in my room at the Mayor's mansion.'

'No thanks.'

'Just give me a couple of hours,' asked Stone. 'No more than that. Have some food, take a hot shower and consider my proposal. If you want to leave after that, you can.'

'What proposal?'

Stone dropped the half-smoked cigarette and clasped his hands together. 'It's simple really,' he told the boy. 'I know that you work with the Resistance. I know that because I've *seen* you. Now that leaves me with a dilemma, Aron. I could let Valefor have you or I could help you out. I don't like the first option, because you impress me. You're strong, smart and single-minded. So I'm choosing option two.'

Aron felt his opposition fading slightly. If Stone knew that he was a rebel, why wasn't he dead already? What was Stone waiting for?

'That's better,' Stone told him, seeing the change in Aron's face.

'I haven't agreed yet,' Aron reminded him.

'Ah,' Stone countered, 'but you will. Because it's either you or Martha . . .' He left his words hanging in the air; enjoying the confusion working its way around the boy's expression.

'But Martha isn't like me,' Aron blurted. 'She's nothing to do with—'

'*Yes. She. Is,*' Stone insisted. 'I've *seen* her, Aron. Either you play ball or I'll go and persuade Martha to help. And I won't be as tactful with her, Aron. I won't be as nice. In fact, I might have to hurt her, maybe try out that lithe body for myself. I'd enjoy that immensely.'

Aron clenched his fists and took a step forward, raising a sneer from the mercenary.

'Don't be stupid, son,' warned Stone. 'I could just kill you here and now, and then I'd still interrogate Martha. I'm offering you a chance, boy. A chance to leave your shitty life behind and become a soldier.'

Aron wanted to kill him, to beat him to death with the bricks that held up his bed. Only he knew that he wasn't strong enough, knew that he'd die before he reached Stone. He felt useless, impotent.

'No tears, Aron,' Stone mocked. 'You're not a baby. Life is about making decisions, son. And sometimes the decisions we make aren't nice. You need to learn that.

I like you, boy, and I want to help you. Leave all this shit behind and become someone. You can use the talents you have and live like a king. Now, are you coming or not?'

Aron shrugged and wondered what choice he had. Much of what Stone offered was enticing, particularly now that his so-called friends had ostracized him. And then there was Martha. There was *always* Martha. How could he let Stone hurt her?

'Yeah,' he mumbled. 'Yeah, I'm coming.'

'Good lad,' replied Stone, lighting another cigarette. 'You won't regret it.'

33

Mias waited until midday before arriving at one of the large factories in the industrial zone. He summoned the lead manager, a short, tubby man with round glasses and tufts of grey hair circling a balding pate.

The man's eyes lit up with fear when he saw who was waiting in his office. Damien Wilson was a company man, a paid-up member of the party that had taken control of the country alongside the demons. He had always followed orders, and worked in many of the smaller protected zones outside the main citadels. Not once had he complained about leaving his family behind, or having to oversee the Unwanted. He did as he was told, and had nothing to fear from Mias, but he was still afraid. The demon underlord before him had a brutal reputation.

'Bring me anyone who has missed a shift or been late this month,' Mias ordered. 'And hurry.'

'May I ask what this concerns, my lord?' asked Damien, trying not to shake.

'You may,' replied Mias. 'I'm in a good mood today. I'm looking for information about the Resistance.'

Damien nodded slowly. 'Why those who've missed days, then?' he enquired. 'Most of these wretched creatures have been ill at some point.'

Mias picked up a photo frame from the desk in front of him. He studied the woman and two girls it showed. 'Are these your women?' he asked the manager.

'Yes, sir.'

'They are not here?'

Damien's left leg twitched. 'No, my lord, they live in the south,' he replied.

'Are they considered attractive?' Mias continued, a cruel smile sweeping across his ape-like face.

'I think so,' said Damien.

'Would they be just as attractive if their eyeballs were cut out? If they were made to eat them, perhaps?'

The manager's right leg began to twitch too.

'I sense fear,' teased Mias. 'Do I scare you, human?'

Damien nodded, unable to speak. His tongue felt like a wedge of sodden cardboard in his mouth.

'Then why do you not obey me?' snapped Mias.

Damien shook his head. 'I'll do your bidding at once,' he spluttered.

Mias replaced the frame and passed wind, his eyes gleaming. 'Gather them downstairs, at the loading bay,' he replied. 'You have ten minutes.'

★ ★ ★

Exactly eight minutes later, Oscar stood facing a line of human soldiers in the factory warehouse with fifteen other workers, most of them men. Most of them Resistance fighters. One of them was Raj, who stood next to him. Unsure of their situation, the two whispered to each other.

'Everyone here is one of us,' Oscar pointed out.

Raj, who at six foot five towered over everyone in the room, turned and studied his colleagues. He saw that Oscar was right, and that meant only one thing.

'We've been rumbled,' he replied, trying not to let his anxiety show.

'Not necessarily,' answered Oscar. 'Could be something else.'

'What else *could* it be?' Raj countered, his deep brown eyes showing alarm. Creases lined his coffee complexion. 'We're in trouble.'

A short mercenary, his thick forearms covered in bright green and red tattoos, told them to shut up. Oscar turned to his left; saw a man called Marko standing next to him. A long scar bisected Marko's olive-skinned face; it led from just below his left cheekbone, across his nose, and almost reached his right ear. Oscar had been with him when he'd received the wound – the result of a fight with an angry patroller.

'What do we do?' Marko asked out of the corner of his mouth.

'Dunno,' Oscar murmured, trying to stay calm despite his fear. 'Just be on guard.'

The warehouse was at least three thousand square metres in size, with giant bay doors to one side. Opposite them, a mezzanine level reached by metal staircases on either side connected the loading area to the rest of the factory. Below this raised platform were smaller versions of the giant doors facing them. To each side of the room were rows of pallets, ten rows of them, five deep. Each pallet was loaded with boxes of clothing, the garments made by people who would never get to wear them. A door clanged open and Oscar looked up to see Mias walking down the steps from the mezzanine.

'Bollocks,' he exclaimed. Things were worse than he'd imagined if the underlord was involved. After his humiliation at Jonah's hands, he would be even more dangerous than usual.

The fur-covered demon loped along, his simian body taut with muscle. With him were a couple of patrollers, already drooling viscous yellow saliva; they towered over Wilson, the factory manager. They reached the soldiers and stood facing Oscar and the others. Raj shifted his weight from foot to foot, feeling apprehensive. The skin around Marko's left eye convulsed involuntarily.

Wilson addressed them. 'All of you have either missed days or shown up late,' he said. 'Lord Mias, therefore, would like to question you. As long as you comply with his demands, no harm will befall you. You have my word.'

Oscar hated Wilson's weasel tone, his often high-pitched words. The man was a disgrace, a worthless piece of crap.

'So listen up and tell the truth,' Wilson added. 'I *urge* you.'

Mias began to walk up and down the line, eyeing each of them in turn. When it came to Oscar's turn, he held the demon's gaze, unflinching, even though his heart was hammering against his ribcage. The demon repeated his inspection twice more before sidling to a stop in front of a wiry young man called Patrick, who drew back, his eyes wild with fear.

'You seem uneasy,' Mias sneered. 'Why are you so nervous, human?'

Oscar shook with silent rage as Patrick began to shake his head, his hands trembling. 'N-n-no reason,' the young man stammered in reply.

Mias nodded and turned to the only woman, Emily. She was a little older than Oscar, around twenty, with wide blue eyes and a pale, freckled face. Her flame-coloured hair was knotted on top of her head. She was Raj's girlfriend and Oscar knew that his tall friend was seething. Unlike Patrick, Emily didn't shy away, keeping her gaze steady.

'Tell me about the Resistance,' ordered Mias.

Emily shook her head. 'Can't tell you anything,' she lied. 'All I do is work here, sir.'

'Then why have you missed so many days?' asked the demon.

'Children,' said Emily, thinking fast, trying to invent a family in her mind. She settled on her own childhood, reimagining her now-deceased siblings as her own brood.

'You have young?' probed Mias, unconvinced.

Both Oscar and Raj took deep breaths, praying that Emily's deflection would work. 'If that hairy bastard touches her . . .' Raj whispered to Oscar.

'*Silence!*' screamed the tattooed mercenary, causing Mias to spring round.

'Who speaks?' he demanded. The soldier pointed to Raj, and Mias strode over at once. 'You dare to interrupt me?' he spat.

Raj kept his eyes forward, looking at some spot several centimetres above the demon's head. Oscar clenched and unclenched his fists. 'No, sir,' replied Raj. 'I merely wish to back my woman's assertion.'

Mias looked back to Emily, then returned to Raj. 'She is your woman?'

'Yes, sir,' said Raj.

'And you have young?'

'We do, my lord,' he replied, backing Emily's story. 'There are two of them, very young, and both have suffered sickness.'

Mias stepped back a touch, and considered Raj's answer. He turned to Wilson. 'Is this the truth?'

'I don't know,' Wilson admitted. 'I have no idea what these people do outside this factory and I don't care.'

Mias picked a bug from his fur and ate it. His eyes were the colour of strawberry skin and held a fair share of intelligence. However, that acumen was wrapped in a blanket of homicidal intent. 'I seek a stranger,' he shouted, now addressing the entire room. 'A man who arrived in your city recently. You may have seen him outside the hotel, engaged in battle with me. You may have heard whispers of his whereabouts. *I want this man.*'

When no one replied, Mias casually sauntered back towards Emily. He stood before her, barely an inch separating their faces. His breath was fetid, like stagnant pond water. Emily fought back a wave of nausea, her cheeks taking on colour. Mias sneered at her discomfort and stepped back.

'I shall return in two days,' the demon said. 'And then you shall tell me the truth. I do not care about your Resistance activities. Your rebellion is no worse than the fleas that live on my fur. I tolerate them because I can

293

remove them at will. You are the same. I seek only this stranger.'

Again there was silence. Oscar exchanged alarmed glances with Raj as Mias sighed and took another backward step. His left arm arced through the air, fingers grabbing Patrick's thin neck. Emily gasped as the demon threw Patrick across the room with ease. A loud crack sickened them all as Patrick's back smacked against one of the pallets, his spine snapping. He hit the floor, and lay unmoving, his eyes still wide with terror.

Mias leaped across to him, straddled his torso. Emily and Oscar turned away, aware of what was coming. The demon clenched his hands together, raised them above his head and then brought them crashing down into Patrick's face, over and over, his arms just a blur. Skin, then layers of subcutaneous fat, and finally bone, split, ripped and cracked apart. Blood pooled underneath the human. Mias' fur grew slick with it, his eyes narrow as he howled in lust.

Next to Raj, an older man puked chunks of bread and nettle soup. Another collapsed, clutching his chest. A third ran for the doors, until a single bullet stopped him dead. Raj darted over to Emily and took her in his arms, shielding her from potential harm.

Oscar glanced over at Wilson. A dark stain had appeared across the manager's trousers, and a puddle of urine surrounded his feet. His face was raspberry-coloured. The soldiers stood impassively, however, as though such incidents meant nothing to them. Oscar felt enraged, and longed to fight, but a survival instinct, honed during countless Hunts, kicked in.

Mias, once sated, rose to his feet and wiped his mouth free of flesh and bone fragments. He roared, gathering the attention of everyone in the warehouse. His eyes had turned from strawberry to a deep ruby.

'Two days,' he warned again. 'If no one speaks of this stranger, I will obliterate five more of you. I will not rest until I have my quarry – or your entire workforce has perished. You have my word . . .'

34

Jonah drove the jeep round a collapsed road bridge, the big, heavy tyres crunching effortlessly over the concrete debris. He'd taken over the driving half an hour earlier, as dawn had turned to morning and tiredness hit Mace full on. The road had widened a few kilometres earlier into a dual carriageway, complete with a wide central reservation.

The only incident after the village had involved a pack of wolves tearing at the flesh of a deer. Jonah had skirted the pack easily in the vehicle, avoiding any conflict. However, the going was slow, the road cratered with holes and strewn with abandoned vehicles.

Mace remembered the route from his childhood, when his parents had taken the family to an adventure park. He wondered what had become of the water slides, rides and stalls since the War, smiling as he recalled hurtling round the tracks of a roller coaster, clinging to his father in excitement. The world had changed so completely that such memories seemed like fantasies now. Mace sometimes wondered if they had ever occurred at all. He would have given anything to be able to take his own children to such places.

'There's a turn-off up ahead, leading to the compound,' Jonah told him as the wind whipped past their ears. 'The track is about one and a half kilometres long, but we can't just drive up to the gates. We'll have to leave the jeep in the surrounding woods and approach on foot.'

'You seem to know it well,' Mace commented.

Jonah nodded. 'I checked it out on my way down to Fire City. It's surrounded by forest on three sides, and there is no demon protection over it. The only danger is the army — there are at least thirty soldiers guarding the place.'

Mace shook his head. 'Well, that'll be simple, then,' he remarked.

'We'll get close and then trek through the trees.'

'What about the wolves?' Mace asked, sounding tired. Jonah looked at the giant and asked if he needed to rest. Mace nodded. 'I'm out on my feet, so to speak,' he admitted.

'OK,' Jonah told him, pulling off the road onto the track. 'Let's get closer and then we'll rest for a while. It might be better to wait until tonight anyway. Darkness will provide the best cover.'

'I only need a nap,' Mace protested. 'We can't wait too long, if what you've told me is true. We have to get to Tyrell.'

Jonah had explained the role of round-up zones to him earlier, making the older man anxious. They had to rescue Tyrell before he was killed or carted off to become prey. Mace knew that he really needed longer to recuperate, but it was a luxury they couldn't afford.

'We'll see,' replied Jonah as they bumped down the gravel track, surrounded by woodland.

About seven hundred metres along, Jonah drove between two ash trees that dwarfed a thick knot of smaller common alders. The ground was moist and rich here, and the tyres threw up clumps of earth as they tracked through the undergrowth. Thirty metres in, Jonah stopped and turned off the engine. He jumped down and asked Mace for one of his machetes.

'We need to cut some branches,' he explained without being prompted. 'To camouflage the jeep.'

Mace drew both weapons and handed one over. Then he copied Jonah, cutting at the point where the thinner branches sprouted from the thicker ones. Thanks to the canopy of taller trees, smaller shrubs such as dogwood and elderberry received only partial sunlight, which meant that they stayed relatively small. Their branches were thick with leaves and easy to cut, and very quickly Mace and Jonah had concealed the vehicle.

'We'll crawl in too,' said Jonah. 'Get some rest.'

Mace went first, his large frame disturbing their

work. Jonah rearranged the cover behind them, until they were seated.

'Give me an hour,' Mace ordered. 'And if anything happens before then, wake me up.'

'Agreed,' Jonah replied.

'And just one thing more,' Mace added. Jonah looked at him and raised his eyebrows. 'If you're half-demon,' began Mace, 'why do you hate the others so much?'

Jonah looked away. 'Because I prefer the human part,' he parried. 'And so did my mother.'

'Your mother?' Mace queried, failing to understand.

'My mother was a pure breed,' explained Jonah. 'She was a true ancient, but from a different branch to Valefor and the others. She left their dimension to live with my father. The demon lords didn't approve.'

Mace screwed up his face, wondering whether the young man was messing with him. It sounded pre-posterous. 'What happened to her?' he asked.

Jonah shook his head slowly. 'They killed her,' he admitted. 'The Lords destroyed my whole family.'

'So you're no different to us, then?' Mace replied.

'No,' agreed Jonah. 'I'm as Unwanted as the rest of you. More so, maybe.'

Mace wondered whether to be honest with the boy. His heritage could cause some serious problems, handled incorrectly. Like Mace, most of the people he knew hated demons with a passion that bordered on rage. 'You know,' he said honestly, 'that many humans won't accept you.'

'I understand,' replied Jonah. 'Which is why I don't tell them what I am.'

'But you've told me.'

Jonah looked into Mace's eyes, and for the first time the giant saw fear in the boy. Fear and something akin to respect too. 'I felt I could trust you,' Jonah pleaded as much as stated. 'You have seen that I'm no threat to you. In fact, my skills are useful.'

'Very true,' admitted Mace. 'But you could easily turn against us.'

'Why would I do that?' asked Jonah. 'Why would I risk my own being to help you, only to betray you later?'

Mace shrugged. 'You've a point there,' he said. 'Now shut up and let me sleep.'

Two hours later, they were hiding by the razor and barbed-wire fence that surrounded the complex, obscured by a large thicket of nettles and bramble. Close by, foxes had burrowed a hole underneath the perimeter. Thirty metres ahead of them stood a line of wooden huts. Each of the five cabins was eight metres wide and thirty long, with a door at either end. According to Jonah they housed the sleeping quarters, mess halls and sanitation blocks for the soldiers.

'The foxes scavenge for food,' Jonah told Mace. 'It's the way I got in last time.'

'Why did you get so close?' asked Mace.

'I wanted to observe the camp,' Jonah replied. 'I needed food and weapons.'

Mace saw that his explanation made sense and nodded.

'They guard the perimeter,' Jonah continued. 'Five patrols, with two men in each. We'll wait until the next time they pass and then go in. The prisoner huts are over near the front but there's cover all the way. If Tyrell is still here, we'll find him.'

Mace indicated a guard tower, fifty metres to their left. 'What about that?'

'There's no one up there,' Jonah told him.

Mace smiled. 'Could be a midget?' he joked.

Jonah's expression remained the same as he pointed to their left. 'Patrol coming,' he warned. 'Stay hidden.'

'How can you know that?' asked Mace.

'Humans smell,' Jonah told him.

Mace was about to reply when he spotted the guards. Two soldiers, young-looking and carrying sub-automatic guns, strolled past casually. One of them was telling the other about a woman and Mace grinned at the boastful nature of the story.

Jonah waited until they were gone before beckoning Mace. He pointed to the foxhole. 'Quick,' he whispered.

Mace followed Jonah's lead as they scrambled to the hole. The entrance was tight but they managed to get through, and a few moments later they emerged inside the fence.

'The first hut,' said Jonah.

Mace nodded and they set off at a sprint. Once in place, next to the rear exit, Mace took a breather, watching out for any movement. Jonah crept up to the door and opened it a little.

'Empty,' he told Mace. 'Come on.'

Inside, Mace counted twenty beds, ten against each wall. Between them were metal cupboards, one chair per cot and shared side tables with lamps. At the far end was the second door, and beyond that the rest of the compound. Jonah led Mace to the next exit and stopped at a map pinned to the wooden wall.

'Plan of the complex,' he said, pointing out their position and then moving his finger to the west. 'And this is where they house the prisoners.'

'There's a lot of buildings between us and Tyrell,' Mace replied. 'And once we get him, we have to get back to the foxhole.'

Jonah shook his head. 'We won't be going back that way,' he revealed.

'So how are we going to get out?' asked a confused Mace.

'We're going to steal a truck,' Jonah told him. 'We'll

need one to transport the weapons back to Fire City anyway. Make up some time on the way back.'

'But stealing a truck might alert the army.'

'Yes,' said Jonah. 'It will.'

Mace gave his companion a look. 'And that's a good thing because . . . ?'

'Because,' explained Jonah, 'we're going to paralyse this compound before we leave. They won't be able to come after us. At least, not these soldiers.'

'Oh,' said Mace. 'The *easy* option . . .'

35

As Jonah and Mace prepared to rescue him, Tyrell was being blasted with a taser stun gun, bound and gagged. His head lolled to one side and drool ran down his chin.

Dr Rogers motioned Boyd forward, telling him to be careful. 'He is top priority,' the doctor advised. 'Senator Wise wants him to arrive in one piece. And Senator Wise likes to have his own way, as I'm sure you know.'

'I can't guarantee that,' Boyd replied, staring down at their captive. 'He's a big lad. Suppose he wakes up and causes a fuss?'

'Then you taser him again,' said Rogers.

Behind them, Kira Hamley showed concern.

'Is there really any need for this?' she asked, her voice faltering slightly.

She'd seen Boyd at work as they'd travelled the wastelands, looking for specimens. Research subjects, Senator Wise had explained to her, when he'd given her the job. The government wanted a study of any diseases affecting the Unwanted population, he had added. It was a top priority, so that they could help the wretched souls. As a research student, hoping to learn about disease, Kira had been asked to find people suitable for study – the suffering *and* the healthy.

With no idea what the research would entail, she had merely been collecting. However, she'd soon realized that her role was a smokescreen. Whatever Wise and his team wanted from the people she had been tasked to find, it wasn't about helping them fight illness. Otherwise they'd be collecting only the sick. No, something else was happening, something that she didn't fully understand and didn't like.

'Do *you* want to deliver him?' Boyd sneered. 'Should be a piece of cake. I mean he's only three times your size.'

'There's no need for sarcasm,' she snapped back. 'I understand that your primary mode of response is violence, but some of us *exhibit* the thought processes that separate us from animals.'

'La-la-la,' said Boyd. 'You keep your higher being, love. Me, I'll just do the grunt work and keep the wolves from the door.'

'Enough,' said Dr Rogers. 'Both of you get on with your tasks.'

Kira looked at the syringe in her left hand; it was filled with enough tranquillizer to knock out a rhino.

She stepped towards the teenager, ignoring the way Boyd invaded her personal space.

'This is nembutal,' she told him. 'Normally it's a sleep-inducing medicine but this is a stronger concentration. It's a barbiturate so its effects won't last too long, but it will pacify him.'

Boyd looked at Dr Rogers and sniggered. 'Thanks for the science lesson, darling,' he replied. 'Just inject him, will you?'

Kira found a vein in the boy's left arm and injected the drug. Withdrawing the needle gently, she wiped the tiny hole with an alcohol swab.

Boyd started to laugh. 'He's from the wastelands,' the soldier reminded her. 'He doesn't change his clothes, he probably craps in an alley and you're worried about him getting an *infection*? Sweetheart, you are one liberal cry-baby.'

Kira ignored his jibes and turned to her medical colleague. 'He needs to be monitored,' she told Rogers.

'Sleep apnoea as a side-effect,' replied her immediate boss. 'Yes, I know. I *did* train for medicine too, Kira.'

'If he stops breathing and no one notices,' Kira continued, 'he'll die. And that will upset the senator.'

Rogers' smile was false and unkind. 'Which is why you'll be going with them,' he told her, enjoying the surprise that exploded across her features.

'But I've got my orders from Senator Wise,' said Kira.

'And I've had new instructions,' Dr Rogers replied. 'Besides, you'll enjoy the trip. You can watch over your subject and enjoy the company of Boyd and his men at the same time.'

Boyd smiled. 'We'll have *so* much fun,' he said.

Kira swore at him and turned away, her face red.

'Get him out of here,' Rogers told Boyd. 'You leave in ten minutes.'

'On my way,' Boyd answered.

'Can you be packed in that time?' Rogers asked Kira.

'I suppose,' she replied. She thanked the stars that she'd remembered to bring her gun, a Ruger semi-automatic pistol. If Boyd stepped out of line, she'd need it. She left the prisoners' quarters and went to pack.

Behind her, Boyd and Rogers exchanged amused glances. 'We should leave her in the wild for a few days,' said Boyd. 'That would sort her out.'

'I agree,' Rogers told him. 'But Senator Wise admires her.'

Boyd grinned. 'By admire, you mean he wants to get his end away?'

Dr Rogers shrugged. 'Quite possibly,' he replied.

Several beds away, Negus watched as Boyd called for some men. Three more soldiers, one pushing a gurney, entered the cabin, their big boots thudding against the floorboards. Together they shifted Tyrell to the wheeled trolley and rolled him out of the hut.

Dr Rogers looked around at the other prisoners, and then he left too. The two guards that remained locked the door behind him, waited a few minutes and then returned to their game of poker.

Negus felt bad about not helping the young man, but what could he have done? The world they inhabited was ugly and forced moral dilemmas upon you. You accepted that and survived, or you fought against it and died. He turned and faced the opposite direction, his eyes meeting those of Jodie. She blinked once, her face ashen, and started to cry. Negus nodded, unsure of what to do. He thought back to his previous escapes, and concentrated instead on his next move. If he could manage it, he would honour Tyrell's promise and take the girl with him. He owed the young man that much.

Mace whistled in amazement as he considered the weapons store. They'd broken in a few seconds earlier, after edging their way past several soldiers and into the heart of the complex. Jonah moved with ease, seeming to know every inch, and once at the armoury he'd removed a panel of pre-cut wood, replacing it after they'd gone through. Now, as they stood in the half-light of the armaments room, Jonah outlined his plan in a whisper. The doors were manned and any loud noise would alert the guards. He pointed at the plastic explosives, and the boxes of grenades.

'You've been in here before,' said Mace.

Jonah nodded. 'I took some weapons last time, I told you. Cut out that access panel we've just used.'

'You'd think they would notice,' said Mace.

'Why?' Jonah asked. 'It's the last thing they'd expect.'

'So what now, then, o wise one?'

Jonah pointed at some explosives. 'We'll use the Semtex,' he explained. 'Wire the sleeping quarters and blow them up.'

'Causing a diversion,' said Mace. 'Yeah, that might work. For a teenager, you're pretty impressive.'

'It *will* work,' Jonah insisted, ignoring Mace's remark about his knowledge. 'But we need to move things into place first.'

'What things?'

'We need to find a truck, load up some of these weapons and leave it near the front of the compound.'

Mace looked puzzled. 'How are we gonna do that?'

'By joining the army,' replied Jonah, pulling out his long knife and picking up a live grenade. He walked carefully to the doors and put an ear to them. A few moments later, he opened one of them slightly and rolled the grenade through the gap without pulling its pin.

'What the hell!' he heard one of the guards exclaim. Jonah stepped aside as the doors flew open and both soldiers stepped in, machine guns trained on Mace.

'Hello, lads,' said Mace, praying that they wouldn't shoot him. Fat chance.

Jonah moved fast, slicing the throats of both guards before they could react. Mace felt dizzy watching him, and wondered whether he was dreaming it all. Would he wake up in the Haven soon, scratching his head? The thud of corpses falling to the floor told him no. He stepped across the bodies, and shut the door. Jonah crouched and placed each soldier on his side, pushing back each head and opening the already wide wounds further. Mace asked what he was doing.

'Diverting the blood flow away from their uniforms. Get changed,' the younger boy ordered. 'Quick!'

Mace looked at the dead men, and sighed. How had he ended up taking orders from someone who could have been his child? 'They're both too small,' he pointed out, trying to reassert a little authority.

'No time for that,' Jonah hurriedly replied. 'Make do. We need to get outside before the guards are missed.'

'Are you sure this is a plan?' Mace asked as he stripped the bigger guard. 'Only you seem to be improvising. Good plans tend to be controlled and thought out in advance. Just saying . . .'

Jonah nodded. 'A good soldier can adapt to ever-changing situations,' he said, sounding like a recruitment officer. The sort of officer Mace had once trained under. It was hard to fault Jonah's logic.

'OK then, soldier,' said the giant as he squeezed himself into a pair of camouflage combats, 'let's adapt.'

36

Stone kept a second room in the Mayor's mansion. It was nothing special, save for the en-suite bathroom and the giant, luxury bed. In fact, Stone disliked the comforts. He'd been a soldier for over thirty years, fighting battles in several parts of the world and then serving his country during the War. Luxuries made people weak, according to Stone, and caused them to want too much. That was why he preferred life outside the citadels, in amongst the misery and destruction of the Unwanted. It felt real, and as close to war as he could get. Stone missed fighting like some people missed their dead parents. Being a soldier was his only need in life – nothing else mattered.

He stood outside his room with two of his mercenaries, waiting for Aron to finish cleaning himself up. The boy had already wolfed down two steaks and six scrambled eggs. From the stink he carried, Stone doubted whether Aron had taken a proper shower in weeks. A maid, one of several servants the Mayor kept, had done as instructed and laid out fresh clothes too – brand-new army-issue fatigues from the central stock kept at the mansion. Stone had picked them out himself, enjoying the process. A simple grey vest, grey jersey boxer shorts, an olive-green, long-sleeved top, camouflage combats and heavy black boots. The final piece, a flak jacket that matched the trousers, finished the ensemble, and would turn the rebel boy into a carbon copy of Stone himself. For a second, Stone felt a strange sensation, an almost paternal feeling of pride, but he shook the emotion away and lit a cigarette.

'Something funny, boss?' asked one of the soldiers.

Stone, who hadn't realized he was smiling, shook his head. 'Just thinking,' he replied.

'What's the plan?' added the other, scratching his grey stubble.

'Talk to the boy,' Stone explained. 'The Resistance have a hideaway, somewhere that the demons can't sense, and I'm going to find out where it is.'

'And then we attack?' the first soldier almost begged. 'I could use some action.'

Stone smiled with intent this time. 'No, brother,' he replied. 'We tell the demons and *they* attack. Our mission is more subtle.'

'Man, that ain't no fun!' the man moaned, flexing a tattoo-covered bicep.

'Don't worry,' Stone told him. 'There'll be plenty of combat soon enough.'

'Better be. I'm tired of this babysitting gig. I'm too old to hold hands with some soft pussy 'cause he's too scared to cross the street.'

'Patience,' said Stone. 'We've got too much experience to fight without reason. That's what those other troops are for.'

The impatient soldier looked at Stone and shrugged. 'Guess so,' he agreed.

The door opened and Aron stepped into the hallway, dressed in his new attire.

Stone grinned, ruffling the boy's freshly washed hair. 'That's better, isn't it,' he said.

Aron pushed his hand away. 'What next?' he asked, his eyes looking from one soldier to the other. 'And who are they?'

'My men,' revealed Stone, before making the introductions.

'You look like a proper soldier now,' the impatient one told Aron. 'One of us.'

Stone agreed. 'You see, Aron,' he explained, 'we're not regular army.'

'I know,' said the boy. 'You're mercenaries. You go where the money is.'

Stone shook his head. 'Not quite,' he said. 'We still work for the government but we don't report to the normal army command. No, our little unit is self-contained, just me, these two, and you – if you want it.'

Aron looked away and shrugged. 'Depends,' he said. 'I'm no collaborator.'

'Which is exactly why I brought you here. My orders come directly from someone high up in the government. Someone with more power than you can imagine. The world is changing, and we're going to be the architects. I told you earlier, you need to stop seeing absolutes, Aron.'

'I don't understand,' Aron admitted.

'Don't worry,' Stone told him, 'you will.'

'And my being here,' continued the boy, 'that will mean Martha and the others are left alone?'

Stone shook his head. 'No, Aron,' he replied. 'They'll join us too. Just trust me . . .'

He turned and led Aron along the passage, past room after room until a small stairwell appeared at the far end. They descended to the ground floor, and then again down into a basement complex. Here the doors were made of steel and the walls were free of decoration and finery. It reminded Aron of the Haven, although judging by the footprint of the building they were beneath, it was smaller.

'This is the army command centre,' Stone explained. 'The troops patrol the city but the orders come from here. There are sleeping quarters, showers, food stores and weapons down here. All of it run from this place.'

'The Mayor,' Aron spat in disgust.

'Not him,' Stone told him. 'He's just a figurehead. I control what really happens.'

'Is that supposed to be impressive?' asked Aron.

'No,' replied Stone. 'It's just a fact. Again, stop the black/white thinking. The Mayor *looks* like he's in control, but not without someone else pulling the strings.'

Aron stopped at one of the many doors, pushing it open. Inside was rack after rack of tinned and packet food. His stomach began to grumble.

'You still hungry?'

'Yeah.'

'I'll get the kitchen to make you some hot dogs.'

Aron looked at Stone in revulsion. 'Why would I want to eat dog?' he asked, causing Stone to laugh out loud.

'It's not *actual* canine,' Stone revealed. 'Hot dogs are sausages in bread rolls . . .'

When Aron remained confused, Stone took him into the food store and grabbed a can of frankfurters from the racks. 'Here,' he said, handing the tin to Aron. 'Sausages.'

Aron studied the can, turning it round to look at the label.

'Can you read?' asked Stone, trying on his best look of concern.

'Mostly,' said Aron. 'Some of the elders taught us enough to get by.'

Stone put his arm round the boy's shoulder. 'That's all going to change from now,' he said gently. 'You join my unit, son, and you become my family. Ask the others about that. We look out for each other and no one messes with us. We're tighter than a nun's underpants.'

'What's a nun?' asked Aron.

Stone grinned. 'Never mind about that,' he said. 'I want you to speak to someone. Come on.'

He took Aron to a small room near the rear of the basement and sat him in front of a computer screen. He connected to the Net and called up his boss. Layer after layer of encryption kicked in until no bug on Earth could have snooped on the link. Aron's face glowed with awe as a face appeared on the screen, an old man with amber eyes and grey hair combed back on his head. The man smiled warmly – something, Aron realized, he hadn't encountered in a very long time.

'Is this the recruit you've told me about, Stone?' the man asked.

To Aron, the man's voice seemed to appear like magic. He looked around the room, searching for some form of amplification.

'Yes, sir, this is Aron.'

'Good afternoon, young man.'

Aron looked at Stone, unsure of himself.

'Just speak normally,' urged Stone. 'He can see and hear you too.'

'Hello,' Aron replied nervously, causing the old man's smile to widen.

'Don't be afraid, son,' the man told him. 'You may call me Brogan. I am a friend.'

Stone took out his mobile phone and began to fiddle with it. Aron asked him what it was but Brogan replied. 'It is a communication device, Aron. There'll be time enough to explain these things later. For now, I wish to set your mind at rest regarding your role in Stone's unit.'

'I haven't agreed to join yet,' Aron told him defiantly. 'I will not collaborate with demons.'

'That is exactly what I wanted to hear,' Brogan replied. 'None of us wish to cooperate with the Hell-kin.'

'So why are you?' asked Aron as his confusion began to grow. 'It's obvious that you work with them.'

Brogan nodded. 'Yes, it is,' he admitted. 'But that is only what the surface suggests. Dig a little deeper, my son, and you'll find another truth, a more profound understanding.'

'I don't understand,' said Aron. 'Stone keeps talking in riddles too. I'm not that clever. The only reason I'm here is so that my friends won't be hurt. I don't care what you do with me. I don't care about anything, not any more.'

Brogan's expression grew concerned. A tear formed

in the old man's left eye, one he wiped away quickly. Aron felt something changing inside. He wondered why Brogan, a man he'd never met, would shed a tear over his plight. Confusion clouded his mind as he thought about the world he knew; the absolute world that Stone had asked him to reconsider. Here was a collaborator, a man who seemed to be everything that Aron despised, yet he was warm and friendly and appeared concerned. He'd shown Aron more kindness than he'd felt in months.

'I am saddened to hear of your alienation,' Brogan told him. 'Let me explain the truth to you. Let me dig through the multi-faceted nature of the world around you and explain our mission.'

'What mission?'

'To rid ourselves of these demons,' revealed Brogan. 'Once and for all.'

Aron felt his mouth fall open. A shiver of emotion ran down his back.

'I see that my words have shocked you,' said Brogan.

Aron could do nothing but nod.

'We are planning a coup, Aron, one that will take time and effort. By working within the government, we have access to the highest levels of information, the best resources. Now we need to contact the Resistance out there, where you are. To fund them with arms and food, and everything else they will need. There is a wasp,

Aron, which lays its eggs inside a caterpillar. When the grubs hatch, they eat the caterpillar from the inside out. That is our aim, son. We are the wasps.'

'But Stone and the others . . . they've killed humans.'

Brogan shook his head slowly. 'A terrible thing, Aron,' he replied. 'Yet it cannot be helped. In order to remain hidden, our agents must behave like collaborators. This is where you must try to rationalize your reactions, son. We are talking about sacrificing some humans in order to save many others. Tell me, how many of your friends have been sacrificed?'

'Too many,' Aron told him sorrowfully. 'Far too many.'

'Yet the ends are justifiable, are they not?'

'I think so,' Aron replied. 'We either fight and die, or we cower and still get killed anyway. I'm no coward.'

'Precisely my point,' Brogan declared. 'Stone is willing to do whatever it takes to make contact with the Resistance, to explain the true nature of our plan. He is just like you.'

Aron began to shake his head vigorously. 'Wait a minute, that's not true,' he accused. 'Stone said he would hurt my friend, to get his information. He said he'd—'

'He'd hurt you too,' Brogan admitted. 'Don't you understand? This mission is more important than any of us, Aron. If you won't give us what we need, you will suffer. Nothing can stand in the way of our revolution.

320

Stone is willing to lay down his life to save the world. Are you prepared to do the same?'

Aron put his face in his hands, mesmerized by the conflicting thoughts and emotions that whirled around him like a typhoon. What was he supposed to do? Stone was hard to trust, but this? If the demons found out what was being said here, everyone involved would perish. Brogan, whoever he was, was taking a huge risk to explain things to him. Why would he do that if he weren't genuine?

'OK,' he eventually replied, looking up at the screen.

'So you'll help us to defeat them?'

'I will,' said Aron. 'I'll help you to bring them all down. Every last one.'

Brogan moved his face closer to the camera. 'I need you to be clear, Aron,' he replied. 'You'll help us to find your friends. To access their hideout?'

'Yes, I'll help you to find the Haven. I'll tell you how to reach them.'

'Good boy.'

'What happens now?' asked Aron.

'Now,' smiled Brogan, 'you get your reward. Anything your heart desires. You have joined us, my son. You are one of ours now.'

Aron nodded as Martha's face appeared in his mind. He wished she could see him now, at the centre of things, helping them all, *really* helping. Not like Jonah, who let so many die without any benefit. Brogan's words were honest and real. His mission was better, more astute, and would truly help the Resistance. And he, Aron, would be the hero, bringing genuine hope to his friends. That would show them his true worth. That would make them see their mistakes. That would make Martha understand that she really *did* love him.

'I only want one thing,' he told Brogan.

'Ask.'

'There's a stranger with them, Jonah. I want him dead.'

Brogan smiled. 'We know,' he said. 'We don't trust him either. He is not what he seems.'

'How so?' Aron asked him.

'Jonah is a spy. He's a special operations soldier, trained by and working for the government. That's how we know of him. We've been tracking him for months.'

'I knew it!' cried Aron. 'I knew something was wrong with him!'

'So it is imperative that you help, my son, and quickly. Your friends are in grave danger. This Jonah, or whatever he's calling himself, is a cold-blooded killer.'

Aron's eyes glazed over with anger and his heart began to pound. He had been right about Jonah all along, and now he would make them see.

All of them . . .

37

The guard seemed dazed as he walked towards them. Mace turned to Jonah, saw that his eyes were closed. Words poured from his mouth in some strange, guttural language that Mace didn't recognize. The soldier, tall and athletically built, knelt before them, his head bowed, weapon placed at Jonah's feet.

'You called?' he droned.

'Enemies have infiltrated the complex,' Jonah told him. 'You must take your platoon and engage them.'

'Yes, sir.'

'They hide in the sleeping quarters. Wait ten minutes and then sound the alarm. Is this clear?'

'Absolutely.'

'Then go,' Jonah commanded.

The soldier stood and shook his head, and then, as if neither Jonah nor Mace were there, he pushed past them.

'What the *hell* was that?' asked Mace, eyeing his companion.

Jonah took a deep breath and then exhaled. He pinched the bridge of his nose with thumb and fore-finger. 'Mind control is something demons can achieve,' he explained. 'My mother taught me how.'

'So that guard will obey you?'

'Yes,' replied Jonah.

Mace wondered why Jonah didn't apply his powers to the entire camp, if that was the case.

'If I were fully demon,' said Jonah, 'I could.'

'Mind-reading too,' said Mace. 'Excellent.'

Jonah shrugged. 'I don't read minds as a rule. It's something that I shut off, most of the time.'

'*Most* of the time?' replied Mace. 'Great. So when *do* you read them?'

'In combat situations,' Jonah admitted. 'Helps me to keep one step ahead.'

'What about when we were chatting earlier?'

'Not then,' said Jonah. 'That would be intrusive.'

'But if you wanted to . . . ?'

Jonah nodded.

'This gets better and better,' said Mace. 'Maybe I should wrap my head in tin foil, stop you spying on my thoughts.'

'I didn't *choose* to be this way,' the other boy parried. 'But I *did* choose to join the human fight.'

'Are you asking me to give you a break?'

'Yes,' Jonah told him. 'I know you want more

answers, and once we've finished here and got Tyrell I'll tell you everything. Right now, we've got ten minutes.'

'How do you know Tyrell is even here?'

'I don't,' said Jonah. 'But his scent is here. Faint but here all the same.'

'His *scent*?'

'Later, Mace. We need to get moving.'

Mace fingered the sonic trigger in his pocket and considered how much plastic explosive they'd used to wire the compound. He wanted to be a long way away when the detonators hit home. Only there was no chance of that, as Jonah had explained. The sonic transmitter only worked within a fifty-metre radius. Nowhere near distant enough for comfort.

They'd spent the last twenty minutes finding and taking a truck, meeting surprisingly little resistance along the way. The only challenge had come from a bored young man with a crooked nose and acne-encrusted skin. Jonah had played his part well, persuading the boy to relinquish his truck and actually help them to load up too. The poor sod was with the angels now, his neck snapped by Mace's hand. Another collaborator gone, thought the giant, unconcerned. Given the chance, he'd kill every turncoat in the complex.

'OK, start it up and drive us to the front gates,' said Jonah. 'And let me have the trigger.'

'Why should you have it?' asked Mace. 'I'm happy to use it.'

Jonah shook his head. 'I'm faster than you,' he pointed out. 'Once we're ready, you engage the prison guards and find Tyrell. I'll go back and detonate the explosives. Then you drive through the gates and keep going. I'll catch you up.'

Mace shrugged and agreed. 'You're the demon,' he joked, handing the detonator over.

The truck rattled as the engine kicked into life but, again, no one paid attention. A patrol passed the wind-screen and Mace gave them the thumbs-up. Both guards nodded a reply, smiled and went about their business.

'These uniforms really work,' said Mace.

'Why wouldn't they?' asked Jonah. 'Hurry up.'

Mace drove slowly between two smaller huts and out into an open zone at the very heart of the complex. Several other vehicles sat in a line in the centre of the clearing. Next to one of them were wooden crates stamped with numerical codes. Jonah pointed to them.

'Food,' he said. 'Tinned stuff, probably, ready for transport. This is more than just a round-up camp, it's a supply base too.'

'Who does it supply?' asked Mace.

'Smaller units dotted about the wastelands,' Jonah told him.

'Be a good place to blow up, then,' said Mace.

'It'll certainly bother them,' replied Jonah. 'See that path? It leads to the front gates. Park up over there.' He pointed out the gravel track, and then the prisoners' hut to the left. 'That's where they'll have Tyrell,' he added unnecessarily.

Mace followed his instructions, coming to a halt within sight of the main entrance. Two guard stations stood on either side of the gates, one of them manned. Both soldiers drew their weapons and approached.

'Think you should handle this,' said Mace. 'My trousers are too short.'

Jonah jumped out of the cab and smiled at the guards. Mace listened through the open window.

'Never seen you before,' one of the guards said to Jonah. Both soldiers looked tense.

'I'm new,' Jonah replied. 'Came in with the prisoners.'

'With Boyd?'

'Yeah,' lied Jonah. 'It's my first time out of the citadels. Got any tips?'

The guards seemed to relax at that and lowered their guns. One of them, about five feet four with a shaved head, shrugged.

'Stay away from the cannibals and don't drink the water,' he offered, showing Jonah his left hand, which was missing the two smallest fingers. 'Got them tore off,' the soldier told him. 'Saw a cat, thought it was cute. My mother has three of them, lovely little things.'

'Private Dick-for-a-brain here tried to pick it up,' said the other one, who was much taller and wore a beige bandana round his long brown hair. All three of them laughed.

'And don't forget about the girls either,' said the first. 'No one cares about them out here. If you see one you like, just take her. Boyd encourages it.'

Jonah smiled again. 'Sounds like fun,' he told them. 'We're transporting later, down towards the southeast. Like I said, we've only just arrived. How many units we got out there?'

The one in the bandana shrugged. 'Five maybe? Never more than that.'

'Thanks,' replied Jonah. 'I wouldn't want to run out of supplies.'

'What did you say your name was again?' asked the first.

'I didn't,' said Jonah. 'I'm Williams . . .'

'Barton,' the short one revealed, holding out his hand. 'This lump with me is Savage.'

They exchanged a few more pleasantries, killing five minutes before Jonah rejoined Mace.

'Nice and friendly,' said Mace. 'Unless you're a girl.'

Jonah ignored him and directed his attention to the prisoners' hut. Heat signatures told him how many soldiers protected it. 'Two guards at the door,' he said.

'Two more inside and maybe eight or ten prisoners. Can you handle it?'

Mace grinned. 'Diplomacy or the gun?' he asked.

'The gun,' Jonah told him. 'It'll be faster . . .'

Suddenly the camp's sirens sounded an alarm. A deep voice crackled from loudspeakers attached to posts around the complex: 'INTRUDER ALERT. ALL PERSONNEL REPORT TO REAR OF COMPLEX. BE ADVISED THIS IS NOT A DRILL. NOT A DRILL. ENGAGE ENEMY ON SIGHT, WEAPONS LIVE. WEAPONS LIVE.'

Savage and Barton responded immediately. Jonah jumped from the cab. 'Do I cover your post?' he asked Savage.

'Yeah!' Savage shouted back. 'You cover the gates. Anyone tries anything, kill them. Got it?'

Jonah nodded. As the soldiers disappeared between the buildings, Mace joined him.

'Your mind-control thing works, then,' he said.

'Let's go!' said Jonah, ignoring his remark.

They walked briskly over to the prisoner hut, weapons drawn. Both guards reacted with alarm, fingering their guns.

'Security breach,' Jonah told them. 'Everyone still inside?'

'Yeah,' said one of the guards, 'but who are you?'

'Your dad,' replied Mace, shooting him through the forehead.

The second guard barely registered before Mace shot him too.

'That was too easy,' he said, shaking his head at the soldiers' stupidity.

'No time for jokes,' replied Jonah. 'Finish up. I'm going to blow the detonators.'

Mace watched him sprint away before kicking the wooden doors open. A bullet smacked against the frame, splintering the wood, and Mace hit the deck, rolling into the building. He got to one knee, saw the shooter ten metres ahead, peeking out from behind a bed, and took aim. The soldier poked his head out again and then again. The fourth time Mace fired, and took him down.

'Like I said, easy,' Mace twittered as he walked towards the prisoners, most of them either screaming with fright or sitting in shocked silence. Another bullet whizzed past his right ear, the gunman by the rear exit, using a toilet block for cover. Mace cursed, crouched and ran between two beds, where a black man with hair twisted into clumps was hiding. He smiled at the giant.

'Need help?' he asked.

Mace shook his head, stood and fired a covering shot. It missed completely, twanging instead against a metal cabinet. Mace scanned the room quickly but failed to see Tyrell. He looked again, giving the soldier enough time to fire back. This time the shot grazed Mace's left shoulder. He dropped to his knees and groaned.

'Give me the gun!' shouted the black man. 'Come on!'

Mace shrugged and handed over the pistol. The man rolled under one of the beds and crawled towards the toilet. Mace rubbed his shoulder and pulled out a second gun. He stood and fired again, before ducking. The soldier stepped out, aimed towards him and returned fire. The man with the strange hair saw his opening and planted two bullets into the soldier's torso. The first one ripped through his groin and into his stomach. He dropped to his knees. The second bullet entered his right ear and crashed around inside his cranium. By the time his face smacked against the floor he was dead.

The black man stood and walked back to Mace. 'My name's Negus,' he said to the giant. 'I'm Resistance.'

Mace ignored niceties. 'Tyrell – have you seen him?' he demanded. 'Big black guy with a shaven head, picked up a few hours ago.'

Negus shook his head. 'They moved him earlier, took him south.'

'*Where?*'

'I don't know,' Negus admitted. 'There was a soldier with him – a man called Boyd, and a female medic.'

'*Shit!*'

'Have you got transport?'

Mace nodded.

'Come on, then,' said Negus. 'Help me get these people out of here.'

Mace snapped out of his frustration and urged everyone out of the room. A couple of prisoners, too sick to move, refused. Mace started to lift one of them, but Negus made him reconsider.

'No time!' he urged. 'If they want to stay, leave them!'

All of a sudden the ground shook violently beneath their feet. Every plank of wood used to construct the hut vibrated.

'What was that?' yelled Negus.

'Semtex!' Mace shouted. 'Come on, let's go.'

They ushered the willing prisoners out and into the awaiting truck, Negus helping people into the back. The last to climb aboard was Jodie, her face full of fear. Negus nodded to her, told her everything would be fine and then joined Mace in the cab.

'Time to go for a ride!' Mace roared, stamping down on the accelerator. As three more powerful explosions shook the complex, the truck fishtailed on the gravel, the tyres fighting for purchase. Without warning, it shot forward at speed, smashing through the gates and out onto the road. Mace kept his foot down as they hit bump after bump until they reached the main road.

There he slowed and turned left, heeding Jonah's orders. Behind them, smoke billowed into the air as the explosions continued.

'He'll be OK,' Negus said.

'Who?'

'Your Tyrell. He's a strong lad, got a good head on him.'

Mace looked out of the side window. 'He'll have to be,' he said softly. 'He's on his own now . . .'

38

Stone watched Aron snoring away. Earlier, the boy had been oblivious to the sedative slipped into his tea. Now that he was out for a few hours, the rest of the plan could begin.

'You want me to watch him?' asked one of the soldiers in Stone's unit, leaning his massive bulk against a wall.

'No, just lock the door,' said Stone. 'I'll come back for him later.'

'Kid folded easily.'

'I knew he would,' Stone replied. 'His sort always does.'

He left the soldier to it, and headed back up to the ground floor. The Mayor was in his drawing room, waiting for news. Stone imagined that he'd been sweating, crapping his pants in case there'd been no breakthrough. *One day soon I'll put a bullet in that fat skull*, thought Stone. Right now though, he was still useful.

The Mayor was drinking an expensive brandy when

Stone arrived, his face flushed and stress lines creasing his brow. 'Well?' he asked impatiently. 'What did he say?'

Stone nodded. 'They call it the Haven,' he revealed. 'It's an old theatre, just outside the protected zone, accessed by tunnels.'

'Do you have the directions?'

'Yeah. The kid gave up everything. It seems this hideout is the centre of their operations. They store food and weapons there. And it's where they take the people they rescue from the Hunt.'

'But they can't hide everyone in there, surely?' the Mayor blurted.

'Depends on how big it is,' Stone pointed out.

'Have you contacted Valefor?'

Stone walked across to the drinks cabinet, an antique piece that was two hundred years old. He took a cut-crystal glass and helped himself to the Mayor's brandy. 'You don't mind, do you?' he asked, gesturing to the glass with a nod.

The Mayor shook his head. The folds of flesh under his chin wobbled. 'Valefor?' he repeated.

'I thought I'd let you tell him,' Stone replied. He swirled the amber liquid around the glass a few times before taking a swig. It was warm and fiery, and tasted rich. Stone raised his eyebrows. 'This is great stuff,' he said.

'Have it,' the Mayor told him.

'So, yeah,' Stone continued. 'Thought that if you told Valefor, you'd be back in his good books.'

The Mayor grinned. It was the charmless smile of a spoiled child winning an argument. Hatred made Stone's left temple twitch.

'That's very noble of you,' said the old man. 'You've returned to your senses.'

The mercenary looked away before he replied. 'I told you I'd sort it out,' he said.

'What about that bitch?' the Mayor asked.

'Who?'

'My stepdaughter . . .'

Stone took another sip of brandy. 'What about her?'

The Mayor set down his own glass and told Stone to look at him. 'Is she part of it?'

'I've already told you,' Stone reminded him, without heeding his request. 'She's a paid–up member.'

'Oh well,' the Mayor sighed. 'I gave up her mother, and I'll have to do the same with her.'

'Gave her up?' asked Stone.

'One of those decisions that can't be avoided,' explained his boss.

Stone fiddled around in a pocket before taking out his cigarettes. 'Mind if I smoke?'

'Open the window first.'

Stone did as he was told, then lit up. 'Tell me more,' he said.

'What's to tell?' the Mayor replied. 'She was having an affair, running with the rebels. When Valefor found out, he gave me an ultimatum. My wife or my position. Like any rational man, I chose the latter.'

'You allowed the demons to kill your wife?'

'Of course,' the Mayor told him. 'She was a cheating slut and a traitor. What would you have done in my place? I didn't just allow them to tear her apart; I stood and watched as they did so. The silly bitch was pregnant too – though not with *my* child. I couldn't let her humiliate me any further. She had to die, as regrettable as it was. There are limits to *any* love.'

Stone nodded slowly. 'I understand,' he replied.

'There are plenty of women in the world, Stone,' the Mayor continued. 'No point in losing your lifestyle because of one.'

Stone took a couple of long drags on his smoke, before finishing his brandy. 'You should contact Valefor,' he eventually said. 'Right away.'

'I shall go to him,' said the Mayor. 'Get the car ready.'

Stone shook his head. 'I've got things to attend to,' he replied. 'Take one of the others, sir, and the credit will be all yours.'

The Mayor considered Stone's words for a moment. 'You don't want any thanks?' he asked.

'*Thanks?*' asked Stone. 'I don't need any. You can have it all.'

'Can you arrange a driver?'

Stone nodded.

'Do so at once, then,' ordered the Mayor.

'What about Martha?'

The Mayor sneered. 'I'll see her once my business with Valefor is concluded. Make her an offer she can't refuse . . .'

'I see,' Stone replied before leaving to organize a chauffeur.

The Mayor's car was pulling out of the drive when Stone called his handler.

'Did you enjoy my theatrics this morning?'

'Yes, sir, I thought you were very convincing as "Brogan",' Stone told him.

'And it worked?'

'Completely. The Mayor has just left to see Valefor, the boy is sleeping and I'm off to talk to the step-daughter.'

'Excellent news, Stone. Is there anything I can help you with?'

'No, sir, everything is in hand. You enjoy your day and I'll update you later.'

'And have you considered where you'd like to take your break, once this matter has been satisfactorily concluded?'

'Somewhere warm,' Stone told him. 'I miss the sun.'

'Done,' said the man who'd called himself Brogan. 'What will you do with the boy?'

'Oh, he deserves a reward too. Let's see how accurate his information is first and then we'll get to that.'

The caller chuckled. 'Let me know then,' he said. 'Good day.'

'Good day, Senator Wise.'

Stone pocketed the phone and went to find his men. Martha would be halfway through her shift by now, and he wanted to see her before the Mayor finished with Valefor. First, though, he needed a computer . . .

39

Jonah caught up with the truck nine kilometres south of the ruined camp. Driving the lighter, faster jeep, he'd made up ground quickly after escaping from the handful of soldiers who'd survived the attack.

Mace pulled into the side of the road and he and Negus jumped out. Jonah followed suit. Mace began to introduce them, but Negus' warm smile made it unnecessary.

'Jonah!' Negus cried, throwing out his arms.

Jonah accepted the embrace and the two of them exchanged some pleasantries.

Mace remained confused. 'How come you . . . ?' he began, screwing up his face.

'Met on the road, three weeks back.' Negus beamed. 'Talk about coincidence.'

Mace looked at Jonah. How many more surprises did he have to reveal?

'Negus and his group are the rebels I told you about,' Jonah explained.

'We've got a settlement,' added Negus, 'due north of your city. There's a good number of us out here.'

'Is that how you ended up at the camp?'

Negus nodded. 'I'm a scout,' he replied. 'Not very good. Been caught three times now – always escape though.'

'How many men?'

Negus thought for a moment. 'Around sixty men, maybe eighty or so women, and Lord knows about the kids. We take in anyone who wants to join us. Quite a few of your people seem to come to us.'

'The people we rescue from the Hunt?'

'Yeah . . .'

'So why haven't you made contact?' asked Mace, relieved that at least some of the rescued seemed to have survived in the wastelands.

'Demon protection,' admitted Negus. 'Most of us escaped similar places and we don't want to go back. It might be dangerous out here but at least our lives belong to us.'

'But what about food and shelter?'

Negus winked. 'You'd be surprised how much you can grow or scavenge out here. And we raid the convoys regularly. Besides, the electricity and water supplies still work. The problem is finding buildings that are still connected. And then, once you do find somewhere, the second you use any power or water, it flashes up a red flag in the citadels.'

'They monitor the flow?'

'Yeah,' said Negus. 'Which is why we're careful not to take water from the same supply more than once. And why we never venture as far as Fire City. Our existence rests on being hard to find, so we live in hiding. Still better than slavery though.'

'I guess,' said an impressed Mace. 'We could learn a lot from you.'

Jonah coughed. 'Maybe we should get to the cache?' he told them. 'This whole area will be flooded with the army very soon and we're way behind schedule.'

Mace raised an eyebrow. 'You didn't kill them all?'

Jonah shook his head. 'No time, and besides, there were civilians – a doctor and some support staff. I locked them in a hut but they'll get out quickly enough. Then they'll raise the alarm. I'm not concerned about regular troops, but if they send planes, then we're in trouble.'

'And they *will* send the planes,' Negus added. 'That's a given.'

Mace looked unimpressed. What was the difference between a soldier and a civilian government worker? Both were traitors, both kissed demon arse. Why kill one and not the other? Instead of broaching the subject, however, he asked how far it was to the weapons hoard.

'Less than two k,' replied Jonah, 'so let's hurry. I can explain my actions later.'

'We should check on the passengers too,' Negus reminded them. 'Some of them looked bad.'

'Tyrell?' asked Jonah.

'Something happened,' Negus told him. 'He was taken away by a soldier called Boyd and some female medic. The order came from another man – probably the doctor you spared at the camp. I couldn't hear too clearly when they took him, but I know they were going south. To someone called Senator Wise.'

'What could they want from Tyrell?' asked Mace.

Jonah looked away. He knew of Boyd – an evil, cantankerous mercenary whose blood ran colder than ice. And he knew what they might want from Tyrell too, yet he kept his counsel. There were too many paths to walk already, without setting off down another. And there were things that Mace and the others didn't *need* to know, things that they'd never comprehend. Not that he'd abandon his friend. No, going after Tyrell would just have to wait.

'I'm leaving Fire City after we get back,' Jonah told them. 'I'll go south and find Tyrell.'

'But what about *our* plans?' asked Mace, surprise evident in his eyes.

'You'll have everything you need,' replied Jonah. 'Once I'm done, you won't need me anyway.'

'Why not?'

Jonah's expression hardened. 'Because you won't,' he declared.

'But—'

'Enough talking,' snapped Jonah. 'We need to move!'

The arms were hidden in an isolated farmhouse about three hundred metres into a small copse of ash and oak trees. They approached with caution, Jonah parking the jeep and going ahead on foot, scouting for threats. When it became clear that they were safe, the passengers climbed out of the truck and stretched their legs. One or two did seem weak, and Jonah checked them over. Jodie helped him, tearing up rags to use as dressings and giving them all water. She seemed calmer now, following Jonah's instructions and asking question after question, most of which went unanswered.

Negus and Mace loaded the truck with as many guns, grenades and ammunition as they could manage. The arms cache was large, part of a shipment that had been ambushed by the rebels. Soon they'd loaded enough weapons to start a small war. However, taking the passengers as well limited the space available, so they decided they would have to ignore some rocket-propelled grenade shells they found. Until Jonah joined them, that is.

'We *have* to take those,' he said.

Mace shook his head. 'Not enough room,' he explained, 'and they're too heavy.'

Jonah approached the weapon, crouched and rubbed dirt from it. 'No discussion,' he insisted.

Both Mace and Negus asked him why.

'Just leave them here,' Negus added. 'We've got more than enough for now.'

Jonah shook his head. 'We can't leave these,' he said. 'These are thermobaric bombs.'

Mace blew out his cheeks and joined Jonah. He'd seen these weapons in action during the War, felt the shock waves they created. 'Wow.'

Jonah nodded, happy that Mace understood his reasoning. 'Bring the launcher too,' he replied. 'I can reconfigure these to detonate without the firing mechanism but it might be useful anyway.'

'These things were crazy,' Mace explained to Negus. 'Even at this size, they'll take out an entire block of buildings. The really big ones flattened whole towns. Only the battlefield nukes were more deadly in a localized fight.'

Negus looked at the bombs and shook his head. 'I used to be a peaceful man,' he said with sorrow. 'Before the demons came, I mean. Never believed in no violence, you understand. But these things? Man, I'd give my right bollock to use one of these on the Hell-kin.'

'You two help the passengers back onto the truck,' said Jonah. 'I'll load these into the jeep.'

'You need some help lifting them?' asked Mace.

Jonah shook his head.

'Stupid question,' the giant muttered.

Jonah pulled Mace to one side as Negus left them, his grip surprisingly powerful. 'They don't know,' he said. 'About my . . .'

'Understood,' Mace told him. 'Your secret's safe with me.'

'That applies when we get back too,' Jonah added. 'You can't tell anyone – not even Martha.'

Mace shrugged. 'Martha likes you, son – *really* likes you. I'm sure she'd understand,' he pointed out, but Jonah shook his head vigorously.

'No one,' he insisted. 'This has to remain between you and me.'

'OK,' Mace replied. 'No problem. But I want to know more about what's going on in your head. Deal?'

Jonah nodded reluctantly. 'Deal.'

40

The Mayor felt a renewed sense of self-worth as he stood in the market square, outside Valefor's lair. Even the presence of a brooding Mias and his patrollers failed to shake him free of his good mood. He had what the demon lord wanted and had proved his worth yet again. This time he would demand respect, not ridicule, and Valefor would once again understand that he was an important player.

As he waited for the demon lord, his thoughts turned to his errant stepdaughter and what he had in store for her. A small cruel smile played across his lips as he imagined Martha begging for her life, offering him whatever he wanted. He'd already decided to resign his post, to talk to the senators in the capital and relocate to the south coast. He'd offer her one last chance to save herself, and if not, if she denied him, then she would die. A wealthy man of his standing would have his pick of women. Martha could either become what her mother would not, or join her. Each option excited the Mayor as much as the other.

'Where is your master?' he demanded from Mias.

The simian underlord showed signs of surprise at the Mayor's tone. 'You should watch how you address me,' he warned.

The Mayor smirked. 'Should I?' he parried. 'Why would that be, then, *under*lord?'

The demon stepped towards the Mayor, drawing a blade, his face stony. A small bead of sweat dropped from the Mayor's hairline onto his brow, but he remained calm.

'Because you are human,' Mias growled at him.

'And I am also higher up the ladder than you.'

Mias looked taken aback. 'Pah!' he spat. 'That is of no consequence here. I could crack open your skull with my teeth right now, suck on your brain, and no one would care.'

The Mayor winced at the mental image Mias' words had created but held his nerve. 'I'm sure the senators would enjoy that,' he countered. 'One of their favourites, a loyal defender of the government, killed by some rogue half-wit with more fleas than brain cells.'

Mias readied himself to attack but something stopped him in his tracks. A shadow loomed over the Mayor. He turned slowly, feeling the air pressure grow around him, crushing his personal space. Valefor, his giant wings fully spread and row after row of razor teeth glinting in the fast-fading light, had appeared from nowhere.

'I—'

The roar sent even the patrollers scrambling as Valefor lifted the Mayor off his feet, claws tight around the human's neck.

'YOU DARE TO SPEAK TO MY KIN SO?' he bellowed, so powerfully that nearby walls vibrated and the atmosphere seemed to buzz with electricity.

The Mayor, fearing a coronary, tried to keep calm. Looking down into the purple eyes and gore-encrusted jaws of an ancient warrior of Hell, however, made that difficult. Valefor was merely toying with him. The demon lord could have ripped the Mayor in two had he wanted it so.

However, Valefor was hot-headed and vengeful but he wasn't stupid. He sensed that the Mayor had information for him, and that even with his demon senses he could not penetrate the Mayor's deepest thoughts. The Mayor had learned early that you could deflect thought-reading by thinking of other things, in this case a woman's breasts. He also understood that demons sensed emotions better than thoughts. The trick was to imagine a beautiful woman, and most men could easily manage that.

'I feel your anger,' the Mayor managed to spit out. 'But you . . . need me.'

Valefor grunted and threw the Mayor to the floor, winding him. Mias stood over him, ready to kill.

'Let him up,' ordered the demon lord. 'Let us hear what he has to say.'

The Mayor got to his feet slowly, holding his left side. A sharp pain cut through his chest, the result of two cracked ribs. He took short, shallow breaths as he spoke. 'The information you requested? I have it.'

'Then tell all,' demanded Valefor. 'It may warrant your continued existence.'

'I doubt even you would kill me,' the Mayor replied in defiance. 'My role is sanctioned by the government.'

'I care not for your human leaders,' Valefor warned. 'The only thing that will save your skin is the information you hold, nothing else.'

'The rebels have a stronghold,' revealed the Mayor. 'A place in which they hide.'

'I discerned as much myself,' replied the demon lord. 'If that is the extent of your knowledge, then you die.'

'There is more,' the Mayor added quickly, his new-found confidence beginning to ebb. '*Much* more.' He took a few more breaths and told Valefor everything Stone had discovered, failing to mention the mercenary once. Once he'd finished talking, the demon seemed to relax.

'This is better than I imagined,' he said to the Mayor. 'You have excelled yourself.'

'Thank you, my lord.'

'Perhaps I have misjudged you recently.'

The Mayor shrugged. 'I have only ever done my duty,' he pointed out. 'We have worked well together for many years. Yet I seem to lack your respect. I should not have to defend myself against your minions. The power rests with you, Valefor, and then in me as your next in command.'

The demon considered his words before nodding his agreement. 'I believe you are correct,' he told him. 'Once the rebel problem has been dealt with, and I have this stranger, you and I will sit and reconsider your role.'

The Mayor sighed. 'That's just it,' he admitted. 'I no longer wish to continue. I want to retire, to find a peaceful place to see out my years. I have worked long and hard and I am growing old.'

'You seek my recommendation to the senators and the council?'

'Yes – that is my reward for your information. I want nothing more.'

Valefor looked into the Mayor's eyes. 'Then it will be done,' he replied. 'You have my word on that.'

'Will you require my men to help you against the Resistance?' asked the Mayor, knowing Valefor's word meant nothing and deciding that he'd approach the council himself.

'No,' said Valefor. 'Mias will handle it. Tonight.'

The Mayor asked if he was free to leave.

'Yes,' Valefor replied. 'You may go.'

Mias approached his master a few moments later.

'You can kill him,' said Valefor. 'Tomorrow, after we have dealt with the rebels. The Mayor wishes a parting gift from me, and he shall have it.'

'Thank you, Lord Valefor,' replied Mias. 'And tonight?'

'Send them a message, Mias. Leave no one alive . . .'

'As you wish, sire.'

'Now go and prepare your troops,' ordered Valefor. 'This stranger is dangerous, so take no chances. Take Saarl with you. If you require my assistance, I will be here, waiting.'

41

As Mias prepared his troops, some thirty kilometres to the northeast, Negus guided the small convoy into a dark field. In the distance eight giant towers loomed, like colossal pepper pots that seemed to hold up the sky. Around them, an invisible shroud buzzed and crackled, a protective field conjured up by the demons. Mace noticed the towers immediately.

'It's a power station,' Negus told him. 'Heavily guarded. Two human platoons are permanently stationed there, plus the workers, a demon lord and his creatures.'

'And you live within sight of it?' asked Mace, amazed.

'Last place they'd look,' said Negus. 'Besides, our efforts are a little more sophisticated than just hiding in a hedge.'

They drove across the field until they reached a small brook. A single rickety bridge provided the only crossing into a vast expanse of trees, so Mace pulled up.

'On foot from here,' Negus informed him, 'and

quickly. They could send troops at any minute. We need to get everyone into the woods.'

Above them a jet roared past, too high to see. Mace ran to the rear of the truck.

'Jodie!' he yelled. 'Get everyone out quickly.'

The young woman jumped down and stretched her legs before helping everyone else out.

'Across the bridge,' Mace added.

'OK,' she replied, her voice calm. 'Will the other one be OK?'

'Who?'

'The big black man,' she explained. 'He helped me when we got caught.'

'His name is Tyrell,' Mace told her. 'And the honest answer is I don't know.'

'Oh,' she said, her face falling.

'He can look after himself,' Mace quickly added. 'And your job is to help these people. It's what Tyrell would do.'

'Yeah,' she replied. 'Will you let me know . . . if he turns up or whatever? I want to thank him. I was mean to him before he left and . . .'

'No time,' he said. 'We'll talk later.'

Jodie nodded as Negus joined them.

'I'll go across,' he said. 'Gather some men. If the passengers wait just inside the tree line, I'll send someone to escort them.'

Mace asked him how close their base was.

'You don't get it,' said Negus. 'Just wait.'

He turned and jogged across the bridge, disappearing into the trees. Somewhere an owl hooted and a fox cried out. Jonah, who had circled the field to look for threats, pulled up.

'What now?' he asked.

Mace pointed into the woods. 'Negus has gone in there,' he explained. 'Said he'd be back with help.'

'It feels too open out here,' Jonah replied. He watched Jodie leading the passengers across, each face bewildered and scared. It was understandable. Forests and other dark areas were perfect hunting grounds for wild animals. At night, only the brave or the foolhardy ventured near them.

She stopped just inside the tree line and turned to face Jonah. 'What now?' she shouted across the brook.

Behind them another owl hooted, causing a monkey to howl in return, and Jonah understood. Several heat signatures, about the size of adult men, approached through the darkness. They had been the source of the animal calls.

'They live in there,' said Jonah. He watched Jodie give a start as Negus and another man, tall and thin with similar matted and twisted hair but lighter skin, appeared at her side.

'Shall we join them?' asked Mace.

Jonah shook his head. 'No – we need to watch the weapons.'

As they drew closer the heat signatures in Jonah's vision morphed into human beings, eight in total, all of them male. Negus led his friends across the bridge and pointed to the vehicles.

'Get everything,' he told them. 'Quickly!' He turned to Mace and Jonah. 'The tribe,' he said, his smile warm and wide.

'You live in the woods?' asked Mace.

'Not *in* them,' explained Negus. 'We live as *part* of them. Come on.' He ran to the truck, grabbed a handful of weapons and urged Mace and Jonah to do the same. Then he led them across, telling Jodie to follow with the others.

The foliage was dense but it was just about possible to pick out a path through the undergrowth. They walked for a few metres, until Negus stopped by an oak tree and pulled apart some bushes. He knelt and lifted a hatch, before vanishing down into a tunnel. A lamp of some sort threw hazy yellow light up into the world. Mace peered in and saw the face of a young boy with ginger hair.

'Follow me,' the kid ordered.

Mace turned to Jonah. 'Wow,' he said.

'Let's do what he said,' replied Jonah. 'Jodie, you go first with the others.'

The girl sat at the edge of the opening and dropped down with a soft thud. One by one the others followed her. Jonah went last, right after Mace's lumbering frame. The tunnel was damp and redolent with the metallic tang of soil. Reinforced with wooden braces every few metres like the tunnels back in Fire City, this one wasn't high enough to stand upright in. Instead, everyone half crouched and edged forwards, one after the other. Jonah wondered where they would end up. It seemed absurd that Negus' tribe would have built an entire cave system under the earth, unless of course there was already an existing cavern.

'These remind me of the entrances to the Haven,' he heard Mace say. 'They must lead to caves or something.'

'That's exactly what I was thinking,' Jonah admitted. 'But the angle isn't steep enough. We're still close to the surface, and the way it twists and turns means that they've dug around the tree roots.'

'Beats me, then,' Mace admitted.

Jonah wondered if the giant man had noticed the hatches every ten metres, openings that gave numerous access points. He knew that if he were walking above ground, none of them would be visible, hidden by bushes and dense undergrowth. No wonder they didn't fear being caught. A few moments later Mace stopped abruptly.

'We're going up again,' he said.

Jonah followed him, back out into the woods. This time there were several lamps and he realized that the tunnel was merely a secret route to the main camp, which sat shrouded on all sides by trees and bushes. Even the canopy seemed roof-like, the dampness of the ground suggesting that very little light penetrated. Jonah saw the floor was covered in flattened bark and leaves, as though people walked about the area daily. To the far left he saw a rope hanging down from some branches. Negus stood by the tunnel opening with Jodie and the taller man. A giant oak stood over them, its branches thicker than most of the other tree trunks.

Jonah walked over to Negus. 'Where are the shelters?' he asked.

'Look around,' came his reply.

To his right, ten metres or so away, one of the thick bushes came forward, revealing a wooden shelter behind. A woman wearing a red headscarf and carrying a baby on her hip came out and smiled. The baby gurgled with delight.

'My two women,' Negus boasted with obvious pride. 'And this here' – he gestured to the thin man who had led the welcome party through the tunnels – 'is Jack.'

The taller man smiled. 'Pleased to meet you all,' he said. His voice was soft, his accent lilting.

Jonah introduced himself too. Behind them Mace whistled as more of the tribe began to reveal themselves.

They came from the undergrowth, from behind trees, and climbed down rope ladders from the canopy.

'This is crazy,' the giant added.

'Crazy and free, brother,' said Negus. 'No one knows we're here.'

Jonah smiled. 'You didn't show me this last time,' he half complained.

'Didn't have time, did I?' Negus reminded him. 'I was scouting with my brother, remember?'

'How do you defend yourselves against the animals?' asked Mace.

'With sticks and knives,' Jack told him, shrugging. 'We've lost one or two but mostly it's safe. There's a wolf pack that lives here, and some lions too, but they stick to the smaller prey – pigs and sheep and whatnot. I seen a zebra grazing by the river bank a few weeks ago. Crazy what happened to all them zoo animals after the War.'

'How long have you been here?'

'Since right after the demons won,' Negus revealed. 'Me and some others. I knew these woods from my childhood. Used to play in them. They weren't as thick then, not around the edges, but nearly twenty years of growing free has sorted that out.'

'And the government never bothered you?'

'They couldn't find us, could they?' He laughed. 'They stuck to clearing the local villages and towns instead.'

Mace nodded. 'So you built all of this?'

'Yeah, and slowly,' said Negus. 'And each time we found humans out on the road, we asked them to join us. That's how Jack got here. We have to go out and look for materials and food, but there are plenty of deserted villages and a town close by. That's what the scouting trips are for. It's hard sometimes, but like I told you earlier, no demons, no soldiers – it's like Heaven.'

'How big?' Jonah asked as yet more people appeared and began to take care of the rescued.

'Three more areas this size,' revealed Jack, 'with a network of tunnels, dug in pairs. We're digging out a larger cavern too – just in case. One way in, one way out. And then some live up in the branches. Not me though – my head can't take them heights.'

Mace looked concerned all of a sudden. 'We should get the rest of the weapons,' he said.

'No need,' Negus replied. 'The men are on the case. Time for us to rest and get something to eat.'

'Ah, food,' said Mace, rubbing his stomach. 'I could eat a demon . . .'

42

Martha was wiping down a table and ignoring the lewd comments of a drunk when Stone walked through the door.

'I need to talk to you,' he told her, his expression serious.

Martha shook her head. 'Take it somewhere else,' she replied. 'I'm busy.'

Stone saw that the large square room was virtually empty. The old man with the cough sat at the bar, smoking, and the woman, Faith, tended to a customer. That left the slobbering wreck hitting on Martha and two middle-aged women in the far left corner, sitting at the last table before the stairs, nursing half-empty glasses. Stone had seen busier coffins.

'Rescued anyone from the Hunt lately?' he said to Martha, who tensed visibly and dropped the rag she was holding. 'Now lose the attitude and come with me!'

Aware that she had no choice, Martha obeyed, brushing off the concern shown by Faith. 'It's nothing,' she told her friend as they passed the bar. 'He just wants to talk.'

'Don't worry,' Stone told Faith. 'I won't do anything she doesn't like.'

Prior turned to the mercenary, bristling with rage. 'You want to try a man for size?' he snapped. The effort caused him to wheeze, his cheeks turning purple.

Stone shook his head. 'Not my thing,' he replied. 'If I was you, I'd conserve my energy.'

'It's fine, Prior,' said Martha, even though she was scared stiff. 'We'll only be upstairs.'

Stone walked on, and Martha followed, the pit of her stomach aching and her head spinning. Stone knew that she was a rebel, which meant that she was in serious trouble. She fingered the knife in the pocket of the grey cargo pants she wore, vowing not to succumb easily. If he hurt her, she would make sure she got her own pound of flesh too.

Stone led her to his quarters, shutting the door behind them. He walked round his sparse desk to the windows, opened one of the blinds.

'How did you find out?' she asked him, remaining by the exit, ready to run if need be.

'Doesn't matter how,' he told her. 'Your reaction proved it was true.'

'So why are we talking?'

Stone shrugged and leaned against the window

frame. 'Would you rather I killed you?' he replied.

Martha's right hand went to her pocket, just as Stone did the same with his left. Her heartbeat gathered pace and her palms grew clammy.

'I've got something you need to hear,' Stone revealed. 'See, you don't really get me, Martha.'

'I don't want to, either,' she bit back, hoping to hide her fear. 'You disgust me.'

'Oh, really?' he countered. 'What – more than these dirty, stinking louts you socialize with? More than your unwashed, shitty-arsed Resistance friends?'

She nodded. 'I'd rather sleep with that drunk downstairs than have anything to do with you. You're a traitor.'

'Yes, yes,' he said, dismissing her with a wave of his hand. 'But what if I wasn't? What if I was actually working for the same side as you?'

'That's ridiculous,' she snorted. 'You work for the demons. How can we be on the same side, Stone? You've lost your mind.'

Stone wanted to smile but held back. Things were just as he hoped they would be. 'Are you prepared to die?' he asked her. 'Really prepared?'

The question made her feel sick. She started to rock on the balls of her feet, ready to move. She thought about her mother – was this how she'd met her end? Sweating and frightened, but defiant too?

363

'Yes, I'm ready to die,' she replied.

Stone ignored the change in her posture and concentrated instead on the intent in her eyes. She was a brave girl, something he admired. He thought about her stepfather and his weasel words, about the tales he'd heard of Martha's mother, her unmatched beauty and huge heart. The gruesome nature of her death.

'Did you know your mother well?' he asked, taking her by surprise.

She hesitated for a moment, unsure of herself. 'Leave her out of this,' she snapped at last, confused about Stone's tactics and where he was going with his question. 'You don't know anything—'

'But I do,' Stone interrupted. 'I know a lot.'

Martha edged further into the room, her gaze fixed on the mercenary, her attention focused. What did he know about Maria? What could he tell her about the mother she'd lost; the woman she'd dreamed of almost every night since?

Stone took out his mobile, fiddled with the touch screen and called Martha closer. 'Listen to this,' he told her. He set the phone down on his desk.

'What's that?' she asked him, staring at the small black device.

'It's for communication,' he explained. 'Everyone in the citadels has them.'

'So why should I be interested?' she added.

Stone touched the screen again and she heard her stepfather's voice coming through the phone's inbuilt speakers.

'*What's to tell?*' she heard him say to someone. '*She was having an affair, running with the rebels. When Valefor found out, he gave me an ultimatum. My wife or my position. Like any rational man, I chose the latter.*'

The next voice belonged to Stone, and she suddenly understood what was happening.

'You . . . ?' she began.

Stone nodded but said nothing. The recording continued.

'*She was a cheating slut and a traitor. What would you have done in my place? I didn't just allow them to tear her apart; I stood and watched as they did so. The silly bitch was pregnant too – though not with my child. I couldn't let her humiliate me any further. She had to die.*'

Martha gasped. Her mouth began to twitch and tears ran down her face. She dropped to her knees and looked up at Stone.

'Is this true?' she wailed.

Stone went to her, crouching so that their faces were level. He held onto her shoulders and nodded.

'Why . . . ?' she asked. 'Why are you telling me?'

'You decide,' he replied. 'Am I friend, foe or something else entirely?' He used his thumbs to wipe away her tears. Then he stood, retrieved his phone and started to leave. At the door, he stopped and turned to her. 'He's on his way here,' he revealed. 'He knows about the rebel thing. I can't give details about how just yet, but I will. I know you hate me, but that matters little. You'll have to trust me. You and your friends are in great danger. You cannot let the Mayor leave this place alive. Do you understand?'

Martha nodded. 'How do you . . . ?'

'Later,' he told her. 'I'll explain everything later.' He walked back to her, pointed to a metal chest to the right of his desk. 'There are some weapons in there,' he told her. 'You do know how to shoot?'

Martha nodded. She hadn't fired a gun for some time but she knew how they worked. Her mother had handled plenty and the elders had shown Martha how to use them.

'Good. I need to check on something but I'll be back shortly. He can't know I've been here, understood?'

'Yes,' said Martha, her mind a tangle of confused thoughts and emotions.

Stone told her to be careful and left, smiling all the way out to his jeep. As his driver pulled away into the encroaching evening light, Stone dialled his handler.

'Where we headed?' the driver asked as Stone waited for an answer.

'Nowhere,' Stone told him. 'Find a spot close by, one where we can keep an eye on the hotel's entrance.'

The soldier, although confused, shrugged and did as he was told.

43

The Mayor arrived moments later, flanked by two stern-faced mercenaries. At the bar, he demanded to know where his stepdaughter was. Faith shrugged and looked away.

'I would urge you to tell me,' he warned her. 'My patience is worn through today. I'll have my men shoot out your knees.'

'She's upstairs,' said Prior from his usual stool. 'Cleaning.'

Prior didn't know what had gone on between Martha and Stone, save for the fact that Stone had left. But he was damned if he was going to tell the Mayor anything that might be important.

'That's better,' replied the Mayor. 'I'll go up and find her.'

'Want me to take you?' asked Prior, a deep, phlegmy rumble erupting from his chest.

'No, no,' the Mayor told him. 'I'm perfectly capable of finding someone in my own premises. You just sit there and choke quietly.' He gestured to his escort. 'These two will stay here. Just in case you decide to get frisky,' he warned. And turning to his men, he added, 'Kill them if they move. Kill everyone in the place if you have to.'

'Yes, sir,' replied both soldiers.

The stairs were wooden and old. Years of use had worn down the centre of each step and scuffed the dark wood to an almost blond shade. The handrail creaked and wobbled slightly. The Mayor made a mental note to get it fixed, once he'd dealt with Martha. He walked up and found her in one of the rear bedrooms, swishing a tattered mop around the hardwood floor.

'Hello, my dear,' he said, his tone sickly sweet, the emotion false.

Martha ignored him and continued her chores. Her stepfather sighed as he walked over to a single bed with frayed yellowing covers and sat down.

'Lost your tongue?' he asked.

'No,' she replied.

The Mayor sighed at the insolence in her tone, the implied defiance. He smiled slightly. He was about to destroy that rebellious streak once and for all.

'You look so much like Maria,' he told her.

Martha felt the fury rising inside her. She saw her mother's smiling face, remembered the spicy scent she'd always worn. To think that this man had watched her die, watched her unborn child butchered – a sibling that Martha had never been given the chance to know. Even in their vicious world, where death was as common as taking a breath, such an act was unspeakable. Two lives, given up to the Hell-kin as though they'd meant nothing. The counterfeit tears that Martha had seen the Mayor cry when he'd broken the news, the bogus sobs that had seemingly racked his body, the phony depression; she would take each of these things and ram them down his deceitful gullet.

'Don't talk about my mother,' she managed to reply, each word catching in her throat.

'She was my wife,' he parried, 'and I will speak of her as I wish. There is so much you don't know about her. You were young, Martha, and besotted with her carefree nature. You never knew the true woman, the one who lied and cheated and stole her way through life. And now you—'

Martha threw up her head, glared at him, a pathetic, insignificant weasel of a man. 'What about me?' she demanded.

'I know,' he told her. 'About you and your Resistance associates.'

Martha gulped down air, felt her heart beating in treble time. Stone, whatever she thought about him, had warned her about this and given her time to prepare. Again, she wondered about his motives. What had he said about being neither friend nor foe? Could he have been telling the truth?

'Your failure to counter my claims tells me much,' the Mayor added, pressing his fingertips together, raising his hands to his mouth.

'You want me to deny it?' she spat. 'Is that why you're here?'

The Mayor shook his head. 'No,' he answered. 'I'm here to give you a chance.'

'A chance?' she asked. 'What chance can you offer me? I'd rather die . . .'

'And you will,' he assured her. 'I know everything about you and your rebels. The Haven, isn't it? The secret tunnels and safe houses dotted around the city. The names of those involved and the patterns you use to avoid detection. Those two people downstairs . . .'

Martha's face dropped. How the hell did he know so much? Someone had to have turned, someone close. As if he'd expected such a reaction, the Mayor nodded.

'Yes,' he continued. 'The informant told us everything. A person you thought was an ally. It's amazing what the lure of basic human comforts can make people do.'

A wave of nausea overcame Martha. She winced and looked away. Who would betray them like this? But even though she tried, she couldn't think of a single person, not one.

'Don't you want to know who?' teased the Mayor.

'No,' she lied, unwilling to give him the satisfaction he craved. Instead, she asked him what he wanted from her.

'I've already told you,' he replied. '*You* can escape the fate awaiting the others.'

A sudden chill hardened the sickness Martha felt in the pit of her stomach. She gulped down more air, her scalp tingling. 'How?' she asked, fearing his reply. What if her compliance was the only way to save her friends? What if he did have her cornered?

The Mayor stood and walked towards her, his arms outstretched. 'You have much to offer,' he cooed. 'I am retiring soon, leaving this place. I want you to come with me.' He stopped mere centimetres short of her, his breath sour.

'Why should I come with you?' she asked him, trying not to breathe in his stench.

'Because the only other option is death,' he explained. 'I've already informed Valefor of the information I received. Your rebellion has less than a few hours left to run. Come the morning, your Haven shall be no more.'

Martha held the mop handle so tightly that her knuckles had turned white. 'So if I stay,' she clarified, 'I'm dead. But if I leave with you, then what?'

The Mayor shrugged. 'Then you live,' he told her.

'No,' she added, 'you're not listening. What do I have to *do*?'

A slimy, stubby-fingered hand took her shoulder, making her shiver in revulsion. 'You will become everything that your mother did not,' he said. 'You will be my woman.'

Martha fought back the vomit and tried to sharpen her mind. She had to stay calm, had to remain focused on her goal. 'Faith and Prior,' she said. 'I want you to spare them too.'

'Who?'

'The two people downstairs,' she explained. 'Aunt May and my other friends too.'

A devious smile crawled across the Mayor's face, like a snake approaching its prey, ready for the final strike. 'You want me to protect your entire group?' he asked her.

Martha fought back tears as she tried to compile a mental list of those she wanted to save. She'd never even thought about having to make such a choice, and the reality of it made her feel helpless and angry.

'Yes,' she told him. 'If you want me, you let my friends leave Fire City.'

'Then remove your clothes,' he whispered. 'Show me that you are willing.'

Martha stepped back and let go of the mop. It fell slowly to the floor, clacking against the boards. She looked down at her feet, her eyes watering. Again she recalled her mother's face and thought quickly through her limited options. All the while, the rage inside her built.

'Come now,' the Mayor told her. 'Do as I ask and your friends will be safe. I give you my word.' He drew a pistol from his jacket pocket, pointed it at her. 'And if you don't, I'll kill you right here and feed your remains to your rebel compatriots,' he added.

Slowly, and with hands trembling, Martha removed her top. The Mayor gasped at the sight of her bare flesh, as she looked away, desperate to find a way out.

'Martha . . .' he panted, invading the space between them.

'Put down the gun,' she whispered to him. 'I'll do anything you want. Just put the gun down.'

She wept as she felt his coarse fingers take hold of her breasts, his slimy tongue slithering across her neck. He held the gun behind her, cold against her back. She turned her head as he mumbled something she couldn't understand. Her mind centred on her mother, on her loving smile. The Mayor's attentions grew rougher, more frantic as he pawed at her like some demented ape; and he dropped the weapon.

Knowing she had only one choice, she reached for the dagger that nestled in the waistband of her trousers, pulling it free. With the other hand she pushed her stepfather towards the bed. He fell onto his back, his mouth open, his eyes full of desire. She walked to him, looked down into his face.

'Did you see it?' she asked, leaning across his legs so that her lips were barely centimetres from his.

'See what, my love?' he replied breathlessly.

'The baby,' she said, her eyes darkening.

The Mayor looked puzzled. 'What baby?'

'The one you watched being ripped out of my dying mother!'

The blade entered his left eye first, and deep crimson blood spouted from the wound, covering Martha's hands. Then quickly she speared the right eyeball too. A frenzy of vengeance overcame her, and the world took on a scarlet hue. Time slowed so that each second stretched itself out like an eternity. The Mayor twitched and convulsed as she tore through his chest and stomach, cutting the flab to ribbons, shredding his insides.

When she fell to the floor in exhaustion, his blood covered her arms up to each elbow and had painted a mask of death across her face . . .

44

Jonah and Mace finished discussing their plans with Negus and told him it was time they left. They were sitting close to the tunnel entrance, having eaten a meal of canned beans with roasted meat, the provenance of which was neither asked after nor explained.

'Better to go now than wait until the morning,' Jonah pointed out. 'Besides, we've got the jeep.'

Negus nodded. 'When will you join us?' he asked Mace.

'Dunno,' the giant admitted. 'We need to gather everyone who wants to leave Fire City and guide them up here. It depends on numbers.'

'I doubt you'll have many,' said Jonah as a young dark-haired woman passed them, her eyes focused on him alone.

'Me too,' said Mace. 'I had this wild idea that we would take everyone, but it's just not possible. Many of the residents are too scared to defy the demons. And then there's the logistics . . .'

'How many in the Resistance?' Negus asked.

'Around fifty, at a guess.'

Negus looked up at the giant tree under which they were seated. 'This was a tiny acorn once,' he said. 'Now look at it.'

Mace stared up at the thick branches and asked him what he was on about.

'Most acorns are carried from their parent tree by animals,' Negus explained. 'I dunno – a squirrel maybe. The squirrel was out in the woods somewhere, ate the acorn and then took a dump here. That's how this mighty tree was born. Slowly and surely . . .'

Mace began to smile. 'Oh,' he replied. 'This is one of those wise old sayings.'

Negus nodded. 'Start with the people you know will leave,' he told the giant. 'After that we can go back in stages and gather any others.'

'You have a point,' Mace told him.

'It's the only way,' Negus replied.

'There should be a fair number gathered at the Haven when we get back. Most of the Resistance.'

'Fine,' said Negus. 'That's your starting point.'

Jonah told them to continue their conversation next time they met.

'Listen to him,' joked Negus. 'Ordering his elders around.'

'He's been doing that since we left Fire City,' replied Mace. 'Very bloody annoying.'

'I'm sorry,' said Jonah. 'It's just that we should be getting back. We've been gone longer than we said.'

'I'll guide you back to the jeep then,' said Negus. 'The men hid it in some bushes.'

'What about the truck?' Jonah asked.

'Same place,' Negus told him. 'We'll run it until the fuel runs out, and then we'll take it apart and bring the bits to camp – see if we can reuse them in some way.'

Jonah remembered the thermobaric grenades. 'I'll need the shells they took from the jeep,' he said, trying not to sound bossy. 'And a few guns too, Negus. The rest can stay here, if you like.'

'Yes, that would be good,' Negus told him. 'Let's get going.'

Mace finished the herb tea he'd been given and stood up, his legs aching. He stretched out his arms and yawned deeply. Not long now and they'd be back in Fire City. At least then he might catch a little sleep – or at least think about it. There wouldn't be time to actually rest – not if their plan was going to work. He took a walk through the camp, acknowledging the people he met along the way. The tribe was a proper community, with women and children, and even some older folks. They seemed happy and contented, full of warm smiles and easy chatter. He wondered whether his own people would feel the same, and saw no reason why that wouldn't be the case. There was a world of difference between his existence and that led by Negus, Jack and the others. His new friends had been right; compared to Fire City their camp was a paradise.

At the brook, Negus handed them a flask of water and bade them farewell. A lamp set on the ground barely lit their faces. Jonah and Mace were already in the jeep, ready to set off.

'Be careful,' warned Negus. 'The army will be out in force.'

Jonah nodded. 'We'll stay away from the main road,' he said.

Mace started the engine, turned back and took a rifle from the rear. 'We've got plenty of protection,' he told Negus, glancing at Jonah as he did so.

'Go, then,' said Negus. 'I'll look out for your return.'

Mace accelerated away, towards the far side of the field and onto the road. The tarmac was in good shape with barely any craters and they made good progress, using the vehicle's headlights at half power. Their unexpected detour after Tyrell's disappearance had yielded at least some positives.

'Shouldn't take more than an hour,' Jonah told him, his eyes focused on the darkness. He wondered what was waiting for them back in the city, and then he thought about Martha and found that he was excited about seeing her again. It was not a feeling he was used

379

to. In fact, it surprised him that he felt that way. That he missed her.

'As long as we don't bump into any troops,' Mace replied.

Jonah said nothing and continued to keep watch and think about Martha at the same time.

In Fire City, Mias had gathered his forces in the industrial zone. Sixty patrollers and three winged demons waited on his word. He ran over the tactics in his mind. They had the locations of every tunnel entrance to the Haven, and he would cover all of them. They would attack from two directions, with cover from the sky for any humans that managed to escape. Not that they would; Mias would make sure that not a single rebel soul survived. A small band of human soldiers stood with them. They would not join the attack but stay and fend off any other humans who were stupid enough to try and intervene. A grizzled and grey-haired soldier called Pipe led the mercenaries. He asked Mias what his orders were.

'You will guard the route,' the demon told him. 'Let no one pass.'

'Understood.'

'And I *mean* no one, human,' Mias cautioned.

'What if the Mayor asks to get through?' Pipe questioned. 'Should I just shoot him too?'

Mias ignored the insolence and shook his head. 'The Mayor is aware of my mission,' he clarified. 'He will not interrupt.'

Pipe turned to his men and gave out some orders. They moved off, in five groups of three, with Pipe joining the last.

'I hate those bastards,' said one of his men, Williams.

Pipe grunted and lit a cigar. 'Sometimes,' he replied, 'I wonder if I joined the right side.'

'Course you did, sir,' countered Kemp, a vicious, barrel-chested veteran. 'Them others can't afford to pay us.'

'You make a fine point,' Pipe told him. 'But it still bothers me.'

'Girls, food, wine and money,' declared Kemp. 'That's all I care about. These useless ones, out here, mean nothing. It was parasites like them that caused the problems, sitting around all day costing the rest of us money. No wonder the old world collapsed.'

'You're a prick, you know that?' Williams told him. 'We're all human, regardless of what happened.'

'I'm paid to be a prick,' Kemp countered. 'It's my job, you shithead.'

Pipe blew out a large puff of vanilla-scented smoke. 'Listen to them,' he said, stopping and turning back to Mias' demon force.

'Sweet mother,' Kemp gasped as he saw the patrollers

pounding their chests, roaring into the night sky. Above them the winged creatures circled, their cries as sharp and piercing as daggers.

'I feel sorry for anyone who gets in their way tonight,' Pipe told them. 'They'll be torn to shreds.'

'Good riddance, an' all,' replied Kemp. 'Bloody Resistance.'

45

Faith looked up to see Martha standing at the top of the stairs. Her face was drawn, the skin pale. Her hands trembled and seemed to be discoloured. Sensing immediately that something was wrong, she occupied the soldiers by offering them a free drink.

'Don't see what harm it'll do,' one of them replied.

The other, short with dark eyes and a receding hairline, eyed her with suspicion. 'We'll have water,' he told her. 'Both of us.'

'Suit yourself,' Faith replied, trying not to let her gaze wander to the stairs as she poured them their drinks.

Prior, sensing her discomfort, asked the first soldier where he was from.

'Up north,' the man replied, taking his glass. He was a few centimetres taller than his colleague, with long thin fingers and a narrow blond moustache.

'We didn't come here to chat,' the shorter soldier barked. 'Just shut up and keep still.'

'There's no need for that,' Prior replied. 'I was just being friendly.'

'I don't need no scum for friends,' the soldier retorted.

Prior looked at Faith, who glanced at the stairs and gave a slight shake of her head. Prior let out a sigh and said he was going to the toilet. He slid off the stool, coughing, and made his way towards Martha, who was descending slowly. As he passed her, she palmed something heavy and metallic into his hands and whispered, '*Follow my lead.*' He nodded and walked round and behind the staircase, where a narrow corridor led to the toilets and a kitchen area. He used it as cover, the gun nestling in his grip. He didn't know what was going on, but understood that it was serious.

Martha ducked under a hinged flap and behind the bar. The shorter soldier gave her a quizzical look.

'Where's the Mayor?' he demanded.

'On his way,' Martha replied, trying not to shake. 'He's just checking on something.'

'We'll have some more water, then.'

Martha nodded to Faith, who looked down and saw Martha place something under the bar – a small pistol. Like Prior, she went with it, despite her surprise. Something must have happened between Martha and her stepfather. It was the only explanation. Faith poured some more water, smiling at the soldiers.

'You're a looker,' she told the taller one. 'Don't get many like you in here.'

'Shut up!' spat the shorter soldier. 'One more word and I'll shoot you.'

Faith shrugged and put the fresh glasses on the counter. The less-friendly man stepped towards them, gaze fixed on Martha.

'Now, if *you* fancy a chat,' he told her, 'I'd be more than happy to oblige.'

Martha forced a giggle, her hands still out of sight. 'I'd like that,' she said, leaning forward.

The soldier grinned and took Prior's stool. 'Don't mind if I sit, do you?' he asked.

'I don't,' she replied. 'Not at all, but Prior might.'

'The old man with the bad chest?'

Martha nodded.

'Like he's an issue,' the soldier smirked.

'I wonder where he is?' said Martha.

'Forget about him,' the soldier told her, leaning forward too. 'Tell me your name.'

Martha giggled again, and ran her left hand through her hair.

'What's that on your fingers?' the soldier asked, with slight alarm in his eyes.

'This?' asked Martha, looking at the reddish-brown stains. 'This is my stepfather's blood.' She whipped out her right hand, and fired once. The echo resounded across the room as the soldier flew backwards, a neat bullet hole in his forehead.

Before his friend could react, Prior pounced, firing three shots into his torso. Two women screamed and ran for the exit. The man dropped to the floor, mouth spitting blood and surprise etched on his face.

Martha came out from behind the bar and knelt by his side. 'I'm sorry,' she whispered, before putting a final bullet through his skull.

The first bang made Stone start. The second caused him to drop his cigarette and reach for his side arm. He jumped from the car.

'What was that?' asked his driver.

'Gunshots from the bar!'

Some female customers burst through the doors, screaming. The few passers-by stopped to gawp.

'*Come on!*' yelled Stone. '*Quick!*'

They sprinted past the onlookers, bursting in to find Martha weeping, a dead soldier by her side. Ten metres away, lying on his back on a broken table, was a second dead soldier. Prior was at his stool, watching them as usual, and Faith was busy cleaning blood from some tables.

'We didn't see a thing,' Prior told Stone.

The mercenary ignored him and helped Martha to her feet. 'Where's the old man?' he demanded.

'Upstairs,' she told him. To the amazement of her friends, she gave Stone a hug. 'Thank you for warning me,' she said. 'I know you didn't have to.'

'I told you because things aren't what they seem,' Stone replied. 'We'll clean this up.'

'Thank you,' she answered, turning to Prior.

Her friend's disgust showed on his face. He averted his gaze, face going red. It was Faith who questioned her.

'Since when did we consort with that monster?' she asked.

Martha turned to her, eyes pleading for understanding. 'You need to hear everything,' she explained. 'The Haven has been compromised. Someone has turned against us.'

Prior's mouth formed a perfect circle. His eyes blazed with anger. '*What?*' he spluttered. He coughed a wedge of thick yellow phlegm into his hand and wiped it on his trousers.

'Stone warned me,' Martha revealed. 'The Mayor came here because he knew about me – about *us*. He said the demons will probably round up everyone else—'

'How could they know?' asked Faith. 'Who would have said anything?'

Martha shook her head. 'They know!' she insisted.

'Who was it?' Prior asked, calming slightly.

'I'll tell you who it was,' came Stone's stern voice. 'The boy, Aron. I have proof.'

The driver, used to the many intrigues conducted by his boss, coughed. 'He's not lying,' he said. 'I was there when he—'

'When Martha's stepfather turned him,' said Stone, finishing the driver's sentence for him, before a well-thought-out plan was ruined. He recalled Senator Wise's warning about uncontrollable variables.

'Was he tortured?' Faith asked in alarm. 'Did that bastard hurt him?'

'No,' Stone replied, cutting her off. 'He wasn't tortured. He couldn't wait to give you up. The Mayor offered him a better life, a job as a soldier. The boy jumped at it.'

'No way,' whispered Martha, her heart seeming ready to tear. 'He wouldn't do that.'

'He was angry,' Stone continued. 'All he wanted was to get at you, Martha. You and Jonah.'

Faith, Prior and Martha exchanged glances. Prior stood and faced Stone.

'These are just words,' he spat. 'I wiped that boy's arse when he was growing up. Martha was like his sister, and Faith his mother. He might be going crazy, Stone, but he's no traitor. He hates the demons more than I do, and I'd sell my soul to burn them back to Hell.'

Stone told Prior that he understood. 'If it was me,' he

added, 'I'd be wary too, but there are things going on, things that you don't understand. I may not be your friend, old man, but perhaps we share a common enemy?'

'Pah!' Prior scoffed. '*You?* You're just a lap dog for these scumbags.'

'Perhaps that's what it seems,' Stone parried. 'But if I'm working for them alone, then why haven't I killed you all?'

'Search me,' Prior replied.

'Martha has killed the Mayor, Prior,' Stone pointed out. 'The *Mayor*. If I was working with him, of course you'd all be dead. But you're not dead and I want you to consider why.' He turned to his driver. 'Go get the car,' he ordered. 'We need to get rid of the bodies.'

Prior watched the driver leave and mulled over Stone's words. It was true that things were odd; he was right about that. Prior had been ready to fight to the death once Stone and his lackey had come through the door. It was what *should* have happened. Only it hadn't. Instead, Stone had warned Martha and now them, and revealed Aron's betrayal. It was like he'd woken up in some alternate world, one even stranger than that in which he lived. Another racking cough worked its way up his chest.

Stone, mindful of what had swayed Martha to his cause, produced his mobile phone. If it had worked on her, it would work on them.

'Listen,' he told them. 'In his own words . . .'

'That's one of them mobiles,' said Prior. 'Do they still work?'

'Only for the Wanted,' Stone admitted. 'I'm sure you had plenty before the War.' Prior nodded as Stone fiddled with the buttons. 'It's not clear who he's talking to but it doesn't matter,' said Stone. 'Here we go.'

He set the phone down on the bar, and enjoyed watching their faces as Aron's voice came through loud and clear.

'*I don't care about anything, not any more,*' they heard him say. '*I'll help you to bring them all down. Every last one . . .*'

Faith gasped, holding onto the bar for support. Martha slowly shook her head, her eyes moistening. She felt her childhood bond with Aron splinter into a thousand tiny pieces. Stone fought back a sudden urge to smile as his controller's voice set up the clincher.

'*You'll help us to find your friends. To access their hideout?*'

Prior started at the new voice. 'Who's that?' he asked.

'Someone the Mayor worked for maybe?' Stone offered. 'I dunno. I just found the recording on one of his computers.'

Prior shook his head in amazement and disgust as he heard Aron reply: '*Yes, I'll help you to find the Haven. I'll tell you how to reach them . . .*'

Stone looked at Martha and shrugged. 'I'm sorry,' he said. 'I'd better go and sort this mess out.'

Martha failed to reply; her mouth was open but any words were lost somewhere. As Stone began to drag the first body towards the door, she doubled over and puked her guts out.

46

Marko jumped down the stairs and across to the tunnel entrance, his face red, his breathing frantic.

'*Demons!*' he shouted down to Oscar.

'What?'

'They're all over the place!' yelled Marko.

Oscar climbed back up into the old office block and drew his blade, his mind racing. Marko was behind him, panting now, trying not to panic; the scar that pitted his olive skin had turned purple.

The stairway was dark but Oscar ran up the steps, desperate to see for himself. Reluctantly, Marko followed. Out in the corridor, Oscar crept towards the access point hidden behind some bushes and an overturned truck. He felt the cool night air on his forehead as he leaned out, scanning the immediate vicinity. He could see nothing, save the same old dilapidated buildings and debris-strewn roads.

'I can't see anyone,' he told Marko, hoping that his friend had been mistaken.

'I'm not making it up!' Marko insisted.

A shrill cry came from above their position and Oscar heard giant wings flapping. It was no mistake.

'*Shit!*' he whispered. 'What's a winged demon doing out here?'

'*Told* you,' said Marko. 'Something's wrong. They never come out here, not in such big numbers.'

Oscar nodded and thought quickly. What would Mace or Tyrell do? he wondered. 'Who's patrolling the other entrance?' he asked as the seed of a strategy began to germinate in his head.

'Raj and someone called Liam, a new one.'

'We have to warn them too,' said Oscar. The only immediate action was to see if the demons attacked. If they did, Oscar knew that he and Marko could use the tunnels to escape, destroying the entrance. However, if they didn't attack and he panicked unnecessarily, then sealing one of only two exits from underground would be foolish.

'Oscar?'

'We'll hang on a while. They might just be passing by.' He stood and ran to another set of stairs, which led to the next floor. Part of the ceiling had caved in here and he had to climb over several piles of steel frame and rubble. The steps were mostly intact though, and he soon made his way to a window that overlooked the street below. Despite the darkness, he made out eight patrollers, their heavy frames with knuckles almost dragging the floor, giving them away. '*Shit!*' He hurried back to Marko, knowing that he had to act quickly. 'One of us needs to warn May and the others,' he said. 'How fast can you make it back through the tunnels?'

Marko shrugged. 'Same as you, I guess?' he replied.

'You wanna go?'

Marko looked out into the night, heard another demonic cry and nodded. It would be safer in the tunnels than out here, and although he was no coward, he wasn't a fool either. He *would* have stayed if Oscar had told him to. He was just following orders.

'Go, then,' Oscar told him, wishing that Tyrell were by his side. 'I'll hold out here. If they discover me, I'll blow the entrance. There's some explosives pre-rigged and I've got matches.'

'Take care, brother.'

Oscar nodded. 'I will – now, get going.'

Raj had already made it back to the Haven, having spotted the Hell-kin before Oscar and Marko. May let him in and his expression turned her blood to ice water. Her pale-grey eyes grew wide.

'Demons!' he gasped. 'Loads of them looking for the entrance. Something's gone wrong.'

May told him to calm down. 'They *can't* know about this place,' she told him. 'Only we know how to get in here. They're probably just passing by.'

'No,' Raj insisted, shaking his head. 'I was watching them. They're going from building to building, searching for something. They're even turning over abandoned vehicles and looking through weed patches. Patrollers and winged ones . . .'

Convinced now that Raj was right, May began to think hard. They had always planned for being discovered. The Haven had only two official access points underground, and they had dug a warren of tunnels to confuse anyone who found them. They crossed and recrossed at regular intervals, and only the rebels knew the correct routes. Mace had rigged the two hatches above ground, using simple explosives that could be ignited with matches. The Haven was also stocked with enough food to last a few weeks, if needed.

There *was* a third, secret access point, known only to May, Faith, Mace and Prior. This was the exit in the event of an emergency. With the other two hatches blown, it would become the only way out.

'What do you think?' she asked Raj, looking up into his deep brown eyes.

'We have no choice,' he told her. 'We blow the exits. If they find their way here, it's all over. We can last down here, can't we?'

'Yes, but it'll be tough,' she replied, her mouth suddenly dry.

'We've no choice,' he pointed out. 'I'll run back now and do it.'

'Is Liam still up there?'

Raj nodded. 'If anything happens before I get there, he'll blow the hatches himself.'

'OK – *go!*' May ordered. She turned and ran for the main chamber . . .

Oscar felt a bead of perspiration creep down the left side of his face. His palms were equally damp and every vein in his body throbbed. The patrollers had surrounded the building now, and he'd recognized the black-coated frame of Mias. There was no longer any question that they knew about the Haven. He edged forward to try and hear what was being said – making the mistake that Mias had been waiting for. The demon underlord sniffed at the air and his finely tuned nostrils sensed the salty tang of human sweat. He spun round, his ruby-coloured eyes catching sight of Oscar.

'*There!*' he roared.

Oscar sprang from his position and ran back to the tunnel entrance, taking the steps two at a time and landing awkwardly at the bottom of the stairwell. A sharp pain jolted his ankle and he winced. He scrambled to the hatch, knowing that Mias would be tracking his scent. He cursed his decision to wait, wishing that he'd just blown the hatch immediately. He went down into the angled drop, feet first. When the tunnel opened up, he took out his matches and searched for the fuse wire. Above him, the soil vibrated with the sound of pounding feet and some of it began to shake loose. He heard the demons shrieking, closing in on their prize.

The lamps used to light the tunnel were fading away so he lit a match. The fuse was less than a metre back from where he'd landed. He was about to approach it when a pair of huge, clawed paws poked through the access. He grabbed his machete and swiped at the patroller's legs. The creature hollered as the blade cut through the skin and severed some toes. Blood, thick and plum-coloured, began to gush from the wound. Oscar struck again, this time causing the patroller to scream and retreat back up towards the hatch. Sensing his opportunity, Oscar grabbed the wire and followed it, only not far enough. Something had gnawed though its length and it was too close to the explosives. There was no way he'd have time to escape. If he blew the tunnel from his current position, the whole thing would cave in on his head.

Oscar had never known his real parents, having lived his entire life with Martha and the others. So, faced with possibly his final moments on Earth, it was his friends' faces that appeared in his mind. He remembered how huge Mace had seemed to his three-year-old eyes. How the giant had thrown him up in the air with one hand, catching him with the other. The time he'd broken his arm, running from a patrol, May fixing it for him, with wooden splints and an old T-shirt, soothing his agony with kind words and soft, maternal kisses.

He thought about walking in on Martha as she changed and how she'd slapped him across the face. How he'd explained that her naked form did nothing for him, his preference being other males, so he hadn't been spying on her. The way she'd begged his forgiveness, insisting that she was sorry until her voice had gone hoarse.

Then, the first time Tyrell had held his hand and told him that he felt the same way. The terror they'd felt at explaining their love to Mace, and the joy at discovering that the elder, the only real father they'd known, blessed them.

Even Prior made it in those last moments: that wizened old goat with his cigarette scent and his yellowing fingers, teaching Oscar how to fight with a blade, urging him to take his first real drink, even if he was a 'poof'. All of it flashed past in the seconds between Oscar lighting another match and putting it to the fuse.

'Suck on that, bitches!' he yelled, turning to run . . .

Above, the explosion threw Mias back into the street as pieces of patroller flesh, concrete and metal showered all around him. Momentarily dazed, he lay on his back, trying to catch his breath. A shard of steel ten centimetres long and two wide stuck out of his chest. He pawed at it, howling when the movement caused him to shudder in pain. He looked around, seeing several half-dismembered corpses, and roared with anger. Taking hold of the shard again, he closed his eyes and pulled it free, this time refusing to succumb to the pain. He summoned his powers, concentrated on the gaping wound, and it began to close over. Satisfied, he got to his feet, shook his head and assessed the situation. This entrance was useless now.

He bellowed at the surviving patrollers to run to the second attack point as one of the winged ones swooped down to his side, towering over him.

'Lord Mias, are you hurt?' it asked.

Its beak was nearly a metre long and curved down at the end. Huge gold-feathered wings flapped behind its eagle's head. Both legs were thick and strong, with five razor-sharp claws on each, all as long as its bill.

'It is only a scratch. Take me to the other entrance,' Mias demanded. 'They will pay for this.'

'As you wish,' the winged monster replied, bowing so that Mias was able to clamber onto its back. He held tightly to its feathers as the ground disappeared and they sped up into the night sky.

The flight was quick and Mias soon found himself earthbound once more. The second entrance was located west of the first, in amongst what had once been a residential area. Four tower blocks stood like giant dominoes in the darkness, one placed behind the other. Around them were smaller blocks, each only four storeys high. Mias saw his lupine-featured number two, Saarl, directing operations. He walked over to him, rubbing at his chest.

'Report!' he snapped.

'We have the location, brother,' Saarl revealed. 'I sensed a single human, no more. We were about to attack when you arrived.'

'They've wired the entrances with explosives,' Mias told him. 'The first is compromised so this remains our only way in. Where is it?'

Saarl led Mias inside one of the tower blocks and down a dark corridor lined with his troops. At the end, another door led them into a courtyard area strewn with debris thrown from the floors above. Beds, televisions, old bicycles, even a bath, littered the area. Over in the left corner, blocking a narrow passageway, sat a six-metre-high mound of rubbish, which Saarl pointed to.

'Under there,' he said. 'We have troops positioned in each doorway, above on the first floor of each building and protecting the passage to the rear.'

Mias nodded. 'You've done well, my friend,' he replied. 'We move swiftly, before the human can set the charges. Can I count on you?'

Saarl put his left arm across his broad, golden-haired chest and bowed. 'I am your servant, brother Mias.'

Moments later, they had snuck around the building to the far side and were standing in the alleyway. The huge rubbish dump blocked the end and Mias saw that a hole had been burrowed underneath it.

'They hid this well,' he said to Saarl. 'Like the devious animals they are.'

Saarl snorted. 'Not well enough, Mias,' he declared. 'They could not escape you.'

Mias crouched and edged towards the hole, Saarl right behind. When they were less than five metres away, he stopped and sniffed the air. This time, above the usual stench and the aroma of human perspiration, he sensed something else. Tears. He smiled as he looked at Saarl.

'*Now!*' he demanded.

Underneath the mound, Liam, barely more than fifteen years of age, peered into the gloom and caught sight of piercing emerald eyes looking back at him. He wished his legs would stop shaking, his eyes streaming. Why hadn't he gone instead of Raj? He knew his orders, understood what he was supposed to have done, but it mattered little. Deep and certain fear had slowed his reactions and turned his stomach inside out. He wanted to vomit, to run and hide, to get away, but he couldn't. He stood frozen, and when he heard the demon roar, his bowels gave way. A wolf-like snout appeared in the entrance, the teeth dripping with saliva. As the demon pounced, Liam closed his eyes . . .

Raj worked his way back towards Liam quickly. His six-foot-two-inch frame counted against him, and sweat poured from his face. Directly in front of him, the tunnels split into four. Three of the passages were decoys and he chose the fourth, turning left. A hundred metres later he hit another intersection and went right. This channel was three hundred metres long and littered with obstacles. His back and legs groaned as he moved through it, his eyes focused on the next junction. As he reached it, he heard a sound that sent shivers crawling across his skin like thousands of tiny spiders. It was the howl of a patroller, no more than two hundred metres away.

'Bollocks!'

He thought through his options, quickly settling on the only course of action. The tunnel entrance had been compromised and Liam was probably about to come scampering round the corner, chased by the demons. He wondered why the boy hadn't followed his instructions and blown the hatch. Perhaps the attack had been too swift, or maybe he'd taken fright. It was understandable, especially in one so young. Raj cursed the fact that Mace and Tyrell had gone with Jonah. Had they been around, the odds would have been far better. Both his friends were experienced rebels, even though Tyrell was young, and they would have been useful in this latest fight.

As it was, they weren't present and there was only one option left if the Haven was going to be saved. He would retreat back to where he'd come from, seal the underground hatches and wait out the storm with May and the others. Hopefully the demons would get lost in the maze of tunnels. Even if they did find the hatch, the barricades might hold them back. Whatever happened, the Haven was the most important thing. Neither his life, nor that of Liam or anyone else, really mattered. Their sanctuary was all, and he would defend it to the bitter end.

He wondered too about who had betrayed them. There was no question in his mind that someone had. The demons had never even come close to discovering them, and yet now here they were, chasing down the tunnels. He heard a thud from the passage that branched left, followed by the deep snarl of a patroller. Something else thudded against the earthen floor and bounced down towards him, once, twice, three times. It rolled into the junction between the tunnels and stopped.

Raj found himself looking at the severed head of Liam, the eyes still wide in fear, the mouth set in a scream. He panicked then, trying to re-swallow the vomit that had worked its way into his mouth. Then, with heart pounding so hard that he thought it might burst through his sternum, Raj turned and ran. The only thing he'd forgotten, the *one* thing that was more vital than any other, was that the demons didn't need to see him to know where he was going. They could simply follow his scent . . .

Marko *hadn't* forgotten to disguise his scent trail. He still had the small vial of lavender, patchouli and wild garlic oil that May prepared for everyone who took part in rescuing people from the Hunt. The sweet, pungent aroma worked brilliantly and seemed to affect the patrollers badly. He'd seen the canine beasts cough and splutter in the past when faced with its odour. They'd also proved too stupid to comprehend that it was being used as a cover. He'd made sure to rub the oil onto any exposed skin as he hurried back to the Haven. The trouble was that he'd stopped paying attention and taken a wrong turn, despite having assured Oscar that he knew the exact route. By the time he'd worked out and corrected his mistake, he'd lost nearly five minutes. He'd ended up scrambling along, trying in vain to make the time up, and finally reached the internal hatch in a breathless state, saturated in perspiration.

Emily let him in, her eyes red from tears and her skin deathly white.

'The tunnel's been compromised,' he told her as between them they frantically resealed the exit.

'I know,' she told him. 'May has already warned everyone.'

'How could she know?' asked Marko.

'Raj,' replied Emily. 'The demons have found both of the entrances.'

'We're dead, then,' Marko said in a resigned tone.

'Where's Oscar?' she demanded, her legs beginning to shake uncontrollably at Marko's words.

'He stayed up top,' Marko explained. 'If the demons look like they're coming through, he's going to set the charges. I'm sure he'll be back any minute.'

'What do we do, then?' she asked.

Marko looked at the hatch they'd been so quick to barricade. 'We wait here,' he said. 'We wait for Oscar.'

Emily shook her head. 'We can't,' she told him. 'May gave orders to seal everything if you hadn't made contact within five minutes. It's been eight.'

'No,' Marko insisted, removing the thick wooden planks that held the hatch in place and throwing back three rusting bolts. 'We can't just abandon Oscar. I'll stay here until he gets back.'

Emily considered Marko's words for a second or two before nodding her consent. They opened the metal door and looked out into the gloom. That was when they felt and heard the explosion . . .

47

Jonah and Mace encountered the army on the very out-skirts of Fire City, where an old fast-food drive-through sat desolate amidst thick weeds. The area around it had been completely destroyed; above, the bridge that had once carried the ring road over the urban area had collapsed into a pile of twisted metal rods and concrete lumps, some bigger than the cars they had crushed. A narrow lane cut southwards through the dense overgrowth – the route they needed to take, but it was blocked by a small platoon of human soldiers; seven visible, and three more staked out in the remains of the restaurant.

Jonah had sensed the soldiers' presence early, order-ing Mace to stop three hundred metres short of their position. He'd spent the entire journey fiddling with the thermobaric grenades, taking out their fuses and re-calibrating them, just as an expert in the north had shown him with normal explosives. All bombs worked the same way but Jonah took extra care with the grenades at hand, having never worked with thermo-barics before. It was no easy task as they bounced along uneven and pitted terrain. Twice Mace had asked him what he was doing, receiving no reply either time. Jonah had wanted Mace to concentrate on the road, not worry about being burned to ashes by a wrong move.

'Just let me concentrate,' he had told him.

'They look dangerous,' Mace had retorted.

'They are,' Jonah replied. 'Which is why I need you to concentrate on the road and avoid any large bumps.'

'If you set one of those things off,' Mace joked as the wheels of the jeep hit yet another pothole, 'I'm going to kill you.'

'Just watch where you're going and shut up,' Jonah had demanded.

Now they were using the undergrowth around the ring road as cover, creeping ever closer to the unit. Two soldiers stood at the entrance to the drive-through, facing east, with a third standing by a lorry, facing west. The other four that were visible stood in pairs facing north, two hundred metres apart, with the city at their backs.

'There's no other way,' Jonah told Mace. 'This is the most remote way into the city. All the other routes are more open and they'll be heavily guarded. We *have* to go through here.'

Mace shrugged his meaty shoulders. 'So let's do that,' he replied. 'Just take the soldiers out.'

Jonah shook his head, thinking about his own, private mission. There was no point in giving Valefor a warning about his return. If his mother had been right about the demon lord, Valefor already knew of his presence. He would have sensed it.

'The minute we show our hand,' he pointed out, 'they'll get on the radio for reinforcements. We have to use stealth.'

'Guess so,' said Mace. 'Use your demon thing on them.'

'My demon thing?'

Mace nodded. 'Whatever you call it, then,' he offered. 'It's not like you've told me anything about it. You'll have to excuse my lack of understanding.'

Jonah sensed his friend's sarcasm and smiled. 'I'm sorry,' he replied. 'It's just that since I told you, we've been on the move. We've got a moment now, so what do you want to know?'

'Everything,' Mace admitted. 'I mean, how is it even possible that your mother was demon and your father human? That's the craziest shit I've ever heard. And then there're all the powers and the fact that you hate your own kind so much you've joined the battle to get rid of them. None of it makes sense.'

'I guess if I was human I'd think that way too,' Jonah replied. 'But I'm not – human, that is – and I'm not completely demon either.'

'See?' Mace pointed out. 'You don't actually answer questions.'

'OK,' Jonah parried, 'let me try and explain a little. My mother was a *succubus*, and when she was killed, she'd already lived for over three thousand years. She fell in love with my father, a human, and I don't know how or why that happened – it just did. My mother gave up her species to be with my father, and that upset the other demons, broke their ancient decrees.

'My parents hid for many years and had children, but eventually, when the Demon Reign began, the Hell-kin, as you call them, came for us. They'd probably always known about us because my mother couldn't hide her true origins. They sensed her presence in the same way that my mother sensed that they were coming.

'She separated us all and sent us away, to members of my father's family. I ended up in the north, around what was called Manchester before the War. That was the last time I ever saw either of my parents or my siblings again . . .'

The explanation hadn't been entirely truthful but it was enough to spark more questions from Mace.

'How do you know they're dead, then?'

'Every one of us, bar my human father, has a connection to the other. I mean, a way of feeling what the other is feeling, directly. I know my parents were slaughtered because I could see and hear and feel everything my mother went through.'

'Because you're half demon?' said Mace.

'Yes,' replied Jonah, trying to shake off the memories of his parents' demise.

'But how?'

'How *what*?'

'*How* could your mother give birth if she was a demon?'

'*Succubi* prey on men,' Jonah explained. 'They appear as beautiful women and lure men into bed. Once there, they devour them. My mother took over a human body and decided to live through it. She *became* the person she possessed.'

'And you?' continued Mace. 'Do you age like us or like them?'

'I don't know,' Jonah admitted. 'The human part of me has aged already. I was born and I grew up like any other human child, but inside there's something else, something my mother taught me to tap. The demon part of me . . .'

'So all those "skills" that you have, they're all produced by your Hell-kin blood?'

'Yes,' said Jonah, 'although Hell doesn't really exist, not in the way most humans think of it. The demons exist in a parallel dimension, one that is always there. That's where they emerged from when the War began.'

Mace looked pensive as he digested Jonah's words and caused the boy to feel uncertainty. The problem for Jonah was that he couldn't allow himself to be discovered, at least not by everyone. His yearning for vengeance was too great, the only true driving force in his life. It was the thing that fed and sustained him, shaped and reshaped his emotions and thoughts. He couldn't let something as trivial as human friendships endanger that. He needed Mace to understand, to react with tolerance and to abide by his desire to be secretive. For Mace's sake as much as his own.

His mother's face took over his thoughts – her pale, porcelain skin, her intensely black eyes and the perfectly symmetrical beauty of her smile. '*They'll never understand us*,' she'd warned, gathering Jonah and his siblings to her. '*They'll never let us be. We don't fit their narrow definitions, and we never will. In order to survive, we have to keep our true selves hidden. You must always remember that. Always . . .*'

'But if your mother couldn't hide from them, how do you manage?'

'My mother didn't have a human soul, she'd only possessed one – it's not the same thing.' said Jonah. 'I *do* have a human soul and I've learned to bury the demon deep inside the human part. I only allow the Hell-kin to surface when I need it.'

Mace's eyes widened. 'So when you fought Mias, you alerted the other demons to your presence?'

'I alerted Valefor,' Jonah told him. 'He's the only ancient in Fire City, and the only one who would have sensed me. He probably knew about it before the confrontation with Mias.'

'And you want to kill Valefor.'

'Not want,' said Jonah. 'I *am* going to kill him.'

'Which is the only reason you came to Fire City . . .'

'Yes.'

Mace shook his head, trying to make sense of what he was hearing. 'I think I'm more confused than before,' he admitted.

'Another time,' said Jonah. 'We've got business to take care of.' He pointed to the nearest soldier, six or seven metres away, standing with his back to the lorry, watching the road. 'There are three humans hidden inside the building,' Jonah told Mace. 'We'll take them down slowly, one at a time.'

'Better get the knives out, then,' Mace replied grimly. 'I'll do the closest one.'

Jonah agreed and they split up, with Mace edging towards the first soldier. Jonah went right, round behind the lorry, using it as cover. He kept low, still concealed by the weeds until he could see the soldier's legs from underneath the vehicle.

Mace was almost within reach now, lying flat on the ground, his machete clenched between his teeth. He waited until the soldier turned before pouncing, jumping to his feet and using his spade-like hands to cover the soldier's mouth and bring him down, breaking his neck in the same movement. The whole manoeuvre took less than five seconds and the rest of the platoon failed to notice. Sure that he was dead, Mace dragged the soldier's body underneath the lorry and past Jonah, leaving it deep in the undergrowth and taking the soldier's gun.

'What next?' he asked Jonah as he rejoined him.

'The far side,' Jonah replied. 'We'll take the four facing this way before we deal with the ones guarding the building.'

'We'll have to be careful,' said Mace.

'We'll distract them.'

'How?' Mace asked him, causing Jonah to shrug nonchalantly.

'We'll think of something,' he said. 'Come on!'

48

Once Stone and his driver had removed the bodies, Martha and the others rushed to the Haven, leaving the customers to take what they wanted from the bar. Not that it mattered any more, with the Mayor dead and their secret discovered. She'd barely thought any more about killing her stepfather, beyond the initial feelings of anger and horror. It had to be done and, even though she felt bad at taking his life, the only concern running through Martha's mind was for the Haven and the people inside it.

She knew that May would be there, alongside Oscar, Raj and a few others, and prayed that they'd understood what was happening and hidden away. However, Martha also knew that an attack was the last thing they would be expecting. The Haven had been a closely guarded secret for so long that any thought of its discovery would be discounted. Not once had the demons or the army come close to finding out about it, never mind raiding it.

She cursed Aron and his treachery, the shock long since replaced by rage. It was doubtful that she'd see him again, but if she did, Martha knew that she would kill him. Nothing excused what he had done – not his anger at being ostracized or his jealousy of Jonah. Aron had destroyed nearly twenty years of secrecy, devotion and sacrifice, belittling every life lost in their cause. All of it done in the service of creatures he claimed to hate.

'That stupid little bastard!' spat Prior, echoing Martha's thoughts.

They'd turned left out of the bar and gone straight over the crossroads into what had been the main thoroughfare before the War. Much like elsewhere, nature had reclaimed every nook and cranny, a particularly fast-growing and invasive knotweed covering walls and floors, weaving around the dense brambles and nettles. The three of them – Martha, Faith and Prior – wanted to run but knew that they couldn't. All around them were soldiers, on foot and in vehicles, and armed to the teeth.

'This is bad,' said Faith as they passed yet another group of soldiers, each one giving them the eye. Faith's usually rosy cheeks were hollow and the bags under her eyes seemed larger than ever. She'd tied her filthy hair back with a length of twine and longed to take a wash.

'Things are going to change for ever,' said Prior.

'Once they find the Haven, that's it. We might as well get shot now.'

'Nothing's ever final,' replied Martha, feeling a sharp pain in her abdomen at the thought that Prior might be right.

The old man half smiled at her, knowing that his illness was certainly final.

'We can't give up,' Martha added. 'If we lose the Haven, we'll have to start again. We can't let these bastards win. That would mean that everyone who has died to protect it lost their lives in vain.'

Faith shrugged and told Martha that she understood what she was saying. 'Still doesn't matter though,' she continued. 'I'm not sure there are enough of us left to care. I mean, who even remembers the days before the demons – me, Prior, Mace, maybe a handful of others? Most of the people around us gave up years ago. They just don't care any more, Martha. They try and get by, struggle and survive, and when their time comes they just accept it.'

'Which is even more justification to fight,' Martha insisted. 'To wake them up and show them a better way.'

'I'm with Faith,' said Prior. 'The Haven was our stand, kid, the one we were all proud to make. If it goes, then we have nothing left. We no longer have the means or the will to begin again.'

'But . . .' began Martha only for the words to die on her tongue.

They had reached the clock tower, a fifteen-metre-high monument that sat at the intersection of five streets, surrounded by armed vehicles and men. Each of the five roads was barricaded and a five-metre cordon had been imposed around the tower. The route that Martha and the others wanted to take was the most heavily obstructed and caused each of them to panic.

'That's it, then,' Prior said in a resigned tone. 'They know.'

'Maybe we can go round?' Martha countered. 'There's *got* to be another way.'

Faith shook her head. 'Forget it, Martha,' she advised. 'It looks like they've locked the city down. We might as well turn back.'

'But what about Oscar and May and everyone else?' asked Martha, her eyes pleading and face almost scarlet.

'I'm sorry for them,' Faith replied impassively, her thoughts already turning to their next move. 'But we have to think about the future now. The Haven can be shut down completely, and hopefully that's what May and the others will have done. There's a secret tunnel that leads out, one that only we elders know about. They can last a week down there anyway, and both May and Raj are resourceful. Only we can't do anything for them right now. If we act now, we'll just be killed and that won't help anyone. Do you understand?'

Martha nodded slowly, sadness and resignation

etched across her features. She knew that Faith was right but still wanted to fight, wanted to get to her aunt. She wondered what her mother would have done in her place, but understood Faith's stoicism. Maria would have reacted in exactly the same way, even if that reaction hurt like hell and caused her heart to fold in upon itself.

'I wish Mace was here,' said Faith.

'I wish that little rat Aron was here,' snapped Prior. 'I'm going to cut out his heart the next time I see him.'

As yet more soldiers appeared, Martha spoke up again. 'We should go back, then,' she suggested, even though everything inside her urged her towards the Haven and May. 'I don't trust these soldiers.'

As they turned and walked away, a voice boomed out from a loudhailer: '*THIS IS A CURFEW – CLEAR THE STREETS! ANYONE DISOBEYING THIS ORDER WILL BE EXECUTED!*'

At precisely the moment that Martha had nodded in resignation, across the city Stone walked in on Aron, who was sitting at a table in the mess, scoffing down hot dogs. The mercenary patted the boy on his back.

'You did good,' Stone told him.

'Martha?' Aron asked, after swallowing his latest mouthful. 'Did you . . . ?'

'She's safe,' Stone replied. 'I warned her well in

advance and besides, there's no way she can make it to the Haven now. Pipe and his men have closed down Fire City.' He looked at his watch. 'The curfew begins in five minutes,' he continued. 'Shoot-to-kill orders. No one will be spared.'

'What about the others?' Aron added. 'The ones at the Haven?'

Stone smiled and shook his head. 'Sorry, son,' he replied. 'They aren't going to make it out alive. That's the price they'll pay.'

'And I made them pay it,' Aron pointed out, shame crawling across his face, discolouring his cheeks. He hadn't meant for them to die.

'You did what any sensible human would do,' Stone told him. 'You took the best available option.'

'Did you tell Martha?' Aron asked expectantly.

'Tell her what?'

'That I'm the one who blabbed?'

Stone didn't answer the question. Instead he told Aron to finish his meal – another plate of hot dogs smothered in baked beans, with two cans of cola to wash it all down. The mercenary felt his own stomach complain about the hunger he'd forced it to endure. 'Who knows when you'll get another chance,' he added.

Aron ignored him and asked again if Stone had revealed his betrayal.

'Yes,' Stone admitted. 'You knew that I would.'

Aron felt his stomach turn somersaults. His former life was over, finished by his act of duplicity. He could accept that his old friends would never forgive him – he expected it, even though he knew that his actions had been those of a true hero. Coping with their hatred would be made easier by the knowledge that he had saved Martha from death, and that alone made everything feel worthwhile. It would sustain him in his new life, running with Stone and his gang and working for Brogan. Maybe one day he'd get the chance to explain to them, and then they would understand how he had helped them.

'Did she say anything?' he asked Stone. 'Anything at all – good or bad?'

Stone nodded. 'Yeah,' he replied. 'She told me to give you a present.'

'A pres—'

The rest of the sentence remained caught in Aron's throat as a bullet punched through his forehead and out the other side, taking bone, flesh and blood with it. The boy fell slowly to his left, his head hitting the table before he crumpled to the floor. Stone pushed him aside with a boot, sat down and opened a can. Yawning, he picked a lone lump of brain matter from the plate and flicked it away before shovelling the food into his mouth . . .

★ ★ ★

Mias and Saarl stood and considered the metal hatch set into the end of the tunnel, where it sloped downward at a thirty-degree angle.

'It is barricaded from the inside, brother,' said Saarl.

Mias kicked at the access but it refused to budge. He tried again with the same outcome. 'Are you certain the human went through here?' he asked.

'Absolutely,' Saarl insisted. 'I can still smell his disgusting odour in the air.'

'How long to punch through, then?'

'Ten minutes, not much more,' said Saarl.

'Then make a start,' Mias ordered.

Saarl backed away from the door. He dropped on all fours, his massive haunches stretching the skin beneath his cream-coloured fur. Mias stepped aside as Saarl growled and ran at the obstruction, slamming against it with gigantic force. The metal buckled slightly but stayed put in its frame. The wolf-like demon grunted, retreated to his start position and repeated his attack. The door held firm.

Unperturbed, Saarl came again and again, each impact bringing him a little closer to his goal as his one-ton mass hammered the hatch. Eventually, it pulled away from the surround so that Mias could see light peeping through the edges. Saarl gave himself over five metres for the final thrust, mustering every reserve of power in his body. On contact, the hatch flew open, crashing against the floor of a corridor with a resonant clang, and they heard a human female screaming in fright.

Mias poked his head through the gap and smelled humans, at least twenty of them, cowering in fear and dripping in their own stench like the filthy beasts they were.

He smiled sardonically and dropped down into the Haven . . .

49

Liam's decapitated and savaged body.

It was the first thing Jonah and Mace saw as they dropped into the tunnels northwest of the Haven, and dawn gave way to morning.

'Demon spore,' said Jonah impassively. 'Everywhere.'

Mace stood perfectly still, eyes wide, mouth open, considering the bloody mess in front of them. Tiny electrical impulses made his right eyelid twitch. 'If they've been here . . .' he began to say.

'I *know*,' Jonah replied.

They moved on cautiously, skirting the tunnel network and looking out for demons. They found none.

'How?' Mace asked a couple of times, feeling the dread fluttering around in his belly. '*How* could they know?'

Jonah ignored him, his concentration total. The demons' scent lingered everywhere, and lots of it. Mixed in were other odours: canine, lupine, simian and . . .

The inner hatch was gone, the metal frame buckled.

Jonah stopped at the threshold, sniffing the dank, sour air. No hint of fresh demon anywhere. Plenty of dead human, however, *everywhere*. He peered into the corridor, the walls seeming even drabber than usual. A single lamp, barely alive, cast long shadows that faded into darkness, towards the inner chamber. With extreme care, Jonah dropped into the Haven, rolled to his feet and drew a blade. Despite what his senses were telling him, he chose to remain guarded. He felt the heavy thump of Mace behind him.

'Slowly,' warned Jonah.

Mace took out both machetes. 'What's the point,' he asked, his face set in a grimace, plum-sized knuckles bulging round his tightly gripped weapons.

'Are you sure you want to look?' Jonah asked him. 'It's going to be bad.'

Mace shrugged his massive shoulders before pointing at the blood trailing away from them into the gloom. 'I can see that,' he replied.

Jonah could see it too and he felt his insides twist. He wondered if he'd find Martha inside, hoped that he wouldn't. 'Slowly,' he repeated, 'and follow me.'

Mace shook his head. 'No,' he insisted. 'This time *you* follow *me*.' He strode off into the darkness, careful to avoid the blood. Round the first corner they found the remains of a woman. Her legs had been torn off, her tongue eaten. She was on her back, eyes open and frozen in terror. A rat gnawed on the exposed bone of her left thumb. Mace kicked the rodent into the wall, snapping its backbone. He raised his heavy boot and stamped down hard. At the next turning, through a door into one of the rooms, Jonah saw another woman – one he recognized.

'Diane,' Mace told him before he asked. 'The one who shouted at Aron when he attacked Prior.'

She was propped up in one of the moth-eaten armchairs, her head lolling to the left. Her chest had been torn open and her intestines sat in her lap, oozing. Mace retched at the stench and backed away, averting his gaze.

'There,' said Jonah, pointing to a small pair of legs sticking out from underneath a makeshift bed. He walked in and crouched, peering at a young boy, his neck broken and the back of his skull shattered. Both arms lay at unnatural angles. Jonah looked up at the wall and saw purple smudges. He matched them to the head wound. 'They broke his body against the wall,' he said, feeling a wave of human emotions crash over him. 'Threw him down when they'd done. He was trying to get away.'

Mace didn't reply.

By the time they reached the doorway to the central chamber, they'd discovered ten more corpses in the rooms and corridors, but not a sign of any survivors. Mace wondered who'd been in charge and whether they'd followed the contingency plans. One of the elders was always on duty, be it himself, May, Prior or Faith. Only they knew about the third, secret exit. That the outer hatch hadn't been blown suggested a surprise attack and the questions kept returning. The Haven had never been compromised, not ever. How then had the demons discovered it? Where were the others? Had anyone escaped the carnage?

'Don't go in there,' Mace heard Jonah say from the entrance to the central chamber. His face had grown ashen.

'More of the same?' Mace asked.

'No,' Jonah whispered. 'Worse.'

Mace pushed him aside, ignoring the warning and immediately wishing he hadn't. The smell alone told of a massacre, never mind the floor swimming in blood and the human heart staked to the wall with a dagger. Something dripped onto his head, ran down his face. He touched his right cheek and saw that his fingers were red. He looked up at the ceiling. Big mistake.

A rope had been thrown over an old suspended water pipe. Marko hung from it, upside down, his throat slashed and eyes gouged away. Chunks of flesh had been torn from his torso, wounds that were inflicted by razor-sharp teeth. Mace looked away, towards the rear of the chamber. There, a raised platform was littered with bodies, young and old. He walked towards them, feeling the fury rising in his chest, hammering away at his heart. How many would they find slaughtered like animals in an abattoir?

Jonah touched Mace on the shoulder and told him to stop. 'There's no sign of life in here,' he said, trying to fight off the human emotions he normally hid so well. 'No hearts still beating.'

Mace shook his head. '*My* heart's still beating,' he pointed out. 'I need to see them, all of them. Need to know who else was here when those *things* attacked.'

'They could come back,' Jonah warned. 'At any time.'

Mace nodded at the corpses on the platform. 'What are they gonna come back *for*?' he asked.

To their right, where they set up the trestle tables when they fed people, Jonah saw the remains of a couple, their bodies entwined. He approached them and felt something akin to sadness. Raj, the tall, brown-skinned man Jonah had seen at the hotel, lay twisted and broken, his arms round a pale-skinned and freckled woman whose head lay by the side of her torso. Jonah wondered how they had ended up in those positions. Whether Raj had clung onto the woman, trying to protect her. He called over to Mace.

'Emily,' Mace said when he saw them. 'I always thought they made an odd couple. She's over a foot shorter than he is. She *was* . . .'

A trail of gore led away from Raj's corpse, and after

427

a moment Jonah understood. Raj, attacked elsewhere, had dragged his shattered body to Emily in a desperate attempt to help her. He saw that Raj's eyes were still open and he reached down and closed them. Raj's skin had taken on a green hue.

Mace knelt at Jonah's side. 'I feel sick,' he admitted.

'These people were your friends,' said Jonah. 'You're bound to feel something.'

'What about you?' Mace asked him. 'Do you *feel* anything?'

Jonah nodded but said nothing. He thought, instead, about how many of Fire City's residents had died since his arrival, and felt the searing finger of guilt work its way into his conscience. Maybe he should have stayed hidden and taken on Valefor alone? He knew that his doubts made no sense, but they prodded at him all the same. It no longer mattered. For this latest act of savagery, and for the many that had preceded it, the demon lord would pay.

With his soul.

'We'll avenge this,' he told Mace.

'Isn't that why you came?' Mace replied, almost aggressively. 'Vengeance?'

Jonah looked away, unable to respond. An image sprang into his mind, something he'd buried deep in his memory. The look of terror on his father's face, the expression of resignation on his mother's as Jonah and his siblings were sent away, too young to fully understand. The deep and lasting sense he'd had that he was losing a part of himself . . .

'Jonah?'

'What if my presence caused all this?'

Mace shrugged. 'Maybe it did,' he replied, much calmer now. 'But it was going to happen sooner or later. You were just the catalyst.'

'But these people, *your* people,' said Jonah as a surge of gloom followed the guilt, 'they'd be alive if I hadn't—'

'*Alive?*' asked Mace. 'None of us were ever really living. We were all moving targets, waiting for that day to come. This world is shit, Jonah. We're all living in Hell. For me death is one of the few blessings—'

'But your people.'

Mace eyed the young man and shook his head. 'Not just my people, son,' he said. 'These poor souls accepted you without question. Their lives changed the minute you arrived and they are dead because of the way things have worked out. The least you can do is make them your people too, Jonah. *Your* people . . .'

'I came here for me,' Jonah replied, his voice changing, taking on a guttural tone. He looked at Mace, who flinched when he saw again the ring of fire around the boy's irises, the way his features seemed to have sharpened, the bone structure momentarily elongated.

'But I'm going to destroy Valefor and his legions for you – for all of you!'

They found May near the second exit. She had been stripped of her clothing and staked to the floor by her hands and feet. Something had torn her open, from her neck down to her nether regions. The skin had been peeled back like butterfly wings, and her insides devoured. All that remained intact was her face, those grey eyes staring back at them. Her death mask was almost calm, even serene. Her left fist was locked in *rigor mortis*, clenched round a tuft of black fur.

Mace sat down at her side, stroked her jet-black hair. The waves of emotion that rose from his stomach made his throat convulse. He swallowed and swallowed but it did no good. Eventually he let it all out, howling like a wounded animal.

Jonah, ashamed by the relief he felt at not finding Martha dead too, closed his eyes. He reached out in his mind, through the invisible cloak thrown around Fire City. Somewhere Valefor and his minions sat, sated and satisfied. No doubt they were feeling victorious, having discovered and destroyed the Haven and killed so many rebels. Time to dampen their mood a little, he decided. Time to do something for someone other than himself. He sent them a message.

I'm coming . . .

50

Jonah and Mace entered the hotel a couple of hours later, secreting themselves from the army patrols. They found Martha, Prior and Faith sitting alone, their faces etched with grief. Martha sprang from her seat at the sight of them, throwing her arms round Mace and bawling. The giant held her gently, tearfully, relieved that she was alive. He looked over at Faith, whose eyes lit up for a moment.

'The Haven,' she began to say, only Jonah stopped her.

'We've just been there,' he explained, unable to make eye contact.

'Are they OK?' asked Prior, with hope rather than conviction.

'No one,' Jonah told him, shaking his head.

'May?' gasped Martha, her face flushed. 'Not Aunt May . . .'

'Everyone,' Mace added, holding the girl closer and letting her take out her rage on his chest, her fists beating at it.

'No! No, no, no!' she wailed. 'It can't be true.'

Jonah reached out and touched her on the shoulder. Martha turned to him, eyes and nose streaming, and looked into his face. 'I'm so sorry,' Jonah whispered. 'This is my fault, all of this.'

Martha let go of Mace and wiped her tears away on her sleeve. Then she shook her head. 'You didn't kill them,' she pointed out.

'If I had never come here, never started this mess . . .'

'It was always a mess, Jonah,' she replied, taking hold of his face. 'You're not to blame.'

Jonah felt the urge to hold her close, and tried to fight it. He found himself gazing at Mace, who gave him a slight nod of the head. Slowly, uncertainly, he put his arms round Martha, half expecting her to run from him. When she did the exact opposite and drew into his body, he felt relieved and something more. Something he didn't understand but liked and welcomed all the same.

'Oh, Jonah!' Martha wailed, the sobs returning as she buried her face in his shoulder.

The others sat silently for a while, the only sound other than Martha's grief coming from Faith as she made coffee. No one had anything to say, so consumed were they by grief and horror. Each of them longed to let their feelings out, just as Martha was doing, but none of them did. When the time came, and she had cried herself dry, it was Martha who broke the silence.

'Where's Tyrell?' she asked, letting go of Jonah.

She thought they'd say he was still at the Haven, maybe salvaging what he could or seeing to the dead.

'He was taken,' Jonah said softly. 'Out in the wastelands.'

'Taken where?' asked Martha, no longer able to cry.

'South,' replied Jonah. 'We don't know exactly.'

'Oscar?'

'We didn't find him,' said Mace. 'There were a few bodies we didn't recognize. They were too badly mutilated. But no one survived, Martha. No one.'

Jonah proceeded to tell them about their trip, slowly and deliberately. Mace sat stony-faced; he felt unable to say anything that might help. Not that anything could. Everything they'd built, as tenuous as it had been, was gone – destroyed in one night. Proof, if it was required, of how fragile their existence had been. Only when Jonah had finished did Mace speak up.

'Who told them?'

It was a simple, obvious question, and both Prior and Faith, despite their seniority, looked to Martha.

'It was Aron,' she revealed, almost spitting out his name. 'Stone told us.'

'Stone?' Mace asked in amazement. 'The mercenary who works for the Mayor?'

Prior tried to lighten the mood with a chuckle. '*Worked* for the Mayor,' he replied.

When Mace gave them a confused look, Faith took up the story. 'Stone seems to have switched sides,' she explained. 'And the Mayor is no more. Martha killed him.'

Jonah glanced at Martha, his eyes searching her face. She nodded a reply to him before explaining everything that had happened.

'You trust this Stone?' he asked when she'd finished.

'I want to say no,' she admitted. 'But he *did* warn me about the Mayor.'

'Not to mention telling us about Aron,' Prior reminded her.

'That too.'

'Where is he now?' asked Jonah.

'He got rid of the bodies,' Martha replied. 'Said he'd be back.'

'We'll wait until he gets here,' declared Mace.

'And then what?' asked Faith.

'Then we leave,' he added. 'But not before we send those bastards back to Hell.'

Stone turned up in the evening, and Mace took him to one side immediately.

'Talk,' he said. 'Talk and convince or, so help me, I'll cut off your head.'

Stone looked at the machete in the big man's right hand and realized that he wasn't boasting.

'Would I be here if I was your enemy?' he asked, repeating what he'd told Martha and the others earlier. 'Would I have helped your friends, or warned them?'

'I don't know,' Mace told him. 'Just seems odd to me – this moral rebirth you've undergone.'

Stone smirked. '*Moral?*' he replied. 'I don't do moral.'

Mace, taken aback by the soldier's candid reply, raised an eyebrow.

'It's my job,' Stone added. 'I'm doing my job.'

'I thought your job was working for the Mayor,' said Mace.

'There are forces bigger than that old pervert,' Stone replied.

'I don't understand.'

Stone lit up a cigarette, and considered the best way to respond. 'The work I do isn't what you think it is,' he explained. 'On the surface I *am* what you think I am. A mercenary, working for the government, taking the devil's coin. But beyond, there are layers that stay hidden. Things that you don't understand.'

Mace tapped the machete against his leg. 'I'm getting bored,' he warned. 'Make sense and make it quickly, Judas.'

Stone flicked away some ash, nonchalant. 'My real

boss is a senator,' he continued. 'I'm working directly for him, on a black op.'

'A black op?'

Stone nodded. 'Undercover,' he clarified. 'You were in the army, you know what I mean.'

Mace nodded as Stone continued his explanation. 'Some people in government are unhappy with the way things are. Powerful people who want the demons gone. The rebellion you have out here is insignificant. My job is to make contact and offer our support. To help you grow and achieve your goals. Secretly.'

Mace shook his head. 'You've been in Fire City for a long time,' he pointed out. 'Why the sudden change?'

'Jonah,' Stone admitted. 'He's changed the game. Things are moving on quickly.'

'What about Aron?'

Stone shrugged. 'What about him?'

'Were you a part of . . . ?'

Mace was unable to finish his sentence, incapable of believing that a boy he had reared as one of his own had betrayed them. Aron was part of their extended family and what he'd done was unfathomable.

'I took him to the Mayor,' lied Stone. 'But I had nothing to do with his interrogation. That was the old man and someone else.'

'Who?'

'There was another voice on the recording. I didn't

recognize it. Probably someone on the council, from the way that he spoke.'

'Talking to Aron?'

Stone nodded. 'Offering him a deal. I can play it for you, if you want.'

Mace shook his head. 'I want Aron back,' he replied. 'Tonight.'

'Too late,' Stone revealed. 'I found him at the mansion. The Mayor had him killed.'

'He's dead?'

'Judging by the large hole in his head, I'd say yes.'

Mace felt a tear sliding down his right cheek.

'He meant something to you?' asked Stone.

'To all of us,' Mace admitted. 'We were family.'

'His betrayal means nothing, then?'

Mace glared at the mercenary. 'Of course it means something!' he snapped. 'But you can't turn off emotions. Not if you're human.'

'Then,' Stone said, after considering the correct response, 'I'm sorry for your loss, Mace. Truly. Sometimes life as a soldier hardens you. But I'm not some demon, I understand what loss is.'

Mace sat back and took a deep breath. 'So you'll help us, then?' he asked.

'Help you what?'

'Take revenge,' Mace told him. 'Against Valefor?'

Stone considered his options and realized that he had

no choice. He *had* to convince them that he was on their side. It was the only way to achieve his goal. He nodded. 'What did you have in mind?' he asked.

Mace smiled. 'Let's just get things straight,' he said. 'I don't trust you. I don't trust your motives and I don't care about your boss. But I'm willing to give you a chance, see how you behave. One wrong move and it's you and me, Stone. You're not the only one with Special Forces training. You put one foot wrong, or I find you're lying to us, and you'll have me to answer to. That OK with you?'

Stone said that it was. 'I would be the same,' he offered. 'I'd expect you to *prove* your worth. I'm happy to take my own medicine, big man.'

'Good,' Mace replied. 'Let's rejoin the others then. You need to hear the plan. We're running short of time.'

The plan, as Jonah explained, had been formulated at the Haven with Mace. In truth, parts of it had been settled long before that. The move away from Fire City, hooking up with other rebels – Mace had been thinking of these for some time. His original ideas had changed due to circumstances, but they were essentially solid. Jonah was the big difference – the catalyst, as Mace had called him. He was their undeclared hand.

'We need someone to round up Mias and his legion,'

Jonah told them. 'Get them all to Valefor's lair, or within the square at least.'

Mace nodded at Stone. 'That's your job,' the giant told him. 'Can you manage it?'

Stone nodded. 'My men can help,' he replied. 'They'll follow my lead and they won't say a word.'

'That's good,' said Jonah. 'We could do with the numbers. The second thing is to lure Valefor away from his nest. That's my part.'

Martha looked scared. 'Why lure him away?' she asked.

Jonah looked to Mace, who raised an eyebrow. His expression told Jonah that he was on his own. If he wanted to explain why, it was his decision.

'He and I have unfinished business,' Jonah said after the pause.

'Why are you looking at Mace?' asked Martha.

Jonah turned to her and half smiled. 'I'll explain later,' he said. 'There are some things you need to know.'

'What things?' she asked.

'You have to trust me,' he replied.

'I do,' she told him. 'You know I do.'

Jonah nodded. 'Later, then?'

Martha shrugged and said OK.

'So that's Valefor and the others,' Mace picked up. 'The last thing is getting out. We need to get everyone together.'

'You mean the few that are left,' replied Faith.

Mace tried to smile but it got lost somewhere inside him. 'Yeah,' he said softly.

'We'll gather at the Haven,' the big man continued. 'It's the last place they'll expect. Although if the plan goes well, they won't be able to react because they'll be dead.'

'What about the human army?' asked Stone.

'You again,' Jonah told him. 'They'll listen to you. We need them to stand down.'

'But how are you going to kill all the demons?' the soldier added. 'It's not possible.'

Mace nodded to Jonah, giving his assent. 'Tell them,' he said.

Jonah gave Martha another look before doing as Mace asked. 'Once they're in the market square, we're going to detonate a bomb,' he explained.

Stone's entire face lit up, a smile crawling across it. 'Tell me you've got a nuke,' he said in excitement.

'Not a nuke,' Jonah replied. 'A thermobaric bomb.'

The whistle that left Stone's mouth was piercing.

'What's a thermobaric—' began Faith.

'The next best thing to a nuke,' Stone interrupted with glee. 'They suck in oxygen, and then blow everything within their radius to kingdom come. The more open the area, the bigger the bang. A giant pressure wave, one massive ball of flame, and *boom*! Instant demon barbecue.'

'Stop it,' said Prior with a sardonic grin. 'You're making my stomach grumble.'

Jonah considered the time, and the certainty that Valefor had sensed his return to the city. To send his earlier message, he'd lowered the barrier between human and demon. Consequently he'd given Valefor a bigger scent to track. There was no guarantee that the demon lord would wait for an invitation before seeking Jonah out.

It was time to act.

51

Stone asked Prior how he was feeling.

'Not bad for someone who's dying,' replied the old man.

They were sitting in Stone's car at the edge of the industrial zone with two soldiers in the back. Waiting for Mias.

'How do you know he's here?' Prior asked, holding down a cough that made his lungs burn.

'I spoke to Pipe.'

'Who is . . .?'

'The man in charge of the army,' Stone explained.

'I thought you were the man,' said Prior.

Stone nodded. 'Unofficially I am,' he revealed. 'But Pipe doesn't know that. He thinks that I pass on orders from command.'

Prior looked bemused. 'Which you do,' he pointed out.

'Do and don't,' Stone replied cryptically.

'You know,' said Prior, 'you do a great line in bullshit. Anyone ever told you that?'

Stone smirked and looked out into the night. 'My mother used to,' he joked. 'In between selling herself to anyone with the money.'

'My heart bleeds,' replied Prior. 'No, truly.'

In front of them stood three huge warehouses, each with its own factory. Five hundred people worked on each shift in each building, churning out goods that they'd never enjoy. Prior reflected on the fall of the Haven, recalled all the people he'd seen die since the demons came. For years they'd been paddling against the tide, consoled by saving perhaps one soul out of every hundred. Had it all been for nothing, some vainglorious exercise in futility? No, he thought, not that. His time was near and he was feeling blue.

May, Oscar and the others mutilated, Tyrell taken away, and Aron's betrayal – all of it weighed heavily on his shoulders and made him feel a loneliness he'd never felt before. He remembered the boyhood dreams he'd grown up with, the feeling that life was there for the taking. Not once had he ever imagined the world as it now was. Who could have? And now that the end was coming . . .

'There he is,' said Stone as Mias appeared from one of the factories. 'Leave it to me.' He turned to face his men. 'Anything looks wrong,' he told them, 'take that overgrown monkey out. Understood?'

'Yes, boss,' both men replied together.

Stone took a deep breath and stepped out of the car into a bracing, chill wind.

Martha and Faith had gathered the few belongings they owned and said a final goodbye to the bar. With the Mayor dead, there was no one asking why it was closed. Most people were scurrying to whatever shelter they had, wary of the curfew. A few customers had knocked on the bar doors, only for Mace to send them packing. No doubt when things became clear, some other collaborator would take over from Martha's dead step-father and reopen the place. Until then, time had been called.

Martha found herself caught between what felt like the end of an era and her growing feelings for Jonah. She had spent her entire life in Fire City, much of it round the bar. Memories of her mother, of Aunt May, of her friends, and even of the drunks, flooded into her head. Yet they fought for space alongside the lingering feel of Jonah's arms, the warmth of his body and his mesmerizing scent. *One door closes*, she told herself as she locked up and set off into the darkness with the others.

The army patrols had lessened during the day, and Martha felt strangely calm. If Stone had done his part correctly, Mias and his minions would be rushing to the market square. The journey across town would be easy, with little secrecy required. Habit forced them into the shadows, as always, as they passed through the streets.

Martha's gut twisted and more memories took hold. It seemed odd that she felt something for Fire City when all she'd ever known was strife and death. Yet, it was there; a nagging sense of loss that she couldn't contain. Everywhere she looked, the faces of dead people stared back – her mother, Oscar, Aunt May. She spotted the little store that Luca's father, Corey, had run. Almost always empty. She remembered trading a set of glasses for a comb, and how Mica Williams had given birth on the dirt floor, May and Faith tending to her as Corey stood on the street and cried. She thought about Luca, wondering where he'd gone after Corey had died, whether he and Mica were still breathing themselves. Felt bad that experience stopped her dwelling on the dead, made her move on quickly. Felt guilt . . .

They approached the clock tower slowly. A single patrol sat at its base, two younger men and a grizzled old soldier smoking a fat cigar stub. Mace thought about turning back but decided it would look too suspicious. Instead, he approached the patrol.

'Looking for a place to spend the night,' he said casually.

The man with the cigar coughed, then smiled, his eyes on Martha. Faith grew tense, expecting the worst, but the soldier soon calmed her fears.

'I've been told to expect you,' he said. 'I'm Pipe. Stone told me you'd be along with the Mayor's daughter.'

'Stone?' asked Mace, praying that Martha would hold her tongue.

'Yeah – you're needing an escort to the rebel hide-out, correct?'

Faith swallowed and said yes. 'Clean-up,' she said, guessing at what Stone had told the soldier.

'Bodies, clean-up – all the same to me,' Pipe replied. 'I bet those demons have done terrible things down there. Seen 'em take out a rebel group out west some years ago. It weren't pretty.'

Mace told him that they'd be fine on their own.

'No can do,' insisted Pipe as a waft of vanilla-scented smoke hit the women. 'Stone has his orders and I got mine. And I *always* follow orders. It's what separates the men from the cockroaches . . .' The grizzled old mercenary grinned at Faith and told them to follow him. His men, taking a little too much interest in Martha, bought up the rear. 'You look like army to me,' Pipe said to Mace.

'I was,' Mace replied. 'Fought against the demons during the War.'

'Against 'em, for 'em,' Pipe replied. 'Who cares as long as you're on the winning side, eh?'

Mace mumbled something unintelligible and looked away.

Jonah stood on the roof of Valefor's lair, his eyes blazing the colour of a setting sun. A cold, fierce wind battered against him but he kept his mind on the task at hand. No sign of Mias and his minions yet, but something else had stirred in the bowels of the building beneath his feet. A deep and ancient evil, immensely powerful.

Understanding that he'd have to trust Stone to complete his part of the plan, Jonah jumped from rooftop to rooftop, crossing the square, concentrating on his own mission. Behind him the air pressure changed and something oozed from the spot on which he'd stood, like a swarm of black wasps, fizzing with kinetic energy.

'*WHY DO YOU RUN?*' Valefor's voice, harsh and metallic, echoed around Jonah's head, making him feel nauseous. His heart rattled inside his rib cage. '*YOU CANNOT ESCAPE ME!*'

Jonah smiled. 'I don't want to,' he whispered. He turned and ran . . .

Mias scratched at his fur, and considered Stone's words.

'How many?' he asked.

'I don't know,' Stone told him. 'One, maybe two hundred?'

'Like ants swarming into a lion's den,' said Mias.

'They're armed,' Stone replied. 'Guns, bombs. It's a full-scale rebellion.'

Mias shook his head. 'We destroyed them in their pit,' he pointed out. 'How could they amass a force so quickly afterwards?'

Stone had always been good at making up stories – an expert at deflecting people away from the truth. He thought fast and hard, the whole process taking less than ten seconds. Mias appeared not to notice, but Stone knew that he might be reading his thoughts. The best lie contains an element of truth, he remembered. He thought about Mace and his rebel band and used their images to shield his true intentions.

'These rebels are coming from outside the protected zone,' he said. 'They've been planning it for months. The stranger that Valefor seeks is with them.'

Mias' eyes lit up with hatred. 'The stranger I fought?'

'The same,' Stone told him. 'Your chance for revenge, to curry favour with your lord.'

'And you are sure of this – *completely* sure?'

'Yes, Mias. It is my job to be certain.'

Stone knew that the next response would be crucial. He waited impatiently, his breathing shallow.

After what seemed like an age, the ape-demon replied. 'I shall amass the legions at my master's lair,' he declared. 'This stranger will pay for his crime. I vow that on my own soul.'

Stone smiled. 'I'll go now,' he said quickly. 'Set up a perimeter.'

'As you wish,' replied the demon. 'But only I will engage the rebels. Is that clear?'

'Absolutely, my lord.'

'Go, then.'

Stone came back to the car and got in.

'Well?' Prior asked, the icy finger of fatality stabbing at his chest.

'We're on,' said Stone. 'It's nearly barbecue time.'

Prior nodded, shut his eyes and, through the pain, thought about his father.

Pipe told Mace that he'd come far enough. 'We won't be helping you out down there,' he added. 'Not my job to scrape up the shit left by Mias.'

'No,' Mace quietly replied. 'We'll do that.'

'You need anything,' said the soldier, 'just holler.'

Mace crawled through the mountain of rubbish and dropped down into the tunnel, landing barely centimetres from Liam's corpse. The rats had been feeding and maggots wriggled across the open wounds. Mace shouted up to the women, telling them to hold back. Fighting back tears and vomit, he lifted the body and dragged it away, leaving it in a dead end. When he was done, he let Martha and Faith enter the tunnels.

'It's not pretty down there,' he told them. 'I want you to prepare yourselves.'

'More than two decades of demon rule already

has done?' asked Faith, feeling a little annoyed.

'I get your point,' Mace gently told her, 'but these were our friends. Our family . . .'

'We have no choice,' Martha told them both. 'I won't leave them to rot.'

'What about the soldiers?' Faith asked. 'When we come out, they won't just let us leave, will they?'

'We're not coming back this way,' said Mace, pulling a grenade from his pocket. 'And anyway, they've served their purpose. Move down to the next junction. Quick!'

The women did as he said. Once they were safe, Mace pulled the pin and threw the grenade out into the mound of rubbish covering the entrance. It was quickly followed by two more.

The blasts caught the mercenaries above by surprise, turning discarded tin cans and pieces of wood into lethal slivers of shrapnel.

Pipe, his ears ringing, a wound the size of an apple in his belly, tried to get to his feet as the big blond man emerged from the smoke. He looked over at his men. Kemp was finished, the left side of his head gone. Williams seemed fine, however, bar some cuts to his face and a single shard of metal embedded in his right arm.

'*Williams,*' he gasped urgently. 'Look lively!'

The younger mercenary rolled onto his side and pulled out his handgun. He watched the giant approach his boss, machete swinging in his hands.

'*Hey!*' shouted Williams, taking aim.

Mace turned to the younger soldier, saw the gun, heard his shout. He froze. Williams fired his gun and the bullet whizzed past Mace's head, urging him into action. He dived to his left, behind Pipe. A second bullet slapped into a wall behind Mace, a third close behind. Mace grabbed the old soldier's pistol and, using him as a shield, shot back three times, catching Williams in the throat, jaw and temple. Then, sure that Williams was dead, Mace throttled Pipe. The soldier's mouth fell open. The stub of his cigar rolled down his chin, across his left shoulder and onto the floor. Swirls of blue smoke rose up into the night.

Jonah dropped down between two buildings and across an abandoned car park. Ahead, a church spire rose into the sky and somewhere beyond it a fox cried out. Behind him, he could feel Valefor gaining ground, a wave of energy surging towards him. The closer the demon lord came, the more Jonah felt his human half receding. He ran straight on, down past the church and right onto a wide road littered with debris. To his left was the railway station and he went in, aware that he was running into a nest of cannibals. He drew his blade and sprinted across the concourse, down some stairs and onto the platform. A single train sat empty on the tracks and rats scattered as he crossed behind it. Over a wall and past the shell of a storehouse, a narrow alley-way opened out into a housing project and he slowed as he approached it, sensing trouble.

'*RUN!*' came Valefor's voice, rasping, grating.

Jonah heard a scream from a hundred metres to his right. He shook Valefor's words from his mind and entered a wide expanse of land, overgrown and danger-ous. His eyes picked up human-sized heat signatures, four to the left surrounding a prone form, and three to the right. He turned left and came upon cannibals tear-ing at the flesh of a young woman. He was too late to save her. They sensed his approach, turning to roar at him with blood-soaked mouths, and Jonah ducked beneath the first blow, spun round and swung his blade, severing an arm. The next swipe sent a cannibal head flying, blood spouting into the air.

Suddenly the cannibals looked beyond Jonah and saw what was coming. They screamed as Valefor closed in. Jonah knew that the demon lord would be unable to pass up the feast. He'd counted on it. As the black cloud surrounded the cannibals, tearing them to shreds, Jonah set off again, sprinting back towards the main road. His diversion would hold Valefor for a few minutes, long enough for Jonah to make it to the park.

To the place where he would finally confront his enemy.

★ ★ ★

Martha gasped as she saw the bodies lined up across the floor of the Haven's main chamber. Each had been wrapped in blankets, a few with faces visible. May's body lay at the end, her face serene, as though she was merely sleeping. Martha approached her aunt and crouched beside her, her whole body shaking. She leaned in and felt her heart breaking as she kissed the cold, waxy flesh of May's face, stroked her once lustrous hair. Behind her, Mace scowled.

'Something isn't right,' he snapped. 'The bodies have been moved.'

'Well,' came a voice from across the chamber. 'If I'd waited for you to do it, old man . . .'

'*Oscar!*' screamed Faith as he emerged from the shadows, limping. She threw her arms round him, kissing his forehead, holding him tight. Martha, unable to speak, stared at Oscar in disbelief.

'We thought you were dead,' sad Mace, feeling his heavy heart soar.

'So did I,' Oscar told them. 'I blew the south-facing entrance and the tunnels collapsed around me. Knocked me out.'

'But you survived?' asked Faith.

'Yeah,' Oscar told her. 'When I came round, it wasn't too bad. My leg was trapped but I managed to free myself. Took hours to crawl down to the inner hatch though, and then I found them. I don't know what happened. One minute it was quiet, and then the demons appeared out of nowhere.'

'We know,' Mace told him. 'Aron betrayed us to the Mayor.'

'Aron?' spat Oscar. 'That weasel-faced, dirty little bastard!'

'Doesn't matter now,' said Faith, even though she knew that it did. 'Aron's dead, they're all dead. We have to get out of here.'

Oscar looked surprised. 'And go where?' he asked.

'We're leaving,' said Mace. 'No time to explain now, we need to hurry.'

'I cleaned up,' said Oscar. 'Covered up May and the others.'

Faith squeezed his arm and kissed his cheek. 'Thank you,' she said.

'Is Tyrell with you?' he asked, looking around.

Faith shook her head and watched Oscar's eyes grow wide with fear. 'He got taken by the army, out in the wastelands,' she explained. 'We don't know where.'

Oscar looked to each of them in turn. 'But he's alive, yeah?' he added hopefully.

'Yes,' Mace told him. 'Alive but lost. We'll find him, Oscar. Jonah will find him.'

'Well, he's better off than May,' Oscar said with a touch of relief and a heap of resignation. If anyone could take care of himself, it was Tyrell. And at least he wasn't dead. Despite that, though, Oscar felt a deep sense of loss.

'I hope so,' Faith replied. 'I really hope so.'

Martha took Oscar by the hand. 'He'll be OK,' she told him, finding her voice. 'I'm so pleased to see you. So pleased.'

'As much as it hurts to leave them all here,' said Mace, looking down at May, 'we need to get going. Gather anything you can carry – food, arms, whatever.'

'But what about them?' Martha asked angrily. 'We can't just leave them to the rats.'

'Don't worry,' Mace told her. 'Before we go, I'm going to set some explosive charges. May was the life force of this place. It'll make a fitting tomb.'

Martha took a final look at her aunt and pushed away her grief. Mace was right – the Haven would make a fine resting place for May.

For them all.

52

Stone pointed at Mias. The demon stood next to the arch in front of the old Corn Exchange, consulting with Saarl. The walls of the building, made of a yellow stone, had taken on an olive tinge. The market square thronged with lesser demons, the vast majority of them patrollers, while the winged ones, ten of them, were perched on the rooftops and around the perimeter, watching with their intense, beady eyes, wings folded behind them.

'There,' Stone told Prior. 'Next to Mias.'

'Are you certain?' Prior asked him. 'We'll only get one chance at this.'

Stone nodded. 'The bomb is big enough to take down this entire block,' he explained. 'Even more than that, I reckon.'

'What about getting away?'

Stone smiled at the old man. 'Don't worry, Prior,' he told him. 'We'll be far enough away when it blows. As long as you get the timing right.'

Beyond Prior's head, Stone saw that Mias and his

troops were growing restless. He turned to his men. 'Be ready to move out.'

Both men nodded, their faces grim. A coughing fit overtook Prior.

'Will you be ready?' asked Stone.

'I'll be fine,' Prior wheezed. 'There's life in me yet.'

Stone checked out Prior's sallow, yellowing skin and the black rings that circled his eyes, the way his hands trembled slightly. 'About ten minutes, I'd say,' Stone told him. 'From the look of you.'

'Twenty minutes will do me,' countered Prior. 'It's all I need.'

Stone considered the timing. In the absence of watches for the others, he knew that much of the plan would be based on guesswork. He calculated that Mace and the women would be finishing up at the Haven, unless they'd taken Pipe's offer of an escort. If they had, then Stone's next step would be much easier. With Mace dead, he'd only have Jonah to deal with. However, something told him that Mace would be too smart for that. Either way, Stone was covered. If Mace and the women were dead, his own plan would be given a short cut. If they weren't, he'd be in for a long-term assignment. Either one was fine with Stone.

'Shouldn't you be going?' Prior asked.

'Yeah,' said Stone. 'But what about you?'

'Don't bullshit,' Prior told him. 'You don't really care

about what happens to me. I'll be fine. Just give me some cigarettes.'

Stone gave the old man his nearly empty pack and then offered his hand. Prior took it in good spirit, and shook.

'Let's move!' Stone told his men.

'See you on the other side,' chuckled Prior, lighting a cigarette.

Jonah ran directly for the centre of the park. To his left, the Mayor's mansion stood in total darkness, silhouetted against a deep purple sky. Grey clouds hid the waxing moon and the wind was strong, the perfect conditions for a thermobaric explosion. His only fear was that he'd tampered with the grenades too much, linking them together into one big bomb without really knowing if it would work. Failure to detonate would leave the demon legion alive and ruin the plan, but he'd had little other option.

Everything rested on Prior getting it right, and on Jonah's own ability to take down Valefor. The demon lord was powerful and there was no guarantee of success. Then again, there was no guarantee of anything in this world. Jonah's mother had taught him well, prepared him for this day, as though she'd always sensed it would come. Her spirit lived inside him – he could sense it – and she wanted Valefor dead as much as he did.

He felt the surge before he saw it, entering the park from the north, destroying what was left of the old pavilion. The black haze, crackling with electricity, moved quickly and purposefully, the embodiment of Valefor's true power. Twenty metres wide and at least forty high, he descended on Jonah like a black tsunami, engulfing him in his rage. Jonah closed his eyes and felt something ancient and primeval course through his bones. Round his neck, the amulet given to him by his mother, ordinarily a lump of granite, began to pulse with an azure glow.

'*I HAVE TASTED YOUR BLOOD BEFORE!*' roared Valefor.

Jonah steadied himself, ignoring the buzzing all around him, waiting for Valefor to understand, to realize exactly who he was. It didn't take long.

'*YOU ARE THE SON OF EISHETH!*'

Jonah bristled at the mention of his mother. His human form began to melt, the demon raging through; his face now had elongated, narrow slits with flame-coloured eyes, a tapered and green-scaled jaw, replete with dagger-like teeth, and his powerful, sinuous limbs ended in razor-sharp, thirty-centimetre-long claws.

'*MY SISTER'S SON! KIN OF MY KIN!*' Valefor bellowed as Jonah's ancestry became clearer still.

'*GREETINGS, UNCLE!*' Jonah heard his demonic voice roar back. '*WELCOME TO YOUR DEATH . . .*'

★ ★ ★

Prior gave Stone and his men the five-minute start they'd asked for. Then, lighting another cigarette and coughing up a chunk of flesh, he broke cover.

All around him patrollers began to snarl and snap, fat globules of saliva, creamy and pus-like, flying all over the place. The air was thick with Hell-kin stench, their pungent faeces and viscous alkaline urine. Above them, two of the winged beasts began to circle, cawing and shrieking. Prior ignored them all, his attention focused on Mias and the lupine creature standing with him.

The demon underlord noticed the disturbance and sprang down into the crowd, approaching Prior.

'HALT!' he demanded.

Prior did as asked and flicked his half-smoked stub at the nearest canine. The patroller dropped on all fours, ready to charge the human.

Mias held up his hand. 'I know you,' he said to Prior.

'And I your mother,' the human whispered in reply.

'What did you say?' Mias demanded, stepping in close, his head cocked to the right, eyes wide.

Prior coughed into Mias' simian face, holding back nothing.

'You are diseased!' spat the demon, backing away.

'Guess I am,' Prior told him. 'I bring a message from Stone.'

'A message?'

Prior nodded.

'What?'

The human closed in on the demon's personal space, so close that Mias' fur tickled his nose.

'He said to enjoy the I D B,' whispered Prior.

'What is that?'

Prior stepped back, pulled out the last cigarette and lit that too.

'WELL?' Mias bellowed. 'SPEAK BEFORE I CARVE OPEN YOUR GUTS!'

The old man took a drag and blew the smoke into Mias' face. 'Instant Demon Barbecue,' he said, grinning from ear to ear.

Jonah felt a rush of energy run through his chest. He roared in agony and fell backwards, landing with a thud. The undergrowth surrounding him was ablaze, crackling with intense heat. The black cloud surged up into the sky, swirling like a tornado and sending the flames outwards, creating a ring of fire around him. Suddenly the buzzing, snapping force changed course, pouring in on itself at great speed, the point aimed directly at Jonah's head. He sprang to his left, knowing that soon Valefor would have to retake his corporeal form. Otherwise the effort he'd expended would leave him weak and open to attack.

Sure enough, as the mass hit the ground, the demon

lord began to reappear. Jonah waited until his reformation was complete before charging at him, swiping out with his claws. A chunk of flesh tore loose from the underside of Valefor's jaw and thick, purple blood gushed from the wound.

Valefor smashed out with his arm, sending Jonah flying. He shook his head, snapping his huge teeth together. '*TIME TO DIE, MONGREL!*' he bellowed, rushing forward.

Jonah took a deep breath and sprang to his feet, balancing himself. When Valefor hit him, the shock wave made the ground shake and the momentum carried them both twenty metres to the left. Jonah landed on his back, with Valefor pinning him down.

'Your stench disgusts me,' the demon lord spat.

'That'll be the demon in me,' Jonah parried.

Valefor drew back his huge head and smashed it down onto Jonah's face. The skin round Jonah's left eye split, oozing yellow fluid.

'Your mother was a disgrace to our kind! She polluted the ancient blood line!'

Once, twice, three times more the demon lord butted Jonah, the force so great it cracked the earth beneath his head. A battered and bruised Jonah, one eye now completely closed over, fought back, throwing Valefor aside. Suddenly he had the upper hand. Before the demon lord could react, Jonah rained in blow after blow, his claws tearing at Valefor's torso, shredding the flesh. The demon lord's screams echoed around the park but Jonah carried on until Valefor was still, his eyes closed.

Jonah mounted him, looked down into his face, snarling. 'I'm going to kill you now, dear uncle,' he spat. 'I'm going to tear out your heart and *eat it*.'

Valefor's eyelids snapped open. 'You cannot kill me!' the demon lord hissed. The giant donkey's jaw, the lidded eyes, the hair-covered torso, the wings – all of it began to dissipate beneath Jonah.

In a moment Valefor was gone, and Jonah found himself staring at flattened weeds. Something took hold of him from behind and threw him into the night. He hurtled towards the thirty-metre stone arch to the north of the park and slammed into it, crying out in pain, the wind sucked from his lungs. He fell in a heap, struggling to breathe, the amulet round his neck burning into his flesh. Getting to his feet, Jonah saw that Valefor had reformed and was speeding towards him, his eyes gleaming. Everything around Jonah seemed to blur, to spin round and round, as though he'd entered a vortex. Air forced its way into his chest and he struggled to think straight, groggy and torn but unbowed. Clearing his mind, he began to whisper his mother's name over and over again.

'*Eisheth . . . Eisheth . . . Eisheth . . . !*'

Suddenly a great charge of electricity coursed through him, throwing back his head, pushing his arms out wide. He concentrated his entire being, centred every impulse in one place. On one thing . . .

Valefor sensed the change in his foe, but a split second too late. As they collided, Jonah opened up his soul, just as his mother had shown him. Valefor tried to turn away but it was no use. He fell into Jonah's embrace as, simultaneously, Jonah allowed his human DNA to envelop the Hell-kin spore, both his and that of Valefor. The demon lord tried to scream, tried to break free, but his efforts were in vain. Jonah had buried Valefor's soul deep inside his own core, had at once consumed it and conjoined with it.

Jonah fell to the ground, rolled onto his back and fought hard to keep Valefor down. His face rippled like a calm pool that had been disturbed by some mighty underground eruption, his human face melting into Valefor's and back again. Over and over, for minute after minute, Jonah fought to keep the demon lord at bay. The cycle went on and on, and on. Fiery, agonizing shards poked at his chest, his stomach, and his loins. He bucked and twisted, his synapses snapping and popping with thunderclaps of pain, his blood boiling and spitting inside the veins. His heart clenched and expanded, clenched and expanded, fifty, a hundred times each second.

And then, abruptly and without warning, everything fell silent and Jonah felt himself begin to drift away . . .

In the market square, Prior threw back the great coat that he'd worn to hide the explosives. He flicked his cigarette butt at Mias' confused and apprehensive face and began to wheeze, to cough, to chuckle . . .

He reached with his left hand for the trigger . . .

. . . and detonated the bomb.

One week later . . .

In the end, we fled Fire City just before the explosion that killed Mias and the demon legion. The bomb took Prior too, although he was so close to death anyway that I was pleased he could control how it happened. He died just like he'd lived for me, as a hero.

Not many other people escaped, however, because the city was in turmoil. Some fled into the wastelands but chose not to follow us; others could only wander the outskirts, looking dazed. Most people simply hid in fright. Even given the chance to leave, the vast majority were too scared to act. Part of me felt guilty for leaving so many behind but it was the best we could manage given how things turned out. I told myself that perhaps more would follow in the days to come . . .

Jonah's arrival had proved to us that we had been losing our battle with the demons. We had the chance to escape the drudgery and danger of Fire City and make new lives out in the wilderness. We had the opportunity to join other rebels and fight as a bigger group, to make a real difference in the struggle to free our people.

We had to take it.

But that didn't mean that any of us could forget the people we'd lost. Losing Aunt May was the one thing that I found hardest to take. For so long she'd been the last remaining link to my mother – the only other person in the world who carried the same blood in her veins. Now I was the only one left and something inside me died with her. I also found myself unable to forget what I'd done to my stepfather. Even through all the rage and the relief, I felt like a murderer, and that's what I was. No matter what he'd done, how evil he'd been, I had killed him, and that was something that weighed down on me during quieter moments. I knew that it always would, no matter how justified my actions might have been.

And then there was Aron. His betrayal had left me feeling cold inside. It was so hard to comprehend that someone I'd grown up with and loved, someone who had been an important part of our family, could have done something so wrong. It made me question the things I believed in, the things I'd been taught. It made me question whether our 'family' was really as close and united as I'd always believed. More than the betrayal, it was the fact that Aron had made me question these things that hurt. That made me wish he were still alive so that I could slap his face until it was raw. And I wasn't the only one. Every one of us felt broken and a little empty because of what Aron had done.

So it was a sorry and tired bunch of us who made the journey north, towards a town that had once been called Loughborough. Stone was as good to his word and led us alongside Mace. Oscar, Faith and me were the only others.

In the confusion, and with Stone's authority, the human army patrols simply let us pass as they tried to work out why half of the protected zone was on fire. By Stone's calculations, the government would send thousands more troops, within hours. We needed to be far away by the time they arrived.

It took us two hours of walking through the darkness to reach our destination – a pre-arranged meeting point that Mace only revealed when we arrived. I spent most of the time staring in awe at the sights we passed. I know it wasn't much – just lots of deserted houses and abandoned cars – but I was still enthralled. It was the first time I'd ever left Fire City, and my first taste of freedom.

The journey was fairly easy and we avoided seeing any army patrols or being ambushed by cannibals. We saw none of the evil things I'd heard lurked in the wastelands, waiting for unsuspecting humans. I know they exist – since we left, I've encountered some of them – but that first night, it was like someone was watching over us, protecting us.

At the meeting point, three men appeared and Mace greeted them like they were long-lost brothers, even though he barely knew them. Their leader was a black man called Negus, who had strange hair and smiled continuously.

'This is our new tribe,' Mace had told the rest of us. 'They're going to take us to where they live.'

I don't know what I'd been expecting, but when we reached Negus' hideaway after another hour-long trek across fields and through woods, I felt deflated. We found ourselves standing in the middle of a field, staring at a forest, just across a narrow stream. It was only when we'd crossed the water and entered a network of shallow tunnels that I began to understand. Once we'd emerged into the clearing and the rest of the tribe had appeared, it all made sense. Negus and his people lived in amongst the trees, hidden away from the outside world.

The tribe was warm and welcoming and we were fed and given water. The food was amazing – roasted root vegetables and soup made from herbs. It was far tastier than anything I'd ever eaten; save for the few meals I'd been given at the mansion as a small child. It was food that Aunt May and my mother would have loved. Just thinking of them brought me to tears and I had to stop myself from sobbing.

The same thing happened when Oscar mentioned Tyrell and wondered what had happened to him. Mace had explained a little, but not enough to stop us from feeling that we'd lost Tyrell too, alongside May and Raj and the others. I was so used to having my big friend around that I even missed his smell. The sight of so many new and friendly faces failed to stop us feeling sad on that first night.

I slept huddled close to Faith, under a tent that had been surrounded on three sides by a mound of earth for warmth. The blankets we'd been given were old and threadbare but they were clean and cosy too. I don't know if it was tiredness or the fresh air, but I fell asleep immediately and didn't wake until long into the following day. On waking, I spent a long time exploring my new home, and talking to the people I met. Some of them were escapees from the Fire City Hunt – people we'd rescued and set free in the wastelands. It was so awesome to find those who had survived because of something we'd done. It made me understand what our rebellion was really worth – much more than Aron or my stepfather could ever comprehend. I began to feel a lot better about things, despite the aching sense of loss I felt inside.

Within a few days I'd settled in completely and begun to help with the day-to-day chores. I took a special interest in cooking and in collecting the ingredients too, maybe to keep the memory of my aunt alive and put the things she'd taught me into practice. Faith and I learned how to distinguish certain plants and roots by their foliage, and which mushrooms and berries were edible as opposed to deadly. We got to know the other tribe members better as we worked, ate and slept alongside them.

Oscar and Mace spent their time talking to Negus and the others, and Stone too. He seemed like a changed man. For the first time ever, I saw him smiling and joining in with the rest. One evening he sat the children around an open fire and told them spooky stories, entertaining them all until they'd fallen asleep. Even though it was a shock, it was good to see him getting involved. Without his warning about my stepfather and his help afterwards, we might still be in Fire City, facing certain death. That was enough for me to accept him, even if I could never completely trust him.

And then, four days after we'd arrived, Jonah limped and stumbled into the camp, his pale face and lithe body covered in bruises, his obsidian eyes sunken and red-ringed and his clothes torn.

It was Negus who spotted him first, rushing to help. I saw him next, and I was so happy that I tipped over a cooking pot in my rush to greet him. I'd spent the previous days praying that he'd managed to escape alive but unsure that he had. In my nightmares, I saw Valefor overpowering and devouring him. No human could match an ancient, but somehow Jonah had, and lived to tell the tale.

To be honest though, by that point I think I already knew that Jonah wasn't completely like me – not totally human. I just didn't want to accept it.

As Jonah rested and a few of the tribe tended to his injuries, I took Mace to one side. 'Let's walk,' I told him.

Mace seemed surprised, but he followed me all the same. We went to the far side of the forest where the small stream flowed into a wide river, and from which we could see the giant pepper pots of the nearby power station clearly. I sat on the riverbank, my feet in the water, and looked up at the only real father I'd ever wanted.

'No more bullshit,' I said to him. 'I want to know.'

'Want to know what?' he asked, looking slightly annoyed at the way I'd spoken.

'Tell me about Jonah,' I told him. 'I know he's not human, so what is he?'

Mace mumbled and turned red, looking away.

'There's no point in lying to me,' I added. 'Your reaction gave the game away. I'm right, aren't I?'

Mace turned back to me and shrugged. 'It's not for me to tell you,' he replied. 'If you want the truth, ask Jonah.'

I nodded and told him I would, just as soon as

he recovered. 'But you did know, didn't you?' I added.

Mace nodded. 'He told me when we left to find the weapons,' he admitted. 'Told me to keep it to myself. I felt I owed him his right to privacy. I'd do the same for you too.'

'What about before that though?' I asked. 'When he first arrived – you know, all the speedy moves and the somersaults?'

Again Mace nodded. 'I had my suspicions,' he said. 'But it didn't matter. I never admitted it, Martha, but we were in a difficult position until Jonah turned up.'

I gave him a quizzing look. 'Difficult in what way?' I asked. 'Our lives have always been tough.'

Mace shook his head this time. 'You don't understand,' he told me. 'We were losing the fight and I knew it. Losing more and more of our people and saving fewer from the Hunt. Jonah's arrival just made all of that more apparent. More urgent.'

'Like a catalyst?' I said.

'That's what I called him, too,' he replied. 'Exactly that. His arrival was like a sign that we had to act, so I wasn't even remotely bothered that there was something odd about him.'

'Because we needed him?'

'Yes, Martha.'

'So he is different then?'

Mace smiled at me. 'I told you, talk to him. And soon

– he's leaving tomorrow and I'm not sure he'll be back.'

'*Tomorrow?*' I felt sick at the thought. He couldn't just leave, not without . . .

'Yeah – he's heading south, says he knows where to find Tyrell. Stone is going with him.'

'To find Tyrell?'

'Jonah feels responsible,' Mace told me. 'Says he won't rest until he finds him.'

'But then,' I said hopefully, 'he'll come back, surely? Bring Tyrell back to us!'

Mace shrugged again. 'Talk to him,' he repeated.

I caught up with Jonah the next morning, as he got ready to leave. Seeing him prepare made me feel sad, and a little angry too.

'Were you just going to leave?' I half snapped at him. 'Not even a goodbye?'

He shook his head. 'There's no time,' he replied. 'I need to find Tyrell.'

'Ever since you arrived in our lives, you've been in a hurry,' I told him, trying to stop myself from sounding like a spoiled child. 'Don't you *ever* relax?'

He smiled, put down the gun he was holding, and took my hands in his. The scent that he carried sent my hormones into overdrive and I wanted to kiss his almost perfectly contoured mouth. My heart was thumping and I forced myself to look away.

'There's too much to do, Martha. The demons don't rest, and neither can we.'

'But,' I said, looking back into his eyes, 'what if I can help you – come *with* you?'

'No,' he said with determination. 'It's too dangerous. The roads south are swarming with patrols, both demon and human. There'll be even more after what we did in Fire City. I won't let you risk your life.'

'But you're happy to risk your own?'

Jonah grinned. 'Last night,' he said, 'I sensed that you and Mace were talking about me. I don't normally listen to people's thoughts but I listened to yours . . .'

The look on my face must have been a mixture of surprise and horror. I looked away again, deeply embarrassed.

'Remember when I told you about the other demons – the ones you've never seen?'

I nodded slowly.

'My mother was a succubus,' he revealed. 'And my father was human.'

'But—'

He shook his head. 'I know what you're going to say,' he told me. 'You want to know why I didn't tell you. Ask yourself a question though, Martha. Would you have accepted me if I'd have told you what I was – on that first night?'

I looked at his hands, holding mine so gently, and I

took in his scent. My head began to spin with questions. 'Probably not,' I admitted. 'But I don't understand why you'd help us if you're a demon.'

'I'm *not* a demon,' he insisted. 'I'm only *part* demon. The human side of my being is the one I choose to live by.'

'But the demon part – how can you control it?'

Jonah shrugged. 'I don't know,' he admitted. 'I just know that I can, most of the time.'

'And when you can't?'

'I can turn it on and off,' he told me. 'When I fought Valefor, I let the demon come to the fore. That's how I defeated him. I know you were wondering about that.'

'He's dead?'

Jonah nodded. 'Consumed,' he added, without explaining what he meant. 'What will you do now?'

I told him that I didn't know. 'Stay here, I guess,' I added. 'Help with whatever we're going to do next.'

'Negus and Mace are going to go further north, to meet the Resistance fighters up there,' he told me. 'They'll need strong people like you and Oscar to guard the camp and take care of things.'

'Then that's what we'll do,' I replied. 'What about you?'

'I want to find Tyrell,' he told me again. 'And then I'm going to find my siblings.'

'To rescue them?' I asked.

Jonah shook his head. 'Not exactly,' he replied. 'They don't need to be rescued. I just want to see my sisters again.'

'What about your brother?'

'Oh,' he said, his eyes hardening. 'I want to find him too. Find him and kill him . . .'

I gasped and Jonah let go of my hands. 'One day,' he told me, 'if we survive, I'll come back to you and explain everything. I didn't choose this path, Martha, just like you didn't choose yours. We end up having to deal with the situations that are created for us. You asked me not to judge your mother, remember?'

I nodded.

'Well, I'm asking you not to judge me. Everything I do, everything I feel – I have no choice over any of it. Life dealt me the hand, Martha. I'm just trying to cope with it.'

'I understand, but I want to be a part of it. If you've been reading my thoughts . . .'

'I don't always do that,' he said, shaking his head. 'Only sometimes.'

'But you know what I'm going to say now?'

'Yes,' he admitted. 'Does that make you angry?'

'No,' I said truthfully. 'It should but it doesn't. All I keep thinking about is—'

He put a finger on my lips. '*Ssh* – I know what you're thinking but we don't have time, Martha. Not now.

There's a long, hard battle to be fought. Most of us won't live to see it end. But we have to fight it, Martha. We *have* to. Otherwise we might as well give up now.'

'Promise me you'll come back,' I almost pleaded, no longer caring that I was making a fool of myself. 'Promise, because I don't want—'

Jonah took my face in his hands and kissed me deeply, and my heart felt like it was trying to burst out of my chest.

'I promise I'll try,' he eventually told me. 'It's the best I can do.'

Jonah

I'm heading south, towards the centre of their power, towards their inner sanctum. The road is going to be treacherous, the journey dangerous, but I am prepared. Nothing is going to stand in my way — not their human armies or their demon legions. I carry the will of my mother inside me and the rage of a son deprived of her love. I carry the blood of both human and Hell-kin, which makes me stronger than them, and gives me a faith they can never understand . . .

The mercenary travelling with me has his uses but I know that he cannot be trusted. Despite his futile attempts at hiding his real thoughts, I can see right through him. I'm going to let him believe that he's got me where he wants me. I'm happy for him to believe it. He's going to take me to the people I'm after . . .

When I've dealt with them, it will be my brother's turn. I know that he can sense me approaching; I'm pleased that he knows. I hope he is ready for me. Consuming Valefor has made me stronger; consuming my brother will make me stronger still . . .

I'm going to need that strength. I'm going to ransack their city, just as they ransacked my home. I'm going to tear them apart, just as they tore apart my parents. I'm going to consume them all and sit and watch as Babylon burns . . .

I hope they're ready . . ..

ABOUT THE AUTHOR

Bali Rai has now written nine young adult novels for Random House Children's Publishers UK. His first, *(un)arranged marriage*, created a huge amount of interest and won many awards including the Angus Book Award and the Leicester Book of the Year. It was also shortlisted for the prestigious Branford Boase First Novel Award. *Rani and Sukh* and *The Whisper* were both shortlisted for the Booktrust Teenage Prize. His latest book, *Killing Honour* won the North East Teen Book Award. Bali also writes the hugely popular Soccer Squad series for younger readers.

Bali was born in Leicester, where he still lives, writing full-time and visiting schools to talk about his books.

**Also by Bali Rai and
available from Corgi . . .**

'Honour,' I repeated, wondering how such a small word could have caused so much trouble.

When Sat's sister, Jas, is married off into the Atwal family she changes, she's quiet and distant. But Sat's too busy with his own life; his girlfriend, his friends, football . . . Then Jas disappears.

According to her new husband, she's run off with another man. Her family disown her; don't seem to care if she's ever found. But Sat doesn't believe it. Something has happened to his sister and he's determined to figure out what. But his investigations take him into dark and dangerous territory . . .

A powerful, hard-hitting teen thriller on the controversial topic of honour killing, by multi-award-winning author Bali Rai.

'Utterly compelling'
Bookseller

Torn apart by violence, united by love . . .

It's 1919 and Amritsar is a city on the brink of violent rebellion.

Bissen fought bravely for the British Empire during World War One. Now he patiently awaits news from England.

Gurdial, a young orphan, is desperate to marry Sohni, the daughter of a rich and evil man.

And Jeevan, Gurdial's oldest friend, is swept up in the revolution and changing beyond all recognition.

Bissen, Gurdial and Jeevan are trying to escape ghosts from the past. But as the fight for Amritsar reaches a terrifying climax, their lives will be changed for ever.

'Powerful storytelling . . . constantly surprising, beautifully compelling' *Scotsman*

Manny wants to be a footballer. Or a musician.
Or write a bestseller. He doesn't want to get married . . .

bali rai
(un)arranged
marriage

Manny is on his way to a wedding – his wedding.
A wedding that he doesn't want, that he
never asked for. To a girl he doesn't know.

At seventeen, Manny wants to do his own thing, to
choose his own path in life. But will his traditional
Sikh family's expectations be too strong to fight?

**'Absorbing and engaging . . . a highly readable
debut from Bali Rai that teenagers of any culture
will identify with'** *Observer*

Sometimes names can lead to terrible trouble . . .

The Punjab, 1950s. A secret affair goes horribly wrong,
and a young girl commits suicide after her lover is attacked
by her family. The two families part in violence and conflict.

Leicester, 2004. Rani and Sukh fall in love,
unaware of the terrible legacy of the past and the
dark history between their ancestors.

Can tragedy be averted this time, or will the
couple be drawn into the bitter cycle of enmity
that has gripped their families for years?

**'Frustratingly honest and overwhelmingly powerful . . .
a heart-wrenching love story that will exert its power
over you long after the book is finished'** *The Bookseller*

*'Mess with one of us – then you have to deal
with all of us . . .'*

Positive attitudes only. That's the Crew: Billy,
Jas, Della, Will and Ellie. And where they
live – in the concrete heart of a big city –
you need a crew to back you up.

Then one day they find a fortune in notes –
and life suddenly becomes very dangerous . . .

'A jewel of a book' *Independent*

Stay in touch with Bali:
www.balirai.co.uk
Twitter @Balirai